Gisèle Pineau

Devil's Dance

Chair Piment

Translated by C. Dickson

University of Nebraska Press
Lincoln and London

Publication of this book was assisted by a grant from
the National Endowment for the Arts ❧

Cet ouvrage, publié dans le cadre d'un programme
d'aide à la publication, bénéficie du soutien du
Ministère des Affaires étrangères et du Service
Culturel de l'Ambassade de France aux Etats-Unis.

This work, published as part of the program of aid
for publication, received support from the French
Ministry of Foreign Affairs and the Cultural Service
of the French Embassy in the United States.

Book set in Adobe Minion and designed by Richard
Eckersley.

Library of Congress Cataloging-in-Publication Data

Pineau, Gisèle.
[Chair piment. English] Devil's dance / Gisèle
Pineau ; translated by C. Dickson.
p. cm. — (European women writers series)
ISBN-13: 978-0-8032-3749-0 (cloth : alk. paper)
ISBN-10: 0-8032-3749-9 (cloth : alk. paper)
ISBN-13: 978-0-8032-8784-6 (pbk : alk. paper)
ISBN-10: 0-8032-8784-4 (pbk : alk. paper)
I. Dickson, C. II. Title. III. Series.
PQ3949.2.P573C4313 2006   843'.914—dc22
2006040433

I awaken.
I think of you.
My bed is so warm.
I want your fingers.
I want your hands.
I want to be drowsy with lovemaking.
I want your penis like a knife
Stuck in my belly.

—Louis Calaferte,
La mécanique des femmes

Devil's Dance

I

She tightened her arms around him. Spread her legs wider so he could penetrate her better.

"You just love it, eh?"

Mina hated for words to get stuck on the motions of love-making. It made her think of those June bugs from the fields in the West Indies that came unbidden into the cabin. Disoriented, dazed, flying crazily at the lamp. Ended their short life, wings singed and roasted to the core, in a flurry of infernal sputtering. In the morning her big sister Rosalia gathered them from the planked floor along with the dust balls, the desiccated roaches, and the red spiders. She tried to count them but never got past three.

One. Two. Three.

One, two, three . . . when the floor was literally strewn with cadavers. One, two, three.

The buzzing of words. You always had to put up with it.

"You just love it! Tell me how good it feels . . ."

Mina wanted nothing but the music of bodies. Flesh rubbing. Skin wrinkling. Juices mingling. Fever. And the shudder that created the illusion of love. She was floating. Rocking. Drifting away, tossed in the waves. Then she was sucked into the purple depths of the sea down where the waves began and old seashells, dead starfish, the wooden skeletons of pirate vessels lay strewn, a burial grounds for fish and cannonballs. Sometimes, giddy as if with strong drink, she thought she heard strange laments mounting from the abyss, women's laughter shot with invectives. She observed her body being aroused. Hoped to come upon some new vibration that would herald the feeling of love she had never known or even come close to. Not even in an ephemeral flash.

"You're beautiful you know . . ."

Unwanted words that joined forces with the rambling circle of her thoughts. Empty words that male voices gave brief meaning to. Words that struck against her flesh, trying to penetrate her. Hysterical words that tried to coax, that played make-believe, and that she despised.

"You love feeling me inside you! Don't you, Mina? Tell me!"

He just had to talk, even while he was sucking at the tip of a breast.

"Say something! I need to hear your voice. Tell me you want more and how good it feels . . . Do you love me?"

"Please be quiet!" She groaned while his question—"Do you love me?"—throbbed and reeled in her head like the lament of a scratched record.

He stuffed the nipple into his mouth and started nibbling on it. She already wished he would withdraw and get off of her. Wished he'd leave . . . But suddenly her breathing quickened. She clenched her teeth. Gasped. Let her body be borne away. Swept up. Swept up high, so very high. Back arched, possessed. She felt both wildly drunk and controlled at the same time. Two in one, her body tensed with orgasm and her mind inhabited with mad, irritating words, uttered by obscure creatures. Borne away. Thrown outside of herself. Swept up high, still higher . . . eyes wide. Borne away. Swept up so high. And then, as if fallen from a cloud, slapped down in the backwash of the wave. Dashed onto the rough cotton sheet.

It was always after orgasm that Rosalia made her appearance, a fleeting visit. Rosalia risen from the shadows on September 11, 1998, the twentieth anniversary of the fire in which she perished. Braids in a fiery crown about her head. Astonished scorched face. Charbroiled skin. Blue nylon nightgown melted into her flesh. Mute screams. Rosalia, an asteroid rushing down from the burning cabin. Charbroiled skin . . .

"Yes! Yes! Mina!" said the man. Tell me how much you love it. Tell me you love me!"

Rosalia was standing near the wardrobe, leaning against the wall with the flowered wallpaper. By God knows what magic, the wardrobe was now a traveler's-tree, gigantic, strangely covered with a scaly mottled bark reflecting shattered images of the room. The blackened, charred palm trees were bowing, crumbling to ashes on the green and white linoleum.

Rosalia looked at Mina. Perhaps she wanted to speak, but had never really known how, even when she was alive. Small flames leapt from her mouth and the words she might have screamed burned up before having time to conjure the slightest sound. Stillborn, asphyxiated words that went up in smoke.

For the last few months her apparitions never varied. Glowing, red-hot eyes, she seemed terrorized and shook her head several times before disappearing.

The first time, Mina was fourteen years old. It was back home, in 1978, right after the funeral. She thought she was insane, hallucinating, because no one else could see Rose. Horrifying in the midst of her flames. Mina was seized with a fit of trembling and screamed for so long that a doctor had to be called in to give her a shot of sedative. When she awoke, Rose was still there, cloaked in those same flames. So then she had to keep from screaming and get used to apparitions. The burning girl followed Mina all the way to France, stayed with her for three years, watching her every move. Then she was finally defeated. Went back where she came from.

When she reappeared on the seventh floor of the Edmond-Rostand high-rise, it was as if Mina had called her back. How? With a cheap candle bought at Monoprix, a small vanilla-scented candle. Foolishly, she'd lit it in her living room on September 11, 1998, in memory of Rosalia, so that her soul might rest in peace. A candle in commemoration of the twentieth anniversary of the fire. A lone, wavering flame in front of which Mina knelt down, signed herself, and mumbled a short

3

prayer before going to heat up the leftover salt cod puree and some canned lentils.

When she came back from the kitchen, Rosalia was standing there in the very same spot as the candle, just like a spirit that had been summoned. Mina started but didn't say a word, for fear of setting the worn cogs to turning again. She closed her eyes and went to her room. Locked the door behind her. Slept through until morning. Thought she'd been dreaming. In the following days, Rose went back and forth between her world and this one. Then reappeared consistently certain afternoons, always when her sister happened to be in bed with a man.

Mina quite naturally sought the help of professionals who associated and collaborated with the forces of Good and Evil. Made an appointment with Sarah Pitagor, a medium and fortuneteller from Martinique whose unemployed son handed out her card at the entrance to the Chateau-Rouge metro station in Paris. The woman lived in an attic room, rue des Poissonniers. She had a reputation for liberating sinners, undoing satanic knots, and striking down Evil. Mina climbed the eighty-five steps of a dim staircase and waited three and a half hours on the landing where clients of all colors crowded around the door. She was told that she was the chain tying Rosalia to this earth. To break the chain, she must either call upon very costly spirits who only rarely circulated amongst the living, pray fervently to God in the hopes of deliverance, or return to the scene of the tragedy — which Mina had no intention of doing.

"It's out of the question . . . I'll never go back home . . ."

"And why not?" asked Sarah who had long been familiar with that "never" and its spectacular about-faces.

"They're all dead," replied Mina in a weak voice.

The fortuneteller squinted her eyes, opened her mouth, stuck her finger into an old hollow molar, pulled out a remnant of food that she showed Mina on the end of a cracked fingernail.

4

"And you don't want to know the truth?"

"What?"

"You see what I pulled out of this tooth that's been hurting me for twenty years. Guess what it is? Every day something gets stuck in there, a bit of meat, a grain of rice, a fishbone . . . This tooth been putting me through hell for the last twenty years. For the last twenty years it's been threatening me, and I can't make up my mind to get it fixed. So, did you guess what it is today?

Mina leaned forward to attempt to put a name on the small harvest Sarah was wiggling under her nose.

"No, I don't see . . .

"No!" Sarah repeated with a sigh.

With a flick of her tongue she retrieved the fruit of her hollow tooth and swallowed it.

"Well, my dear," she pursued, "you'll have to start seeing one day, whether you like it or not!"

So, without guaranteeing any results, Sarah supplied her with seven marvelous prayers to recite forty times every Sunday at six o'clock, two phials of anti-zombie containing a yellowish liquid with an alkaline smell, and three sugar powders to scatter on the site of the apparitions morning, noon, and night, taking care not to confuse the vanishing powder for evening with that of the morning, and thereby throw incontrollable elements into a trance. After a year, despite Lysia's pleas, Mina tired of the rituals and allowed Rose to come and go as she wished.

Rosalia would lean up against the wardrobe to observe what men called making Love . . . Straddle Mina. Press her. Turn her this way and that. Spread her legs. Penetrate her, hard. Sweat . . . A battle of bodies that Mina engaged in fearlessly. She opened up. Arched her back. Let herself be turned this way and that, penetrated . . . Asking for more. Wanted to feel them hard inside of her.

Who? Casual acquaintances picked up between two cars in

the project parking lot or led astray from their daily routine in a wing of the shopping center. Bachelors. Young men, old men. Family men. Good husbands. Blacks, Whites, Arabs . . .

They penetrated her, free of charge, tested her flesh, tasted her skin. She needed to be taken. Possessed. Speared, wordlessly, by hard male organs.

She couldn't remember their names, or their faces either . . . Didn't want to know anything about their lives. It came over her just like that, like a fever. And then she couldn't control her body. She consumed sex, erect penises. Asked for more. Dreamt about it sometimes. And awoke with a start in the middle of the night, longing for a man's body fitted tightly to hers. She needed to be taken, possessed, speared . . . Sometimes she went through periods of smooth-sailing, thought she was ready to lead a decent life, cast off the skin of the man-hunting female. Swore to herself she would put the brakes on the wild machinery, be reasonable, wouldn't succumb if the fever returned . . . After work she double-locked the door to her two-room apartment, imagining that unknown forces slipped into her place to drive her outside in search of a man. She spent her nights alone, in front of frantic television images, documentaries, wars, horror films, Miss so-and-so contests, variety shows, American sitcoms. She fell asleep on the couch. Dreamt of Rose. Had nightmares that bore her off to Morne Calvaire. Woke up feeling spent but always ready to confront the high school cafeteria. And then one day, try as she might to be defiant and resist, she was caught up again in the macabre dance of love . . .

"When can we see each other again Mina? I'm free Saturday afternoon . . . Hey, I'm talking to you! What planet are you on now?" He blew out a smoke ring.

"I'm not free."

Rosalia opened her mouth one last time and then disappeared, taking her flames and her shadows along with her.

6

"Hey Mi, say something!"

"Don't ever come here without calling first . . . You have to go now."

Irritated, Mina threw back the sheets.

"You have to go," she repeated.

"You're one strange girl . . ."

"I know."

She sighed.

"I really like you, Mina."

"Stop, please anything but that . . ."

She pushed him out of her room.

"It's true, Mi. We don't know each other very well. How many times have we seen each other, two or three times already? In my own dumb way, I thought we could travel down the road a ways together . . . I'm not involved with anyone, you know. Wouldn't you like to go to the movies one of these days? What about the provinces, have you ever been to the provinces? Normandy . . . what do you say about a quick trip to the provinces . . ."

"I don't like to travel."

"You said you were thirty-five, are you still waiting for Prince Charming or can you make do with a guy like me? You're a mystery, you know. I like mysterious women . . ."

"I know I'm thirty-five . . ."

"What were you staring at a while ago by the wardrobe, a ghost?"

He was jumping up and down, tangled up in the legs of his jeans.

"Your eyes were wide as saucers!"

"You don't know how right you are . . ."

Christian started laughing.

"You are one strange girl."

"Hurry up!"

"Yes, Madame Mina. But I want one last cuddle before I go."

She couldn't stand the stupid airs some men took on after

lovemaking. Endless goodbyes. The last cuddle called for a little pawing. Their eyes filled with a flood of promises that disgusted her.

"Good bye!" she said hurriedly.

"Kiss me and say, 'Goodbye Christian!' Say my name Mina!"

"Goodbye!"

"Walk me to the door. I'm afraid of running into the ghost in the hallway."

He burst out laughing.

"Don't joke about that!"

"Cool down, see you soon."

"Maybe . . ."

"Call me, I'm not the bed-hopper type."

"I'm not asking anything of you."

II

From her seventh-floor window, Mina learned everything about the project. Her universe for the last ten years. Three diffident old high-rises sculpted in concrete. Five oblong blocks rising between scrawny stands of trees. And six boxlike buildings covered with graffiti. Behind the façades blossoming with satellite dishes were the apartments — chicken coops and rabbit hutches — where families lived. As high as the eye could see, the project was poised between rack and ruin. If you had time to kill, you could set about counting the broken windows, unhinged doors, graying curtains. Or else the laundry flapping in the wind. Jeans and sweaters, sheets and dishcloths floating like so many nationless flags. And at the foot of the buildings, gutted, black and blue garbage bags on the sidewalks where the asphalt dimpled and buckled before crumbling to pieces. Garbage bins overflowing with filth and busily scurrying rats. Sometimes small kids chased them, hurling insults and gravel. Their older brothers ran after other demons, other pipedreams, gilt footballs, envelopes of grass, jealous

8

gods, social integration programs, occasional jobs, chicks they called bitches. Or slued around in scraggly gangs, slouching into their dark parkas, cigarettes dangling from their lips, grimy Nikes on their feet, rap tunes and rhymes filling their heads.

Once said to be futuristic, conceived in architects' offices for housing part of humanity, the project was today a place of exile that had been marked for demolition years ago. Most people were awaiting the end of the nightmare and constantly looking for a way out. Even though they pretended to busy themselves with their daily occupations—picking up the kids in front of the school, carting groceries, or catching the train for Paris forty miles away—they felt trapped there, trampled under life's foot. Forever watchful, always on the alert, some seemed to be pursued by evil spirits similar to Mina's. Haggard, striding swiftly along, you could watch them turning into the maze of dead-end streets with warped sidewalks that led nowhere. Others hung around in the parking lot graveyards where the burned out hulls of cars slept their last sleep. Stripped of their wheels and fenders, hoods gaping, the carcasses were still continually plundered. For there was always one last fool who lived in the hope of ripping a treasure from their rusty entrails, plucking out a precious part, a radiator still intact, a horn in excellent condition, a handful of sparkplugs, two-three pistons, a camshaft that he could sell to some crooked dealer for a good price, trade for a CD or a dose of something.

Sometimes Mina stood for hours with her nose against the kitchen window, watching from the seventh floor the comings and goings of the project's inhabitants. They came from everywhere and anywhere . . . Embittered exiles, sodden with nostalgia. Welfare collectors of all sorts who lined up in front of the social services. Retirees, pensioners, laborers, unemployed, minor public servants. Left-wingers, right-wingers. Far left-wingers or far right-wingers. People from the North and from the South. From every corner of France and the rest of the world. Good guys and bad guys from the movies. Jaded people, fanatics, rebels, fatalists. Old women with plaid shopping bags. Skinheads. People of every kind and color. Blacks, Whites, Arabs, Asians. Espousers of grand humanitarian causes, loners with bewildered looks who prepared for the Apocalypse every morning.

Long ago, in 1988, her first year in the project, a man fell for her. He swore he was in love with her. She played along, simply to have his body. She had no feelings for him. Soul as cold as a slab of marble. The words he uttered slipped over her heart without ever touching it. "I love you, Mina! Do you love me?" She didn't answer. He whispered in her ear that he saw stars plastered on the elevator door whenever he went up to her place on the seventh floor. "With you, I'm in seventh heaven, right next to paradise," he said. "I love you...Do you love me?"

The metal doors of the elevator were covered with graffiti and always closed with an infernal clamor when it wasn't out of order, forcing her to make it up the seven floors on foot.

"I love you Mina! Do you love me?" She felt nothing. No feelings. Just wanted to be taken, possessed, speared by the hard penises of men, just reach orgasm with them ..."Do you love me?" There were others after him. They all used the same words.

1978—the year of the fire back home, up there on the hill, Mina was fourteen years old. Olga, her only relative, had been living in France for nine years, married to Douglas, no children. They paid for her airfare. Came to pick her up at the airport. Took her into their home, a stone house in the northern suburbs. Ile-de-France. Mina had left them ten years later for the project and her little apartment on the seventh floor in the Edmond-Rostand high-rise.

She'd been stringing one season after the other in France for twenty-one years now.

Twenty-one years of diabolical whispers filled her head. People spoke to her in her dreams, accused her of having lit the fire with her own hands, of coming from evil stock, of being responsible for her sister's death. Her nights were peopled with creatures that tried to kill her. Visions of cabins in flames and flambéed banana groves. Ballets of tormented spirits roaming the earth, green strangling snakes.

Rosalia had gone away, and then come back.

Rosalia, loyal as the Creole she-dog in the story they used to tell around Piment. The Creole she-dog that the children adopted in a surge of compassion on a beach in Grande-Terre and that they brought back to Côte Sous-le-Vent. Three hours by car. But generous feelings flagged since the dog was not of porcelain and cried for her food every morning. One day, they decided to get rid of her. They left her at the farthest point of the island, Trou-au-Diable, high cliffs lashed by the sea and the wind. Abandoned, she roamed about for a month, that dog did. Finally she found the way back to her masters in Piment. Teary-eyed, came to lean against their legs. Licked their fingers. Laid at their feet, tail low, scrawny and mangy, gashed and wounded.

When those uncharitable thoughts took root in her mind, Mina asked her sister for forgiveness. No! You're not a she-dog, my Rose! I swear you're not a she-dog . . . You just don't know where to go, do you? You got lost along the way, didn't you? But if you would just tell me why you came back on that anniversary of the fire . . .

III

The morning Mina had arrived in France, Olga said, "You're starting a new life."

Mina believed her. Olga was the very incarnation of the New Life. She sprouted twenty arms to show off her world and weigh the fruits of her success: cherry wood dining room set, leather armchairs, porcelain knickknacks, prints of classical paintings, crystal ceiling lamp, champagne glasses in the china cabinet, library . . . After inventorying the house, she held Mina's hand and led her into the blue room fitted with curtains to match the wallpaper.

"See your bed Mina! We were waiting for you, see? And now don't think about your ordeal anymore. Your new life begins today!"

She spoke in a bright voice. Smiling as she smoothed the blue bedspread.

"No one will bother you. You have your own little desk to do your homework on. This is your home now."

The day after the fire, Olga hadn't come rushing to attend Rose's funeral. She'd sent a wreath of white flowers with a red satin ribbon stretched across it—"To my beloved sister"—that cousin Tibert carried in the church in Piment and later laid on the fresh earth that had been thrown over Rosalia's coffin in the cemetery. It didn't take long for the airplane ticket to come.

In those days Mina's memory of her half-sister was double-sided. Sixteen years her elder, Olga was the only child from Melchior's first marriage. Her mother, Marie-Perle, a chabine from Anse-Bertrand, had perished in the waters of the Goyave River one winter afternoon.

Olga was eight when Melchior married Médée. The child never called her stepmother mama, never considered her as an upstanding woman that could live up to Marie-Perle. She rose in the morning glaring at her and forced herself to keep a hostile attitude till evening. In her eyes, Médée was a freeloader that didn't deserve to live. A heinous stand-in for Marie-Perle that went and got herself knocked up good and quick for Melchior . . .

For two days the cabin on the hill endured Médée's cries. Screams of pain that hushed the birds and came ripping through the silence.

Two nights during which Olga put her two knees to the ground and prayed that death would bear Médée away.

On the morning of the third day Médée gave birth to a child

with a deformed head who came into the world without uttering the slightest cry, half strangled by its umbilical cord. A long, very long cord, longer than normal. And green. Greener than green. Gangrene. Fetid. Putrefied. The mid-wife recommended baptizing her immediately in the church in Piment. It was true, just laying eyes on her, you assumed her life on earth would be short. Médée named her Rosalia. She lived five, ten, fifteen, twenty years . . . Stood up on her own two legs the day after her third birthday, pronounced her first words at six, made herself understood—somewhat—at ten.

Olga never took her on her lap, never kissed her, never spoke to her. She got even with Médée through Rosalia, who became her tortured plaything. When she spoke of her little sister Olga said "she". And howled, "She peed in the middle of the cabin! She broke the vase! She took my sandals! She threw my cat on the pavement! She dropped the rotten bananas in the water jar! She scribbled in my notebook!" So many pretexts for beating the child. All the time. With a shoe, a belt with buckle, an acacia switch. Olga lashed out at her with her nails, her fists, her feet. Most often, Rosalia just sat under the blows, her eyes trained on her world, a dazed smile drifting over her purple lips. When she was really frightened, able to see only out of one eye, she pissed in her panties, but remained rooted there, petrified in the face of Olga's rage. Later—at around seven or eight—she learned to flee, yelping like a puppy.

If she was anywhere in the vicinity, young Médée put her two hands to her head, closed her eyes for an instant to muster strength in her soul and then ran to tear Rose from the clutches of the little harpy, beckoning for Melchior to come to her aid. The man just nodded his head with an air of *fouté-pamal*, couldn't care less, and stared at her with a haunting look in his eyes. At times like that Médée felt as if she'd created Rosalia all on her own. She'd just have to assume the consequences, cope with the seed he'd planted. And it was just her hard luck if the harvest was rotten. He, Melchior Montério, wasn't going to get all worked up over a creature with no future.

The man wasn't a bad sort, he simply had a moody and melancholy temperament. He endured his life on earth like the land endured cyclone weather, the torrential rains in the hills, or the drought in dry season. He opened his mouth willingly only to relate the saga of Ancestor Séléna of whom he was the proud descendant. And especially to evoke Marie-Perle, his copper-skinned chabine who'd been — he avowed — the light of his life. As soon as he spoke of her, golden pearls formed in the brown of his eyes and his face lit up with radiant nostalgia. He'd married black Médée — thirteen years his junior — out of pure necessity, because a man can't remain alone in this world. She was there to replace the lost soul mate. Only there to cook his food, wash his clothes, ensure his posterity, and serve as a mother for Olga.

Médée thought she could heal a bruised heart with love's simple remedies. Youth is foolish and eager for illusions, as everyone knows. Two–three days after their marriage, the man took the wind out of her happy dreams and Médée traded her bright face for the dreary mask that so delighted Olga.

Love did not light Melchior's eyes. Fleshly desire caught up with him from time to time. But only when their bodies touched in bed. In spite of himself, a force drove him to mount Médée and penetrate her in an abrupt and enraged manner, as if possessed. In the middle of the night, the motions of love burst in like a gang of thieves, wasting no words or caresses. One would have thought his days were counted. Had to get it done quickly. Unhook the door. Go in. Then get out. Go in and out of Médée's body. Go in and out, with a guilty conscience and repenting already. Petty larceny. Vile thrill, given the meager spoils. And their bodies separated in the morning. Both went their separate ways.

Médée could have walked tall on this earth. You could still perceive trapped sparks of joy deep in her black eyes. Smoth-

14

ered bursts of laughter in her throat. Alas, since her marriage, she drifted along through life like a creature slighted by fate. A tall negress, she went stoop-shouldered, broken-backed, and her legs always wobbling just a bit in the dresses she made for herself, hastily, without giving much thought to being attractive. Though the winds of the hot iron and hair curlers had blown over the land, converting all women in that single fanatic blast—those from Piment first and foremost—Médée persisted in wearing her hair in the braids of backwoods–broads. And though the only person who spoke to her, Silène Couba—known as The Crab due to the deep lines furrowing her cheeks—tried to give her beauty advice, Médée continued to behave like one of those old women whom death has overlooked. She went down into the center of town with her hair tied up in stiff old rags that could have terrorized the rattail combs and boar-bristle brushes that styled the straightened mops of those days. When Rosalia came, things only got worse. And the feeling of having committed some crime she couldn't remember began to weigh silently within her, like a bullet wedged near the heart that is too dangerous to extract.

After five years and as many miscarriages, Médée found herself pregnant with her second daughter, Mina. Up until then her life had been meaningless and the way people in Piment looked at her only made it all the more clear. Yes, what had she contributed to the world? She'd given birth to a retarded child. A creature that frightened the other kids with her disjointed movements, her broken words, the horn-braids standing up on her head despite their being soaked in carapate oil. An unspeakable thing that could turn into a crazed top for hours, whirling, whirling, whirling around the courtyard, arms outspread and eyes blank. Or else stand smitten and despondent, a ghastly stone statue in the garden, her two feet stuck into a rotting breadfruit . . . Or still yet, start talking in an unknown tongue and tell stories of snakes and dolls shut up in boxes that drew tears to her eyes. Sometimes she banged her head till bumps swelled on her forehead and blood spurted everywhere.

People whispered that Médée beat Olga . . . Sheer lies. In truth, Médée was blamed for everything that went wrong because she hadn't been able to console Melchior. That was perhaps her greatest fault. He had made the mistake of choosing her, when during his period of mourning interested parties—girls in full blood from Piment—did not neglect their duty, helped him with the housework, brought him hot soup and syrup cakes, offered their bodies to his grief. Suzon Mignard was the favorite for a long time. The one everyone had a presentiment about, the one who was always rejected. Always just a gallop behind.

What drove Melchior to hook up with that drab Médée whose relatives and origins were unknown? What blind star guided Melchior to that birdbrain? And to what end, Lord!

And why not Suzon Mignard whom Melchior had chosen on the school bench?

The birth of Mina finally brought meaning to Médée's life. Not a cloud darkened the skies of the pregnancy. She was born without a hint of suffering. Healthy little *ti moun* child. Médée felt it was a sign from heaven. And heaven doesn't lie, that's what they say back home. Mina became her pride and joy, the dawn of her life, her sunshine and her heart's consolation. To everyone's surprise, the child brought the disparate members of the family together. Mina was the link between them all. She seemed to draw them to her like light draws lost travelers in the night.

Olga turned a kind face toward the child. Rosalia's whirligig sessions became less frequent. And even Melchior, who'd been hoping for a son, fell to worshipping her. He said that Mina would be the staff of his old age. He was thirty-seven that year. Only eleven more years to live. His name was written in boldface characters in the Book. In those days he believed deep in his soul that their misfortune had abandoned them and gone off to torment other folks. Incapable of showing gratitude, he never went out of his way to grant two–three words of thanks, but he felt indebted to Médée and did attempt a few smiles that, from lack of practice, quickly turned to grimaces. Whenever he started back up toward the cabin, he'd call out the child's name. Mina! Mina! Mina! She jumped into his dirt-stained arms. He pressed her close to his heart so she might hear the pulsing of his blood and caress the tangled hairs on his chest. He begged for kisses, watched for her first words and never tired of glorifying the work of art that had sprung from his loins.

Thanks to benign providence, a heaven-sent gift, Médée laid down her tormented mask and learned to like herself again in no time. Her metamorphosis was spectacular. Now when she went down to Piment, people turned as she passed. No longer to find fault with her, confabulate or gossip behind her back. But to contemplate her, for it was no small miracle. Madame had straightened up her carcass, paraded around, head, titties, and bottom high.

Madame looked the sun straight in the eyes, it was downright outrageous. Madame pressed her hair. Primped herself. Perfumed herself, just like Silène Couba, hardly a commendable friend, guilty of seventy-five abortions in the lean-to of her courtyard, just a few steps from the church ... And much to the dismay of Melchior, painted her thick lips with blood-red lipstick she'd taken a liking to and that gave her a provocative femme fatale pout, like Ava Gardner, like Marilyn Monroe ...

At the Syrian Habib's store — Worldwide Fabrics — she and Silène chose remnants of gay material from which she cut out stylish patterns purchased over the counter at the bazaar. She seemed to have entered into a new loop of her life, took to women that people pointed fingers at, floozies with flaccid *coucounes*, worn out by the rods of too many black men. Swear to God, Médée respected Melchior. She went to confession the first Thursday of every month and father Michel could bear witness, laying his hand on the Old and the New Testament, that the woman didn't offer her body to anyone. Even if he thought Melchior, her God-given husband, was an old, embittered, repulsive man . . . who'd robbed her of her youth . . . An accursed tree upon which no bird wished to light.

The year that Olga left to go to secretarial school in Point-à-Pitre, the Palace Cinema was inaugurated with great fanfare in the town of Piment. Madame became a regular. Madame no longer felt guilty for having brought a retarded child into the world. Lord, you should have seen her on Saturdays with her girls, Mina and Rosalia! They were the first to arrive at the ticket booth. While they waited for the usherette, they sat down on the steps and talked, kissed each other, and laughed so you would have thought that life was smiling upon them, that Rosalia's head wasn't elongated, and that the twisted words that came from her mouth were totally comprehensible. The people standing, holding up the poster-plastered walls with their shoulders and hands, glared at them with steely looks that didn't faze them. They'd come for the dream that Technicolor cinema offered, its thrilling suspense, and its bigger-than-life kisses. And who cared if the films were shown a few years late. Italian, American, and French productions preceded by newsreels about major world events: the fairy-tale of Farah Diba, Doña Fabiola's marriage to the King of Belgium, the assassination of John Fitzgerald Kennedy, De Gaulle in Martinique, the Goitschel sisters at the Innsbruck games, Tutankhamen in Paris . . . Médée watched all the films passionately. Though she admitted she had a particular weakness for Italian actresses, she'd have thrown them all over for just one Marilyn Monroe. "If I'd been born in America, I could have been like Marilyn," she confided to Silène.

At the age of six, the year that Mina entered first grade, Rose was still somewhat subject to her crazy spells, her whirligigs, her quirks. However, she now spent her leisure time contemplating her sister, imitating her gestures, and repeating her chatterings. She'd become so well behaved that she ended up gaining Melchior's confidence and, since she wasn't going to die anytime soon as had been predicted, she became Mina's official escort to school. She didn't know how to read or write, but she watched over the Adored Child better than a guardian angel. When they passed, people fell silent, froze in comic postures, both surprised and fascinated by the fantastic pair that they watched until it disappeared in a bend behind a cane field, one girl following in the footsteps of the other, copying her every move and swinging the bag full of books from right to left.

At first Rosalia waited for Mina all day long with her fingers clinging pathetically to the bars of the school gate. Her little sister was in a classroom. She knew that. She'd brought her there. She'd been asked to. But why? "You don't go in! No matter what, don't go in! It ain't the Palace! Miss Rutice won't like it!" Médée told her. Yet extraordinary things seemed to be happening in there, a strange type of cinema that was off-limits to her. Something mysterious was gathering behind those walls, allowing, at times, songs to escape that flew rapidly out to fill the courtyard like a cloud of pigeons. Endlessly chanted A's, I's, and O's slipped between the blinds and began to bounce, bounce, bounce till they reached Rosalia who, feeling vaguely guilty of abandoning her sister, waited for hours for Mina in the sun or in the rain, head filled with songs, heart racing, face dismayed. Old Clarissia, who lived across the street from the school in a two-hundred-year-old cabin, tried to tell her more than once that it was time for her to leave, that her sister was there to learn how to decipher words, recite the tables, and reproduce life on paper. Life, with its complex words, its explosive colors and its strange forms. But Rosalia didn't hear a word. During recess, Mina felt sorry for her and came to touch her fingers through the wrought iron bars. She gave her a quick kiss and a piece of her bread and chocolate.

"Go back to the house!" she ordered. "It's not finished yet, understand? Go back to Mama, Rose! Come back later . . . everyone's looking at you! The principal doesn't want you to stay here!"

Rosalia didn't budge a finger, her eyes begged for one last show of affection. So then Mina went back to jump rope or play hopscotch with her schoolmates. And Rosalia lost sight of her again, for all the children wore checkered smocks of the same orange material that made them look identical from a distance. Her face grew even longer and, clinging to the gate in that way, she looked like a scarecrow that the schoolchildren spat and jeered at for fun. Sometimes Clarissia handed her a piece of bread spread with guava jelly. Or Suzon, the good soul, brought her a mango.

Around five o'clock in the afternoon, Mina finally reappeared. Rosalia's throat was dry, her lips cracked, and her stomach full of wind. Even so, she grinned widely and her heart pounded with joy. She grabbed the book satchel, took her sister's hand in her own and didn't let go of it until they reached the top of Morne Calvaire. Mina told her all about her day. Echoing her sister's words, Rosalia tried diligently and fervently to reproduce the sounds.

What finally brought her back to the cabin was the sudden passion she developed for painting. The first time Mina began to paint in front of her, Rosalia yanked the paintbrush out of her hand and splashed her work with ugly streaks. She seemed to think that the color, some miraculous oil, came from the hairs of the paintbrush.

Mina gave her a clean paper, a codfish tail, and her palette of colors. Rose covered her eyes with both hands.

Mina called gently to her, "Rosalia! Rosalia! I'll teach you, all right?"

Rose didn't bat an eyelash. But her wild braids, whipped in the wind blowing up on the hilltop, said yes and no. Yes! No! Yes! No!

After a minute, she spread her fingers. Her little sister dipped the paintbrush into the water in the old Nestle's milk can, stroked it on the cake of yellow paint and made a picture of a sun. They were lying side by side on the bare floor of the gallery. Big, twelve-year-old Rosalia and little Mina who was only six. Sole guardians of the cabin. Médée had gone to buy some fish at the market and Melchior was off in his banana grove.

From the veranda, they could see Piment, the white church, the abandoned sugar refinery and its ruined chimney with broad-leafed plants twining up it, the black snake of the main road running between the yellow flamboyant trees, the cabin roofs of red corrugated iron, and at the far end of town, the venerable hundred-year-old royal palms. On some days the two sisters watched the sailboats drifting over the sea in the trade winds. Mina played at counting the cruise ships, barges, sand freighters, banana boats, trawlers. She gave lessons to her sister. "Count on your fingers, One. Two. Three . . . Go on! What comes next, Rosalia?" But the other girl simply stammered, one, two, three . . . Eyes brimming with gratitude, she waited for Mina to pronounce the other numbers she couldn't recite.

"What do you want to paint Rosalia?" asked Mina in a bright, schoolmistress voice.

The other girl pointed to a lone boat in the middle of the sea. She stuck the fish tail resolutely into the water, smashed it onto the indigo paint cake and smeared it over the paper.

"Blow on it now! Blow! It has to dry!" exclaimed Mina.

Rosalia was already washing the paintbrush, rubbing it into the white paint. She painted something that, from a great distance, might look like a boat. A large straggling mark, a wild mane in the two intermingling blues of the sea and the sky.

From that day onward, Rosalia was able to quell her madness by painting what she saw from high on the hilltop. When she dashed out a painting of a tree, she lay down in the grass and, with her head thrown backward, swiped at her bit of cardboard with the paintbrush. The tree became in itself an inextricable forest like those the discoverers of the New World penetrated. A greenish imbroglio of branches and leaves that could shelter terrifying fauna. She was inspired by everything except the sun and humans, which were not depicted in any of her pictures. Never a face. Not a body. Little light. But many trees with no trunks, boats on stormy seas, enormous flowers and dark, barren hills.

Médée, who went into ecstasy over her older daughter's artwork because she saw it through eyes blinded by maternal love, sometimes thought she recognized a mouth in an avant-garde corolla, a nose, a hand with three fingers, an ear or a toe hanging from a branch. The truth was that in admiring Rosalia's lifeless paintings, Médée wanted to prove to herself that the child wasn't so terribly retarded—perhaps simply misunderstood, like the great artists who live and die amidst the general indifference of their contemporaries and are later discovered by future generations. So she spotted things that were invisible to others, animals or parts of human bodies she could pin a name on, as one picks out—if he takes the trouble—shapes in the movements of clouds . . . The profiles of emperors, camels with six humps, catfish, herds of elephants, celestial seahorses, ancestors' faces, or smiling angels in frayed robes.

Each evening brought a new work, created on pieces of cardboard gleaned in the boutiques of Piment, painted in gouache bought with the pocket money Melchior provided each week. Inevitably, Médée became a collector. It never would have crossed her mind to throw out a single one of Rosalia's pictures. Day after day, up until her death—in 1975— she conscientiously put them away in old crates that had once contained salted cod. She quickly gave up trying to show them to Melchior. He stared at the pictures in disgust, for all he saw in them were wasted francs, madwomen's monkey tricks, and a bunch of hogwash.

In December of 1969 Olga climbed up the hill for the last

time on Douglas's arm. He was a young professor of mathematics setting sail for a future as a functionary in France. In the same visit, they announced that they were married and would soon be departing. Olga was wearing patent leather high-heeled shoes. Her hand remained nestled in her husband's during the whole visit. In those days Douglas sported a proud mustache and two-toned moccasins that gave him the air of a dandy. The newlyweds stood in the middle of the courtyard smiling. And in front of Melchior, who kept a closed mouth and a frown on his face, Olga snuggled up to her sweet love, smothering him with kisses. Rosalia watched the scene from the veranda. Médée was only half-listening to the diva, but watching her closely with a sad expression, thinking that love did exist elsewhere than in the cinema. It was inside of Olga's body, it was blowing over Morne Calvaire. If she'd dared, she would have touched Olga, touched her palpitating flesh. Even wished she could become Douglas's very hand, so extraordinary was the bright blaze of that love.

"Don't cry, Médée, we'll see each other again. And you, come here!" Olga said to Mina. "I'm going away to France, honey. I'm giving you my gold cross as a present so that you won't forget me. Say goodbye! We'll see each other again, I promise."

She took Mina in her arms and granted her a kiss drawn from the infinite reserve destined for Douglas. Then she marked a pause, brushed back a strand of hair with a studied gesture and, for the first time in her life, pronounced Rosalia's name.

"Come on! Let's have a kiss, Rosalia!"

Till then, Rose had been following the conversation with the same remote look that froze her face as soon as she sat down nice and quiet in the Palace between Mina and Médée. At the sound of her name, she started. Backed away. Then began to scream and run, run and scream, trying to disappear into the banana grove.

Lovely Olga's mask cracked. Her legs buckled and she clung to Douglas's arm. Suddenly the pebbles that had gotten into her shoes just then made her feel uncomfortable. She smoothed her hair.

"I didn't touch her . . . I didn't touch her . . ." She mumbled, calling her husband as a witness, while Rosalia's screams bounced from hilltop to hilltop.

"What's wrong with her?" stuttered Douglas.

"She's throwing a fit as usual . . . Well, I'll be saying goodbye to you, Papa. And goodbye to you, Médée . . ."

At those words she spared them two little kisses, a stiff smile on her face, refusing to let Rose's screams shake her.

After those events, Melchior went through life ever more limpingly. Wounded in his heart by some mysterious weapon, his mood varied like the weather. Some days he proclaimed loudly and clearly that if he were wearing his body out with labor, it was for Mina alone. And that he didn't give a damn that Olga had gotten married behind his back. That he couldn't care less about having a crazy daughter and a wife who thought she was Marilyn Monroe. Other times you'd have thought he was besieged by an army of mischievous spirits that were driving him into the boiling bath of jealousy. Then he'd follow Médée everywhere. You'd see him lurking at the back of the Palace Theater. And it was pitiful to see him in the marketplace or the church hiding in the shadow of a column. He now surmised — convinced by some well-sharpened tongues — that Rose was not his offspring, for she was the spitting image of a man named Bélisair who they said had sown long-headed and soft-brained creatures in every town in the country. When he badgered her with his imprecations, Médée just shrugged her shoulders. Most often she left him to deal with his misery on his own. Sometimes she sent Mina to see him.

The child had an infallible method of placating him. She'd

ask him to tell her about Ancestor Séléna and the days when the first goats were in need of a home. Melchior protested just to be polite, grumbling into his perpetual three-day beard. Then he began, suddenly relieved at being able to escape his earthly life, happy to lend his tongue to a bit of family epic, and straightening up gradually as he narrated, you'd have thought that Ancestor Séléna could see him from up in her paradise. His smile lit up and he himself marveled at the tale told so many times over. But these interludes were only a soothing balm that was of little help. At the close of his story, Séléna's decadent end was a rude awakening for him. Faced with his own inglorious destiny and the bankrupt dreams of his youth, the words died slowly on his lips. And when he started in on the life and times of his father, Gabriel, it was best to stop questioning him and look the other way, try to find an occupation, think about some poor neglected dishes, a tubful of wash to scrub, a floor to sweep, worry about the mood of the sky ... For Melchior's mood suddenly changed, sometimes into incontrollable anger, other times into a fathomless melancholy. So it was wise to stay out of his way ...

When the villagers asked, he declared he'd even forgotten his elder daughter's face. But oddly enough, when the postman, Délos Mignard, showed up at the top of Morne Calvaire, his heart always skipped a beat and he got as nervous as a filly in heat. His fingers started fidgeting with his straw hat. His eyes fluttered. And his belly pulled in of its own accord, which forced him to tighten his belt buckle with a mechanical gesture, looking irritated, and check to see if his green snakeskin wallet was still where he left it, in the back pocket of his pants.

All Médée could do was put her assumptions and interpretations end to end. According to her, Melchior got into that state because his fondest dream was to open a letter coming from France. A letter from Olga. Alas! Délos never brought anything but mail from Basse-Terre or Pointe-à-Pitre: professions of faith from candidates up for election, tax assessments, ever more exorbitant water bills. Mignard didn't need too much goading to sink into a gushing account with assorted gossip that he often briskly pursued alone. Melchior answered him with sluggish nods, inappropriate grumbling, and throat clearing. During these monologues, Délos never failed to whisper two–three words in Melchior's ear concerning lovely Suzon, who was growing older. It was like an old ritual between the two of them. Melchior bowed his head as if to say that there was nothing he could do about it, and Délos—a knowing smile on his face—hitched his mailbag back up on his shoulder.

Mina could still see her father turning his back on the postman, his dispirited face, his pants bagging over fleshless buttocks, weighed down by the green snakeskin wallet. Near the end of his life, Melchior sat on the steps of the veranda every morning. Waiting for Délos and the letters from Olga. Hoping, until the sun was rooted in the very center of the sky.

IV

Three years after Melchior's death, Olga's letter finally arrived. Nine years of silence . . . And Olga was talking as if they'd seen each other just the day before, as if the life she'd lived in Piment belonged to someone else, as if Mina had lost her memory . . .

"I hope you're a good student . . . You're fourteen now . . ."

Olga chatted with a calm face, and Mina remembered her scowling at Médée, refusing to pronounce Rose's name, whom she ranked in a class with animals. Olga bestowing smiles, kisses, sweet words upon her alone: "Mina, my pretty girl . . . Mina, my baby . . ." Olga and her two faces.

"You'll like it here. You'll get your bearings quickly, you'll see . . . Isn't that right, Doug?"

What ever became of Douglas? wondered Mina. Maybe Olga got tired of saying his full name. But Doug lay heavy on the tongue like an undercooked dumpling, Doug! Rang too short in the ear, Doug! A whack over the head with a stick ...

"Isn't that right, Doug?"

The man seemed lost in his thoughts. What had become of the dandy of 1969?

"Yes, yes, this is your home. We're delighted to have you," he exclaimed.

His missing mustache accentuated the thinness of his pink-colored lips. He spoke without smiling and his words of welcome sounded hollow.

"Take her suitcase, Doug! And you, make yourself comfortable! Take off your sweater! Come sit by me so I can get a good look at you. You have no idea ... I'm so happy. You're pretty, my little Mina. Even prettier than I remembered."

Rosalia let out a little moan. Terror welled in her eyes. She leaned her back against the china cabinet, the look on her face imploring Mina to take her away, far away.

"Doug! Bring us something to drink!" Olga shouted into the apartment.

Rosalia raised her arms as if to ward off invisible blows. The flames in her hair doubled in intensity.

"So tell me, Mina! What do you want to do later on? You have ambitions, I hope ..."

Olga threw her left leg over the right. The dangling tip of her toe tapped out a rhythm in the air. She didn't ask a single question about Piment, nothing about the circumstances of the fire. She'd turned the page. "You know, ever since I left, I never stopped thinking about you. I saw you in my dreams sometimes ..."

Looking worried, Rosalia waggled her head.

"We'll go shopping when you've rested up. I took some days off for you."

For the first time, she looked straight at Mina. Her gaze didn't falter, but showed the desire to read in her sister's eyes whether the past had left marks. Whether Mina could clearly remember the torture Rosalia had endured. The disdain with which she'd treated Médée. Her silence after Melchior's death . . .

"Fruit juice," Douglas said apologetically as he set three glasses down on the table.

"No! Doug! No! We're going to celebrate Mina's arrival! There's a bottle of champagne in the fridge."

Terrified, Rosalia immediately spread her wings and flew to the other end of the room.

Very quickly, thanks to Douglas who proved to be loquacious in Olga's absence, Mina was able to reconstruct the nine years of silence that had made up their life in France. Seven years of struggling to have a baby. When the verdict was pronounced —irreversible sterility—Olga had not shed a tear. She'd lived as a recluse for a few months. Refused to go out. No longer had the strength to go to Paris. She felt as if people saw through her, knew that God had not given her the means of bringing a child into the world. In the beginning of those years, she'd renamed Douglas as Doug, as if it were his fault and he were no longer but half a man in her eyes.

The first few days Olga was beaming. She anticipated everything Mina could desire. She kissed her. Took her in her arms. Doted over her. She had a fourteen-year-old child in the house and she couldn't get over it. A heaven-sent, flesh and blood daughter living in the little room that had remained desolate for so long. Olga imposed her joy authoritatively. And it was just too bad if grief and fire were its arrogant parents. Several days in a row she took Mina out to the large Parisian department stores ... Printemps, Bon Marché, Samaritaine, Galeries Lafayette. She laughed as she paid for Mina's wardrobe, as if she could buy back her weight in nasty deeds of the past. Be free at last. They walked up the wide boulevards, strolled around Saint-Michel, ate lunch in brasseries, Chinese, or Greek restaurants, visited museums, took the bus and the metro. Lived a life of pleasure.

And Rosalia tagged after them. Ran and flew behind them, looking distraught, eyes glowing red.

Olga had great plans for Mina. Confronted with her report cards, she was quickly disillusioned and had to accept her sister's modest ambitions. A Brevet d'Etudes Professionnelles (BEP), a vocational diploma in the health and welfare services for a lackluster future.

"Remember how much you used to love school, baby? Tell me what happened? You had a lot of ability ..."

Mina had turned her back on Junior High School after Médée's death on April 18, 1975. She'd grown suddenly disgusted with it as if she'd been stricken with a stupendous revelation.

What use was it to acquire knowledge? Death could strike at any minute. It lay in wait for the living. Laughing at their petty joys. What use was it to fill one's head with dates, theorems, great men, and grammatical rules? What use, since life was one long, endless war?

On April 18, 1975 Médée had gone down to the center of Piment and a Titan truck had cut her down. Dragged her body for several yards. Torn off an arm. Thrown her into the ditch. She was still warm when they found her, poor Marilyn from Piment. Blood on her lace blouse. Skirt thrown up and torn.

Some people carried her up to Morne Calvaire and laid her in her bed. Melchior didn't say anything. Didn't shed a single tear. He pulled a chair up next to the bed and with both hands pressed between his emaciated thighs, remained there, stricken, back stooped, head bowed. Médée was dead. Médée had abandoned him. Médée had gone off, leaving him alone with Mina and Rose who were crying with shared grief. From that moment on, he knew he would no longer have the strength to survive what he'd long considered as a curse. During the funeral, he walked alone at the head of the procession. Dressed in black, Mina and Rosalia held hands three steps behind him, followed by the women of Piment, who had never liked their mother. Rosalia was calm during the mass. But when they reached the cemetery, she started screaming and whirling around. They let her be until she tore a conch shell from Grandfather Gabriel's grave. She was going to bang herself over the head with it but Suzon Mignard held her arm back. Melchior looked at his daughter in complete surprise. He lifted a finger to the sky in a gesture that no one could interpret. Soon after, the sky darkened and it began to rain.

Despite Suzon's show of loyalty to him, Melchior had no desire to remain in this world. He was awaiting death. You could sense it in his behavior. His way of imploring the heavens with a mute prayer. The new way in which he looked at Rosalia, believing she was the bearer of higher knowledge. His suspicious interest in a pair of goats that he'd acquired for a very high price in Lamentin and that people saw him caring for with morbid affection. The post mortem instructions given to Mina every day . . .

On July 18 of that same year, three months after Médée's death, one of the Haitian laborers found his already stiff body in the banana grove. His cutlass lay next to him just like the sword of a valiant musketeer. And his old green snakeskin wallet was clutched in his left hand. Melchior was buried with no grand ado, but grieved by a procession of women from Piment.

Mina was eleven years old. She'd just entered junior high school. Up until that year, 1975, the beloved child had never really known suffering. Save for Rosalia's madness, Melchior's lunacy, Médée's whims, and Olga's two faces, she'd enjoyed her life on Morne Calvaire. The world that lay ahead of her now was bleak and cruel. She had lost her mother and father. All that remained were poor Rose and Olga who'd gone off to France ...

After Melchior's death she only went to school occasionally. She felt obligated to stay on the hill, as if she were the guardian. Take care of Rosalia and the young goats. Observe Piment, the tiny cars in the middle of the village, the clouds that formed in the sky, the rain on the islands, the boats sailing away to other lands.

One, two, three.

Also keep a lookout to make sure death didn't come looking for them ...

Banana trees proliferated everywhere up on the hill. The guinea grass grew to gigantic proportions. Vines strangled the trees. Rotting fruits vied to be the first to decay. A few people still ventured to climb up to see the two girls, take them a nice hot meal, half a baguette, some meat stock soup, or a piece of cake. They came back saddened, unable to find words to describe the total neglect that reigned on the hill. Of course there was Tibert, the loyal cousin. And also Délos and his sister Suzon Mignard, who was slowly beginning to go blind, but wasn't averse to climbing the hill to see how the orphans were getting along.

For three years they lived like that, making do with their loneliness and eating mostly cassavas with coconut that they picked up Friday evenings at Momonne's. And fruit—oranges, bananas, guavas, and avocados picked in the orchards running wild. When Mina received letters from the principal, she left the hill grudgingly, begging Rose to wait for her and not to get dejected or into mischief and to always keep on the lookout for death.

31

The girls were hardly ever seen in town. They went down to go to the post office and withdraw their relief money. And to the Palace where karate films had replaced American and Italian productions. It was like a pilgrimage for them, in memory of Médée. They always sat in the third row, leaving an empty seat between the two of them. On the way back, they collected old cardboard boxes from the shops in Piment for Rosalia's paintings. People took the opportunity to fill their baskets with Vache qui rit cheese, Kohler chocolate, bread at the Dotémar bread shop, paint boxes, pots of strawberry jam, Blédina flour, remnants of fabric, and France-apples.

V

A few months after she arrived in France, Mina could see that Olga's enthusiasm was beginning to wane. Her mask cracked pathetically. In truth, the eldest Montério girl was constantly struggling with ghosts from the past and all of the little angels she'd been unable to conceive. Neither of them had anything to share with the other, no mother, father, or sister. They never mentioned Piment and kept the doors to their memories from back home tightly locked for fear of being swept away in the winds of regret and bitter words. They lived in the present, wary of one another.

When alone with Mina, Olga's husband took on several different characters. First of all there was the strict Mr. Bétel who taught in a high-priority secondary school; he made her study her lessons and explained mathematical problems to her. Then Doug made his entrance, a man haunted with dreams of a family, grieved in his conversations with his confidante. But after a little while, Douglas eclipsed the others. He smiled at the mistakes that Mina scattered through her assignments. She laughed. Suddenly Douglas looked younger. He grew curious about her life. He asked questions about Piment. Mina told him about the days before the fire, Rosalia's crazed drawings, their breakfasts of fruit and cassava. She never went any further than that, because Rosalia was always spying on them. If he insisted, trying to discover what the circumstances were, Mina fell silent or she asked him to talk about his own childhood in Grande-Terre where he'd been born, about his meeting Olga.

Rosalia blinked her eyes and nodded her head.

They spoke very openly about everything. And Mina found it hard to believe she could talk like that with the dandy who'd climbed up the hill in 1969, his hand clasped in Olga's. The thin mustache had disappeared, but he was still the same man all right, with the same elegance, that starry-eyed look about him, the blissful smile of someone who still believes in paradise on earth. He no longer thought about the desired child. He was Douglas and not Doug. The Douglas six-year-old Mina had known. The one who'd made Médée cry.

Sometimes, when he no longer controlled his gestures, he took Mina's hand. Held on to it for a long time. Then she felt her heart speeding up. Her body tensing. She no longer paid any attention to Rosalia, no longer saw her fiery mane.

After three years, in May of 1981, Mina decided to risk telling him about the night of the fire. She was seventeen years old— no longer a child. Her body had taken on womanly form. Sometimes she dreamed of Douglas. She described Rosalia. Her burnt nightgown, her red eyes, the flaming braids on her head. She told him that she was there. There all the time, had never left her since the fire. Douglas of course couldn't see her. But he didn't laugh. He was dumbstruck for a moment, his eyes glued to the span of wall Rosalia was supposedly leaning against.

"She's always there?" he asked.

"All the time. Night and day. Everywhere . . . She even sleeps next to me. With her flames. Her burnt nightgown . . . I can feel her breathing on my neck . . ."

He pulled Mina toward him. Pressed her to his chest. He kissed her. First on the forehead as one does with very young children, with old people. Then on her cheeks. Her lips were silky and soft. That was exactly what she'd been waiting for. She offered him her mouth.

"We mustn't do this!" he moaned, pulling suddenly away. "We have to stop now. If not . . ."

"But I want to . . ." Mina heard herself responding, as if the words didn't really belong to her. Even though they were coming from her mouth, they seemed to be dictated by someone else.

"Kiss me again."

He drew away. Stood up. Stood for a moment facing her, trembling and stuttering.

"We have no right to do this to Olga. We have no right. Not in her house. She took you in, Mina. She's unhappy enough as it is . . . I don't want to hurt her . . ."

Rosalia cowered in her corner.

"She won't know. Come here, I want you," pleaded Mina.

She felt possessed, that was it. Possessed by a voice, a breath, a desire that overwhelmed and terrified her, but also gave her a feeling of power. Douglas shook his head. He looked like a sinner being offered the Holy Communion.

"She hated Rosalia . . . She beat her, scratched her, slapped her . . . Believe me, she's no saint!"

"What's come over you Mina, stop it!"

"I want you! I want you to take me . . ."

Rosalia lifted her arms as if blows were going to rain down upon her.

"Mina, you're mistaken . . . You're my sister-in-law. I still love Olga."

With both hands pushed deep into his pockets, he backed away.

"I told you about Rosalia. I've never talked to anyone about it . . . It's as if I were naked in front of you . . ."

"I'm going to go out, Mina. I need to get some fresh air."

He glanced warily at the corner where Rosalia squirmed, peered at Mina as if he no longer knew her.

"Forget what happened! We should never be alone together again. All right, Mina?"

"No, it's not all right, Douglas. Kiss me again! One last time . . ."

But he disappeared into the hallway leaving her alone with Rosalia, who was rocking her body back and forth from one foot to the other.

1981 . . . For three years Olga had been playing the part of a mama and Mina that of a docile child. Three years of charades and playacting. That evening at dinner Douglas ignored Mina.

Olga related the story of a couple in the throes of divorce proceedings.

"Bernstein is sick of them. One day they're on good terms, the next their cursing at each other."

Mina asked for some wine.

"Just a drop," Olga ordered.

Mina took a deep drink.

"They came back again this morning. You should have seen them Doug! Two turtle doves . . ."

"Why don't you ever talk about Rosalia?" interrupted Mina. She was staring straight into her older sister's eyes.

"Why should I talk about her?" asked Olga dryly.

She served herself another glassful of wine.

"Why couldn't we talk about her?"

"Because it's in the past, that's all!" replied Olga before turning toward Douglas . . . "Yes, what was I saying . . . This morning milord and milady arrived arm in arm. You can bet your life, Bernstein didn't want to let them in. He kept them hanging around in the waiting room and . . ."

35

"It's not in the past!" Mina said coldly.

"Then what is it?"

Olga's fingers were drumming on the table. Exasperated, smile frozen, she was searching Douglas's eyes for support.

"You never loved her, isn't that right? You beat her whenever you had the slightest excuse because she was retarded and ugly and her head was deformed. Did you tell that to Douglas the day you came up on the hill? Did you explain her screams when you were walking back down to Piment? Did you tell him that you terrorized her? That you never called her by her name? That she was so terrified of you she pissed her pants? Did you tell him about the blows, Olga?"

"That's enough!" Douglas cut in. "It does no good to drag up the past. You have to calm down, Mina: You really need to calm down! I don't know what's gotten into you of late but ..."

"No, let her be," groaned Olga.

She threw her head back and held her empty glass like the pommel of a cane. Her eyes were intensely bright.

"You have no right to judge me, Mina ... I was a child. I'd lost my mother. You know what it's like to lose your mother, baby. Rosalia was my scapegoat ... It's true, I beat her ... With whatever I could lay my hands on ... But I'm not the one who killed her ..."

"You're trying to say I killed her!" retorted Mina in surprise.

"I'm not trying to say anything ... I live in France. I never went back home. I don't ever want to hear about Piment again. I have nothing but bad memories of the place. I don't want to poison my life with it!"

Having said that, she pushed back her chair and left the dining room.

Douglas's anger was silent. He stayed away from her for a week. In the afternoon, when he came home from work early, he closed himself up in his office. Mina tried a hundred times to rehabilitate herself in his eyes, through her actions and words, acting the part of the model child who adored Olga.

36

Smooth smiling face. But deep in her heart, and in the loneliness of her room, she prayed that Douglas would desire her and take her as a woman. It went all the way back to that period in her life, that desire to be taken by a man's body, to feel herself being penetrated by a man, any man, Douglas or someone else . . .

Over by the window, eyes half shut, Rosalia seemed to be asleep on her feet, like a weary guardian. Mina pretended not to see her, telling herself that the burning girl would soon disappear if she stopped talking to or looking at her. She'd put up with her for three years. Looking back on it, Mina realized it had been all too easy for her to grow accustomed to Rose's presence, her muffled wails, the flames surrounding her—that only she could see. She now wondered if Rosalia had remained on earth in order to take revenge upon her stepsister. Mina shuddered, believing that she too was a tool in Rose's charred hands. A well-sharpened knife, ready to be sunk into Olga's heart.

VI

When it came time to face the coming winter, Mina felt sorry for Rose, who either flew about half naked in her ragged shroud, or slipped along at her side, with her burned, bare feet on the frozen sidewalks, in the melted snow and the brackish gutter water. "You're going to catch cold!" Mina kept saying, as if she were addressing a living and breathing creature. "Stay home in Olga's warm house, at least until spring."

But Rosalia never left her, latched right on to her steps. If she stopped wailing for a moment, Mina grew concerned. "Tell me what's bothering you, my little Rose . . ." Sometimes, when they were alone at Olga's, Mina talked about the way things were back home, back in the days when they were both alive. Rosalia smiled faintly, waggling her head. Her flaming braids seemed

37

to shudder with pleasure and glow a deep red like the cane stalks in the evening trades when men rally at harvest time to fire the fields and drive the ravenous rats from the sweet reed. Rosalia melted onto the bed, her black fingers, in which the whitened bones could be seen, clutching Mina's hand. And her eyes begged to go further and further back into the days of old, to reveal the legend of the cabin, the follies of her youth . . .

For her, Mina climbed back in time, all the way back to the days before she was born, through dark corridors echoing with the voices of ancestors who opened the book of their lives to pages that had remained intact for the sake of posterity and the magic of memory.

Do you remember, Rosalia . . . At nightfall, the wind wrenched cries from the trunks of old banana trees growing behind the cabin . . .

A wild growth of trees, abandoned to the weeds and the whims of the heavens. No one ever set foot in there after Melchior's death. A hilltop where two inseparable sisters lived. Single-handedly, young Mina took care of her older sister, Rosalia, who remained as simple-minded as a five-year-old child all her life.

Do you remember, Rose . . .

The banana trees proliferated in total anarchy, dropping their bunches under the windows of the cabin. Enormous batches ripened in the trees and fell apart without shedding a tear. The fallen fruit rotted and one day filled the air with a sweetish, fetid fragrance that was a joy for bluebottle flies, worms, rats, and various scolopendra.

Nights, Rosalia often had nightmares and her screams mingled with the moaning of the briny wind and the terrifying cries of the banana grove that we believed was haunted by fraternities of tortured spirits. She-devils loosed from the olden days. Cursed souls who'd been refused their passports for hell, wearing suits of ashen dust and expressions from beyond the grave. Veterans who were cut down in the Dardanelles and resuscitated in the islands. All peoples from the Realm of Darkness rambling about, each in search of his own dream, accompanied by the ghastly, ear-splitting trills of insects. You could also hear the barking of stray dogs tearing the remains of a wayward zombie to pieces, the frantic flight of *soucougnans* and bats in the breadfruit trees, the dwarf Ambarellas, the mango, guava, and papaya trees that the old folks had planted for their daily fare and to aid a penniless neighbor. Processions of chains, clanging of bells, screaming suffering souls . . .

That wooden cabin was at least a hundred years old. What remained of its strength was being wasted in the unequal combat it was waging against the vines, the tall guinea-grasses and the banana grove that robbed it of sunlight. Its lower planks were slowly being gnawed away—rain, termites, rats—and were cracking like an old woman weary of dragging her body and the bits and pieces of her life around. It had seen a few generations of living beings come through there . . . How many had been born between its boards and gone out feet first, stone dead, in their wedding clothes? It had never taken pleasure in silence, not in the daytime or at night. For the cabin, silence was a mystery that was more easily concealed than fleshly sin in faraway, desolate, unimaginable lands.

Joy and grief at the same time.

Morning laughter, evening laments.

Screams. Words cast up to the saints in heaven. Whimpering. Imprecations. Voices clamoring in unison. Agonized rails. Great outpourings of words to sugarcoat life's cavorting, explain the unfathomable, unscrew the cogs of destiny.

Malign. Mislead. Maltreat. And then scheme. Calculate. Promise to tie the eternal bond with a belle or a beau and for an instant believe oneself to be immortal, an angel fallen straight from heaven.

A hundred years of sounds.

Day and night.

Night and day.

Before the cabin on Morne Calvaire left this world consumed by the flames.

～

Their father Melchior used to tell the story.

Around 1870, the hill had been acquainted with a pair of goat kids that Ancestor Séléna—who saw far and clear—had purchased on credit. The goats mated and had six kids in the first litter. Séléna sold four. Bought another pair. And that's how she built up a fortune. Fed on the succulent grass that grew on the hill, the creatures founded a peaceful strain that reproduced effortlessly and endlessly. After six years, Séléna decided to make a bid for the land she was then renting from a mulatto, whose exact name has been lost over the centuries. They saw each other once a year. Séléna paid him the rent for the land and he renewed the lease. When she got it into her head to become the owner, the man laughed in young Séléna's face. Decades later, having reached the last rounds of her existence, paralyzed, drooling and feeble, Séléna related the epic tale herself, with a glint of pride swimming in her eye. "The mulatto," she said in her quavering voice, "couldn't believe his eyes or his ears." She imitated him, wagging an accusatory finger. "'You! You want to become owner of the land that I lease you! And where will you get the money for that, you poor wretch?'"

Her time-shattering laughter burst forth.

"Ha! Ha! Ha! God be my witness, that man wanted me to pay the rent on his land every year and he didn't never want it to be mine! And one day Massa would decide not to renew the contract! And I'd go off empty-handed, with my herd of goats at my heels!"

She fidgeted in her rocker. Her back straightened miraculously. Her tiny feet began stamping at invisible thieves. With the back of her hand, she wiped away the foam that had formed at the corner of her lips. Then resumed the story of her life, sniffing at the air like a nervous dog.

"When I pulled the three hundred francs I saved after selling my goats from my blouse, the man went green and then blue before turning red. 'Not enough,' is what he said. 'I want double that. And anyway, who says I'm selling?' He called his dog. Pulled up a tuft of grass with all of the roots stuck in a clump of earth. He caressed that earth like the nipples of a virgin and turned his back on me. I remember," Ancestor Séléna said, "that day lightning streaked the sky. Behind the hill, gray clouds scudded by so fast you'd have thought the angels of Beelzebub were pursuing them. But there was also a large white patch, a door to the Kingdom of Heaven. The Good Lord was sending me a sign, letting me know the cards were in my favor. I mustered all my courage and ran after the man. I grabbed that mulatto by the sleeve. 'Sir,' I says to him, 'please, you promise to let me have this land if I get the money up . . . It's for my goats, see how well they like it here!' He jerked abruptly away and gave me an odd look meaning, above all, that I wasn't to touch him—him the arrogant mulatto in his white drill jacket. The dog growled at me and bared its teeth before rubbing against the legs of his good master. 'You'll have your money in three months, Sir.'

"Above us, cracks ran through the sky, it was ready to just bust wide open. Thunder and lightning. The man looked down at me. It wasn't something he was in the habit of doing. That race of men dealt with small folks without ever seeing them. Back in those days I ranked among the hungry poor— worn pockets, empty stomach, holed up in a one-room cabin. 1873, you wouldn't believe it! In those days, blacks didn't own nothing but their aching soul and the freedom that trailed after them like some grim shadow. Niggers was waiting to see if slavery wasn't coming back, in some form or another, some law or decree conceived of back in France by the first cousins

41

of the white folk from here. So you can imagine how they kept each other company while they were waiting!" grunted Ancestor Séléna, picking yellow crusts of rheum from the corners of her eyes. "You should have seen the gaggles of niggers lazing on the steps of their cabins . . . Rum, idle talk, and tambours. Prudence, vigilance, romance, and somnolence. Eyeing the sails out on the horizon. Jumping at every bark of a dog. Waiting for tomorrow. Waiting for day-after-tomorrow. Waiting for sunrise. Waiting for nightfall. Not walking the path through the cane fields. Working for their daily bread. Not filling their head with too many dreams. Living for the moment and filling their life up with cheap pleasures that made one tougher: the flesh of women, the fire of rum, the magic of the *ka*. Owned nothing. Weren't looking to get their feet out of poverty. Were just waiting . . .

"When that mulatto finished looking me up one side and down the other, he asked, 'Why you want to become landowner, black woman? You ain't happy the way things are?' I repeated that it wasn't for me, just so my goats would have a place of their own. He let out a laugh that cracked louder in my heart than thunder in the sky. 'A place of their own! Ha! Ha! Ha! You niggers don't even have a place of your own and you want your goats to be taken into the ranks of possessors! Upon my word, you making fun of me!' His face clapped shut like a coffin over its corpse. 'All right for the three months,' he said before turning away. 'I want six hundred francs, I'll have you know!' And he left me there with my oversized dreams and my landless goats."

Melchior used to say that each time Ancestor Séléna reached this part of the story she paused, left a long silence punctuated with sighs to mark the three months of waiting.

Do you remember, Rosalia, how proud our papa was of Ancestor Séléna? He used to say, "She was a mighty commanding woman for those days!"

42

And knowledgeable and wily to boot! Three months later to the day, Séléna went to the mulatto's notary, purse full of bills, head full of worries. Wearing her sarcenet church dress over her fustian petticoat, she had style, queenly bearing, face smooth and shining. An ebony statue.

Six hundred francs! It was quite a sum! Just imagine, through sacrifice Ancestor Séléna had succeeded in saving nine hundred francs. Nine hundred francs! And why in the devil did she save nine hundred, when the man wanted six hundred? Well, you see, there were rumors in Piment that the mulatto had put the land up for sale and was asking nine hundred francs. They said he was looking for a taker on the double so he could get that negress Séléna off the hill. He couldn't stomach the fact that she had grand dreams and took him for an outright fool, with her story about goats looking for a place of their own. All of a sudden he suspected her of being underhanded and dangerous like white leprosy or smallpox, a bad example for Negroes. But Séléna had ears everywhere.

As soon as she showed her face at the notary's office, he squared himself in his Empire armchair and, with his hands resting flat on the mahogany desk, sized Lady Séléna up with a mocking smile.

"Yes, I see, Madame. You wish to become proprietress of the land you are presently renting."

He adjusted his gold rim glasses, opened a thick file and started leafing through a stack of papers bearing official stamps.

Séléna curled her fingers into her fists as she observed the impeccable manicure of the notary. Her nails were black and worn from work in the fields.

"My client has given me the power of attorney to sell to the first buyer. He wants a ready cash payment, you are aware of that, are you not?"

Séléna nodded her head.

"How much did he ask you for?"

"Six hundred francs, Sir," Séléna whispered with her heart racing.

"Six hundred francs!" objected the notary. "You are gravely mistaken, Madame. I'm terribly sorry."

Cunningly, he feigned to be looking for the price in a wad of papers yanked out of another file.

Séléna held her breath.

"Here I see the sum of nine hundred francs, Madame."

"He told me six hundred francs," sighed Séléna.

"I seriously doubt that. This is the fixed, definitive price."

Séléna put on her cowering negress air, which she'd inherited from her mother.

The notary rose to his feet.

Séléna remained sitting, hunched herself deeper into the cane-seated armchair and wiggled her toes that were imprisoned in the overly narrow patent leather shoes.

"If I can get the money together, will the land be mine?"

"Why yes of course," murmured the notary softly. "Of course, Madame, unless someone buys it before you."

"And you'll give me the deed at the same time?" insisted Séléna.

Standing at the open door, the man was beginning to grow impatient.

"Come back as soon as you have the nine hundred francs, Madame."

Séléna marked a moment's pause and, bursting with controlled jubilation, she took the bills from her bag and began to count, stacking them in piles of one hundred francs on the notary's desk.

When he finished with that part of the story, Melchior was transfigured. Séléna's glory made him beam.

Nine hundred francs! She laid out nine hundred francs! And her face was chiseled in the hard rock that the Soufrière spits out when it gets cross. Clenching his jaw, the notary closed the door. Obliged to give in, he sat back down, assuming the dignified bearing of those stricken by the sword of righteousness. He was twitching with rage, sweating and quivering behind his little glasses.

"Here are your nine hundred francs, Sir. Nine hundred francs to pay for my goats' land."

Later it was rumored that when the mulatto learned the news, he locked himself in his office, put a pistol to his head and sat like that for long hours, suspended between life and death. When he finally decided to pull the trigger, in the same fraction of a second, a providential gust of wind banged a window shut. The bullet then followed an extremely fanciful course. It went through the man's green left eye, glanced off his skull, sparing his brain but still carrying away a tuft of light brown and white hair rooted to a patch of scalp. Alerted by the detonation, his wife and family found him sitting behind his desk, face covered with blood, his remaining eye staring at the tuft of hair blasted onto a shelf in his library between Plato and Socrates; it looked uncannily like the tuft of grass he had pulled up three months earlier on Séléna's hill. Short one eye, but of a sane mind—albeit somewhat melancholy—he withdrew to Grand-Terre where, according to him, blacks did not indulge in such vice. He died at the age of seventy, leaving three children, nineteen grandchildren, an illuminated widow, and a disconsolate dog.

"And what happened to Séléna after that?"

Melchior did not relish venturing behind the curtain of the events that followed. He would begin to stutter. His words grew suddenly incoherent with the flip side of the story. Séléna's glorious reign became frayed. If he was pushed a little, not too much, he would disclose that Ancestor Séléna went through a period of decline. She seemed to be affected by a bizarre malady. She had an uncontrollable urge to buy. She had a morbid and frantic tendency to hoard, to acquire more and more

45

land, which made her hateful in the eyes of her fellow black people. It was said she was possessed, bewitched by evil forces. She called herself the landed mulattress, which—due to her black skin—made people smile. She built the cabin on the hill in 1878 and locked herself into those miserly ways of hers. She lived for many years on dry bread and water up there with her goats, without friend or lover. Her money fructified in the bank, but she never took advantage of it. Then one day, a new priest came to Piment...

And Séléna, who had never even been slightly enamored, became slowly infatuated with the man of God at the Sunday mass week-in and week-out in Piment. That was in 1888. Strangely enough, the priest happened to be looking for a Mount Calvary in order to act out the divine passion of Christ. After many prayers, the Holy Ghost visited his dream one full-moon night and designated Séléna's hill. And that is how, guided by the Lord's finger, he met the woman who was awaiting him as if he were a Messiah. Séléna was already forty years old and had no descendents. When he explained his request, luring her with the promise of a peaceful spot in celestial paradise, Séléna succumbed to the charms of the handsome priest. He didn't ask her to relinquish the hilltop, simply to authorize its access to the faithful in Piment. She signed for fifty years. A few days after the last cross had been planted on the hill, which had been renamed Morne Calvaire, the priest was unceremoniously defrocked and fled to spend the rest of his days in a village that, with a good pair of eyes and a large magnifying glass, can be located on a map of southern France. He was never heard from again.

After his departure, in 1889, Séléna gave birth to a son, Gabriel, whom she loved with all her soul yet never disclosed to him his father's name. The child grew up amongst the goats, lulled by the stories of past glory and the mystery of his birth. Séléna lived to be over a hundred and gradually forgot large portions of her life, even her liaison with the priest. At the end of her life she almost never left the cabin on the hill.

Every day she related the story of the bygone century to her grandchildren, as if she were searching the ruins of her memory, trying to drown herself in the holy waters of her past grandeur, maintaining that her passage on earth would leave the mark of a saintly woman. The faithful who still climbed Morne Calvaire—more out of a desire to gossip than an expression of faith—mumbled between two prayers that the madwoman who lived up there had dipped her soul in the devil's ciborium.

Upon her death, it was discovered that she willed her fortune to the Pope in Rome and to the episcopate in general. Thank God, she forgot to mention Morne Calvaire in her testament, and Gabriel, Melchior's father, was able to snatch it from the clutches of the church. The evening of Séléna's burial, the disinherited son took up a pick. No one was able to hold him back, and though Nana, his wife, wept and begged, threw his three children underfoot, he uprooted the crosses and planted a sign forbidding the fervent Catholics of Piment access to the hill.

"So much struggle to come to this," moaned Melchior. "We would be rich now . . ."

That's where the story ended.

VII

After ignoring her for a week, Douglas finally decided to break the silence. He gave three light raps on Mina's door. He had the strict professor look on his face.

"We need to talk, Mina."

Lying on her sister's bed, Rosalia shook herself and sat up, her braids sent sparks flying across the room.

Mina observed her warily. Would Rosalia succeed in entering the world of the living one day and cause a real fire?

Douglas stepped into the room.

"Is she here?" he asked nervously.

"Yes."

"What's she doing?"

"She's watching you," answered Mina closing her book.

"Does she have powers?"

"I don't know."

"What does she want of you, Mina?"

"I have no idea. She probably couldn't find her way to the other world. At times I get the feeling that she has a mission to fulfill, a job to finish."

"Does she frighten you?"

"No, she's there, that's all. She has never hurt anyone. You know, when I was little, she used to walk me to school. She waited for me for whole days, hanging on the gate. We got along well together. She liked to paint, Rosalia did. She died trying to save the crates of her paintings. Old salt cod crates that our mother used to keep her paintings in. The cabin was already collapsing in flames. She went into the fire. I called out to her, 'Rosalia! Rosalia! Come back, my little Rose! Come back!' She went into the fire, Douglas. Then she came back out. I'd fixed her hair that morning. She wanted to have braids like mine. She looked pretty with her braids. We were already outside but she went back into the fire, Douglas. With her nylon nightgown, her pretty hairdo and her bare feet . . . We never found out what started the fire. But she went back in. She went into the cabin and the fire swallowed her up . . .

Rosalia started to wail, she hid her head under the sheet.

"She came back out of the cabin like a living torch. She was running with the crate in her arms. She ran for a long time, Douglas. We couldn't catch her. We could see the crazed flames rushing through the banana grove. It was Rosalia . . . She ran for a long time, Douglas . . . Letting out animal-like cries. When I thought I had her, she tore free again and again. And I screamed out her name, 'Rosalia! Rosalia! Wait for me!

It's Mina, Rosalia! Your little sister Mina . . .' But nothing could stop her. We found her body at dawn at the bottom of the hill."

"And when did she come back?" asked Douglas.

"After she was buried. Suzon took me in. I've already spoken to you of Suzon. You remember, the mailman's sister . . . She was truly in love with my papa. She went into mourning as if she were his widow. She waited for him all of her life . . . She was the one who took me in when the cabin burned down."

"And you didn't have any other relatives?"

"Olga didn't tell you? My father had two brothers that were younger than he was. Ferdy and Gregory. They went away to live in Grande-Terre with my Grandmother Nana when they were children. I never knew them. Only Ferdy's son, my cousin Tibert, used to come and see us from time to time. My mother was raised by her godmother. She had some aunts and nephews and nieces, but we never got to know them. We hardly had any visitors."

"And it was at Suzon's that you first saw Rosalia again?" asked Douglas.

He leaned his elbow on the secretary. The story seemed to fascinate him.

"Yes, she was waiting for me . . . When we came back from the cemetery, I saw flames burning in Suzon's cabin. I screamed that her house was on fire. Suzon looked at me as if I were crazy. 'Where do you see fire, Mina?' But I just kept on screaming, 'My God! Call the firemen, everything is going to burn! Water! Quick! Help!' Suzon gave me a hard slap and sternly ordered me to wake up. She was bellowing, 'Ain't no flames! Ain't no fire! Ain't no smoke! Ain't no flames! Ain't no fire! Ain't no smoke! Do you hear me, Mina?' And yet I could see them anyway, red and yellow in Suzon's cabin . . . But I was the only one who saw them. And I understood when I stopped crying, stunned by the slap and Suzon's shouting. No one was running, the street was peaceful. There were people walking calmly along their way. Two men were even talking in front of

49

the cabin next to a woman who was tying her daughter's shoe-laces."

"What happened next?" asked Douglas, in a hurry to get to the crux of the story.

"Suzon was angry. She said I wasn't being ladylike. I had no right to make such a scene on the day of my sister's funeral. She dragged me down the street. I was shaking with fear, Douglas. I couldn't put one foot in front of the other. I saw the flames dancing in the windows. I tightened my fist around my gold cross, the one Olga gave me the day she left. Do you remember, Douglas? I still have it . . ."

"Yeah. Yeah, I recognize it," Douglas admitted.

He shot a quick glance at the chain Mina wore around her neck.

"Suzon stopped in front of the door and rummaged around in her purse looking for the key. Suddenly I had a stomach-ache. The fire was roaring inside the cabin. But she noticed nothing. She opened the door. I closed my eyes. She took me by the hand and forced me to go inside. I felt like vomiting. I thought I was in a nightmare. I tried to resist. She pushed me inside and locked the door. She said, 'This is too much, the girl's not right!' She called to her neighbor from the window. 'Hey! Clarence! Call the doctor! Melchior's little girl is sick!'

'What doctor?' the other woman asked.

'Whichever you like!' answered Suzon. 'Hurry up! She needs to have a shot of sedative!'"

"And where were you then?" Douglas asked worriedly.

"I was frozen in the middle of the living room, in the very place Suzon had left me. Eyes closed. I didn't dare move forward or backward."

"And when did you see Rosalia?"

Captivated by the story, Douglas sat on the bed near Rosalia, who immediately slipped out from under the sheets. Went quickly over to a corner of the room. Her mouth formed an O of stupefaction.

"I heard someone wailing. So I opened one eye. She was in front of me, head cocked to one side. With her burning nightgown, her braids in flames . . . I screamed. And I crumpled to the ground. I must have fainted . . ."

"You just have to stop it," Douglas sighed.

He asked no further questions for a while. Seemed to be thinking of a way to solve a difficult mathematical problem. He had to analyze the givens, figure out the value of the unknowns, link the positive and the negative elements.

Mina remained silent, torn between the fear of losing Rosalia and the desire to be rid of the visions. She didn't understand what held her sister here and depending on the day, she tended to be either filled with curiosity, or with lassitude. Rosalia was her companion, the staff of her grief, her shadow, her memory. But she also embodied mystery and madness. Sometimes Mina found herself praying deep in her heart that Rose would suddenly disappear from her life, leave her in peace at last. But then she changed her mind immediately and begged the other not to leave her.

"Mina, you have to get rid of her!" Douglas suddenly exclaimed.

His lips curled into a knowing smile. Eureka! As if he'd just uncovered the roots of an obscure equation.

He had the key, but where was the door?

How could they make Rosalia disappear?

"It's not easy, I've already tried prayer . . ."

"What happened after that? The doctor gave you a shot?"

"Yes, I think so . . . When I woke up I was lying in Suzon's bed. She told me that I'd slept twelve hours, that I'd had nightmares. She asked me if I remembered anything. My head was full of cotton. She brought me some coffee. 'Everything's all right now, you not having no more visions?' It was more of a statement than a question. I said, 'No, no more flames . . .' And yet they were still there, Rosalia standing amidst them. I was calm. Maybe because of the medication . . .

"And then?"

"You know, I soon got used to her company. It's funny how your eyes can grow accustomed. I see her burning in perpetual flames. She stares at me in a strange way, but I don't really feel threatened. At first I was startled to see sparks dancing around her head. There are always one or two that go astray. Sometimes I play at catching them. They don't burn me, Douglas. For a long time I thought they disappeared in the palm of my hand. Magic! In reality, they don't exist. I . . ."

"Okay, so you left Suzon's house. Then what?" grumbled Douglas.

"Right," resumed Mina. It was Cousin Tibert, Ferdy's son, who took me to the airport. I hadn't seen Rosalia once that day. She'd disappeared into thin air. From the car window, I watched Piment whizzing by. I looked for a fire somewhere, in the cane fields, in the town, and even in the trees. I thought that Rosalia had appeared at Suzon's just long enough to say goodbye to me. And that she'd finally gone up to heaven. I was sure the hallucinations were over with. But no! Just when Tibert was giving me his send off, a column of flames rose above him. It was Rosalia! She had never gone to Pointe-à-Pitre in her whole life, had never been in such a large crowd. She stumbled with every step, her wild eyes darted from left to right. Her head was cocked to one side. It looked as if her neck were broken. I was happy to see her, funny, isn't it? When I went through the checkpoints, one of the policemen gave me a strange look. He turned my ID card over and back again and couldn't bring himself to give it back to me. Rosalia was jumping up and down impatiently behind me. He glanced over my shoulder. 'What is it?' I asked. 'No, nothing. I thought I saw someone . . . A shadow. It gave me goose bumps. Look! Look!' He showed me the hairs standing upright on his arm. Then he held out my papers as if I were a leper. In the stairway leading to the airplane, Rosalia disappeared again. I found her again in the cabin. She was flying over the passengers, bumping up

52

against the windows like a blind bird in a cage. The journey was hell for her. She likes to lean against furniture, hang around in corners, you know Douglas."

"Then what?"

"We arrived at your house. That's the story, Douglas. She never left my side. I started talking to her here. She listens to me when I talk to her. She loves stories . . ."

"You have to stop it, Mina!" Douglas interrupted, suddenly sobered. "She has to leave you alone! This madness has gone on long enough!"

"All right," Mina breathed, feeling once again the voice that was not hers asserting itself.

Douglas stood up and put his hand on Mina's shoulder.

"I'll help you if you like."

Mina held on to his hand.

"You're not angry anymore?"

He stroked her cheek.

"No, Mina."

In the following days, Douglas was generous with his recommendations . . . Ignore Rosalia. Stop speaking to her. Kick her out of the bed. Forget about the fire. Pray to make her disappear. Fill your mind with mathematical thoughts. Concentrate on passing the final exam.

Mina willingly submitted to these new rules. In the beginning, Douglas's advice even took the form of a catchy and exasperating song that kept popping back into her mind from morning to night.

Rosalia I must ignore
I will not see her anymore
The blazing fire has now gone dead
She is not to sleep in my bed

My thoughts are mathematical
Yes praying is quite practical
Soon is examination day
And I must go along my way

But as it went on, new words magically took the place of these, creating a gruesome complaint.

If Rosalia goes away
She'll take me off with her to stay
The night ablaze and bright with fire
Will always be a burning pyre

I am burning, I am frying
This is mad, it's terrifying
Her hand takes mine, doesn't hesitate
And I must go to meet my fate.

After a week, Douglas made a fresh attempt.

"So? Is it over with? Did she disappear?"

He was standing in front of her, like a second-rate witch-doctor with imagined powers. It was almost funny to see the professor of mathematics racking his brains with an irrational problem. Mina shook her head, opened the door and glanced toward the wardrobe. Rosalia was playing at counting the flowers on the wallpaper. One, two, three. One. Two. Three. Like when she used to count the boats out at sea, the dead roaches on the floorboards.

"We should just leave her be. She'll leave some day," said Mina with a touch of compassion in her voice.

"No! She won't go away!" bellowed Douglas. "She's in your head! You're imagining it all! No one can see her! It's up to you to make her go, Mina. Be careful, she'll end up driving you crazy . . ."

"So that's what you think! I bet you've talked to Olga about it!"

"No, I made you a promise. Olga is already struggling with an army of ghosts, I didn't want to make things worse . . ."

"Olga could care less about me. When I get my degree, I'm getting out of here, Douglas. It's obvious I'm not welcome."

"That's not true, not at all . . ."

He took her hand in a way that, at first, was simply meant to be comforting.

Mina's body flushed warm, tensed.

Douglas quivered.

"No Mina . . . No . . . ," he murmured.

"But why, Douglas?"

"You know why . . ."

He attempted a weak smile. Then took off his glasses.

"I'm old, Mina. You want me to believe you're not interested in boys your age, Mi . . ."

She laid a finger on the man's lips. Seductive, womanly gesture.

"Don't talk, listen to your heartbeat."

And Douglas fell silent, like so many others after him. They remained holding one another for a long time before their hands began moving and tracing imaginary lines on their clothing. Circles hemming them into desire. Parallel lines and curves that were a prelude to lovemaking.

"No, Min . . ." he attempted once again.

"Don't say anything," she begged him as she unbuttoned his white shirt. "I want your mouth."

They were alone in the apartment. Alone with Rosalia. Their only witness. When their lips met again, a fire kindled deep in their bodies. It was already too late. Douglas picked her up and carried her into his office. There was a small sofa there where he sometimes stretched out after reading. He lay her down on it. Knelt before her.

"I'm crazy," he said with a sigh.

He had that love struck look on his face from back in 1969. She was almost eighteen years old, he was nearing forty.

"I'm crazy, you've put a spell on me," he repeated, stunned by what was happening. By what he felt was coming . . .

55

Mina spread her legs. He plunged his head between the open thighs. She held his head there. He succumbed, threw himself furiously, drunkenly, and desperately into lovemaking. He proclaimed his innocence with tender gestures and pleading eyes. He was innocent, Lord! An innocent lamb thrown to the wild dogs.

Rosalia didn't take her eyes from them for an instant. Leaning against the locked door, she seemed calm and quiet, hardly even surprised.

"How is everything?" Olga asked that evening when she came in.

Ever since the dinner in which Rosalia's name had been thrown in her face, Olga had avoided all conflicts. Mina thought she was pitiful. She wanted to see her wounded, crushed, wanted to scream, "Your Doug laid me! Doug two-timed you! We were in bed together! Right here, in your beautiful house!" I've avenged Rosalia, she thought, to justify herself. Yes, Olga deserved it all. But she was immediately overwhelmed with shame and remorse. Olga had taken her in. Olga had never done her any harm. Olga loved her as best she could. And Mina felt as if she were nothing but a worm hidden in the fruit, a snake coiled in her sister's heart. Then she resented Rosalia and stared at her in horror.

Rosalia had seen them. You might even have thought she was smiling behind the flames. She'd remained there the whole time that their bodies were intertwined. She'd listened to Douglas's sweet words. She'd watched him wash Mina's private parts. She hadn't budged.

"Now you're going to leave, Mina murmured. You're happy now. You got what you wanted. It's over now. You're going to leave me . . ."

Rosalia shook her head. Sparks showered onto the furniture in the room.

"I never want to see you again. You're mean. You're a demon! Olga was right to beat you . . .

Rosalia drew nearer to the bed.

"No, I don't want you to sleep with me anymore. Go away! Go away, Rosalia! Go back to hell!"

Saying that, Mina clutched the cross that was around her neck.

"Out of my sight! Go away! O dear God! Make her go away!"

Dear God, preserve me from evil spirits, Lord, ward off the fallen angels.

O God in Heaven, You, who reign on earth, drive the phantom of my sister from my life.

O Eternal All Mighty!
Make Rosalia go away!
Dear God! Dear God!
Deliver me from Evil!
Save me from Rosalia!
Forgive me my trespasses!

The next morning, Rosalia had disappeared.

Douglas and Mina gave themselves to one another for almost a year. It was their way of proving that they hadn't been puppets in the hands of a phantom. But the initial ecstasy soon wore thin. Douglas was constantly struggling with his conscience, always felt as if he were falling under a diabolical, almost mechanical charm. They had become like the actors in a two-man comedy show that drew to an end with their own yawns and worn jokes stuck in their throats. They learned to avoid one another, as bored couples do, while Olga noticed nothing, or pretended not to.

When she was twenty-four, Mina found the job at the high school cafeteria and rented a two-room apartment in the same project. She met a man. After him, she seduced others, developed a taste for the unknown, got used to it, wanted more. It was her way of getting high. Going from one man to the next with no ties, or passion, or love. No words. Flee words. Enjoy the variety of men. Seek them out. Be taken aback by the beauty of bodies and the fury of embraces. Touch the mystery of erect penises.

VIII

Of the thirty or so women from varied countries who stood behind the hot tables and washed the pots and pans in the high-school cafeteria, six were from the Antilles. Mina never forgot how Salima, the Algerian, and Maria-Rosa, the Portuguese woman, had welcomed her. From time to time, the three women saw each other outside of the cafeteria, told each other about the torments of their lives sitting over a cup of coffee or mint tea, shared a couscous dinner or took the train, and then the metro to Barbès, to buy clothes, material, pots and pans.

Salima was fifty years old. She'd come to France in the sixties. She married an Algerian man who was twenty years her elder. She had five children and struggled through life alongside a retired man who spent his days in front of the television and complained about the state of the world and its wayward youth every time he opened his mouth. Maria-Rosa was divorced. Raised her two children alone. Took in a little sewing to supplement her income.

Lysia, Mina's best friend, had left Guadeloupe and her village of Sainte-Anne in 1987. After a few hard falls, dreaming of becoming engaged, a near marriage, and a slew of training courses and work placements, she found herself in the project with three mouths to feed. She was hired on at the cafeteria shortly after Mina. Though they were very different, physically as well as mentally, the two women had been drawn to one another straight off. Not because of their common origins, but due to a certain mutual recognition, a simultaneous attraction.

People often took Mina for Lysia's daughter. having borne three children, Lysia's figure had grown heavier with each pregnancy. She now weighed a hundred and ninety pounds and blamed it all, almost down to the last ounce, on life's tribulations. She had abdicated in the face of fate. So she contained her breasts by fair means or foul, in wide-strapped, underwired, size 105 bras. She wore men's shoes into which she crammed her splayed feet, slipped on knit pants that didn't need to be ironed but that mercilessly molded her buttocks and legs. She had a collection of large blouses and huge cardigans that did not easily dissimulate the thick folds of her flesh. She laughed loudly and often, talked a great deal, was always dreaming up projects to better her sort, find ways of bringing in money or saving it. So it happened that one day, after having calculated and recalculated, she set out toward the university to post ads on the bulletin boards. She proposed a room for an English–speaking student. That same evening, she received some thirty calls and had difficulty choosing. One week later, Ashwina, an Indian girl in a sari, was moving in to Lysia's apartment, which had only three rooms. Jessy, Sofia, and Manon, her three daughters, stayed in their room. Lysia relinquished hers to Ashwina and grew accustomed to opening out and folding up the futon in the living room every night and every morning.

Ashwina was from Mauritius, she'd grown up between Reunion and Mauritius, as she had relatives on both islands. For bed and board she paid fifteen hundred francs a month and in addition gave English lessons to the three girls and helped them with their homework. Though she lost in comfort, Lysia couldn't get over how resourceful she was and felt she gained on all fronts. The food didn't cost her anything because she always brought back oodles from the cafeteria, not to mention the fact that Ashwina ate like a baby bird. She saved a thousand francs each month, which enabled her to get twelve thousand francs together each year, enough to pay airfare for their vacation. Of course, she didn't declare a penny to the internal revenue service. At night, instead of running to the corner supermarket, she opened plastic containers brought back from the cafeteria, threw their contents into a pot and let it heat slowly as she slumped her body onto the folding sofa in front of the television and her favorite shows. In the meanwhile, Ashwina took charge of homework and speaking English, sweet music to Lysia's ears.

"So how's your love-life?" Mina always asked in lieu of a greeting.

It was a game between the two of them. Ever since they'd known each other . . . Talking about love as if they might one day know it.

Lysia swore she would hang herself if she were ever caught dreaming of a man.

"Oh no! Believe me, I won't have the wool pulled over my eyes again, Mina. I can't stand the taste or the smell of men anymore, I'm just fine the way I am, you can take my word for that, and I don't know how you can stand all those men . . ."

And as she was spitting out those bitter bits of phrases, her laughter suddenly swelled and exploded amongst the women, amid the vapors and smells of cooked food. Ha! Ha! Ha! The sort of delirious laughter one hears in psychiatric wards and jails. Broken-winged, bent-cornered laughter. Laughter that comes from bile, that sticks your insides together, that breaks your eardrums.

Lysia was never short of sayings and predictions, of sermons and precepts. She knew the addresses of all the Creole fortune tellers established in Paris and she collected visiting cards for African witchdoctors (natives of the great forests) that seamy-looking black beanpoles distributed at the exit to the Barbès metro station or on the street corners of Boulevard Sebastopol where she went to have her hair straightened by a Senegalese hairdresser. She had left a good deal of money in witchdoctors' dens listening to tales and legends about her own life. In the process she'd lost half of her illusions, but remained fundamentally optimistic. She was a good friend, the kind that knows how to keep a secret. She was the only person who knew Mina's secret, that of her love life.

How's your love life?

That morning they laughed as usual. Then Salima said that her oldest daughter, Aïsha, wanted to leave home and live with a Frenchman, a Christian, without even getting married. Salima understood young people. But the girl's father was against it. He threatened to go back to Algeria. He'd been thinking about it for a long time, seeing as how he was retired. It was the straw that broke the camel's back. "All right, we'll take you all back to the village, and then you'll see," that's what he said. "We have a house back there. We wouldn't be any worse off than here. I'm tired of watching French people's TV. I even think we've waited too long. And it's not the puny salary you bring back from the cafeteria that'll keep me in France ..."

Mina had not been seized by a fit of what she considered to be madness for nearly two months. She was going through a calm phase, didn't need to go out hunting at all hours of the day or night. Most often went home after work, or stayed with Maria Rosa who enjoyed relating the story of her life. Sometimes she went for a walk over by Barbès or Châtelet, strolled down the wharves watching the Seine slip by. Had a family dinner at Lysia's, listened to the girls babbling under the authoritative eye of Ashwina who fiercely denied her Reunion origins and in her reedy—but firm—voice bragged about Mauritius, an independent state, snatched from the clutches of the French and the English. Nothing like the French overseas departments, France's poor relatives that were still not ashamed to beg, whining about their history that the Indians in Mauritius had masterfully reversed.

During those two months Rosalia had visited her only three times and every day Mina promised—as usual—not to give in to temptation, to resist, to be reasonable. She even caught herself dreaming of a love affair, a real one, the kind she used to see at the Palace with Médée and Rosalia. A simple love affair, that happened all the time to simple people. But when she left Lysia in front of her building that afternoon, Mina recognized the first signs of the tension that heralded the fever, the insurmountable urge to get a man into her bed, feel a penis jab into her belly.

"Say my name, Mi! Just once! Hey! I exist, Mi! My name is Christian. Why don't you ever say my name?"

And what about her, did she exist? Was she treated like a person? She was invisible, simply a phantom like Rosalia was.

"Oh! That's funny, I dreamed about you. I was going to call you . . ."

"Can I come over tomorrow? I want to see you, Mi . . ." Christian murmured on the other end of the line.

"At what time?" asked Mina.

"Around three. Is that okay?"

"Yes! You can come at three o'clock sharp and leave at seven . . ."

"Will you be glad to see me? Do you love me just a little, Mi?"

Mina imagined him smiling idiotically at his own questions. "I wouldn't let you into my place if I didn't like you," she answered.

And it was on again. The hunt. She had to have men. The hard flesh of men. Their bulk on her body. Their sweat. She would go out hunting again, a solitary warrior. After the cafeteria. She'd hang around in the park, on the banks of the canal, in the parking lots. Anywhere . . . She'd take the bus at rush hour, simply to rub against men. She loved Paris for that. Most men were docile, easy prey. Guys she'd brushed up against in the metro or in the street. Surprised men at whom she smiled back. It was always the same story.

"Where do you come from?"

Always the same question, because of her black skin.

"The Antilles, you ever been there?"

"No, but I dream of making it one day. It's a beautiful place . . ."

They looked at each other for a moment without saying anything. Mina already soaring, imagining their bodies struggling, limbs intertwining.

"Yes it's a beautiful place," she repeated politely.

They saw each other once or twice in a café in the project, on the way to the high school, or sometimes in the shopping center. Then she'd invite them up to her place, in the seventh heaven of her high-rise. They were soon in the bedroom and the snare of sheets under Rosalia's sidelong gaze. It never lasted . . .

Mina made those particular men observe strict discretion, she kept her distance. She chose them like vegetables from a vendor's stand. She didn't become attached, ever, so she could be free at any time to close them out of her life. Above all, she didn't want to know anything about them. Not hear anything about their little problems that she refused to resolve with pillow talk. They were all alike. After bed play, they felt like confiding. Needed to talk about themselves, share their suffering and pour the burden of their misfortunes on her heart, without even asking her permission.

She made them shut up.

Stop gabbing about your divorce, your ex-wife, your custody and alimony problems. Don't talk to me about it! I'm not interested! I couldn't care less about the lovers who flew, fiancées who were untrue, your childhood beaten blue. Don't say a word! Please, no confessions. I don't want to hear about it!

Incomprehensible Mina who had been living with her phantoms for twenty-one years and—crazy, oblivious to the danger—who let strange men into her apartment. Gave them nothing of herself, save her body that they penetrated. Tried hard not to think too much about death, even though fear of a violent death, like that of everyone in her family, constantly tormented her.

Médée run down by a truck.
Melchior struck by lightning.
Rosalia burned alive.

Her sister Olga was the only one left. Douglas had left her in 1990 and was now living in Toulouse with a Spanish woman who had borne him two children. Olga still lived in their suburban house. In the beginning Mina used to visit her. Unfortunately, neither of them was able to act like a friendly sister. When they got together there was nothing but play-acting and beating around the bush. Their words were stilted, their movements fumbling, and their eyes fixed on thoughts of Rosalia and Douglas. For those two always came between the sisters, like resentful and ghostly birds that they no longer tried to stave off. Little by little, they gave up trying to see one another. Only called each other once a year, to exchange new years wishes of good health and prosperity.

"If I were black, would you love me just a little, Mi?" Christian suddenly asked in a tone he hoped was nonchalant.

He lit a cigarette. His fingers were trembling.

"What's gotten into you?" Mina asked.

"Nothing, I just wondered . . ."

"What difference does it make?"

He wasn't getting undressed. Just stood there with his cigarette. Looked at her like a prospector sizing up a bit of land.

"Would you marry me, Mi?"

Mina sighed.

"That has nothing to do with it . . . Listen, we agreed from the very beginning. We don't get attached. We don't talk about our past. We go to bed together and that's it. You promised me that . . ."

"I know, I know," Christian interrupted.

"But what."

"Well, you know, Mina . . . We say things . . . And then . . ."

"I don't want any complications, Christian!"

"See, you can say it . . . See, it's not so hard . . ."

He repeated his name like a chant, gently stepping nearer to her, hands stretched out, offered to her.

"See, it's not all that difficult," he repeated. "I just want to love you, Mi. Just want you to love me a little. I just want you to let me into your life."

Jaws clenched, Mina dragged him into the bedroom, following the ritual of their lovemaking. But he still needed to talk.

"Would you be willing to share my life, Mi? Please think it over . . ."

"You wouldn't be able to stand me. I'm not easy to live with. And there are a heap of ghosts trailing after me . . ."

"We're all the same, Mi. We all have our phantoms. Do you want to marry me?"

She started laughing.

"You don't know what you're talking about . . . Come here now! Stop torturing yourself . . . Come and make love to me, right now . . ."

A few minutes earlier she'd taken a quick shower. She'd perfumed and prepared her body for a party. She'd put on her long blue denim skirt that opened down the front and a white sweater with a large blue star on it. But Christian was being emotional, he wanted to talk, was asking her to marry him. He was ruining everything with his romantic babble and she had no time for it. She simply wanted to be taken, now, to feel herself being submerged, the ground slipping out from under her feet . . . She needed to console the grief that was inside of her like she would a child.

"Come here," she whispered making one last attempt.

"Why don't you take me seriously, Mi? Why won't you answer my question?"

His voice was filled with sadness. Mina observed him for a moment. Her thoughts vacillated between anger and compassion. She softened.

"What would you do with a wife like me? You'd soon be exasperated!"

"I swear I wouldn't. We understand each other . . . You're only thirty-five. If you want, we can have a baby . . ."

"What!" Mina broke in. "A baby!" She burst out laughing. "A baby! You must be joking! Come on, come make love and forget about all of that."

She'd taken on Lysia's bruised laugh.

When Christian's lips touched hers, Mina closed her eyes and abandoned herself to her desire. Finally! That's what she wanted. Nothing more. For him to take her and keep quiet. For him to wrap his body around hers, caress her, penetrate her. For him to be nothing but the mute object of her desire. And for the thrilling feeling to engulf her. Submerge her in the waves coming up from the depths of her entrails. One, two, three . . .

One. Two. Three! Keep going Rose! What comes next?

Count the boats!

Go on! One, two, three . . . fo . . .

You can do it!

One. Two. Three! Rosalia exclaimed.

One. Two. Three. Nothing more. The world was summed up in those three numbers. One, two, three.

Birth. Life. And death.

The past. The present. And the future.

One. Two. Three.

The sky. The water. And the earth.

One. Two. Three.

The Father. The Son. And the Holy-Ghost.

One. Two. Three.

Paradise. Purgatory. And Hell.

One. Two. Three.

Médée. Melchior. And Rosalia.

One. Two. Three. And Christian wanted to wrench open the perfect circle of that trilogy. Stick his spoke in the wheel . . .

"I love you, Mina . . ." he sighed.

"I love you too," answered Mina.

On the ceiling large birds formed arabesques. And standing before them, leaning against the tree-wardrobe-mirror, Rosalia had taken her usual post.

"Is it true that you love me, Mi? Will you have me . . ."

"Wait, let me get my breath . . . Please wait . . ."

He kept quiet for a minute, groped for his pack of cigarettes with the tips of his fingers.

"I can wait if you want," he continued as if he were talking to himself.

IX

When he closed the door to his studio that morning, Victor felt as if destiny would soon give him a sign. On the sidewalk, the owner of La Rose d'Ouessant Hotel was humming as he pushed a broom out in front of him. The sweepings floated away in the blackened waters of the gutter. Victor greeted the man and crossed the sunlit street. With blood-red roses filling his head, he walked past the Mundo Night, closed at that hour, and planned to go that very night to see Omega, a famous salsa dancer, who, three months earlier—on a night when Victor was particularly depressed—had found him drunk on the sidewalk and taken him to the emergency room of Saint-Antoine Hospital.

He walked gingerly along, feeling lighthearted, undoubtedly due to that new generation of anti-depressants his psychiatrist had prescribed and also because new hope of finding

67

a cure had been endlessly blossoming in his mind ever since he met Bénédicte. And that feeling, mixed with a sense of fulfillment, delighted him. *I'm walking on my own two legs and I'm on the road to being cured.*

From Saint-Antoine, he was transferred to Esquirol Hospital. He'd just spent three months in the old wing known as Charenton, where so many poets had been interned, he thought to himself as a consolation. Three months with a bunch of loonies of all kinds from all places, for depression. What had the doctor said? *Melancholic state, chronic depression. You'll have to follow your treatment closely, Victor* . . . The nurses were nice. He made friends with some of the patients.

He'd been trying to live with depression for years now. Forever, according to him. Sometimes it spilled over like a large river—the Nile or the Ganges—and prevented him from enjoying life, kept him home, leadened down in front of the TV, tied him to the bed for days on end. Didn't wash anymore. Didn't eat anymore. Drank red wine to bolster his courage in case he ran across a rope or a bridge to help him escape the world . . . Three months at Esquirol and he was starting back in life standing on his own two feet, with fewer black thoughts and a permanent job in a supermarket . . .

Even when he was on medication, the black thoughts never disappeared completely. There were still some remnants, traces, trails, smells, feelings, a pain that shot through his head, possessed his body and moved around like a freshwater snake in the sand, between two rocks . . . Elusive pain.

He didn't let anything show, refrained from flaunting it, crying out, pretended to simply ignore it so it would ignore him, the same as a man and a woman sometimes do after a long married life together. He wanted to be loved. Oh, not all that much! Just a little . . . It wasn't too much to ask.

Bénédicte, his friend who lived in Charenton, had told him that all the odds were in his favor. Being loved. A little, just a little. Bénédicte was originally from the Antilles. For ten years she'd been going back and forth between Esquirol and her two-room apartment on Avenue Daumesnil. She was a regular. Her illness came over her in fits. She could spend a year with no problem, a charming neighbor in her building, fine co-worker at the post office. And then one day, the demons would come back. They were everywhere. Ghastly faces coming back to circle around her, whisper insults in her ear, talk to her on the TV or the radio, give her orders. She had to defend herself, answer them . . . They were all over the streets, in the metro, the drugstore, stopped at the red lights, window-shopping in front of Samaritaine, lazing in the sun on the benches of the Jardin du Luxembourg, until some of them entered her body. She tried to resist, of course. But everyone knows that Evil is more powerful than Good . . . So then she screamed, threw herself to the ground, drooled, bit her tongue, lacerated her face. As long as she remained in that state, no one got too worked up about it. She went home and took a week or two off on sick leave. The only danger was that she might crack her head open or break a leg. However, hospitalization became necessary when Bénédicte began insulting others, uttering verses from the Bible, waving her arms about wildly in the bus or the metro at the risk of hurting another passenger, pulling her skirt up above her waist to show the flabby flesh between her fat thighs, looking at people as if she were going to chop them to pieces.

Bénédicte never remembered these episodes of pure madness but she believed more in witchcraft than in medicine. She pronounced her own diagnosis: possession. But there was nothing to do about it. The problem was too old, the demons too well rooted.

Coincidentally, Bénédicte and Victor were hospitalized on the same day. Bénédicte was raving deliriously that she could see demons with the naked eye and even while fasting. In the corridors of the hospital ward she'd counted hundreds of old ghosts in rags that dated back to the turn of the century, one-eyed soldiers from a lost war, shrunken cripples, toothless amputees. Three of them were trailing Victor just like bodyguards. She informed the nurses, but they just laughed, jaded.

"Poor boy! There are three of them, Lord Jesus! Three of them walking right behind you, poor boy. Holy of Holies! Dear Jesus! Our Father who smites the darkness, descend to earth and liberate my brother, poor sinner . . ."

Impressed, Victor listened to her attentively, at least as attentively as his state of total collapse allowed. The day before he had attempted for the nth time to, at long last, put an end to his life (that old gray wife he'd been with for forty years) but he was resistant. He wanted to die spontaneously, meaning unexpectedly. Be taken unawares. Not have to make the first move. Right in the middle of the street, be struck down by a sudden attack. Cut down in an ethylic flash. Pushed under a train, no time to think it over. Killed by a stray bullet in the forest—it happens to some lucky ducks—during a stroll in the shade of the tall trees. Be the victim of his death and not the artisan. Die to rid himself of the invisible chains, chronic moroseness, corrosive listlessness, defunct desires. Sick and tired of being in the skin of this guy, a sinister person no one cared about, no one ever invited, godfather to no child, best man to no groom.

Since he himself could make no sense of the illness that consumed him, Victor took in the words of the woman who claimed to be some sort of prophetess, disheveled and scruffy to be sure, but whose voice did not tremble at the sound of warning shots. And why must her words be necessarily questioned? There is no smoke without fire, he thought, or if so, of what use are popular sayings? For thirty years now he had been ingurgitating bitter potions and a variety of different-colored pills that were supposed to help him enjoy life and feel lighthearted again. He had listened to the tortured metaphors of his psychiatrists and followed their recommendations precisely. He had played out the film of his childhood three hundred times to the point of even feeling his dear old mother's milky nipple on his lips. He had participated in relaxation exercises with both obese and anorexic women. Had talked in talk groups in which each word was figured in and figured out, dissected, analyzed. Had played his very own role in role games in which teary-eyed people spilled their guts. Had learned all about health food, banned from his refrigerator all depressing foods: turnips; endives, leeks, chicken breast . . . And eaten orange and yellow sun-colored foods that in civilizations the world over signify happiness, joy, health: pumpkin soup, carrots fixed every which way, oranges, lemons, apricots, peaches. He had become a fruitarian and had a natural leaning for yoga, tai chi, for remaining Zen in all seasons, in all situations, Asian style. And then he'd changed again. Had gone through his nightlife period, discotheques, alcohol, and piano bars. Numbing himself with drink and music. Living by night, sleeping by day . . . He learned to dance the salsa, to throw his moodiness into reverse and turn into a jovial, happy, lively person just like those damned party-loving Cubanos who continued ingurgitating rum, smoking Havana cigars, and getting the most out of women and life after three centuries of Castrist castration . . . He'd lasted two months. One day someone said to him, "If you have time to be depressed, it's that you are turned exclusively in upon yourself, the hero of your story, now it's time to reach out toward other people." For the first time in his life, at the age of thirty, he felt he'd finally found his vocation. Reach out to others, forget his middleclass Parisian self and all his petty moping. So he'd joined a group of volunteers, soldiers fighting poverty who served soup and handed out blankets to the homeless in winter. When he found a way of escaping, the old depression always subsided for a little while. The inextricable forest of desolation in which he lived thinned. He believed he could see the horizon. He saw people, shared a vision of the world, was part of the group, the movement, the committee . . .

71

Sadly, these intermezzos never lasted long. It was like eating olives and peanuts at the bar, or antipasti at an Italian place. Only tasty for the few seconds they remain between the tongue and the palate, just before being swallowed. Once in the stomach, they prove to be indigestible and start your entrails to moving. After nights of rum and salsa, for example, he was near death when he got back home. If he was unlucky enough to pass his reflection in the mirror, he invariably saw the same pathetic character—totally worthless to the world. The face of a zombie that cannot make up its mind to crawl back into the grave. Or else at the end of a yoga class, he always had the unpleasant feeling of being the future pawn of a sect, the consenting victim who paid his dues and learned to breathe from the abdomen to serve the invisible guru hidden behind the twenty-five-year-old teacher with a syrupy voice and the body of an aesthete. With the anti-poverty committee, though he was reaching out to others, he wasn't forgetting himself. On the contrary, every night he suffered from insomnia, he imagined himself walking amidst them, a huge funereal procession of beggars, a poverty-stricken army of shades that stopped on Pont-Neuf and threw themselves unceremoniously into the Seine one after the other, their pallid moonlit faces looking like the death-masks of very old clowns. Braced in the stirrups of her ancient nag, Old Lady Spleen immediately took the opportunity to gain a little ground. She nimbly charged in on his rear guard, casting her large lasso. The slipknot tightened inexorably around Victor's neck. He immediately had the morbid sensation of suffocating, the feeling that death was imminent. Then it all depended, some days he put on clean pajamas, called an ambulance and dragged himself to bed to wait for death to grip him. Or sometimes he raced down the stairs, ran out into the street amid the passersby, haggard, teary-eyed. When the attack had passed, everything had to be rebuilt, started over from scratch . . . Shrinks of all sorts, pills of all colors, group this and group that were suggested left and right . . .

While Bénédicte, surrounded by three nurses, screamed out her injunctions, Victor meditated on the turn his life was taking as he waited for the overworked psychiatrist on duty to find a minute to talk to him. I've come to seek refuge, to save myself from myself. I, who am my own worst enemy, he said to himself in an apparently serene voice, it was the classic case of a victim of depression on the verge of suicide. Once again he'd touched rock bottom, had wanted to take his own life. I'm a failure. My mother made a mess out of me. Everything has gone wrong since the day I was born. They could have been happy if I hadn't been born. Edmond was a handsome man. My mother liked him a lot. And then he hangs himself from the light fixture in the middle of the living room and . . .

"Three demons are walking right behind you!" screeched Bénédicte, her eyes flashing and fixing on Victor. "I swear I see them, brother."

"Now, now, Ms. Hypolite, leave the gentleman be. Calm down, Ms. Hypolite!"

"Why do you want to keep me quiet? From time out of mind, the just have always been gagged. You'll remember Bénédicte as you remember Moses announcing the Déluge! You'll remember my words . . ."

"Calm down, Bénédicte!" hissed one nurse who had known the mad woman for twenty years.

"I will speak the Truth and you will quake!" Bénédicte barked in answer to the other woman. "Life never dies, never! Never! Everyone is here together, living and dead! I have eyes to see them with, a nose to smell them with, ears to hear them with! Blind! You're all blind!"

"Please be reasonable, Ms. Hypolite," the doctor will see you in a minute . . .

"You and your gang of cronies, you're all deaf and blind and you want me to calm down!"

Then as she turned her back on Victor, she said, "You can be saved. Don't listen to the charlatans! I can save you! I CAN

DO IT! You have to believe me! I can see them as clearly as I see you. Three demons that have left you no peace since you were born. Remember Jesus-Christ! Demons are waging war against us, you hear! But you can't see them . . . They get inside your heart and hollow out endless, bottomless tunnels, stations and platforms like in the belly of Paris . . . Stations and platforms, I tell you. But you don't see them, you're all blind!"

Then she began to sing a hymn and fell to her knees.

"Remember that Jesus Christ was raised from the dead! He is my savior, my prophet, and my cross . . ."

Sprawled out in his chair observing her, a glimmer of hope suddenly lit Victor's dull eyes. At this stage in the game, he preferred to be burdened with three identifiable demons rather than a faceless illness that had ruined his whole life. When one knows his enemy, it's easier to maneuver, he reasoned.

After three days on tranquilizers—horse pills as some would say—Bénédicte miraculously calmed down. Behind the nurses' backs she still spoke of the most virulent, recalcitrant invisibles. As for Victor, every morning he would relate a bit of his story to the psychiatrist who listened to him in silence while glancing at his watch and licking his lips every three minutes.

"How are you feeling today, Mr. Clément?"

"Well, I'm fine. I'm coming out of it gradually . . ."

"Are you handling the medication all right?"

"Yes, fine."

"Do you wish to speak with me about anything in particular?"

"About my mother, for example," began Victor.

"Very well, go ahead."

"Well, it sure must not have been easy for her on a day to day basis. After my father hung himself. There were just the two of us. She was very ill. I get my chronic depression from her. She spent all of her time in bed smoking . . . You see Doctor, I was four when he hung himself . . ."

74

"Right. Do you have any plans for the future, Mr. Clément?"

"I do temporary work. I work in supermarkets. I'm quite competent in my field, you know. I . . ."

"What exactly is it that you do, Mr. Clément?"

"I work in the warehouse. I take care of the stock, the merchandise. When I'm not sick, I'm in charge . . ."

"So you'll go back to your job after the hospitalization?"

"Yeah, sure, I'm not lazy . . . If I could just get over this illness . . ."

"You'll get over it, Mr. Clément," the psychiatrist always concluded, running his tongue over his lips. "You'll get over it, but you'll need medical treatment to do so."

Victor and Bénédicte became inseparable. Those two obviously respected one another. She wanted to save him — had the means to do so — and he believed her, was already grateful. She sometimes spoke to him with gestures so that the demons would not understand, or sometimes simply with her eyes that she opened and closed, blinked, or rolled backward. They were one behind the other when medication was distributed and face to face in the cafeteria, or often side by side, sitting on plastic chairs in the courtyard with their eyes turned in the same direction, silently puffing in smoke and blowing it out around each other, as if in some prior life they had belonged to the same brotherhood, the same tribe. When she was besieged by the demons that kept her hair mussed and her head thrown back, Victor repaired to a corner of the courtyard and waited for the high winds to pass. A truly strange couple, whispered the nurses. He, forty years old, an atheist, white, blank-eyed, the melancholy air of a nineteenth-century poet who had strayed into the dawn of the third millennium. And she, fat negress in the full bloom of her fifties, bolts of white running through her hair, mustachioed, caked with gaudy make up, exuberant, talkative, as vulgar and vituperative as she was a fervent Christian.

The day he left, she clung to Victor's sleeve. The purple polish on her long nail-claws was chipped in places. "Don't forget! You have to go get the spell broken in Guadeloupe, Victor."

Her lipstick, hurriedly applied, went far over the edges of her fleshy lips, which made them doubly thick. "Don't forget! Your demons aren't too old, you can still shake them. This is your last chance. All you need is a good guide. I'm sure you'll get rid of your ghosts. I have a vision of you cured from head to toe, Victor . . . Watch for the signs . . . And don't listen to the doctors! They keep giving us drugs that feed the spirits instead of striking them down . . . You must remain pure until you have completely recovered: no women, no alcohol, no evil thoughts. Go to Guadeloupe, you hear, promise me . . . And as soon as you're cured, send me a post card. Don't write anything but, 'Beyond the clouds.' Just those three words. I'll understand . . ."

"And how will I know I've been cured?" asked Victor for the last time.

Bénédicte had answered that question time and time again. But Victor was her protégé, she could refuse him nothing, he believed in her.

"I've already told you . . . You'll see beyond the clouds with your own two eyes, that will mean your demons and all the evil sorts have gone back to where they came from. Seeing beyond the clouds means that what was once hidden emerges from the folds of darkness and filth, the truth finally appears to the eyes of our Lord. Two huge projectors trained on the darkness in which we walk. Not many people can see beyond the clouds. I've only met three in my whole life. An old Moroccan man who sold sardines in Belleville. A man from Guadeloupe, a veteran soldier who wrote a famous poem that the schoolchildren still recite today. And an unknown painter, Igor Dostovich, my upstairs neighbor. That's all he paints on his canvases, what is beyond the clouds. And . . . can you spare me one last cigarette before you go?"

"And how will I know that I'm seeing beyond the clouds? I don't quite understand what beyond the clouds means . . ."

"Victor, when you put a sweater on inside out, can you tell it or not?"

"Well yes, I can tell it . . ."

"That's the way it is with the clouds too. They have an inside and an outside. When you're on the other side, they've got seams, threads that hang down and knots, like sweaters . . ."

X

The landscape whipped past the window of the bus. Victor watched the clouds in the sky, searched for signs in the trees and looked for his guide amongst the bustling passersby. Billboards spoke to him. Traffic lights blinked for him. Clouds in the sky unrolled their parchments. It's all right there, all you have to do is open your eyes, he thought, to muster his courage.

~

"So he asked you to marry him? That's pretty incredible, after all," sighed Lysia, feeling half turned-on, half amazed. "What do you intend to tell him?"

"I told him that I loved him. But that was in bed, see . . ."

The other woman smiled. Her eyes shone like those of women who know—from having experienced it a hundred times over—the power of an embrace and the scope of the visions that fill your mind in those moments. And that, most importantly, will turn the fire that flares up and goes out so suddenly in the body into definitive words.

"Yeah, I see . . . You don't love him, but it was good!"

Lysia started laughing, thinking of her old lovers. Yes, it had been good to make love and experience a feeling in her body that was probably akin to the state of grace that the first beings born to Creation knew. Love that was like a blinding stab. The bliss of eternity. The divine flux. Instants of perfection rocking the body and dying away in a brief orgasm. Always too brief, paling, frazzling away in the belly as quickly as clouds in the sky fade after a storm.

"Yes it was good. But it's just impossible . . ."

Lysia chalked all of Mina's lovers up to youthful reckless-ness. The things her friend confided stirred her blood and slipped through her pleasantly like sweet vice, sweeter than the Barbara Cartland novels she read in her futon before going to sleep. Secretly, they aroused her. But sometimes, seized by the fear of God and of Sin, seeing herself in painful flashes taking her first Communion in her immaculate white dress, she got a hold on herself and urged Mina to behave.

"It's really not right. That's no kind of life to live. You'll go to hell, my poor little Mina. For sure, you'll end up in the Devil's big cauldron. Just saying it gives me the shivers . . ." She grabbed Mina's arm. "Maybe this man is your only chance . . . You wouldn't want to give it a try?"

"I don't love him . . . But it's true, he is very nice . . ."

"So, if he's nice, what more can you want? That's good enough. Nice men are rare. I've known real brutes. A chance like this doesn't come along all that often in a woman's life. Look at me, I don't expect anything anymore. I'm an old, fat, ugly, fifty-year-old woman. The well-being of my girls is all I live for now. But you're still young, good God! You have to keep the faith! I've wilted. Three kids is no small feat . . . I've made my contribution . . ."

"You know, I've been thinking. I'm going to Guadeloupe, to . . ."

"What!" exclaimed Lysia. "When? Oh Lord, you want to go back home at last . . . Right here and now, you've gone and made up your mind! But everything is almost all booked up at this time of the year. Planes are full for the summer vacation. I made my reservations in January and . . ."

"Calm down, Lysia. I'm not going now . . . I've got plenty of time . . . Maybe in December . . ."

They separated in front of the high school. Lysia had to go to Tati on Boulevard Barbès. She went there regularly all year long to avoid feeling rushed just before leaving for Guadeloupe. Gifts to take back to her mama and her old aunts: Nylon nightgowns, 100% cotton underpants in extra large sizes, slips, and slippers made in Taiwan. T-shirts and shorts at ten francs for her nephews. Polyester sheets and stretch dresses at twenty-five francs for her two sisters who had never wanted to join her in the mother country where — Lysia was absolutely convinced — they could have found work in the civil services. The result was they were vegetating back home. Living on minimum welfare payments and family allowances.

Two years ago, leading a gang of single women, they had succeeded in squatting some small houses intended for other poor folks. No one was able to get them out of there, neither the mayor nor the Prefect who even sent in the gendarmes. Those rebels had taken root there. Taken possession of the premises. It was owed to them, they said. Very rapidly they began renovations in which they took immense pride. Each year another addition was built on to their little two-room cabins constructed by some crooked company that turned up after cyclone Hugo passed in 1989. They were proud to have braved the law, still laughed about it in the evenings, sitting on their doorsteps, pink and green hair rollers stuck with yellow pins on their heads.

They had children. Five each. No official husband. Doriane, the elder, did odd jobs to improve her ordinary fare. But Eléonore, the least good-humored of the two, the ringleader, was happy just to get by — which Lysia found unscrupulous — on government money. As far as men were concerned, she was certainly no better off, but Lysia felt she had been more successful, even though she was only a cafeteria employee at a high school in the outskirts of Paris. She was able to pay for five airplane tickets for Guadeloupe every year; the State financed the trip every five years. She called no man Honey, like

Doriane did, simply so he would give her a made-in-China clock of imitation varnished wood, decorated with horrid gilt work that would up and die in a month, or even a radio for ninety-nine francs. She had her dignity. Her wallet was heavy with money earned by the sweat of her brow. Her head was screwed on tight and set straight on her shoulders. As a result, though she didn't have much education, her daughters were learning English in order to be able to face up to tomorrow's world. Her life was not simply an experiment, and she prided herself on having led it as she pleased. Sometimes, observing her sisters, she felt as if she were glimpsing a deformed image of the Lysia she would have become if she had not left Guadeloupe. At the mere idea of it, a shudder ran up her spine.

So, each year, she loaded herself down with presents, because of the pity she felt, but also to show off her success in the Métropole, Métwopol, as her sisters said, to prove that she'd made the right choice in not stagnating in Guadeloupe. Doriane, Eléonore, and their children made a circle around her open suitcases and waited silently for her to hand them packages. They literally ripped them from her hands, the heathens. And as an afterthought let out a forced thank you, as if the money she'd spent had fallen into her lap. Her presents were never expensive enough, never pretty enough, not worthy of them. Crumbs from France that didn't even whet their appetites. Cheap articles that would run and shrink in their Calor washing machines whose drain tubes convulsed as the cycle progressed and spat out dirty water into the cemented courtyard to mix with the dregs of the wheelbarrow. T-shirts and shorts the kinds of which—they did have eyes in their heads after all—Lysia didn't buy for her own children. Those kids who rolled their *r*'s and put on airs, strutted about in clothes with American brand names. And, faced with their condescending yet contrite looks, not even masked with hypocritical joy, Lysia promised herself never to sacrifice to the ritual again, but she always gave in. It was her tribute, her minimum duty, her visa as a negropolitan as well.

Mina didn't want to go to Tati. She didn't feel like rummaging around in the bins. Not the slightest inclination to get a good bargain, talk clothes with Lysia, yank at the material to test the quality of the clothing. Just wanted to go back to her room, stretch out on her bed. Sleep and dream about a man's body. Bite his flesh. Sniff it, sink her nails into it.

Bread. First she had to go by the bakery. The good bread they sold in a bakery two blocks from the high school. Mina felt like spoiling herself. She would take the opportunity to get herself some strawberry pie. Yes, a fresh piece of old-fashioned pie, with puff pastry and strawberries covered with a nice sweet coulis. Yes, she was going to console herself. Eat some good pie alone in her bed. And forget about the rest: Christian declaring his love for her, asking her to marry him. All the men whirling around in her head . . . Yes, a good piece of pie to taste sweetness on her tongue. To sink her teeth into something and then lick her lips and fingers.

After the pie, I'll call a travel agent. I have to go back to Piment.

The prospect cheered her up considerably. She was already imagining herself stepping off the airplane, driving to Piment in cousin Tibert's car. Visiting Suzon. Was Suzon still alive? If so, she would spend a few days at her place. How many people had died in these last twenty years? Twenty years! Twenty-one years without asking for or offering any news . . . She'd cut all ties with Guadeloupe. Twenty-one years she repeated to herself as she pushed open the door to the bakery. Twenty-one years! It made her head swim. How could I have spent twenty-one years without going back there . . .

The pastries, in trim little lines, awaited on trays covered with lacy white paper.

In Piment the baker, Dotémar, baked bread with a wood fire. His cakes were of course flavored with vanilla and cinnamon, doused with rum, and marbled with cocoa, but they cloyed the palate and bloated the belly. After Melchior's death, when she would go down to the post office to pick up their pension money, Mina always went past Dotémar's to buy a loaf of bread, four coco sugars, and two syrup-candies. The sweets seemed unique to her, marvelous and incomparable, just as Momonne's cassavas with coconut were. But a few years later, France had led her to discover paris-brests, chocolate cream puffs, napoleons, The Tatin sisters' famous tart and the . . .

Near the cash register, standing behind a man wearing a raincoat, two women in damask djellabas were talking to each other in Arab. Their hands were covered with tattoos. Mina took her place in line. The bell on the bakery door tinkled. An African man in a boubou with a plaid baseball hat on his head came in, followed by a woman carrying a child on her back. He looked a little like Délos Mignard, the mailman in Piment.

As soon as I get to Piment, I'm going to see Suzon, Mina thought. If she's dead, I'll go visit her grave. I'll write this evening . . . If she's still alive, I'll ask her to put me up . . . She won't refuse.

The African man nodded at Mina as if they were relatives. Brother and sister of color. Distant cousins that found themselves in a strange land and, wordlessly, each knew what had become of their extended family dispersed in the four corners of the world. Secretly shared the pain of past tribulations. In that single, knowing glance, flowed the whole story of the black people, from the very beginnings. Mina responded with a smile. Then she abruptly turned away. Break the parental ties just as abruptly. Quickly remove herself from the fraternity of color. I have no family. I'm alone. Alone as an island in the middle of the ocean. Alone in my life. Alone in my body. Each person is unique and as desperately alone as an island. People are islands set adrift. The idea amused her and she looked up at the people who were in the bakery, just to count them. Six islands . . .

"Thank you," Victor said to the baker woman who handed him two–three small coins.

A vibrant, heartfelt thank you. Too vast a thank you for a loaf of bread. Mina started. A thank you that seemed to be addressed to God rather than the baker woman.

"And have a nice day, Sir!" called the women in a rasping voice, giving a toss of her helmet-like lacquered permanent.

A thank you that Mina had already heard one day, up there on the seventh floor of the high-rise.

Her heart started thumping hard in her chest. She buttoned up her sweater mechanically.

She leaned over the display case and started inspecting the pastries. She didn't feel like eating a delicate strawberry pie anymore. Or a napolean. She felt nauseaous, wished she could disappear. The apple turnovers were daubed with a crude layer of varnish, half flaking off. The chocolate éclairs looked like strange dead phalluses. The cream puffs were enormous naked buttocks, lined up for a collective spanking. She would have liked to slip into the last black forest cake, sink into the thick icing, smear her face with it so he wouldn't recognize her, feel obligated to talk to her. I have nothing to say to that man.

The bell tinkled. A woman with slanting eyes accompanied by a child held the door open and stepped aside for Victor. Mina straightened up. The two North African women ordered six large loaves of bread and one of them dug out handfuls of coins from a gigantic grimy leather coin-purse that had once been green.

Green like the snakeskin wallet Melchior carried in the back pocket of his pants. One time he'd looked for it for three days yelling that someone had stolen it. He blamed Rose . . .

"Show me where you hid it! If not, you'll feel my belt strap on your back!"

He walked threateningly toward her.

"Bring my wallet back, or I'll make you regret the day you were born!"

83

Rosalia backed away from him.

"My wallet, you rotten crook!"

We searched through the cabin, turned the garden inside out, inspected every tree. Nothing. During those three days of terror, Rosalia had not eaten anything. Nothing. Not even a crust of bread. Drank nothing. Nothing. Not even a drop of coconut water. She wandered around looking for the word *wallet* that she didn't understand.

She brought back one of Mina's notepads with questioning eyes.

Is a notepad a wallet?

No, Rosalia.

She broke off a guava branch.

Is a guava branch a wallet?

No, Rose.

She took up the crude broom with the handle whittled from *ti goman* wood tied to a bouquet of starwort leaves.

She held it up triumphantly.

No, poor girl.

After three days of fasting, Rosalia's eyes and cheeks began to look sunken. Happy ending, the wallet, having remained hidden like a true serpent under the little bench where Melchior laid his gamebag, was suddenly brought into the light by a magical sweep of the broom. Melchior didn't even ask Rose to forgive him. He meticulously went over the outward appearance, then the contents of his treasure. Yes, the wavy-edged photo of his defunct Marie-Pearl was still in place, he smoothed it with his dry fingertips. His French ID card was still there. His electoral card was intact. The tangerine seeds from January 1—heralding good fortune—were counted and recounted as well as the three fifty-franc bills folded in four. Even after this inspection, he was unable to say sorry, my apologies, I'm to blame. Rosalia didn't deserve the slightest apology. Sorry was perhaps the most difficult word to say, along with thank you.

Sorry for the offence.

Thank you for your patience.

Those are never simple words. They burn your throat, sighed Mina. It takes practice to learn how to say them naturally.

I'm sorry.

Thank you.

If the ocean could talk, it would say thank you. If it were able, it would say I'm sorry. Thank you to those who cross her waters to reach other lands. I'm sorry to all those it has swallowed up since the beginning of Creation. If the earth could speak, it would say thank you. If it dared, it would cry out I'm sorry. Thank you to the women who never tire of peopling it. I'm sorry to the men rotting in her belly to fecundate her.

I'm sorry.

Thank you.

I'll say thank you to Suzon as soon as I get to Piment, if she's still alive. Thank you for having taken me in after the fire. I'm sorry for having forgotten you for such a long time. Not even a letter in twenty-one years . . .

And this evening in my prayers, I'll also ask Rosalia to forgive me for having let her go back into the flames.

I'm going to ask for a baguette. No strawberry pie. No pastries. I need to sleep. Forget about Christian's idea of getting married. Forget that man she'd brought up to her apartment. She couldn't remember his name anymore. Only the thank you he had addressed her with before closing the door behind him. Thank you for having given me your body for nothing, Ma'am.

Leaning against the lamppost, Victor was waiting for Mina in front of the bakery. Next to him, tied to a scrawny tree, a fox-terrier tugged at its leash. She bumped up against his smile as if it were a wall. A flashy, well-polished smile. The glossy, lustrous smile of an old actor playing his last role in front of his last audience.

85

"When I woke up this morning I knew something was going to happen," he began, without abandoning his mask of amazement. "I was waiting for you . . ."

"Who? Me?" exclaimed Mina.

"Yes, you've forgotten . . ."

"What? I don't know you."

"Yes, I followed you back to your place . . . We made l . . ."

"Be quiet! We did nothing at all. You are mistaking me for someone else."

She glanced around. People were already looking at them.

"I assure you . . . It really was you. The Edmond Rostand high-rise."

"Just leave me alone now."

She fumbled to button up her sweater, but it was already done. Button it up because her heart was racing, had forgotten how to keep time, was thumping, sinking into the depths of her chest, quite near to stopping dead, then suddenly swelling, thudding, leaping, chafing, growling . . . Her throat went dry, dryer than bedrock that had never known rain or dew. She was cold too. Couldn't control her hands that were now trembling, clutching at her sweater. Couldn't control her fingers that kept sticking into the buttonholes, fidgeting with the buttons. And her legs! All wobbly, Lord . . . Every time she ran into one of the men she'd offered herself to, she wanted to disappear she was so disgusted with herself.

"I never stopped thinking about you," Victor continued. "I owe you a lot . . . I've been ill, you know. Depression. I spent three months in the hospital. There's another woman, Bénédicte . . . A lady I met over there, in Esquirol. She helped me too, like you did. A woman from Guadeloupe . . . We have to see each other again! We really need to talk! I'll introduce you to Bénédicte, if you like. She's getting out soon, I think . . . I'm feeling a lot better now you know . . . I'll tell you all about myself. We'll take the necessary time. Still some anxiety and the blues sometimes, but I'm slowly coming out of it. I'm taking care of myself, in a word. You're from Guadeloupe, I'm not mistaken am I? But we'll have to wait . . . When I can send her a post card from Guadeloupe, it will mean that I'm truly cured. You remember, I was in bad shape. I was dead inside . . . You helped me so much . . . I felt alive. That's great, alive . . . But it didn't last. I had to go to the hospital, the next day . . . We have to see each other again, it's very important . . ."

Mina could not recall exactly where she had met him, maybe over by the shopping center. Incoherent talk. Choppy speech sprinkled with "Have to this! Have to that!" Each time she ran into one of these men she avoided their eyes. Crossed the street. Feigned to be completely astounded. Flabbergasted that they should confuse her with someone else, a wanton woman of easy virtue who invited men to come up to her place.

"I don't know you, Sir."

She turned her heels. Sometimes they called her a slut. Get lost, slut! She walked away standing very straight under the insults, ashamed, afraid, telling herself she was crazy. A mad-woman that picks up men in the street and that would one day be found in her apartment with her throat cut. At those times, she always swore to herself she'd get off the merry-go-round, stop giving in to the temptation of men, console herself on her own, dominate the impulse that pushed her out looking for them like a dog in heat. But she was unable to stop, and went hunting a little further away, beyond the project, in the devel- opments with individual houses, so she wouldn't run the risk of ever passing them again in the dirty alleyways, at the foot of the project buildings, of running into a fanatic of some sort, someone violent, a fetishist . . . She'd imagined herself dead more than once. And ever since AIDS had become a problem, she took precautions, demanded that they put on condoms. There were the casual encounters, and those she could depend upon, who knew how to pass her on the street without saying anything, who had her telephone number.

"I'm sorry, Sir, I don't know you . . . You are mistaken."

She had only brought this one up once. He had a blank look

on his face, seemed to be wandering around, just like she was, lost. First she followed, and then accosted him. She played it up real sweet to entice him. He hadn't resisted. When they reached the seventh floor, she held him close to her breast and he wept before taking her, awkwardly, as if he were dealing with a colossus. He cried while he was making love, as she guided his sex inside of her. He said thank you on the doorstep. Thanks to you I felt as if I were somewhat alive. Thank you, see you soon. I would like to see you again. Thanks for what you have done for me . . . Thank you again for having given your body to me for nothing, Ma'am.

"Leave me alone!" she repeated.

She wanted to disappear, fly away like Rose did. But all she had were her two feet. She would have like to be sucked up into the wind in the street before he started cursing her like all the others. She took a step backwards.

"Don't go!" Victor pleaded, holding on to her arm. "Don't be afraid. I really did want to see you again. I told you I was in the hospital. And I was waiting for a sign too. Something extraordinary happened to me. I have to tell you about it. Bénédicte told me to keep my eyes open, for there would be signs . . . I met you the day before I was hospitalized. I thought of you every day, that's the honest truth. It's been three months now. Three months to the day . . . And here we are . . . It's been three months!"

"Three months!"

Mina's anger suddenly vanished. She remained silent for a moment. Then she allowed her mouth to fill with laughter while the exasperated dog yapped in indignation and tugged harder on its leash.

It's the story of Ancestor Séléna, she thought.

Sir, you promise to let me have this land . . .
So my goats will have a place of their own . . .
See how well they like it here!

The characters were all in place:
The white man, the dog, and the Negress.
They were playing out the same scene.
Had given each other the same amount of time:
Three months of waiting.

All right for the three months, the mulatto had said.
And he left me there with my oversized dreams and
*   my landless goats, grumbled Séléna.*

"All right for the three months," Mina murmured.
"All right for the three months . . ." repeated Victor.

In 1873 the mulatto had exclaimed:
Not enough. I want double that.
And anyway, who says I'm selling?

Victor frowned. He patted his pants pockets, "No! No money!
Not three hundred, or six hundred, or nine hundred francs . . ."

People were staring at them. The dog had stopped barking and
was licking the hands of his young master.

"Can I invite you to have a cup of coffee with me?" Victor
drew closer to her.

"No, I have to go home."

"I have to speak with you, Ma'am."

"Another time . . . I'm running late already . . ."

"When? Let's make a date! We could have dinner some
evening . . ."

XI

Mina said no to everything Victor suggested.

No to coffee.

No to tea.

No to lunch.

No to dinner.

89

No to the stone bench in the project park where they could sit down to have a friendly talk.

No to his telephone number: 01 43 35 etc., etc.

She felt petty and pathetic. Dirty most of all. Dirty on the inside. Wished this madness would be over with.

They had gone their separate ways, disoriented, baguette under arm, like actors who have gotten their lines wrong, know their performance was poor, the film was a flop.

As soon as she reached home, Mina called a travel agency. Flights for Point-à-Pitre were booked up through September. She reserved a ticket for December 20.

"And the return trip?" asked the voice at the other end of the line. "January? 3, 4, 5? There are still vacant seats, but you're wise to be booking now. Everyone wants to kick off the second millennium in the sun."

"January 5," Mina replied.

Up until the death of her mama Médée in 1975, Mina loved numbers. Back when she was in school she used to enjoy combining them, listening to the racket they made in her head before falling into place. Miss Rutice, her first schoolteacher, said she was gifted in arithmetic. Actually, for Mina, adding, subtracting, or dividing was an insignificant game—like jumping rope, reciting "The Sleeper in the Valley," "The Ant and the Grasshopper," singing "Humpty Dumpty." As soon as she closed her notebook the numbers stopped their fuss. Afterwards, she thought about them from time to time, when she decided to teach mathematics to Rosalia, when she needed to check the change after running errands . . . They never grew unwieldy, never signified anything but money, signs in a notebook, the hours of the day, or the boats to be counted out at sea.

And then the numbers turned into dates.

04/18/1975, Médée run down on the road to Piment by a Titan truck.

07/18/1975, Melchior struck by lightning in the banana grove.

Mina could neither add up nor subtract those particular numbers. Only look upon them with fear and suspicion as one does wild animals, infernal machines, lightning flashes in the sky, or monstrous plants that can do nothing but bite, crush, grind, smother, or smite dead. She could hear them grumbling and mumbling and feasting on Médée and Melchior. She saw them come bowling down the road and inscribe their macabre dances on the black crosses in the cemetery. 41819757181975.

And then came September 11, 1978. 9/11/1978. The day Rosalia went back into the flaming cabin. 9111978 . . .

Twenty-one years she hadn't been back to Guadeloupe. 21 years . . . She was leaving on December 20, 1999, and would spend the first day of the year 2000 in the sunshine.

12/20/1999, depart for Piment.

01/05/2000, return to France.

All through the Easter vacation of 1999, Mina repeated the dates to herself. She found them handsome, with their round numbers. She felt like sharing them with someone she knew. She'd been bumping off the walls alone in her apartment for a week.

She called Lysia three times. Very busy on a new project. Christian? No, she refused to see him.

Salima had too many problems just then. Aïsha had gone off to live with the young Christian man and her father was preparing to take the whole family back to their hometown in Algeria, but no one wanted to follow him. There was a constant battle at Salima's house. Maria-Rosa had found herself a fiancé. A Frenchman around forty who had fallen so deeply in love, he never took his eyes off her.

Alone, rattling around in her two-room apartment, watching images of war on the television, of children starving around the world, fanatics of all types in trance, she zapped from one channel to the next, American sit-coms, million-dollar game shows, pop stars, science-fiction films . . . Alone while visions of Guadeloupe superimposed themselves upon those of the television. Burst forth. Filled the rooms, piled up on the shelves in the refrigerator, blotted out the faces on the television screen. Guadeloupe was everywhere. It had never ceased being there. And Mina had always refused to allow herself, even with Lysia, to refer to the country by its name. Guadeloupe. Hung from hangars in the wardrobe. Mixed with the flowers on the wallpaper. Shut up in the jars of guava and pineapple jam. Put away to dry along with pieces of cinnamon bark and nutmeg seeds in metal boxes that had once contained butter cookies from Normandy. Preserved in the pulp of orange and grapefruit juice. Locked deep in her heart and memory. In Rosalia's apparitions.

Yes I'm going back to Guadeloupe. And I'll walk with my head held high through the streets of Piment. I'm going back to my country, far from men.

Alone with the dates that no one wished to share with her.

Alone with this shaky feeling of peace taking root in her heart.

Alone with the exuberance she felt at the idea of starting out the year 2000 on the island of Guadeloupe.

Wait for Suzon's answer. Go back to Morne Calvaire. Take Rose home . . . That's a promise, Rosalia . . .

Alone in her bed on the evening she ran into Victor, Mina tried to summon her. Her fingers sought out the place of orgasm between her open thighs. Her hands became Victor's lips, his silent, greedy tongue. For him, she murmured the dates a hundred times over: 12/20/1999 and 01/05/2000. She opened her eyes, looked over toward the wardrobe where Rosalia always stood. But there was no traveler's-tree, no Rosalia. No flames. No ball of fire. The flowers on the wallpaper were not damaged. And Victor was not there.

Mina decided to call him. His telephone number, which she had not written down anywhere, came back to her as she was sitting in front of the television eating a hard-boiled egg, she was watching the lottery being drawn. 3. 9. 12. 16. 18. 36. 37. 43.

The number was easy to remember: 01 43 35 etc., etc. She dialed it without thinking. Got Victor on the third ring. She forced herself to say something.

"It's me, Mina, do you remember me? The bakery. I'd like to see you again," she said.

"I'd like to see you too," answered Victor without the slightest hesitation. "This evening . . ."

"Yes . . . This evening . . ."

"Would you like to have dinner some place?"

"Yes . . . Dinner"

"Is there anywhere in particular you would prefer?"

"No, nowhere in particular . . ."

"Then I suggest the Mundo Night. It's a jazz and salsa club, but they have a dining room. Good food . . . International cooking . . . You'll have plenty of choice . . ."

"Yes . . . Plenty of choice . . ."

"I was waiting for your call," said Victor. "We have so much to talk about . . ."

"What time this evening?" asked Mina who felt like her head was full of hard rocks.

"Let's say nine o'clock. What do you think?"

"Yeah, nine o'clock . . . I'll be there . . . Okay, see you this evening then . . ."

"See you this evening. And thanks again for calling . . ."

"Right, see you this evening . . ."

"Wait, I'll give you the address . . ."

When she hung up the phone, Mina took a deep breath and slumped onto the couch. She felt like drinking and smoking. Giving her body to a man. And dying. She felt overwhelmed and more fragile than a cabin beset on all sides by a hurricane.

In Guadeloupe, she had known some pretty mean cyclones . . . When Médée and Melchior were still alive. Melchior ran back and forth fifty times with buckets of water, his ladder, his cutlass, his hammer . . . He talked to himself as he filled up the water jugs. Nailed bars in a cross over the doors and windows. Heaved old cinder blocks and bags filled with sand onto his shoulders that he put on the corrugated metal roof. In the meantime, Médée forgot that she might have been Marilyn if she had been born in America. She busied herself in the cabin. Kneaded the dough and fried the *dunkit*-cakes as her mother had taught her. Checked the kerosene and the wick in the lamp. Put the provisions and the linens away in barrels and boxes that she stowed up high. Above all, she opened her Bible, implored Jesus to be clement, begged God's pity and asked forgiveness for all the venal and mortal sins of black people on this earth. Rosalia didn't understand anything about the general agitation because before the fury is unleashed, the sky does not announce what is to come. It is always clear blue in the hours before a cyclone. The clouds are immaculately white and the sun is as resplendent as a pubescent bride on the steps of the church. So just when Melchior was hooking up the last door, Rosalia always wanted to go out and paint in the garden. Strategies had to be devised to convince her to remain quiet, closed up in the cabin. That was Mina's big chore.

"If you like, Rose, we'll paint those pots and pans there! Look!"

Rosalia looked in the direction of Mina's finger. Then bowed her head before pointing to the barricaded door.

"Go on stick your brush in the water!"

Rosalia grew more sullen as time went on, sobbed and fidgeted under Melchior's gaze who was starting to grumble and sigh heavily.

"What would you like to do? Tell me. Sing a song! Take a nap! Oh, I know, Rose! You want me to tell you a story . . ."

When Melchior decided it was time to start hurling insults to make his people keep quiet, Rosalia started shrieking, kicked the pots of paint away. She seemed to be battling with invisibles, knocked her elongated head against the corners of the furniture and spoke in a tongue known only to her.

"Calm down, calm down, Rose . . . Listen to the wind outside. Hoo! Hoo! Hoo! It's the cyclone. Hoo! Hoo! Hoo!"

Mina made her mouth into an O and blew on her big sister's face to dry her tears and turn them into laughter. Outside the wind rose. Rosalia sought refuge in Mina's arms where she was rocked and consoled with soft words, as furious torrents of rain riding on the gale-force winds pounded at the sheet metal roof.

"He thinks he's going to get in, the fiend!" fumed Melchior, battling the fury of the elements with mere imprecations. "Go on! Get the hell out of here you blasted devil! Off with you, heathen!"

"Easy now, easy, sweet Rosalia . . . Go to sleep my little Rose . . ." whispered Mina.

In the end Rosalia calmed down. And as soon as she sunk into sleep, a smile stemming from the mystery of her dreams formed on her face—innocent of all the sins Médée believed the human species capable of, deaf to Melchior's gloomy theatrics, and the renewed assaults of the wind, suddenly liberated from her condition of helpless demented girl.

When the cyclone grew weary of Guadeloupe and set its sights on other lands, islands farther to the north, Melchior did some more pounding, unnailed everything without a word. Then he inspected the cabin, its surroundings, the garden, the orchard, and above all the banana grove, where the most damage was done. He took the mortally wounded banana trees in his arms, like brave soldiers who had valiantly stood their ground before giving way. Faced with the disaster caused by the cyclone, Melchior sometimes wept in silence, lopping off in one swipe the useless, scrawny little bunches, barely good enough to give to the pigs.

Mina arrived too early for her rendezvous with Victor. She went and hid in a smoke-filled pari-mutuel bar from where the door to Mundo Night could be seen. At a neighboring table, a man lit up one cigarette after another. The ashtray was overflowing with stubs. If she hadn't refrained, Mina would have asked him for one. But that just wasn't done. She hadn't been brought up like that. She ordered a cup of coffee and then a glass of red wine. Drink and smoke, that's what she needed. She had never been tempted by Christian's cigarettes, not even after lovemaking. That's a sign, she said to herself.

"I was waiting for a sign!" Victor had confided to her.

He's ten minutes late! sighed Mina from her post across the street.

Victor had just pushed open the door to the Mundo Night. She swallowed her third glass of wine, paid the bill and stood up unsteadily. A thick fog-like cloud hung in the room filled with men talking loudly over their beers and discussing horses as they leafed through the *Paris-Turf.* A few of them gave her a wink.

They think they're dealing with a second-rate whore. Yes, I'm a whore, take a good look! I've seen a lot more than you can imagine! The only thing that interests me is being taken, speared by men! And, throwing her shoulders back, she left the premises holding her head high. She arrived at the Mundo Night teetering slightly, having the odd impression that she was a puppet being manipulated by a superior force. A poor mindless doll that never makes its own decisions and goes wherever others choose to lead her. And the feeling that she had never had to choose her own path. Never been given the chance to undertake or accomplish anything. That she had always just endured life.

Endured having been born to a taciturn father and a mother who dreamt of being the Marilyn Monroe of Piment.

Endured her childhood in the company of one retarded sister and another who was two-faced.

Endured her adolescence filled with dead people and licked by flames.

Endured life in France alongside Olga, Douglas, and Rosalia...

And all the men she laid in her bed...

She stood there, a little lost in the entrance to the Mundo, looking around for her date. The door to the restaurant was set in a vault of large bare stones covered with tendrils of creeping ivy. The mirrors threw her image back to her and she thought that she wore her wine well. She found that she still looked young and shapely at thirty-five. Nothing betrayed the fact that she lived with ghosts. Nothing in the way she walked or acted related that she had grown up on a desolate hill in Guadeloupe where the glorious ancestor had made a fortune and given land to her goats and then—for the sake of posterity— her body to an apocryphal priest. Not a single wrinkle on her face revealed that she had seen death at such close quarters... on three different occasions.

One, two, three.

One. Two. Three.

Seen Médée's broken body. Dragged for several meters by the Titan truck. Blood on her lace blouse. Skirt thrown up.

One. Two. Three.

Seen, that very same year, poor Melchior struck down in his banana grove, like a valiant musketeer.

One. Two. Three.

Seen Rosalia come out of the burning cabin and rush down the hill, a living torch.

No, right here and now, no one could betray her. It was magic! She could invent a serene childhood for herself, build a life free of torment. Lie and tell stories ad infinitum. No one would know. No one knew.

Victor had reserved a table in the middle of a tangle of imitation and real tropical plants: philodendrons, dwarf banana trees, tentacular, sprawling rubber plants, giant rhododendrons, tree ferns, ficus with leaves that gleamed in the muted lighting. The customers, people between thirty and fifty years of age, seemed to be regulars and addressed the waiters—cheerful men with suave gestures and sleek shiny hair—by their first names.

"This is a nice private place," said Victor.

"Yes," said Mina, taking on the air of a young girl on her first date.

"Would you like something to drink?"

"No alcohol for the time being . . ."

"Perfect. I'm not drinking at the moment either."

He ordered two fruit-juice cocktails.

Victor sat down next to a banana tree whose leaves kept drooping down over his ears, as if they wanted to keep him from hearing the stories Mina was cooking up to seduce him. She shelled the sautéed shrimp and drank little sips of the Evian mineral water he had ordered. But her eyes remained trained on his face, trying to decipher the interest, the disbelief, the boredom, the desire most of all.

She portrayed her imaginary childhood in a well-to-do house in Pointe-à-Pitre. Her make-believe brothers and sisters. Her arrival in France after obtaining the baccalaureate. Her romantic love affair with a Frenchman, Bruno. And then, just to add a few frills, the mental depression which forced her to quit the university. The bitter disappointment it had caused her parents, who were still living. And finally, the job serving food in the high-school cafeteria.

Mina spoke in a whisper so that her voice would not carry over to other ears, not anger the banana leaves. Her own words made her head reel. They vibrated with the rhythm of a reconstituted life that was surprisingly convincing, even seemed genuine and credible to her. She talked, talked, talked, reconstructing her existence with an assortment of almost mythical characters, with no souls or faces, or toes or tongues, painted with wide sweeps of color that dried almost immediately into brittle crusts. Ephemeral heroes wandering through an imbroglio that the sun had never shone upon. As she went along inventing, she began to feel as if she were actually in that world. An amorphous creature, buffeted about by the elements. The farther she wandered from the path of her true story, the more her lies awakened old pains that led her back to the straight road of her tormented loneliness.

Once, up on Morne Calvaire, Rosalia had painted the world in a similar way.

Victor seemed sincere when he began to relate his life. A depressive, hypochondriac mother who spent her life in bed, smoking and lamenting about her widowhood and humankind. A father who committed suicide by hanging himself. The first signs of depression—the first bond between them. Imperious thoughts of suicide, anxiety, medication. Both fear of and longing for death rolled up together in his mind. His last stay in the psychiatric hospital in Esquirol . . .

Listening to him, Mina felt wretched.

"I have to go now," she said, suddenly sobered by the sight of the crème brûlée desert, feeling nauseous about the time she'd wasted lying.

She threw her napkin down on the table like a boxer chucks in the sponge after having bungled a fight. She would have liked to begin all over again. Reveal herself to him without a mask, but she'd already said too much.

"I'd like to go to Guadeloupe, you know . . . I have to. I have to be cured over there. Bénédicte saw the ghosts marching in my shadow. I have to go to Guadeloupe . . ."

All through dinner she'd found him a little odd, but thought of only one thing: touching him, getting him into her bed. She stretched her hands out on the table between the bread and the water. Victor ignored them.

He had other things on his mind. His own urgent matters. Getting the spell he was under broken. Getting cured. And while she spoke to him of love with her eyes, he was telling her of Bénédicte and her diagnosis of bewitchment. He introduced her to Omega, his friend, and related their first encounter, back in the days when he wanted to be a salsa dancer, an amateur of rum and cigars. Then he went on about the women he'd been with: Gloria, Catherine, and the others . . . And then there was his job in supermarket warehouses.

"I have to go now," Mina repeated. She rose to her feet.

"No, not right away! Please," he held her back by the arm, "we're going over to the other side now, to the jazz club. You'll see how relaxing it is. It's the kind of music that speaks to the soul."

In the dimly lit room, Omega took Victor and Mina by the hand and led them over to a reserved booth. The very place where Victor had passed out drunk, three months earlier, the night he was hospitalized.

"We don't shake good habits, do we?" whispered Omega with a knowing smile.

"Bring us something to drink instead of spilling my life story . . ."

"What are you afraid of, Vic? I'm no snitch!"

"Would you like some champagne, Mina? I'm sticking with water myself, I shouldn't drink alcohol . . ."

"Yes, Victor, I'd love some," she said, surprised that she'd got his name out without a hitch.

Omega disappeared between the tables, gracefully swinging his hips, pretending to grab notes of music here and there coming from the quartet playing that evening.

"He's a great salsa dancer you know. He's also a good friend. I owe him my life. He's the one that saved me from certain death three months ago."

It was the first time Mina had ever been to this kind of place since she'd been living in France. The people there were incredible, the kind you never run across in the streets of Paris during the daytime. Night zombies with bleached hair. Men kissing each other mouth to mouth in front of everyone. Women in brassieres or transparent blouses exposing their

100

breasts jiggling over candleholders on the tables. Scattered groups and loners poring over their drinks. Shadows floating on a tiny dance floor swept by projectors that turned their faces green or pink or purple . . .

"Do you like the music, Mina?" asked Victor after a moment.

She nodded. She was afraid to speak in case lies should force themselves on her tongue.

"Are you having a nice time here with me?"

He smiled.

He seemed to be talking to himself.

So Mina didn't bother to reply. There was enough noise, loud bursts of voices, laughter, and music to fill all of their silence. Hanging on the walls in gilt rococo frames covered with sculpted rosettes, paintings portraying pink and black thighs and legs intermingling, armless hands cupping breasts, modern still-lives depicting vacuum cleaners, underwear and toothbrushes, old fridges, bashed up American cars and scooters with blown-out tires. The champagne was making Mina sleepy while the water was loosening Victor's tongue.

"I have to listen to my instincts. This might be my last chance to be cured. I have to go to Guadeloupe. But I can't go alone. I need a guide . . ."

"But you're seeing a doctor here. Why do you insist on believing this poor woman? She's deranged . . . Do you really believe there's a spell on you?"

"Of course I believe it. Bénédicte and I talked about it a lot. She's obviously clairvoyant. I've been swallowing drugs for years. Tranxene . . . Lexomil . . . Prozac . . . I know I need them, but why shouldn't I try something else . . ."

"I'll be your guide," sighed Mina, having exhausted all arguments. "I'm going to Guadeloupe on December 20, 1999, and I'm coming back to Paris January 5, 2000 . . ."

Once again she had said the dates that she was yearning to share with the entire world.

One too many times.

At the wrong time.

And above all to the wrong person.

Victor didn't react immediately, mired down as he was in his monologue. But step by step, the idea wormed its way in. First he sat up in the booth. Shook his head from right to left like a horse readying to rear. Then he opened his eyes wide.

"To Guadeloupe! On December 20, 1999 . . ."

"If you'd like, of course . . . Nothing binding . . . If I go . . . Nothing is certain yet. I still don't even have the tickets . . ."

She was already changing her mind.

"If . . . If . . . If . . . I want to!" bellowed Victor. "If I want to!" He burst out laughing.

"If . . ."

And he was weeping. He wanted to kiss Mina.

"If . . ."

He ordered her another glass of champagne, endlessly repeating that *if*, as if he had captured it, like a butterfly with fairy wings that had appeared in the jazz club just for him, Victor. A lyrical and luminous *if* like a note drifting out of a saxophone. An *if* in the shape of a key that could open the golden door of recovery to him. An *if* as tender as a woman's lips . . .

Mina made a feeble attempt to calm his ardor, but it was out of her hands. However, the disaster had totally sobered her. She'd spoken without thinking. Where in the world did her claim to be a guide come from?

Guadeloupe.

First station: the spice market.

"Sweety, buy some of my cinnamon and vanilla! Give me a sale honey!"

Second station: Meet the fishermen as they bring in their catch. redfish, catfish, sunfish, sea bass.

The gommier canoes are marked with women's names or those of saints.

They are painted in bright gay colors to brave the ocean.

Third station: l'Allée Dumanoir

Capesterre-Belle-Eau. Royal palms.

A photo-op one mustn't miss.

Fourth station: beaches, sun and sand guaranteed.

From North to South on each wing of the Guadeloupe butterfly.

Fifth station: A touch of history.

The first inhabitants: The Caribs left rock engravings.

Christopher Columbus landed in 1493.

The Africans reduced to slavery for French sugar.

1848: The abolition of slavery.

1946: Guadeloupe declared an overseas department of France.

Sixth station: Geography.

La Souffrière, legendary volcano.

Island: Land surrounded by water.

An Archipel: Marie-Galante, Iles des Saintes, La Désirade.

Seventh station: A mosaic of peoples.

"Who are we? Where do we come from? Where are we going?"

Eighth station: Piment.

Morne Calvaire.

Rosalia, the cabin blazing in the night.

"You see, Bénédicte was right. It's a sign! Our roads crossed three months ago, under rather strange conditions, you might say. Now I've found you again and you will be my guide . . . You are on my path, Mina. You're not there by chance."

"If I go, I'll let you know. Nothing is for sure . . . One never knows what might come up in the meantime . . . You know, we really don't make any choices in life . . . I already . . ."

"If you go!" Victor cut in. "But of course you're going. We're both going!"

He hammered out the dates, rolled them on his tongue, repeated them with the same ecstasy and fervor that had filled

Mina these last few days. He made the dates his own. He robbed her of her joy.

Mina hadn't the slightest desire to serve as Victor's tour guide. Even if she had felt the desire to have his body next to hers, to touch his naked skin. For her big homecoming in Piment, she had to be alone. Alone to face Morne Calvaire and the remnants of the burned down cabin, the ruins of her past, the banana grove given over to the vines.

Victor accompanied her in a taxi to the foot of her high-rise. He had insisted upon it, begged her to accept. "Three o'clock in the morning, it's all my fault! I can't let you go home alone . . ." But he hadn't risked the slightest move when they found themselves on the back seat, surrounded by darkness conducive to preliminary petting. When she slammed the door of the Mercedes, despite one last smile, a big thank you, and a vibrant See you soon!, Mina decided to never see him again.

XII

She called him three days later.

She hadn't stopped thinking of him. She needed to rediscover Victor's body. Then break it off. She swore to herself this would be the last one, the one that would bring her around full circle before going back to Piment. After making love, leave Victor to his eccentricities. Goodbye, my dear man! Find yourself another guide! And bon voyage!

She hadn't slept well. Had dreamt of him . . .

He appeared on Morne Calvaire, searching for relics spared by the fire. She ran into him by chance, naked, swimming in the river in Piment. She saw him sitting at Cousin Tibert's house, a guest at dinner. He was everywhere in Guadeloupe, as if the trip had already taken place.

Mina resented the idea that he could coerce her, with his wide grins, to undertake this expedition with him, that she should have to bow to his every whim and that everything was already in the cards. Victor just had to let her use his body, take her, penetrate her. Give her some love, a few minutes of loving. She would not be his guide. His majesty could think only of himself and being cured! He'd swallowed all of her lies without raising an eyebrow, without even trying to distinguish the truth from the falsehoods, without asking any questions. He wasn't interested in her. The only thing that counted was Victor and getting his spell broken.

He just has to take me, Mina said to herself while picking up the telephone, she was a fury, a woman half mad, possessed, driven by the urgent desire to have a man's body on hers, a man's penis stuck in her belly like a knife. What's that white man got in his mind? He drops me docilely off at the foot of my building, instead of taking me in his arms and going up to the seventh floor with me. He didn't even feel an inkling of desire and there I was offering myself to him. She went back and forth between seeing herself first as a repudiated woman —ranting and ruminating—then as a novice torn between God and the Devil. I swear he will be the last one if he takes me! I swear! May death strike me down if I break my word . . .

Victor answered on the fifth ring.

"I was waiting for your call."

"Would you like to come for dinner at my place tonight?" she heard herself asking him.

"You're marvelous Mina. Really a good, generous person . . ."

"What time, Victor?"

"Is eight okay with you?"

"Fine, eight o'clock. See you tonight, Victor."

"See you tonight Mina. And thanks . . ."

I'm a whore, Mina kept telling herself as she prepared dinner. A whore who gives her body away without asking to be paid. I'm a whore who lures men in. A whore who takes some pleasure, but knows nothing of love. A poor girl begging for caresses from the first man that comes along . . .

We'll see if he can resist this time, she thought as she changed the sheets on her bed. If he can keep his distance and his detached state of mind ... And she slipped on a transparent beige silk blouse that had cost her thirty francs at Monoprix, put on her make-up carefully, doused herself abundantly with perfume. And glancing one last time in the bathroom mirror, she prayed to heaven that Victor would succumb.

The bell rang at exactly eight o'clock. Victor brought blue flowers. He was wearing a suit the same color of beige as Mina's blouse.

"I'm very moved," he began. "If my poor mother could only see me now ..."

"If your mother could see you?" Mina replied. "What would she do, give you a spanking?"

"No, she would simply be shattered," said Victor in a neutral voice.

"She's already dead and buried, so let's talk about something else ..."

She wanted to make him angry, but Victor was the very image of blissful innocence, a polished stone statue that her spit simply ran off of.

"Sit down there! You're in my territory now."

She laughed, just like a genuine Guadeloupe she-devil who's trapped some poor fool in the lakes in order to cut him up and eat him raw after having befuddled him with her tales. Victor obeyed serenely, even crossed his legs as if they were going to chat and dream about going to Guadeloupe together.

"I love the way you laugh, Mina."

He stretched and relaxed in the easy chair covered in corduroy, patted a satin cushion.

"I'm so happy. I feel so much better now that I know I have a guide. I still have anxiety attacks, but I'm sure it will be fine when I'm in Guadeloupe. And it's all thanks to you, Mina. Thanks to you!"

And he repeated that bit of phrase with a gleam in his eyes: Thanks to you ...

"You want to go to Guadeloupe, are you sure?"

"Yes," said Victor without batting an eyelid.

"You really believe what that crazy old woman told you? What's her name again . . ."

"Bénédicte . . ."

"In Guadeloupe there are cruel and jealous people, just like with White People. Thieves and narrow-minded folks."

"Yes, I know."

"There are people who could kill you!"

"Yes, I know."

"You know everything, don't you? You're one of the chosen few!" She looked him up and down.

"No, I'm just a man, Mina. Just a man who's trying to get cured."

"All right, I'm going to tell you a story . . . The true story of my life . . ."

~

For a few days Bénédicte pretended she no longer saw the horrid creatures prowling in the corridors and sleeping in the rooms beside the patients. Her psychiatrist allowed her to go home on leave, accompanied by a nurse. Offensive therapy. Mail was waiting for her in the mailbox, it was overflowing with bills, advertisements, and game contests that she had been entering since she first arrived in France. She was in the habit of reading everything carefully, pencil in hand in order to jot down the addresses of sales, slashed prices, unique special offers. She was always surprised to discover she was the winner of a contest, a lottery, or a raffle that she hadn't entered, even in her wildest dreams. Yet there her name was, written as plain as day: Mrs. Bénédicte Hypolite, the grand winner, will receive the sum of 300,000 francs, a Ford Escort, a Renault Space, a gift certificate for 5,000 francs, a micro-wave oven, a dishwasher, a trip around the world, a diamond, a piece of gold jewelry worth 60,000 francs . . .

At first she had swallowed it all, hook, line, and sinker. She even tried to take a mail order giant to court; her colleagues at the Post Office and her dead husband, who smiled and nodded his head sometimes in the frame sitting on the dresser, had dissuaded her. Since then, she simply collected the certificates and framed, as if they were the most spectacular diplomas or honorary titles, the ones where her name appeared in boldface type, the ones that didn't skimp on the zeros. That day she was the lucky winner of a one-week trip to Morocco, a coupon for a 20% discount on any carpet purchase, and a menagerie of Chinese statuettes. When she finished inspecting the ads, she carefully opened the envelope she had set aside. It contained a post card, the Arch of Triumph against a blue sky.

Paris, June 8 1999

My dearest Bénédicte,
*   I am almost cured.*
I awaited the signs and I have met my guide: Mina, you recall . . .
She's taking me to Guadeloupe.
I'll be leaving December 20.
*   Yours sincerely,*
*   Victor Clément*

Bénédicte lit a cigarette, blew the smoke into the face of a triad of demons who were looking at her in a strange way and sank deeper into her armchair. Surrounded by three succubae and two imps with corkscrew horns, the nurse — outrageously oblivious — was pouring water into the coffee filter. Bénédicte remembered Victor, her protégé, perfectly well. A tall white man with wild hair, looking as if he were possessed with his eyes turned yellow by satanic forces. You could see with the naked eye that a spell had been put on him and that he would go from the frying pan into the fire if he didn't start looking for a good *gadèzafè*-conjuror to rid him of the demons that walked in his shadow. As a good Christian, Bénédicte had warned him, same as she would have any black man.

"Ah! Good, he listened," thought Bénédicte. "All right, that's not the end of it, now I'll have to make sure he falls into the right hands . . . A medicine man able to deal with this kind of affliction. There aren't many left in Guadeloupe . . ."

On the back of the envelope, Victor had written his address. Bénédicte copied it into her small black address book and circled Victor's departure date in red.

XIII

Suzon Mignard was now seventy-two years old. She could still distinguish shapes and people's movements, the fire on the stove, the flame of a candle. But there was no remedying it, her life had sunk into twilight.

In the late '70s she hardly paid any attention to the fog hovering around the edges. Thin veils of muslin that she thought she could draw away by rinsing her eyes with weak coffee. Very soon, these eyewashes no longer sufficed. Regardless of how hard she strove to open her eyes wide, or knit her brows, the veils grew thicker, became curtains, weighed more heavily each day.

Berlus, the *gadèzafè*-conjuror whom she consulted without further delay, called upon the clairvoyant spirits floating in the time when yesterday, today, and tomorrow all run together, the place in which the living and the dead coexisted without seeing it, breathed the same air without believing it. For him, they frantically sounded the troubled waters of Suzon's past and in an instant, they unanimously pointed out the beginnings and ends of the disorder. Berlus pronounced his diagnosis so pitilessly that Suzon was stricken with a fit of trembling.

"You asked that they be plunged into darkness. The job was effective, even more so than you hoped. Alas, the man who served you used the wrong dosage. Now you come to me, but too late. If you'd made the move earlier, I might have been able to help . . . For a long time darkness has been casting its wide net, unshackled and unchecked. It proliferated like a weed that smothers and devours everything in its path. When it found no more flesh to consume, it turned on you, who had first summoned it. Turned on you like a starving dog attacks its master. The evil has not been satiated . . . What can I do against the powers you yourself have unleashed?"

Berlus, a gloomy man of great notoriety, signed himself and then, taking a fistful of ashes, rubbed his long black hands together.

"I won't steal your money, Mignard. There's nothing I can do for you . . . Try praying," he suggested in his booming voice.

Suzon had withdrawn five hundred francs at the bank, taken from her little nest-egg toward retiring at l'Habitation Mézières. She would have paid twice that to get her sight back. Chastened, she put her billfold back into the bottom of her basket.

"You can't do nothing for me," she moaned. "So that's your last word . . . I got to pay my debt to the past. I an old woman now and I ain't got no more hate in my heart. I swear, I've already atoned. I've asked forgiveness a thousand times. I swear it on my life . . ."

"When they put your body in the ground, you will still not have paid your debt, Mignard . . . You will still not have paid your debt—far from it—when you are nothing but a pile of bones and decomposed flesh, food for the worms. You could live a thousand years and say a thousand pardons, Mignard. Two thousand years and you would still not have paid your debt, far from it."

Suzon shuddered. Though she had been expecting it, actually hearing the indictment was a blow. Still, she found the strength to stand up straight, breathing heavily. As if those final words were not enough, she could feel the full weight of Berlus's gaze on her head. The disgusted gaze of a devil's advocate or—worse—of a priest bound to the secrecy of confession. What he had seen in the ashes, the coffee, and the earth mixed together, was more horrific and gruesome than the memories of his most epic consultations.

She extended her hand so that he might touch it, press it, a gesture that would signify that he still considered her to be part of the human race, despite all of her evil doings. But Berlus skillfully avoided it, leaving Suzon's limp hand clutching at emptiness. Thrown off balance, the poor dim-sighted woman bumped up against the altar where tapers of brown wax had been lit. She burned her fingers groping for a branch, a charitable hand, an invisible crutch. Her legs barely held her up. She stumbled, did not fall, by the grace of God, and teetered out of Berlus's office. To her, the street bathed in the noonday sun seemed dark, treacherous, peopled with zombies. "I already paid my debts," she repeated to herself. "I repented before God."

Suzon remained shut up in her house for a week, ruminating over her punishment, mumbling prayers, and roaming the dark corridors of her youth.

In the early '80s, egged on by the neighbor women who actively criticized her for resigning herself to her fate, yet hypocritically assured her of her righteousness, she made an appointment with the M.D. in Piment. The man had the reputation of being a miracle-worker. Alas, he immediately admitted he was powerless and recommended that she see a specialist in La Pointe. For three years Suzon kept the letter the doctor had entrusted to her, addressed to one of his colleagues. Her sole company was the low humming sound of Berlus's cruel words in her ears: "A thousand years, two thousand years, and you would still not have paid your debt, far from it . . ."

She had been struggling against the semi-darkness for nearly twenty-one years now. Sometimes, when she awoke, she saw rays of light streaming before her eyes, like falling stars leaving trails heavy with hope. Sharp pointed branches to pierce the bubble of misfortune and rip open the curtains that barred the light. She prayed all the more fervently hoping to appeal to God's mercy. Alas, night fell quickly over that deceitful sky. Her visions went up in smoke. And the new day, whiter than a promise, inexorably grew as black as soot. She beat her breast, endlessly repeating, "It's my fault! It's my fault! It's all my terrible fault!"

~

When, in August of 1999, the mailman who was named Teddy, informed her of a letter from France, Suzon shook from head to toe.

"Who's writing me?" she cried out, panic-stricken, clutching the three crosses she wore around her neck.

"Mina Montério, Edmond Rostand high-rise, Apartment 7005, 7th floor ... I can read it to you, Madame Mignard, I don't mind. You don't get mail very often. Montério," the prying fool repeated, "wasn't there a Montério family right here in Piment back in the old days ..."

"No!" hissed Suzon at the blurry mass standing three steps in front of her. "You have your route to finish ... I got someone who does my reading for me. Give me my letter!"

Teddy, a young man brought up to venerate and respect his elders, believed she was embarrassed to ask. He insisted compassionately.

"It will only take me a couple of minutes, Madame Mignard. You won't have to wait for a pair of neighbor's eyes ... It's a pleasure for me to be of service to you. There now, I'll open it and ..."

"No! No!" roared Suzon, "Give it to me right now! It's my letter, you impudent good for nothing! Give it to me!"

Suzon leapt forward, pushed her rocking chair aside and strode toward Teddy's shadow. She tore at the air trying to get hold of the letter that was floating—a bright white patch—in the hands of the ill-mannered boy. Suzon's fingers were opening and closing like the claws of drunken crabs, veritable razor blades that ripped at the smooth skin on the mailman's face before snatching the letter. No one had ever warned him about the Mignard woman, only about Mr. or Mrs. So and So's dogs . . . That is why, under his trousers, he was wearing a pair of puttees he had found in the attic in a metal trunk that had belonged to his grandfather, a hero from the second-to-last war. No! No one had told him about the savagery of certain old negresses whose wrinkles and white hair directly conferred upon them an air of virginal saintliness.

At his young age, Teddy was naïve and pretentious. He considered elderly women to be inoffensive creatures, abandoned in their rocking-chairs, frail, defenseless little dolls who had no sins or regrets. And so he stopped on their doorsteps, offered them a few comforting words. Even if there was no mail, he gave some of his time, feeling he was the most generous of the generous. Piment now counted five mailmen who made their rounds by car. In twenty years, the town's population had more than doubled. Huge housing developments had replaced half of the banana groves. Five mailmen compared to the lone Délos of the past, who died two days after he retired. Teddy was the latest addition, and he thanked the good lord for having found him that job. At the end of his workday, he went over all the faces he had seen, the loneliness he'd encountered, the small torments he had come in contact with. And he fell asleep blissfully, with a more contented heart than that of the Lord on the seventh day of Creation.

When her hands finally got hold of Mina's letter, Suzon calmed down and flopped back into her rocking chair. She ate nothing all day long. Didn't even have the strength to swallow a bowl of milk. With Mina's letter slipped into her pocket, she remained sitting on the porch until evening, squinting her eyes and trying to watch the shadows stretch out in the street. Then she went into her cabin and locked the door just as the sun was disappearing behind the crest of Morne Calvaire.

Twenty-one years since Mina had left. Not a word since

then. When she'd gone she'd taken Suzon's past along with her. Paradoxically, in spite of her madness, Suzon had always considered the people on Morne Calvaire as part of her family; a family she had both loved and hated with the same pulsing of her heart.

Twenty-one years of reprieve in the peace of bitter waters . . .

As far back into her childhood memories as she delved, Suzon's life had been tied to Melchior's. Both born the same year, they were baptized on the same Sunday. They went to the village school together. Though they never happened to be in the same class, they joined each other in a corner of the playground and made up games and conversations just for two. Hand games that left no place for anyone but them and in which they had to hug and touch each other. And conversations in which they were supposed to whisper sweet words in each other's ear. Very early in her childhood dreams, Suzon saw herself unmistakably married to Melchior. Her younger brother Délos was their confidant, who as a small child already served as a messenger between the two friends.

At the age of twelve, Suzon firmly believed in her destiny, pictured herself as a wife and mother, a passel of children at her feet because Melchior had run his fingers over the tips of her titties, filled her head with whispered promises.

To turn her off or make her change her mind, Lucinda—her mama—told her the old story of Séléna, the boy's ancestor, a cursed negress if ever there was one, who thought she was a mulattress and caused a priest to fall into her bed. Suzon laughed with Délos about it and sent the past and its phantoms packing back to the other side of time. So what if Melchior was the descendent of a defrocked priest? How did any of that change the present? Suzon couldn't care less about the old days. She embodied the youth and the future of Piment. The only thing she was sure of was that she would be in love with Melchior for the rest of her life.

Lucinda threatened to whip her a hundred times. But nothing worked. On the eve of her sixteenth birthday, chaperoned by Délos, their faithful accomplice, the two lovers met at the foot of the blooming mango tree. Melchior promised her the moon and a good many other planets. For him, in the warm friendly darkness, Suzon slipped off her immaculate white panties. Trembling, Melchior slipped his hand between the thighs of his beloved. He pressed, caressed, fondled time and again before shoving his man rod into the body that was already rocking and rolling. I've conquered him, thought Suzon, sure that her battle had been won. Utterly confident, she gave him her treasure. They mingled their flesh. She allowed him to tear open the veil of her virginity. She bled for him, for him alone. And the blood she spilt in the name of love was like a signature at the bottom of a parchment. A pact uniting them till the end of time.

Melchior penetrated the intimacy of her body three times. Three times all in all.

And then, without her having the slightest notion why, he grew distant, invented mountains to climb and storm-tossed seas to cross. He pretended she'd said something wrong that she apparently couldn't remember. He promised a hundred times to meet her in some hidden love nest. She waited, starting at the slightest crack of a leaf, at the sigh of the wind in the cane fields, at the cry of a wounded animal. She wished he would come for days and days, heart racing, throat dry, head filled with foreboding. She tried to approach him, to revive the extinguished flame with whispered honey-words. She wrote him in approximate, error-filled French, passionate letters packed with questions and entreaties, which remained unanswered.

One morning she stationed herself on his path—a grieving stone statue. He gave her a little wave of the hand and went along his way, magnificent, princely, indifferent, filled with such coldness Suzon was devastated. In a single glance, she realized he no longer had any desire to stick his head or his rod between her open thighs, or to suck sweet oil from her titties either.

"Patience!" urged Délos. "Men always throw things into reverse before taking the plunge. He'll be eating out of your hand in no time. You're a woman, you can't understand. Hopping on the train of life isn't all that easy for men..."

Alas, Melchior let the years grow heavy and pile up, forgot the caresses and promises. He received the strict orders of the banana grove, worked himself silly, declared he would devote his life to hard labor while the townspeople who recalled the games for four hands between Suzon and him remained perplexed and called him a renegade, secretly laughing at the girl's misfortune. That's what males are like, sighed the old war-hardened negresses.

But Suzon did not admit defeat. Time and again she sent Délos as a delegate. He always came back empty-handed but with a mouthful of that unbearable patience, easy to preach in conversation, but hard for a broken heart to live by. Suzon felt uplifted for a while. She mustered all of her patience, got to her knees and prayed to God, telling herself that time—as her brother assured her—would bring an end to her torment. She called upon the saints, implored them, each in turn, to deliver Melchior from the diabolical elements that had turned him away from her... That was, in any case, her presentiment and it was the impression most people were under, because the man coveted no woman. For a long time the mystery added fuel to the two-bit stories that would burst into flames at the drop of a word in the evening, or at a late-night gathering.

1948, thunder clouds in the sky over Piment! At the age of twenty-one, Melchior fell in love with a certain Mamzell Marie-Perle, a salt-water chabine fished out of a hole in Anse-Bertrand. He married her in two days and then brought her back to Piment, proud as any heathen.

The bitter news awaited Suzon in the marketplace.

Bitter in the bitter mouth of Silène Couba whose heart had once beat for Melchior.

As soon as she learned of the offense, Suzon snapped.

Brought back to her cabin under heavy escort and thrown into her bed, she was delirious for two moons, sweated, pissed on herself, scratched, spit, screamed, screamed, screamed . . . They had to tie her down, wash her, force-feed her. She almost lost her mind. People took turns sitting by her for it was feared she would drink something lethal, decide to hang or drown her body . . . Or still yet, be tempted to cut her own throat, jab a cutlass up her grieving *coucoune* . . .

Her mother was of no help. Poor Lucinda seemed to have been hit over the head with a sledge-hammer. She started out by cursing Suzon, reminding the girl she had been warned.

"What did I tell you, damn fool? You had no business with that nigger from the hills! You're nothing but a bitch in heat!"

And then suddenly Lucinda collapsed, right on the spot, forgot how to speak in the space of one day. She wiled away the hours sitting on the veranda, face frozen into haughty indifference staring out on the storm-tossed sea, while people came and went in the cabin amidst Suzon's screams.

The two women were wasting away together, one might have thought that grief was feeding upon both of their hearts with equal eagerness.

A new mystery that no one was able to decipher.

After the time of screaming and crying, Suzon passed into the stage of petrification.

The girl remained petrified in her bed for six months, laughing though her mouth did not laugh and crying though her body did not shed a tear.

Petrified, that was just the word for it . . .

The priest at the time visited her often, prayed lengths of rosaries at her bedside to exorcise the evil from the body of the supposed virgin.

"Leave this world!" he exhorted Satan, brandishing a cross. "And you, Suzon Mignard, daughter of Lucinda Mignard, offer your life to the Almighty Lord, ruler of heaven and earth. Become the bride of Christ, who is calling you . . . There is a place for you with the Carmelite nuns . . . Go knock on their door; they are waiting for you now."

Suzon got back on her feet.

Pétrified, that was just the word for it, Délos repeated to all who would listen. For she returned from her journey through pain as hard as rock. Promoted as regional mailman, he carried Suzon's health report to the four corners of Piment leaving humbled faces and bent backs behind him.

Suzon got back on her feet.

Several times—zombie—she went down to Basse-Terre. Stood guard in front of the tall black wooden door closed upon the women who had chosen a saintly life. She waited feverishly in the hot sun for the Calling, straining her ears, torn between Good and Evil, two tyrants of equal, Herculean strength.

Good murmured, "Knock on that door, Suzon. Join your sisters who are waiting for you in your abode. Disappear forever in the merciful whirlwind of prayer . . ."

Evil roared, "Return to the ruins of your shattered life! You can make the wheel turn the way you want, control its rhythm, and choose the music it will follow . . . Listen! Do you hear it? La la la la la . . . It's playing for you, Suzon! La la la la la . . ."

During the period of indecision, Suzon very nearly stumbled into eternal ecstasy, a thousand times over, almost went to take her solemn vows and renounce both carnal pleasure and venal sins. But she dreamt a lot, and that is what saved her from the convent.

Did you know that dreams are built with the dust of days, the kind that is trapped in the spider webs woven deep in people's souls?

Did you know that sometimes dreams feed the spirit a bitter milk taken from the thick bark of ageless trees?

Did you know that dreams can poison those who enter the webbed prisons and innocently partake of that bitter-sweet milk?

Suzon dreamt.

In her dreams she marched along boldly. Wearing a cotton print dress with French-grown paradise flowers, daisies, roses, lilac . . . She watched herself victoriously climbing Morne Calvaire. She felt the weight of the gold—twenty-four karats!—wedding band on her left ring finger. Ecstatic, she could hear herself being called Madame Melchior! Madame Melchior here, Madame Melchior there. Her waters broke in the night, she felt labor pains. And saw with her very own eyes, eighteen little black babies come out from between her arched legs. She was everywhere Melchior was, in his shadow and in his male flesh. In his strong arms, lying on his chest dotted with coarse hair. In his smell and in his breath. In the rum that burned deep in his throat. In his plate, she was the eye of the catfish lying lifelessly next to the squares of breadfruit covered with brown-butter sauce. She was his ox and his cart, his cutlass and his hoe, his sun and his moon in plenitude and perfection. She was sweet mango and water coco to his mouth and also love's song to his ears. She was his half and his whole, his universe and his eternity.

That is how, after another six months of procrastinating and making pilgrimages between Piment and the Carmelite nunnery, into which the priest was pushing her as if into a lion's den, Suzon came to her senses and chose life and the torments of the world.

She got back on her feet.

No, Lord! She did not succumb to temptation.

She got back on her feet.

Halleluiah!

And she understood in the deep swampland of her heart, that the only man awaiting her, the chosen one whom she elevated to the rank of king, was her beloved Melchior and not the crucified Christ.

That negress got back on her feet.

And she rid her mind of Marie-Perle, rubbed the filthy marriage out of her memory, hung her grief on a nail, far from her soul.

She got back on her feet.

And even if—from then on—her smile seemed a bit stiff, tight at the jaw, she looked as if she had recovered well enough, reconciled herself to life.

Marie-Perle is but a comet, Suzon hummed at her reflection in the mirror as she cupped her firm titties in her hands.

I'm the prettiest
I'm the prettiest
A comet in the sky is but a jest
La la la la la
Never comes to stay, and we soon forget
La la la la la
It's a long and lovely pirouette
La la la la la
As fleeting as an amourette
Marie-Perle is but a comet
I'm the prettiest
I'm the prettiest

Suzon got back on her feet.

Harnessed with patience, caparisoned with hope. She was twenty-two years old, had large hips from which eighteen children would spring. She had seen it in a dream.

Melchior's first marriage lasted seven years. And then . . . You already know that bit of the story. Coincidence, miracle, witchcraft, or curse, the salt-water chabine—poor girl!—was swept away in the fresh waters of the raging river. A providential drowning on an ordinary washing day.

And then 1955, Melchior once again free, single . . . and prepared to don the cloak of his destiny and take Suzon for his
legitimate wife. "Justice does exist!" people whispered, escort-
ing Marie-Perle's casket in a somber procession. Especially
since the beauty from Anse-Bertrand had left a daughter,
Olga, who was in dire need of a mother.

Encouraged by go-betweens who predicted her future
would be true to her wildest dreams, and convinced that she
had a legitimate claim, Suzon climbed back up on the steed
that for seven long years had been champing at the bit in front
of the doors to her heart. Once again, she began hoping to find
love in Melchior's arms. And, nine days after Marie-Perle's funeral, she walked up the hill, barefoot, just like in her dreams,
with her heart on a platter and her thoughts head over heels
with three hundred thousand visions, memories of being
touched between her legs, longing for a tongue in her mouth,
and the promise of eighteen lives in her belly.

With her heart racing, she called out to him hardily, hugging a marble cake—grenadine syrup—to her heart.

"Here I am, sweet Melchior! I'm yours forever . . ."

Melchior came out of the grief-stricken house, little Olga
clinging to his pant leg. He closed the door behind him, a
gesture Suzon rightfully thought portended she was not welcome. Her smile widened, became a stiff grimace. Her fluffy
France flour cake, wrapped in a white linen cloth turned to
brick. And the words which had flowed through her lips in a
babbling stream all along the path, rushed back into her throat
before welling up again in hot tears, rumbling at the edges of
her eyes. Melchior did not flinch in the face of the icon. He
observed her without showing any feeling, forgetting yesterday's intimacy and the hypocritical oaths he had woven for
her, night after night under the mango tree of their youth.
Suzon held back her sobs. Recomposed her fallen queen smile,
which seemed to make Melchior feel more comfortable.

"Who's that lady?" Olga asked then.

"It's nothing," replied the renegade without even batting an eye.

He laid a hand on the child's head.

"I just came to bring you a syrup-cake," mumbled the woman with clenched jaws.

Dull pain. She lifted a corner of the cloth, which revealed the golden crust of the lovely cake.

"Give it then!" whispered Melchior.

He made as if to step forward. Olga tightened her grip on the stiff cloth of her father's pants. He immediately stopped.

"May I come forward?" Suzon ventured.

"No, I'll come for the cake. Wait a minute, I'm coming!"

When he was near her, he whispered in her ear, "How old are you now, Suzon?"

"I'm the same age as you are, Melchior. Twenty-eight years old and . . ."

"And what you waiting for, black woman?" he interrupted sharply. "You never going to have any children at this point in your life if you is waiting for me . . ."

"Why you saying that, Melchior?" she protested.

"I in mourning for my Perle. What you come here for? You need to find yourself a good black man, Suzon. I don't think our paths will cross again . . ."

Two weary folds formed at the corners of his mouth. He glanced worriedly at Olga.

"I came to tell you my heart hasn't changed, Melchior . . . And also, I want you to tell me what happened between us. Why did you reject me? What I done for you to treat me like this? For you to turn your back on me? You look at me like I make you sick . . . Why do you push me away, sweet Melchior? I been waiting for you all this time . . . If you want me, I . . . I can take care of the little girl, and . . ."

Tears tumbled down her cheeks. She grabbed his arm, which he jerked cruelly away from her.

She fell to her knees at his feet, covering them with kisses, tears, and snot.

"I'll have your children! Eighteen! Eighteen, I swear it! I seen them in a dream . . . And you can take my body every which way you like, Melchior!"

He pulled away from her. She clutched at his boots.

He dragged her for several yards. She let go and then rolled in the dust.

"Eighteen little black babies! And no one could separate us again!"

"Go away, Suzon!" shouted Melchior in lieu of saying good-bye. "Don't go scratching around in the past no more! Find yourself a black man that's worthy of you! We should never see each other again. . . Your mother was right . . . And don't be crying! That's just the way life is and we can't change it. Our paths weren't meant to cross."

Suzon remained in the courtyard for a long time, weeping and moaning, rubbing her *coucoune* with dry grass mixed with the smashed remains of her cake. Melchior never came back out of the cabin and he forbade Olga to stick her nose out the window. On that day Suzon's cries rose up as high as flames, silenced the birds on the hill, and mingled with the sharp calls of the insects till late into the night.

XIV

Forty-four years later, thinking of those bitter moments, the burning feeling that had been devouring Suzon ever since that day rose in her throat again and began throbbing between her legs. She had been repudiated three times. She had known abandonment, petrification, years of waiting, and burning hatred.

Picture that fortress of patience in ruins! Its finely hewn stones cracked, eroded by the rain and the wind, given over to the brambles and vines. Picture the endangered masterpiece ablaze!

And you will have a clear picture of Suzon Mignard.

The fiend she had become in the secrecy of her cabin.

The bitch with yellow fangs smiling into the mirror.

The witch that visited fifty-four *gadèzafè*-conjurors and ten sorcerers so that Love would triumph.

The vile creature that called up evil water spirits, locked the brakes of a Titan truck, summoned madness, lightning, and fire to her side.

The heinous shrew that prayed for woe to descend upon Morne Calvaire. The snake that lived within Suzon Mignard's love-starved body.

The demon that smiled in the face of adversity, never knew the joys of childbearing and fed upon the dry crusts of misfortune without complaining.

The crocodile-woman who wept abundant tears at every funeral and remained hidden under the mask of Benevolence.

The cowardly old woman who, twenty-one years after her last crime, was afraid to open Mina's letter and saw the past spread out before her, as fresh and clear as a December morning . . .

It wasn't the same as nowadays. Back then sorcerers knew their business. Professionals, their skills had been handed down to them over thousands of years, they were masters of their art and with steady hands they wielded herbs and roots, stardust and the silt of troubled waters. They controlled the elements in heaven and on earth. They worked in conjunction with the sun and the moon. Spoke with defunct spirits and read the future in the yolk of a fertilized egg. Counted the children in the bellies of virgins. Tied women's tubes. Made and broke marriages. Mastered the improbable and diverted destinies from their course. Gave life or took it away just like the Almighty Creator.

The ten that Suzon consulted had names that made your hair stand on end.

Botinious, great-grandson of a Congo black man, sum-

moned his ancestors in an African tongue and made nightmares come true. He had a small monster working for him
that he sent away on missions to the four corners of the world.

Verdigris fed upon the putrid and pink flesh of stillborn
children. He claimed to belong to the rare race of immortals
but died at seventy-five after agonizing for twenty years.

Serpicon changed into a kite in the middle of the dry season. His concoctions were patented and had a five-year guarantee.

Chalamort, both man and woman, was familiar with three
hundred sorts of bamboo and harvested fibers from them every Good Friday. That was how he was able to get away with
the assassination of a half-dozen politicians.

Lautréamont de Maldoror was a mulatto with a gray beard
who used white or black magic indifferently. In 1978 Suzon fi-
nagled a lease for twenty years of malediction on Melchior's
descendants. At the end of his reign, the sorcerer turned himself into a dog and spent thirty moons in the company of the
spirits in the cemetery.

Hellfire and Brimstone was master of thunder and lightning. With a single glance, he could make the sky turn black.
He swore he had seen the Apocalypse three times. He unleashed, for Suzon, the waters of the Goyave River that swept
Marie-Perle away.

Apolythe Trident was born with black skin and died whiter
than milk. He was a traditional sorcerer who appreciated mo-
dernity. Mechanics was his particular specialty. He caused ac-
cidents without leaving his sweltering little office, spoke to
brakes, pistons, and carburetors. He put drivers to sleep at the
wheel of their cars, made imaginary obstacles appear and created roads that led nowhere. Suzon called upon him when she
wanted to be rid of Médée.

Solstice III was blind. Darkness was his trade! When it came
to dosages, he groped about, proceeding by trial and error . . .
When he opened his eyes, the darkest depths of his soul spilled

out into the world. Suzon commissioned him to throw Médée into eternal shadows.

Branquignol spent his time laughing. But behind his ever mirthful, doll-like face, lurked the worst breed of demon. He laughed as he poisoned. He laughed as he strangled or drove children mad in their mothers' bellies. He laughed as he assassinated. He laughed as he decapitated. He laughed as he amputated. The day they took his casket to the infidel's cemetery, people had to put cork plugs in their ears so they wouldn't hear his laughter echoing out for a long time underground, imprisoned in the purple satin and white pine. For a long time . . .

Heart-Stoker did not deserve his reputation. A hundred times over, he had promised to marry Suzon to Melchior. A hundred times she believed his prophecies. Together they counted the eighteen little black babies hanging in her belly. He said he saw her going into the church in Piment as Suzon Mignard and coming out as Suzon Montério. She opened her billfold a hundred times for him.

In the last month of 1956, Melchior married Médée.

When Suzon passed him with the new woman on his arm, she did not go into a trance, nor did she petrify. To everyone who tried to patch up her soul with syrupy words she responded with a smile and, "That's all ancient history, I got over Melchior long ago! What on Earth are you thinking of? My mama just died, you think I still got time to be running around after Melchior . . . Trust me, I better off alone than in bad company. I thank the Lord every day for having spared me his company. You seen well enough for yourself, when Melchior marries a woman, something bad happens to her. This one don't know what's in store for her . . . He who laughs on Friday will weep on Sunday." But instead of taking the road to the cemetery where her poor mama lay, she got on a bus like some sort of robot, to go you know where . . . To see Solstice III, the blind man, and Branquignol, the laughing sorcerer.

When she was half way there, she got out of the bus. Walked for three hours, head empty, heart deeply wounded.

A thousand Melchiors paraded before her eyes with women of all colors, sizes, ages, heights on their arms. Every tree trunk she passed was a woman. Sometimes Suzon thought she saw herself in one of them, took heart, told herself that in the long run, the man would end up choosing her. "Just a little more patience, girl!" She repeated to herself, nearly turning back when she was in front of Branquignol's office. But her feet would no longer obey her. She moved forward like a soldier, mind blank, stomach hollow with hunger, the taste of blood on her tongue. She was twenty-nine years old . . .

> *I am only twenty-nine*
> *And my hips are nice and wide.*
> *How can Melchior fight his fate?*
> *I'll carry his eighteen black babes.*
> *Time is still on my side.*
> *Yes, dear God!*
> *Women of fifty have often begot*
> *Into the world their last little tot.*
> *Time is still on my side.*
> *And this Médée will not remain.*
> *Before God, I have ordained.*
> *When Melchior has finished straying*
> *By my side he will be staying.*
> *I am only twenty-nine.*

She waited five years. Ran from sorcerer to sorcerer, seeing her titties drooping, her hips thickening, and the skin on her buttocks and face sagging . . .

Five years of unfulfilled joy, dashed hopes, sleepless nights, and hurt pride, during which Médée paid thirty times over for having robbed Suzon of her destiny. Darkness swooped down upon her as surely as night follows day. Five miscarriages.

1964. The arrival of Mina broke her.

Suzon had just turned thirty-seven. She was tired of waiting. She felt as if all her efforts were in vain, as if all the years she'd lost had gotten her nowhere. Mina was just too pretty. Perfect from head to toe. She was growing like a weed. She was the pride and joy of her father, the triumph of her mother, who now thought of herself as Piment's Marilyn Monroe— imagine that! And Médée was actually strutting! You had to see it to believe it, that mug of hers all shiny and red . . . Sashaying this way and that in full flowered skirts . . . And madam went to the cinema with her two princesses . . . And Suzon had to smile at her and say, "Good day Madame Melchior! Oh! Goodness gracious, that young one certainly has grown! How old is she now?" And act like her heart was made of steel. Make believe that honey flowed in her veins. When in truth her back was against the wall, she was getting rustier as she stood there, twitching with hate.

1975. Time was passing. Disasters did not come showering down, darkness did not settle in, misfortune refused to take root on the morne.

"She'll be twelve soon!" answered Médée.

It was a knife stabbing Suzon in the heart. And I'm forty-eight! I'm forty-eight, dear Lord!

"Twel-el-el-elve soo-oo-oo-oon!" Suzon turned pale. Then quickly pulled herself together. Grimaced a compliment and even slipped a coin into Mina's hand. "You'll split it with poor Rose!"

Branquignol had been buried along with his laughter and his infamous secrets. Verdigris, the immortal, was in the throes of death. Serpicon had gone away to France to get treatment for the elephantiasis that prevented him from flying. And Solstice III claimed that conjuring darkness took time . . .

Suzon heard about Apolythe Trident in the Saint-Antoine marketplace in Pointe-à-Pitre where she'd gone to buy some plants to put in her bath as a pick-me-up. The man's notoriety

128

had grown in proportion to the number of automobiles on the roads of Guadeloupe. Trident lived on a disreputable street in the town. Suzon was let in by his mother. Now retired, the old woman ruled over the clientele whom she supervised from the corner of her eye as she nostalgically leafed through the pages of a large black ledger recording all of the great deeds she'd accomplished during her illustrious life as a sorceress.

Already, eleven people were waiting their turn, sitting in a row on the lone bench in the waiting room. Five black men, two puckered up chabines who looked like twins, a *manawa*-whore mulattress caked with make-up, and—sitting under their straw hats—three negresses of around fifty whose faces seemed to be cast in bronze masks of meanness. They kept their mouths shut but were evidently chawing on despicable secrets.

On the dusty shelves, ex votos, collections of hymns, and crucifixes were discarded pell-mell alongside filthy boxes and broken baskets. The floor of the adjoining room was strewn with automobile parts and different sized monkey wrenches.

Suzon was ushered in after a three-hour wait.

"I'm forty eight years old," she said softly to Trident. "I still have one last chance to marry Melchior, you understand . . . But Médée will have to disappear in the coming year . . ."

The modernist sorcerer was softhearted and easily moved to tears. Touched, he listened to Suzon's story with his eyes closed, his right hand laying on the New Testament, the left on a handbook of general mechanics. After thinking it over for a few minutes, he decided to do his utmost to help her.

"Your problem will not be easy to sort out," he began, wiping away a tear. "You've done the right thing in coming to me. In this day and age, thank God, man has been given the means to do Good. In the past, our ancestors resorted to plants, as for myself, I try and stay abreast of the times, of technology, of speed. Today, we can't hang back with old-fashioned practices. I studied for a long time before reaching this conclusion. I have many degrees and a myriad of certificates. My methods are scientific. Men go to the moon, you know . . . I am of the new generation. No, I do not deny the legitimacy of my peers, but I know what I'm talking about, believe me. Have you heard that in America they can pierce the eye of a cyclone? You watch television, don't you? You must have seen that now they can descend into the center of volcanoes . . . One must remain informed . . . There are so many things happening in the world! I could give you thousands of examples . . . Today medical professors can replace a human heart with the heart of a pig, there's nothing to it, it's like a mechanic changing a rotating piston . . . Every second, scientists discover new remedies to save mankind. We will soon be immortal. In your opinion, what do they use the rats and the monkeys in laboratories for, eh? The world is not coming to an end, I can guarantee you that . . ."

"Is it going to cost a lot?" asked Suzon after his presentation.

"The price of a life. How much do you think the life of this woman is worth? You place a value on her life. I have no standard tariff . . ."

Médée's life was worth nothing in Suzon's eyes, not even an old stocking with a runner, but she knew she had to appear generous if she wanted a good clean job done.

"I have twelve hundred francs right here in my bag, Monsieur Trident . . . Will that be enough?"

"You will be the one to know how much you spent to have that soul removed from the world of the living . . ."

"If it's not enough, I'll bring you the rest when the job is done and . . ."

"You'll come back in three days with eight hundred francs," interrupted Apolythe.

"That means it will all be done in three days, Monsieur Trident?"

A small flicker of hope lit Suzon's eye.

"Off with you! And come back in three days . . . Give the cash to my mother. I don't touch money myself, only the Holy Scriptures and mechanics manuals."

When Suzon returned to Piment in the rickety bus owned by Calamoussamy, a seventy year old Indian who could not make up his mind to let a younger driver take his place, she felt lighter than when she was fifteen. Her mind was swimming with happy images: flowers and suns, children's laughter and nights of lovemaking . . . She had new faith in life and told herself that what had been written in the stars the day she was born would soon shine out in all of its glory. Trident did not betray his reputation and masterfully demonstrated that he did indeed belong to the new generation. He sent out a truck whose will and brakes he'd been neutralizing for two days. On the afternoon of the third day, the Titan crossed Médée's path.

After Médée's burial, the women of Piment—who for lack of more interesting subjects of conversation had taken a keen interest in the epic love story from the very beginning—cast sly looks at Suzon when she walked through the village. She stooped a little, trying to appear grief-stricken. She was forty-eight years old and felt young in the body that had known no other man but Melchior, her king, her beloved. Closed up in her room, she stood planted in front of the mirror and did not notice any significant difference between the forty-eight-year-old Suzon and the blossoming young girl of pre-petrification. A few gray strands streaked her head, but they were lost in the thick dark mass of her hair. Her hips were wider, which was a good sign after all, her eighteen children could come in twos. Her titties were heavier and drooped a little farther onto her stomach each day, which meant they promised an abundance of milk. And even if her face seemed to be stiff and cast in stone, she could still smile and laugh and sing.

Délos often brought her news of Melchior and she knew that he and Médée had never shared the miracle of love. Though the man had sometimes epitomized the jealous husband, following Médée like a mad dog through the streets of

Piment, everyone confirmed that their marriage was in ruins.

"This time, Melchior won't say no," Délos whispered to her at the gathering the night before the funeral. "He like a broken branch. All you got to do is pick him up. I swear, he'll let you do as you please. He waiting for you. Before he was widowed, when I mentioned your name, his eyes brightened up straight away. He never said why he didn't marry you, but he loved you more than the others and you always been in his heart. One morning last dry season, he told me face to face that he thought of you all the time. Said he'd been obliged to give you up due to circumstances beyond either of your control . . ."

"What circumstances, dear God? I can't see what could have separated us . . ."

"Circumstances, that is all he said to me . . ."

"And you didn't question him any farther than that. You ain't in the least bit curious . . ."

"No, you know how he is . . . Afterward, he closed back up and I went down to the village to finish my rounds."

"So you don't think it's too late?"

"No!" said Délos reassuringly. "He alone with Rose and his last child, Mina. Go on, don't wait around too long . . . I guarantee you, this time it's a cinch . . ."

Délos's hair was already white, but he still had enormous faith in hope. In 1964 he had married Gina, one of Hermancia Girois's girls. Flawless union. She had borne him four children who were his pride and joy and a daily confirmation of his belief that life was just a bag of pleasures and blessings into which one simply stuck his hand to bring out love, health, prosperity. Life had always smiled upon him and he couldn't conceive of bad luck hounding Suzon indefinitely. He firmly believed every word he spoke, each rang clearer and truer to his ear than the Spirit of Good. He had never known anything about the commerce his sister carried on with evildoers.

Suzon never missed a prayer. Night after night, for nine days, she climbed Morne Calvaire along with all the praying women, their torches formed a long serpent of light in the night. She returned to town after midnight and went back up in the early morning with provisions: coffee, candles, rice, peas, salted pig's tails. Afternoons she sang of her grief and resurrection in Paradise as she was cooking the soup up there for Melchior and his two orphans before going back down at vespers. Gentle, she dispensed smiles and caresses, consoled, appeased, comforted. Nine days of climbing up and down the hill three times between sunup and sundown. Nine days of play-acting during which Suzon made a point of being charitable, respectable, and marriageable.

One month after the funeral, when she decided to adopt an even more offensive means of winning her man back, Piment lay in pitch-black darkness. Suzon did not make a cake this time. She had the intention of offering herself to Melchior like a stick of candy. She felt pretty, desirable, and already imagined the prince biting hungrily into her flesh. Under her dress she had slipped on the twenty-year-old lace nightgown she had sewn for her honeymoon, even before Marie-Perle had departed this world. Around seven o'clock she knotted the three crosses of eternal protection bought directly from Botinious around her neck. She soaked herself in an herb bath. From under her bed she drew a phial of perfumed oil (called the seven essences of love) concocted by Serpicon—touted as being aged ten years and guaranteed five. She took a swallow and rubbed some on her body.

"No one can resist this ointment, Suzon! If he touches you, he's a goner!"

At ten in the evening, prepared for their reunion, she covered her head with a madras cloth and locked the door after herself, making sure no one saw her, gossiping women standing watch behind their blinds, men either roaring drunk or turned into dogs. Serpicon had sworn that the phial truly contained the seven essences of love, no one could resist it. A bitter taste in her mouth, her skin shiny, she went across town at a run in the middle of the night, her head buzzing with the words of Master Serpicon . . .

If he touches you, he's a goner!

If he touches you, he's a goner!

If he touches you, he's a goner!

She followed dirt paths taken by dogs yelping out of their tails.

If he touches you, he's a goner!

If he touches you, he's a goner!

If he touches you, he's a goner!

She plunged into cane fields where soulless creatures dwelt.

If he touches you, he's a goner!

If he touches you, he's a goner!

If he touches you, he's a goner!

At one point she was escorted by three niggers, maroons armed with old muskets. Suzon didn't see them as one sees ordinary human beings, but her nostrils were filled with wafts of molasses and mangroves, mixed with the strong smell of gunpowder. They spoke to each other in a language with no *A*'s. The first had a voice like a blackbird. The second mooed. The third was the exact echo of the other two. They strode along. The grass squidged under the calluses on their heels. At the foot of Morne Calvaire, the small troop disbanded. The maroons whispered Serpicon's words to her, or at least that's what she thought, then they continued on their way to beyond some other time . . .

If he touches you, he's a goner!

If he touches you, he's a goner!

If he touches you, he's a goner!

The cabin was locked. Suzon went around to the back. She knew by heart where each room was. Bars of light shone under the doors. She drew nearer, put her ear against the window behind which Melchior slept, recited three verses from the bible and began to meow.

She had thought of several ways to announce her arrival:

134

throwing rocks on the roof, giving a serenade, beating on the door, or calling out her beloved's name. In the end she preferred to appear to him like a lost kitten. For that is exactly what she was underneath her shell of hate, in the landslide of her despair, in the secrecy of her heart. A kitten in a nightgown, reeking of the evil oil of sorcerers.

If he touches you, he's a goner! She repeated to herself between meows, her mouth dry and foul-smelling.

If he touches you, he's a goner!

Suzon meowed for a minute and a half. Then, without really understanding what was happening to her, she suddenly found herself in the skin of other, less gentle, creatures: snake, tiger, agama, mongoose, spider, elephant ... The poor woman didn't even have time to curse Serpicon who had sold her an adulterated potion! Seven essences of love, my foot! Rather, the seven trumpets of the Apocalypse ... Suzon recognized herself in each animal. Her life flashed before her eyes as if in a nightmare. She was both hot and cold. She slithered and squawked, growled ... Melchior was sorting through his official papers when the zoo arrived under his window. Bravely, he unhooked the shutter to see what was going on outside. At that moment, Suzon was an elephant. Melchior jumped, stammered, and immediately tried to close the shutter. Suzon grabbed him by the sleeve and began to trumpet. Her free arm was raised like a majestic trunk. That didn't last long. She turned into a tigress and began to roar through her fangs, drool dripping from her jaws.

"You is mine, Melchior Montério! The game's up!"

"What's this all about? You gone crazy, Suzon! What you doing here? Upon my word you out of your mind ..."

Melchior's eyes had turned purple.

"You always been mine! You don't remember your promises, do you? You done forgotten everything! I let you touch me back then, didn't I Melchior? I gave you my newly opened flower! I gave you my blood ... Go on! Touch me again! One day you going to have to tell me what turned you away from me . . ." she begged, turned agama, opening her nightgown to display her wilted flesh.

"Go away, Suzon! It's too late . . . Don't blame me. It ain't my fault."

Suzon's huge titties swung pitifully back and forth, like two leather game pouches, worn with the years.

"It ain't too late! Look at me, I not that old. Tell me why it's too late! I been waiting for you for thirty years, Melchior . . . Thirty years . . . Forty-eight years . . . I been waiting for you since the very first day, Melchior . . . We was promised to each other, don't you remember? Under the mango tree . . . I never knew no other man since that day . . . You the only one who has possessed me, Melchior. The only one who stuck his rod in my body! The only one! And I swear I forgive you for everything."

Clinging to the window, Suzon, mongoose, was sobbing. Bitter tears streamed down her anguished face smeared with Serpicon's rancid oil as she thought of the evil deeds she'd committed in the name of love.

Melchior ran his hand over Suzon's face, "Don't cry, sweet girl! I'll tell you the story. Don't cry . . ."

The man had softened in the face of the sad mongoose.

"If it be any consolation to you, know I always loved you," he whispered, finally admitting his crime. "That's right, you, Suzon Mignard!"

"And why didn't you marry me, Melchior?" interrupted Suzon.

"Let me finish! Listen . . ."

That night, coming down from Morne Calvaire, walking sideways like a crayfish, Suzon was shattered. She wasn't even frightened when she passed some she-devils in a cane field. She didn't even answer a dog that asked her directions. She didn't notice the two moons playing hide and seek in the sky. She was like the soul of a dead woman wandering the countryside in search of a body where the rest of her destiny might dwell.

At first, Melchior's confession had staggered her. Everything became clear in her mind. Each enigma found its key. But when she reached her cabin, serpent curled up on her bed, Suzon realized she was inconsolable. She could no longer bear to see a new woman hanging on her Melchior's arm, someone other than her, even if that was how things were meant to be.

Could no longer bear the looks of the women in Piment.

No longer bear to think that some Manawa-whore slept in Melchior's smell and in his sheets.

No longer bear to have another woman take his sap and bear his children.

No longer bear Délos's pity, his fine words of hope, the latest news he brought.

No longer bear growing old with the thought that Melchior lived up there, so near to her and yet out of her reach.

No longer bear to know he was alive . . .

The next morning, blank-eyed, Suzon wiped the oil from her body with the dried orange peels that she kept for the Christmas *schrubb*-cocktail. Her skin dotted with pimples, but free of Serpicon's malodorous oil, she went knocking at the door of Hellfire and Brimstone whom she hadn't visited since back in the days of Marie-Perle. She ordered thunder. Three months later, Melchior was found stricken down in the middle of his banana grove.

Suzon Mignard had never, even in the secret of the confessional, revealed her evil deeds. At seventy-two years of age, half-blind, she awaited nothing but death. After the fire in the cabin and Mina's departure in 1978, she had not consulted another sorcerer. Except one, to be truthful—Lautréamont de Maldorer who had long ago promised her a twenty-year curse upon Melchior's descendents. Though she had resorted to two–three *gadèzafès* in the last few years simply for her eyes. She had implored the Lord to be merciful, and he had forgiven her trespasses. All's well that ends well. She would wed Melchior in Paradise, for that which could not be accomplished on earth would be fulfilled in the Kingdom of God, she said to herself every morning upon awakening, surprised to find herself alive in her bed.

Just when she believed she had escaped being judged by mankind, Mina suddenly reappeared, sent her back to the mad love that had consumed her entire life. What does she want of me? Suzon wondered, feeling the past hot on her heels. Maybe she's learned something . . . She wants to settle some scores . . .

In September 1999, having made up her mind to face Mina, the old woman mustered her courage and bought a large magnifying glass at Gwa Bricolage, Piment's new hardware store. Back at her place, she didn't dare use it and put it away, far away, deep in a dark cabinet in her kitchen. Fear . . . The letter remained in her handbag for a month. From time to time Suzon held it between her fingers. Tried to estimate its weight, assess its contents. Sniffed it to become familiar with its odors. Pressed it against her ear, like a seashell found on the beach, until she heard a long murmur, a cantilena or a complaint. Then one Sunday in October, it occurred to her that it would be more prudent to hide the sealed letter in the feathers of her pillow. Which is what she did. Before going to bed, praying to God always reassured her. She asked for very little. Only that the truth would not come out before death nabbed her. She couldn't make up her mind to open the cursed letter, or to have it read by one of the gossips who came to sit on her veranda and tell her rumors, when Suzon didn't feel like talking to anyone. Burning the letter would have been a solution, but one never knows . . .

That is how, in the middle of the night, the letter started waking the woman up. The cotton pillowcase suddenly became burning hot. Drifting up from the feathers, soft moans could be heard. These were small inconveniences compared to the nightmares that the letter caused. Nightmares that made Suzon's life miserable from October through the beginning of November of the year 1999.

Nightmares during which Rosalia would suddenly appear

exactly as she had the day after her funeral. After twenty-one years, there was not an extra wrinkle on her burnt face. Not a white hair in the flaming braids in which pillow feathers remained stuck. Not the slightest trace of rheumatism in her charred bones. Then she ended up leaving the envelope once and for all, barged in right in the middle of the day. A constant presence that in the beginning only Suzon saw despite her blind eyes, Rose observed her every move. Though Suzon invoked the saints, lit candles of all colors and shapes, sprinkled holy water in the four corners of her cabin, Rosalia did not leave her side, it was as if Mina had sent her along with the letter . . . A terrifying living torch, that seemed to have come straight up from hell.

XV

When Mina told him her story—the real story of her life plagued with the ghost of Rosalia—Victor didn't seem surprised. He listened to her without saying a word. For him, she poured out the legend of Ancestor Séléna, the epic story of the goats in search of a home, and the misfortune of the defrocked priest. She withstood the winds of time and tears so that he might enter her heart, enter the place where Médée's sorrows, Melchior's black moods, Olga's sterile womb, and Rosalia's madness lurked. She rekindled the flames in the cabin and described Rose with her hair standing up on end, her burned nightgown, her roasted flesh.

"You've only got one ghost. I have three trailing after me. Can you imagine? Three! My friend Bénédicte isn't all that crazy. She can see them too. Maybe we can arrange a meeting when she gets out of Esquirol . . ."

"No, Victor. No, I don't think so . . . It's not a good idea . . ."

"Whatever you like, Mina. But as you can see, the two of us aren't all that different."

He took her in his arms. Whispered that she was like a com-

139

panion in misery to him. They would make the journey. Go up to the top of the hill. She with her burned sister. He with his three ghosts. And maybe that's what Bénédicte intended when she advised him to go to Guadeloupe to be cured. Maybe he needed to leave his phantoms over there. And Victor seemed to get high on his own words. Yes, together they would come out of this expedition victorious. Would support each other. They both deserved a new start.

He kept saying, "In 2000 we'll be free, Mina. In 2000, we'll be liberated. Our ghosts will stop waging war on us, Mina . . ."

And when he said "in 2000", his eyes shone with a thousand stars, a thousand flames, a bonfire into which he cast his old sad self, his anxiety, his morbid thoughts, the corpses of Rosalia and his father Edmond.

Mina watched and listened to him like a fascinated child, dazzled by the story-teller who bewitches his audience, places mad words beside wise words and makes the unimaginable believable. So she didn't hold it against him when, making one last attempt to offer her body, she found him rejecting her.

"No, Mina . . . I can't . . . I am not supposed to . . . I promised not to touch a woman until I've been cured . . . That was the deal. Bénédicte told me I was to remain pure, no alcohol, no women, no . . . And even if I wanted to, you know, the medications I'm on sap my sex drive . . ."

He went home in the middle of the night leaving her alone with bright images of Piment and her abandoned body throbbing with frustrated pleasure.

In August, her vacation month, Mina went down to check the mail every day—Suzon's answer—and went to the shopping center only when her refrigerator was empty. She didn't feel like doing anything, seeing anyone. She lay stretched out on her sofa for hours, waiting for time to pass, counting the days that remained until December, sunk deep in reverie and refusing to come out of it. Sometimes the telephone rang. It was Maria-Rosa or Lysia (on vacation in Guadeloupe with her daughters), sometimes Christian, Victor every evening, calling from Troyes where he'd been sent to work temporarily. Mina picked up the receiver, said hello, asked how everything was, and then good-bye. She didn't hear the sound of her own voice again until the next call.

Once, only once, one evening, she called Christian to the rescue.

He held nothing against her and came rushing to her side like a knight in shining armor. She led him into her room immediately without a word.

He stuck his penis into her. A blade. Mina allowed herself to be swept up, borne away. Then she opened her eyes and stared at the place by the wardrobe where Rosalia usually stood. She waited a minute, imploring Rose with all her heart.

One. Two. Three.
Yoo hoo!
Come on Rose!
Where are you?
One. Two. Three.
Rosalia!

She pushed Christian away. Sat up. Got out from under the sheets naked. Walked over to the wardrobe that hadn't turned into a voyager's tree. Ran her hand over the flowers on the wallpaper that had remained intact. Searched for the smell of charred flesh, two-three sparks drifting in the air.

"What's wrong with you?" Christian asked.

Mina was pacing and wheeling about the room, looking under the bed, opening and closing the wardrobe, rummaging through the drawers.

"What's going on, Mi?"

But she didn't answer, continued mumbling through her teeth.

Yoo hoo!

141

Where are you, Rosalia?
Why are you hiding?
Come and count with me!
Yoo hoo! Rose!
It's Mina!
Your little sister Mina . . .

Christian caught up with her in the living room. Shook her.
Took her in his arms.

"Calm down, Mi. Come and sit down here and tell me what's
wrong."

"I've lost Rosalia . . . I've lost my sister . . . for the second time . . ."

"What? What sister? Who's Rosalia? You haven't lost anything. Wake up, Mina! Wake up from this nightmare!"

"She always came to see me . . . She's gone now . . . Vanished
. . . Disappeared . . ."

"Who?"

"Rosalia . . . My little Rose . . . She's left me . . . We were supposed to go back to Guadeloupe together. The two of us. Usher
in the year 2000 in Piment. She didn't have the strength to wait.
The two of us . . . Rosalia and I . . . I promised I would take her
back to our home, up on the hill . . ."

Mina had wished that Rosalia would disappear from her life
so many times. Had prayed she would slip off into the other
world so many times. And now it had happened. With not so
much as a goodbye. Not so much as an adieu. Not so much as
an explanation. After twenty-one years.

~

In September, it was time to go back to the cafeteria and the
usual humdrum. Now that she was rid of Rosalia's ghost, Mina
could feel free at last, make plans for the future in peace. Alas,
now that she was gone, Rosalia seemed all the more present.
Every other second, Mina thought she saw her, heard her
laughing behind Lysia's laughter. Even Ashwina, back from her

142

Island of Mauritius, seemed to be in on the scheme. Her piercing looks, her weighty silences evoked Rosalia. At Mina's place, the smell of burned flesh would suddenly fill the rooms. Mingling with the flames of the gas burners, sparks drifted up from under pots. Shadows loomed here and there at the foot of the building, near the mailboxes, behind a shopkeeper's stall, next to the women in the cafeteria, and even on the TV during the variety shows.

Mourn the loss of Rosalia.
    Prepare for the trip back to Piment.
    Wait for Suzon to answer.

Was the old lady already dead? In her letter Mina had asked forgiveness for the twenty-one years of silence and thanked her for her affection. Also a few words announcing her homecoming. A polite message that ended with a question, "Could you put me up at your place, my dear Suzon? You know better than anyone that I have no family left in Piment."

Poor Suzon, who was once the only memory of Piment that Olga would willingly evoke, talk about, and laugh over. Suzon, the only person she could mention comfortably because she'd seen her pining over and sighing for the love of Melchior. Suzon Mignard, the mailman's sister. Loyal old Suzon who'd gone to all the funerals, who had taken Mina into her house after Rosalia's death.

Poor Suzon, thought Mina, recalling the woman's generosity after Médée's death. The meat soup, the cakes, the songs. She didn't ask for the slightest payment in return. She did it for nothing, free as the wind. Just to do good, out of Christian charity.

Poor Suzon who still found strength to climb up the hill after Melchior's death carrying baskets heavy with grub.
    Get my life in order.
    Prepare for my trip back to Piment.

Wait for Suzon to answer.
Write to Tibert.
Forget about Rosalia.
Change my life.

No I'm not in love with Victor. I just need to have his body. I'm through with throwing myself into the arms of the first man who comes along. I'm going to think things through and find out what's wrong with me.

Get my life in order.
Prepare for the trip back to Piment.
Calmly.
Break up with Christian.

Had Piment changed?

French television sometimes showed images of Guadeloupe in the hurricane season or during carnival. There were still old cabins of boards and sheet metal, even though fine wide roads ran from one end of the country to the other. There were still fishermen, even though hotels had sprouted up wildly on the beachfronts. The tourists interviewed—bare-breasted women, men in flowered swim trunks, beaming retirees—posed amid brightly colored canoes, swearing they had landed in Paradise. You still ran across ox carts, but there were thousands of automobiles tearing around. Depending on the type of program it was, Guadeloupe came off looking either prosperous or poverty-stricken. Rich with concrete houses, businesses equipped with computers and modern machines. Yet at the same time inescapably bound to misfortune, extremely pathetic, even when people laughed, danced, and sang as the cameras looked on.

Had Piment changed?
Would she recognize the streets she used to know like the

back of her hand when she was a child?

Was the village, the town hall, the church still standing?

Were all the old people dead?

Would she find the Piment bakery right where it used to be along with the smell of warm bread?

Did people still wear straw hats all the time?

Did men still walk the streets armed with long cutlasses?

Was good old Suzon Mignard still of this world?

"Don't worry!" Suzon had told her twenty-one years earlier. "Don't worry, if it's meant to be, you'll see Piment again. Don't cry, we'll wait for you. We won't budge. Nothing going to ever change in this land full of demons. Nothing has changed since the day my mother went into the cane fields for the white man. Nothing has changed for centuries, since the days they brought the Negroes here from Africa. And Piment is the place where they put the meanest ones. They mated like beasts at the foot of the Cross. And the angel Gabriel was the most insatiable at the feast of the flesh . . . They let fall the cursed seed of misfortune and fatted Satan's pigs. I don't advise you to come back here, Mina . . . As long as you are able to, stay over there in France . . . Far from Evil and its thirty-two thousand tentacles . . . Twenty years at least. As long as possible . . . Far from dark spirits and Lucifer's acolytes . . . You an innocent child, Mina, you ain't learned the ugliness of this world . . . If you decide to come back to this pigsty one day—you the only one who knows what you must do—you remember my words, surely I be gone from this world. Your father was like you, an innocent. He was above the rest of the lot, and I loved him for his nobility and righteousness. People said I was mad for the love of him and that I spent my life waiting for him in vain, chained to a love that was too great for Piment. They laughed at me, behind my back, I know. I know all that, better than you do, girl. Run far away from Piment, where nothing but hate and the flowers of Evil grow. There are too many dead folks around you. So many that you even see the flames of a fire that went out three days ago. Go! Save yourself before they start coming after you . . . I'll pray for you, Mina. I'll pray all my prayers for you . . . And maybe I'll wait for you if my heart is strong, right here in my cabin, if you get the idea to come back one day . . .

After twenty-one years, those bitter words spoken by Suzon Mignard, words that Mina thought had left her memory, been buried in forgetfulness, came back to her in the very same order as before. In the same incantatory tone, defying the years. Exhumed from the past, they called to Mina from across the seas.

Was Suzon waiting for her as she had prophesied?

Then Mina let herself get caught up in the colorful images of Piment, back in the days when Rosalia reinvented the world in her paintings and counted boats on the sea with her. In the days when the cabin perched atop Morne Calvaire was still standing, even if it was a hundred years old. In the days when Médée thought she was Marilyn Monroe and walked through the narrow streets of the town with her head held high . . .

XVI

Fall was already drawing to an end. At the foot of the highrises bitter winds now prevailed, stabbing you in the back just like a knife. Gusts came ripping through the scrawny trees sending leaves soaring high into the dark sky, whirling for long minutes, always making one last loop before joining the others in damp dead piles on the sidewalks where people passing between apartment blocks seemed haggard, like survivors of one catastrophe that were hurrying toward another.

Lysia said she didn't mind the bad weather, the gray sky, night falling at five in the afternoon, rain, sudden showers, snow, frozen feet, and the rest. "As long as I have my own well-heated place and I know that summer will follow . . . I'm not like those niggers who whine all year round about the sunshine from back home. I adjust to France and its four seasons. It's the price I have to pay for my freedom and it's not such a

146

high price . . ." Mina had reluctantly left her high-rise and affronted the cold weather. There was another birthday party at Lysia's, this time it was for the youngest girl, Manon. Mina hated West Indian drinking parties. They always left her feeling dreary in the early morning hours, head heavy with talk, hearty laughter, and music. She'd done her best to refuse the invitation, but her friend gave her the kind of look that needs no frilly words to be understood.

It was barely nine o'clock and a multitude of more or less black young faces, more or less known to Mina, were already crowding into the apartment. People were sprawled on the futon that Lysia opened out every night. Others were standing near the table that was pushed into a corner, converted into a rum bar, a blood sausage and akra sideboard. There was talk, an effusive encounter here, a wary sidelong glance there. Powdered women dancing in overly tight silky dresses, lavish display of gold jewelry and patent leather high heels. The men over forty had taken out their three-piece suits, knotted their ties, and shined their shoes. They were grinning, close-shaven, sprinkled with expensive perfume. The younger ones wore designer jeans, T-shirts and track shoes. Music was blaring out of huge speakers stuck in the four corners of the living room.

For Lysia, celebrating her daughters' birthdays was always a challenge, a battle to be won. In truth, the parties were a pretext. Make everyone forget their day-to-day lives. Driving the bus or the underground metro from stop to stop. Caring for the sick at the hospital. Delivering the mail from door to door. Washing the pots in the cafeteria. Serving clients time and time again . . . Forget the journey of their ancestors, the cane fields, and the whip . . . Dance and stamp out the malediction and the images of niggers eternally down on their luck . . . Dance, shake your body and sweat out the old laments . . . Glory in life today and tomorrow . . .

And people had to shake it up, and drink, and eat to please Lysia, who went from one guest to the next asking how everything was, if they were having a good time, if they'd had enough dinner to pop their shirt buttons and burst their zippers, if the music was all right. And when people answered with a kiss or a smile, she let out her earsplitting laughter and silently repeated to herself that she'd done the right thing in choosing France, even if it was so bitterly cold outside and the project so hideous, even if she could sometimes see in white people's eyes that she was ugly and fat and black.

Mina gave her present to Manon—the latest MC Solaar, the new prophet whose smile was pasted on the walls of the room where the three girls slept. She stood in the middle of the party for a moment, looking for a corner to slip into, avoiding peoples' looks, wondering what she was doing there, feeling awkward about her hands, feigning to be absorbed in the naive paintings hanging on the walls. Guadeloupe in all of its holiday splendor. Guadeloupe in full make-up, the dream destination of people from around here. Beachfronts strewn with fishermen's canoes nonchalantly hauled up on the yellow sand. Majestic coconut trees buffeted in the trade winds. Green hills studded with typical cabins made of tropical wood and red tin roofs. A batch of Creole women in traditional garb striking suggestive poses, orange madras, white teeth, and lace.

She exchanged a few stiffly polite remarks with two women who swore they knew her, declined three invitations to dance a zouk, refused the punch offered by a chabin with slicked down hair, his face glowing with Nivea cream and stamped with a thousand reminders of bygone acne. She was jostled by dancers who'd already worked up a sweat. Then she made her way through the narrow hallway crowded with guests with glasses of planter's punch in their hands, appropriate smiles on their faces. Finally she reached the kitchen and found herself with Ashwina who was busy fixing finger foods with plastic toothpicks. A green pitted olive, a cube of cheese and a small white onion. Pursuing her work, the girl from Mauritius greeted Mina with a brief nod. An olive, a piece of cheese, an onion.

148

She was standing very straight, her shoulder blades jutting out under the pink silk sari that she'd put on over a black sweatshirt and leggings. Everything about her bearing suggested she was simply enduring Lysia's party, but her face remained smooth, inexpressive. Her fingers seemed to be practiced in carrying out that type of repetitive task.

Ashwina had been living at Lysia's place for two years now. If Lysia found it worth her while, despite the inconvenience (being evicted from her room, opening and closing the futon morning and night), her lodger—in order to be willing to serve as help at the party and give up her sleep—must surely obtain some secret advantage from the deal, thought Mina. Apart from the fact that she spoke fluent English and denied any ties to Réunion, nothing was known about Ashwina, who seemed to be appreciated by the girls and conscientious about her work with them. Ashwina never raised her voice, preferred silence to all other forms of expression. If she was asked how her parents were, she answered with a pat phrase: "They are fine, thank you." If one enquired about her studies at the university she said she was doing well. Lysia was satisfied with those kinds of responses. In fact all she worried about was the monthly payment and her daughters' progress in English. According to her, Ashwina's mail was delivered to a post-office box. She was never expecting a telephone call, and no one knew any of her student friends. Olive, cheese, onion . . .

"Ashwina, do you have a secret?" Mina asked her point-blank.

A question she hadn't expected to ask, a question that just popped out, go and figure why. Across the hall, the dancers repeated in unison the refrain of the frenzied zouk tune.

Ashwina's hands stopped in mid air and she turned toward Mina who stood with her back leaning against the refrigerator.

"Who doesn't have a secret, Mina?"

"Will you tell me your secret . . ."

"Secrets aren't for sharing."

"I don't want to share it, just to know it . . ."

Ashwina straightened her sari on her shoulder and put down the olive she was preparing to stick on a toothpick.

"I don't want to know your secret, Mina."

"Do you believe in ghosts?"

"I didn't ask you to tell me your secret," Ashwina responded. "Why don't you go and be with the others? Why are you hiding in the kitchen?"

"Are there ghosts in your country?"

Ashwina gazed at the tips of her babouches, then lifted her eyes to Mina, just like a schoolmistress faced with her poorest student.

"How old are you, Mina?"

"Thirty-five, why?"

"At your age, you still believe that ghosts . . ."

Lysia chose that very moment to make her entrance into the kitchen. Her face, well-powdered earlier in the evening, was gleaming with sweat like that of a hangman at confession. Her carefully pressed hair, slicked down in the style of Josephine Baker, was now sticking up in all directions. Her titties, that had docilely remained in the enormous cups of her brassiere in the beginning of the party, were now spilling out on all sides. She must have snagged her black knit dress on rings with large artificial stones or on broken fingernails—loose threads were hanging down here and there. She'd taken off her shoes and, standing there on her huge feet with callused heels and black toenails, she looked like the fish vendor, wife of a fisherman Mina used to know in Piment. But to make things worse, she'd mixed her drinks, rum, whisky, and wine. Her voice was changed, she was swallowing her words. It was as if her mouth were full of fog.

"Miiinaaa . . . Now jesss what yoou doooin heeere? We bin loookin for yoou ever place! C'mon en dance! Theys a niiice youungman I meanin you to meeet, heee aaaskin for you couple-times. Jessmite be luuuck comin you way tonight. Don't let it

150

sliiip on paasst, girl. Good Lord what you doooin in here? I want you havin fun, understand? Ain't no holiday ever day! Ain't no feastin ever day . . ."

"I'm coming right away, Lysia . . ."

"Don't go makin me come back lookin for you, hear? Theys callin me the other siiide! Whooo caaallin? Seeee? They can't get by without me . . . I takin these tidbits, Ashwina . . . Don't make no more there's plenty enough for this tiiime of niiight . . . Okay, I waitin on you!"

At those words she teetered off to rejoin her guests, hugging the plate full of appetizers to her breast like a treasure.

Mina and Ashwina remained for a moment facing one another in silence. Then the young woman from Mauritius turned away and began to wash the plastic cups piled on an abandoned tray.

"Where do ghosts live?"

"I'm twenty years old, It's not my place to teach you that," sighed Ashwina scrubbing the cups in the sink.

"Pretend that I'm ten . . ."

"Why are you suddenly interested in what I think or believe? We don't have to make conversation, you know. You can just stand there quietly without talking. You're at your friend's house . . ."

"Pretend that I'm ten years old, please."

Ashwina turned off the tap water and slowly wiped her hands with a dishcloth. When her eyes settled on Mina, she looked thirty years older. The lines of her face had hardened. Her lips were trembling. The music, songs, laughter, and shouts continued to drift into the kitchen but before crossing the threshold, they seemed to lose momentum.

"They are in all of us. The spirits of the dead live in us, Mina. The spirits become ghosts and take on form and color in our eyes when the heart no longer has the strength to bear grief. You see them to ease your heart. You see them so you will believe that you're alive when you feel dead too. Seeing them is

151

like a crutch for you and you would limp even worse through life if they weren't there."

"She disappeared, Ashwina . . . And I feel empty. I feel so empty. Drained . . ."

"Empty?"

Ashwina shook her head. A thin smile drew up the corners of her mouth.

"Nothing ever remains empty for long. We always find something to put into our body or our heart. It's like a house. See how we pile things up? We accumulate things. Fear of echoes in empty rooms. Furniture, pretentious knickknacks, mountains of dishware that we'll never use, new sheets in the closets, useless electrical appliances. We surround ourselves with faces and landscapes. We hang straw hats, crosses, plastic dolls, on the walls . . . It's like silence, listen to them! People can't refrain from filling up the silence. It is so frightening . . . So much like death . . . So they talk, play music, sing, and shout . . . All of that just to feel alive . . . Ghosts are like words sitting in the silence and . . ."

"Miiinaaa, why youou don't come listen to the mean things they tellin me. I not worth nothin in this world. I taaalk lotta foooolishness. I good for nothin."

"Now, now mama!" sighed Jessy who was holding her mother up as well as she could, keeping her from lunging into and bumping against the cupboards.

Lysia's face, smeared with tears and the vestiges of makeup, was twisting into all sorts of expressions. First screwing up pathetically. The next minute, swelling, moonlike. Then deflating before pulling itself back together.

"Whooo got started talkin negropolitans, huh? Whoooo was it?"

"It was Edouard, Mama."

"Bad chabin! He want to ruin the party, does he? That's it!!!"

"No, mama. We were kidding. Listen, your party isn't ruined. People are still dancing and having fun . . ."

"Yeees, that IS it," Lysia cut in.

She crumpled onto the kitchen tiles, her flesh spreading every which way, and—at Ashwina, Jessy, and Mina's feet—she started to relate a bitter tale that gradually brought her out of the fog she was in.

"Oh! Miiina, if only you'd seeen how they treated me in Guadeloupe . . . My sisters, you should have seen them . . . You remember, I took them plenty of presents. Well, they didn't ask me over to their place even once. Not once! Eeevery time I called on them, they were getting ready to go out. 'You should have phoned first, Lysia. You should have let us know you were coming . . .' And the nasty sneaks giggled with each other. And their kids didn't pay no attention to mine, except to call them names. 'Negropolitans! Neg Zagonal! Oreo!' They spoke Creole on purpose as soon as their cousins came around. Can you believe it, Minaaa? My own relatives . . . Even you would have been hurt . . . It would have shocked you. On top of that you've been in the Metropolis too long. You'll see, they don't want to have nothing to do with us anymore back home. They say we're half white-washed . . . They think we're worse than foreigners . . . As soon as you run into someone you know, he don't ask you how you are, he wants to know when you're going back, you hear . . . I swear, they treat white folk better . . ."

"Don't cry mama. We don't care if they don't like us. We don't want to live back there. No point in going back anymore."

"Yes there IS, that's our home, back there," grumbled Lysia.

"No, it's not our home anymore, mama," Jessy retorted.

"Our home is in France!" cried Sofia who had just walked in. "I don't want to go back anymore. They're all crazy. Next year, I'd rather go to summer camp."

Negropolitan.

Neg Zagonal.

Oreo.

When Mina left Lysia, she took those three words along with her. Three iron balls at the end of long rusty chains tied to her feet. Three words to fill her thoughts and the early morning silence.

XVII

When she wasn't at Suzon's, Rosalia wandered Morne Calvaire or strolled around here and there, nose in the air, eyes red and ravished. Her return to Piment was somewhat of a resurrection. She wasn't immediately identified, but since she'd come out of the envelope, more and more people had seen her. They called her "The Creature." And The Creature appeared everywhere, in town as well as in the country, decked out in all her flames, scandalously incandescent. She would come surging up from the water in the river, sit on a rock and have a wonderful time watching the women around her scatter and disappear, evoking gods and devils, proffering loud prayers, abandoning their sheets, wash powder, and tubs. The Creature also enjoyed prowling around the primary school. She stood near the wrought-iron gate. Melancholy, awaiting God knows what while the schoolteachers hurriedly gathered the terrified children together in the classrooms, swearing there was nothing outside, it was simply the play of sunshine, a bright patch of light, not a burning woman.

All sorts of theories went around about her. Historico-scientific-philosophical declamations purporting she had come back from the slave days because she'd been awakened by the commemorators of the year 1998, celebrating the one hundred and fiftieth anniversary of Abolition with great fanfare and little folderol. Those people shook the rusty chains of yesteryear for a long time, much to the dismay of the man in the street who had been struggling for a hundred and fifty years to digest History in his own way and learn, as best he could, to let the past centuries of servitude sink into oblivion. Too many debates on television about black slaves, insisted the descendants of shame, ungrateful folk who had proclaimed themselves free of shackles since they'd been observing the world perched high in air-conditioned, four-wheel-drive vehicles. Too many morbid parables about the year of Abolition, lamented others, convinced that they were billions of light years from the old niggers who had their arms crushed in the wheels of the sugar mill or their legs devoured by the master's hounds. Too many pious thoughts for old man Schœlcher and his reckless love for blacks, too many speeches and memories, too many statues and monuments, too much sniveling and saltpeter. That's what had brought that poor creature back from the shadows.

For a few days an even more extravagant version went through people's tortured minds. Cane-woman, that's what the creature haunting Piment was . . . As usual, to drive out vermin and burn dead leaves, fires had been lit in the fields of the *béké*-white man who owned most of the land in the district. But it had been so dry that year that sparks borne away on the wind leapt over the roads and almost set fire to cabins standing on the other side of the cane fields. Called to the rescue, the firemen whipped out their hoses and order was restored. The woman in flames appeared shortly after these events, which supported the idea that she was a stalk of cane that had escaped the fire. A stalk of cane that might well have been the product of some witch's revengeful spirit who had a score to settle with the *béké*. A black stalk of cane with eyes, hair, arms, and legs . . . That's how Sidoine, an old cane bundler, described the creature. The convoy of trucks had just pulled away from the factory. Sidoine was taking a break. She had already tied up fifty bundles of cane. Was taking a swallow of water observing, from under her hat, the immensity of the dark cane stretching before her, like the tangled mop of Lucifer's hair. Rosalia came up and planted herself right in front of her, arms raised to the sky. Sidoine jumped, froze, and then ran, stomach heaving, throat clenched tight. Though she'd never known anything but work in the fields, the woman was sound of spirit. No one questioned her prophetical words.

In the end it was an old retired fireman who recognized The Creature as soon as he saw her.

"Why, that's Rosalia! You can take my word for it, that's her all right. I was only a couple of inches from her the night of the fire and my eyes have never played tricks on me . . ."

In barely half a day, the townspeople had heard the news at least three times. By nightfall, all the distant villages had, in one way or another, been informed. In nothing flat, a wave of terror washed over Piment.

"Good Lord! It really is her, it's Rose! Melchior's Rosalia, escaped from hell . . ." people whispered through the blinds.

"Poor Médée's Rosalia come back to claim her due . . ." they muttered in the depths of their cabins.

"The mad spinning whirligig of a girl, Lord! After all these years . . ."

"How many? Twenty years . . . Twenty-one years . . . What did she come back here for?" mumbled—before beginning their evening prayers—those who spit and threw gravel at her as children on the playground at recess. For two–three days, the few who had seen her were thought of as lucky survivors with an interesting tale to relate; they inspired profound admiration dampened by jealousy. The blind, who had not yet run across her, swore that they wouldn't want to lock eyes with her for anything in the world but, deep down inside, they really wished with all their soul that they could, even if they did tremble at the mere mention of her name and shudder at the slightest unusual sound: the cracking of the beams at the peak of the cabin roofs, the whistling of a kettle, the clucking of a hen . . . In short, Rosalia was the very center of conversation, present in everyone's mind, standing watch behind every thicket, crouching in every hole like a hideous rat, hiding, rustling in the leafy treetops like a bat. She was everywhere.

Here and there.

In several places at once.

Those who despaired at not having glimpsed her yet found themselves obliged to invent fables in which they played the role of hero. They beat their chests, vowing they had chased Rose, had thrown buckets of water at her to put out the flames, had fought and subdued her.

One morning, armed with rifles and following a pack of five large dogs, a group of hunters organized a memorable search on Morne Calvaire. They came back to town in close rank at nightfall, heads hung low, with three young rabbits, two scrawny ringdoves, and a bunch of bananas. One of them, Judor, swore he had seen Rose, could have killed her if a wild pig hadn't run out just as he was aiming his rifle. But the stinging silence of the others belied his words.

The next day, Judor went bravely out to hunt alone. Two days later they found his body by the riverbank, or somewhere thereabout, guts torn out, hair in a rout. The police made out his death certificate and conducted a brief investigation. *France-Antilles*, the local daily paper, reported the death in the miscellaneous column along with other fillers, on page six. The case would have been wrongfully forgotten if Charly, a self-educated reporter-journalist working for an underground television station, hadn't left Point-à-Pitre, shouldering a camera and clutching a microphone. As a specialist in supernatural matters—the legacy of his storyteller grandmother—and being a reputed sleuth, he questioned Judor's family, his friends, and his foes. Tongues started wagging. Every word led back to Rosalia. The reporter climbed the hill, following her trail, searched the burnt ruins of the cabin, wandered around for a whole afternoon in the banana grove. Worn out, he came back without having filmed a thing, to the great disappointment of the people of Piment who watched him leaving on the road to La Pointe along with their last hopes and a sinking feeling of solitude and abandon filling their hearts.

Neighbors asked Suzon if she had encountered Rosalia, if she could in any way explain the apparitions. Mignard shrugged her shoulders, gripped her cane and sighed. "Fabulations! I can't see straight, but you are blind. Thanks to you, Piment will always be three steps behind the modern world. Demons won't never stop haunting you . . . Lord! Those things don't belong to this century . . . You got eyes, don't you watch television? Sweet Jesus, men have walked on the moon, they descend into the belly of volcanoes, they change people's organs like spare car parts . . . We can live with a pig's heart today I tell you."

But when she went back into her cabin and found herself more often than not nose to nose with Rosalia, Suzon was filled with dread. Bearing up under Rose's gaze, if only for an instant, was veritable torture that made terrific visions and chaotic worlds suddenly loom before Suzon's dead eyes. For she knew better than anyone the source of Rosalia's madness and the person who had cast the Montério family into misfortune and misery. Then Suzon traced two hundred and fifty signs of the cross in the air. Sprinkled the plants, the furniture, and the floor with ammonium. Lit consecrated candles. Asked a thousand pardons for her thousand sins.

November was drawing to an end. The man who had murdered Judor, the lone hunter, was unmasked and incarcerated. His name was Macaillat. A hardened criminal that the gendarmes ran down in a rum bar in Basse-Terre while he was bragging about having killed, just for fun, a crazy hunter in whose company he had spent the night observing a creature enveloped in flames. At first the business had amused him. Then, as time passed, he began to get irritated with the man who constantly motioned him to keep quiet, picked his nose disgustingly and wiped his harvest of boogers and snot on his pant legs. Macaillat condemned him at dawn after having decreed, beyond the question of a doubt, that he was of no use to this world.

Once Macaillat was arrested and thrown into jail with no tomorrow, people were no longer fearful or wary of Rosalia. She faded into the landscape. Even became a sort of attraction in early December. On Sundays, people came out from La Pointe, Abymes, Saint-Anne, Côte sous-le-vent, to try and get a glimpse of her. Two–three natives from Piment acted as tourist and historical guides in exchange for a small contribution, a meager tip. Hunters went back to their usual prey and people who ran across Rose hardly even jumped anymore. She could hang on the school gate for hours, the schoolmistresses carried on their lessons and the children recited, without stuttering or shuddering, couplets and multiplication tables, which seemed to delight the poor girl. In the market, she stood rooted in front of the women vendors, reaching out toward the *pakala* ignames, sweetsops, apple-mangos. People stopped beside her, gazed at her for a moment before hurrying off to their own affairs. Everyone knew she was there—a revenant amongst the living—as inoffensive as she was in the days she used to walk in her little sister Mina's footsteps. Wise soothsayers said she would leave as she had come, disappear as she had appeared. Sometimes souls in purgatory lost their way and came back to earth instead of going to paradise . . . It had happened before . . . Just had to give time some time . . . One day— God only knew the date and the time!—she would leave Piment to join her loved ones.

They weren't mistaken. In mid-December Rosalia climbed up Morne Calvaire and, weary of drifting on the roads, lay her body down at the foot of the traveler's tree, the one under which Melchior had buried the pieces of her umbilical cord. No one saw her wandering the town again. Days, she sat on a rock contemplating the fields or counting the boats on the sea, the birds in the sky.

One, two, three.

One. Two. Three.

Evenings, those who raised their eyes saw a pillar of flames rising and falling, coming and going, running and leaping over the morne.

XVIII

Cousin Tibert came barreling into Piment on December 17. He parked his pick-up in front of Suzon's cabin, gave a quick honk of the horn, rolled up the windows and locked the door. Due to the vagabonds invading Guadeloupe since the beginning of the '80s, he'd gotten over his habit of leaving a door open or a window down. With a sigh, he knocked on Suzon Mignard's door. A chore he would have preferred to avoid. When he received Mina's letter, he had immediately pictured himself twenty years earlier, driving his young cousin to the airport. He hadn't received any news of her until that surprising letter announcing her impending visit. Mina was worried about Suzon's silence.

Has she passed away?

I'm coming to Guadeloupe for a few days.

I wanted to stay at her place. I wrote her a letter but she didn't reply.

Can you fill me in?

I'm arriving December 20 to spend Christmas in Guadeloupe, in Piment.

If she's no longer living, could you put me up in Trois-Rivères?

Tibert had just left Trois-Rivères and Tiphaine—his legitimate wife, his concrete house, and his two German shepherds. At forty-five years of age, he'd given up the material comfort he'd endured twenty years of sacrifice and privation to accumulate. He was starting out from scratch again and had just set up house with Cindy, a twenty-year-old beauty with the body of a goddess, who helped him find his youthful spirits once again. He dyed his hair and touched it up every Sunday so that the white roots growing in wouldn't betray him. He sweated in a tracksuit every morning running after the silhouette of a dream playboy who was always at least fifty strides ahead of him. He'd already trimmed some fat off his belly and he still believed he could get the muscles he'd had at twenty-five back. The couple was subletting a modest apartment in a new, hastily constructed housing project, where he could in no way lodge Mina. He'd received the letter in the beginning of the month and had been putting off visiting Suzon every day.

After he repeated it three times, Suzon finally understood the name of her visitor: Tibert Montério. She clutched her cane like a club, ready to grapple with the nasty past that was coming back to knock at her door. She took on the sweet voice of the wolf in the story of Little Red Riding Hood.

"Who's there?"

"Tibert, Mam Suzon. Tibert Montério."

"Oh, just a minute. I be right there. What brings you out this way? It's been a long time . . . What a pleasure . . ."

On the other side of the door, Tibert straightened up, smoothed down his hair, blacker than a priest's robe, and patted the pocket of his Lacoste T-shirt to make sure he hadn't forgotten Mina's letter. He didn't bother to answer Suzon. His mind wandered to thoughts of Cindy's titties, her waist, her buttocks. The material objects he had accumulated for twenty years held no weight compared to the pleasures and thrills he derived from that vigorous, ardent body. Nevertheless, in spite of this newfound happiness that grew in his heart by the hour, painful images and nagging regrets were constantly popping up. How, he chided himself, was I able to live twenty years with a creature so stingy with caresses that she only consented to lend me her flesh with clenched mouth and tight-closed legs, sagging titties and dry *coucoune*? How could I have stayed for so long in that life, begging for love like a dog begs its daily pittance?

He'd seen Suzon five or six times since Mina had left. Usually at funerals. One morning three years ago, coming out of mass where his ex-wife had dragged him so that the Lord might patch up their already failing marriage. One day last year, in the waiting room of the town hall in Piment.

Tibert had never much liked Suzon. When she extended her cheek to him, he felt as if his face were bumping up against a stone wall. He also hated her mournful, tearless eyes. He wasn't easily taken in. In his humble opinion, old Suzon was no saint. Rather like one of those stinking slop pails people used to use that fouled the air as soon as it was uncovered. Certainly, to her credit, the woman had always shown—and quite ostentatiously—absolute loyalty toward Melchior and his family. But something evil, something unhealthy emanated from her. He knew that she was almost blind now, yet he didn't feel in the least sorry for her.

Smile! You've come to visit. Smile! You are a messenger! Smile at poor Suzon who never knew love! Smile even if she can't see your smile! Smile to drive away ugly thoughts! Think of how privileged you are. You're living with a young woman while Mignard spent her life waiting and lonely . . . That's what Tibert was thinking as he walked into Suzon's lair.

First off, as is customary, she asked how Tiphaine and the children were doing since they'd all gone to live in the Metropolis. Suzon said the Metropolis instead of France. Or rather, in truth she said: "Métwopole". The word came back to her lips ten times over, an old dream, like a piece of candy she made last as long as possible to put off the moment when Tibert would bring up the real reason for his visit. Courteous, well mannered, the man played along with the polite conversation, docilely and unhurriedly answered all the questions. Imperturbable, he endured the fetid breath coming from Suzon's mouth whose lips had not parted for three and a half weeks, except to talk to herself. Even though he'd staked his life on a wild shot, he was no fool and could smell the savage beast

162

behind the walls of politeness and conventional affability. As they chatted, just like the closest of friends, Tibert was inspecting the premises.

Suzon had seated him on the sofa in the parlor. Like an aristocrat with a financial setback, she had slumped her flabby body down in the only rocking chair, fist gripping the pommel of her cane. She sat rocking gently like someone who has paid her debts in life, someone with an immaculate conscience and a peaceful heart.

The room that served as a parlor was bathed in a tepid semi-darkness swimming with dust. The half-closed blinds barred the sunlight, let only choppy sounds in from the street, and cut off the light breeze. Suzon had been born in that cabin. She'd grown up there, with her parents whom she'd watched die and her brother Délos whom she'd allowed to leave. She'd never known any other sheet metal, any other planks, any other roof beams . . . All of her life she had tread on that same floor, she knew it's every flaw and loose board. As a child she had slept on it, rolled up in old France-flour sacks that had been sewn together. Morning after morning she had pushed open those never painted or repaired rickety old doors that seemed to be waiting for her to depart before crumbling to ashes. She had been sleeping in her mother's room for over forty years now. Alone in her solitude. Alone with her face and her body that had gradually capitulated as she waited and the years went by. Alone with her demons and the ugly faces of the sorcerers she had closely associated with. Alone with her nightmares, until Rosalia came back . . .

"So, there you have it! I stopped by to tell you that Mina wrote to me . . ."

Tibert cleared his throat, smoothed down his hair and patted one of the faded cushions lying next to him.

"Ah! She wrote you . . . So what's new?" ventured Suzon hunching further down in her rocking chair so as to better embody innocent, vulnerable old age. "But, perhaps you'll be wanting something to drink, Tibert?"

163

She made as if to rise to her feet, stiff-boned, body filled with pains.

"No! No! I won't be staying!" cried Tibert who was already counting the precious minutes spent far from Cindy.

Suzon fell back heavily.

"You see, I nearly blind ... I just an old lonely blind woman ..."

"That's just it!" cried Tibert, catching the ball on the rebound. "That's just it, Mina is coming home. On vacation. She wrote to you too. You didn't answer. She was worried ..."

"I didn't get no letter," lied Suzon, rubbing her chin.

"As you know, she has no family left in Piment. She always thought of you as . . . She wants to see Piment again. The school, the town, the hill, see ... She told me to give you a kiss ..."

Suzon nodded her head, looking very pensive. So that was it, she thought, that was all. The survivors of the Montério family hadn't unmasked her yet. Rose hadn't come to revenge the dead. In a way, she was simply a coincidence, the kind you run into at every turn in life, she had simply been passing through and—thank God!—time had sent her off to Morne Calvaire that she now haunted without being able to make up her mind to return to the realm of shadows.

"Ah! She sent me a kiss," said Suzon, moved. "She's kind, ain't she?"

A smile like a poorly mended scar, lifted her ashen lips.

"She'd like to stay at your house," Tibert continued. "She has no family left in Piment, see ..." he repeated again.

"But I am her family, Tibert! My house is her house!" Suzon declared with a firmer voice, in a surge of generosity that surprised Tibert despite the aversion he felt for the old woman.

"So I can tell her you agree? I'll give her a call this afternoon ..."

"I always keep my word, Tibert. I didn't receive her letter, but you tell her I'll be waiting for her ..."

Tibert shrugged one shoulder. Time was slipping by. He was relieved and his problem was solved. He pulled his feet together in front of him and slowly began to stand up.

"Tell her that I can barely see, dear Tibert. Tell her that I can't make her any big meals. Tell her too that there's dust everywhere. But most of all tell her I'll be waiting for her . . ."

Then she fell silent.

"You won't be leaving without having some punch . . ."

"No! No! I don't drink alcohol anymore!" protested Tibert. "I'm not thirsty," he huffed, lifting his buttocks up from the sofa.

By the time she could tear herself from the rocking chair, drag her body into the kitchen, grope around in the buffet in search of a greasy glass that hadn't been washed in ten years, find a grimy dishcloth to wipe it with, get her hands on a dubious looking knife, a piece of wilted lemon and the sugar bowl where the roaches slept and the ants ran, he would have lost an hour of his life. Just then the smell of unwashed womanly flesh that permeated the room filled his nostrils once again. An unbearable stench.

He jumped to his feet, using an important appointment in Pointe-à-Pitre as a pretense. With closed eyes, Suzon stretched her chin bristling with white hairs out to him. Just as he was about to kiss her, Tibert noticed the three crosses hanging at her neck. One was plain, made of dark wood. Another was gold with a silver Christ. The last cross was made of two twigs of acacia, knotted together with a red ribbon. The smell of long-dried sweat wafted up in sour vapors. Tibert kissed her on the forehead. Her hair reeked of ammonia and carapate oil.

He hurried out into the light of day and the fresh air of the street. On his way back home, and back to his divine Cindy, he felt ashamed. No, he had no right to hand over his cousin to that unkempt woman, who was surely a witch, hiding her ugly nature behind a veneer of piety. But at the same time, he felt buoyed. Relieved of a difficult problem. At any rate, he concluded, that's what Mina wanted: to stay at Suzon Mignard's and nowhere else . . .

XIX

Mina let out a sigh of relief when the taxi finally let her off at
the Orly airport with her two suitcases and three bags in the
freezing December morning. During the ride, the driver—to
whom she'd unfortunately revealed her destination—had
constantly lamented his sort and endlessly related his West Indian love-affairs. "Guadeloupe! You're very lucky! I'll never get
to that bit of paradise! I have friends, neighbors of mine, who
come from there . . . I almost even married a girl from Réunion
. . . It's all the same, isn't it?" He loved chicken with colombo
sauce, akras, and hot spicy blood sausage . . . He danced the
zouk . . . Once he'd picked up Jocelyne Béroard, the singer
from the group Kassav' . . . She was really nice . . .

Up until then Mina had dreamed and dreamed of the trip.
And now the day had come. Here she was, Mina Montério, at
the Orly airport. She was really going away and not just
dreaming about it. She was going to fly to Guadeloupe. And,
with her heart racing, her mood swung from joyous to fearful
in the space of an instant. First, she would allow fear to jab
brutally through her and rip out her insides, then would sink
into joy's silken sweetness. She placed one foot in front of the
other. Was standing up straight when she felt herself being
thumped on the back and jerked forward by obscure forces.
She moved along like everyone else, pushing the baggage cart
in front of her, hugging her handbag under her arm because it
contained all of her treasures: her airplane ticket, her passport,
credit card, two thousand five hundred francs in cash. She was
aware that she wasn't being careful enough. But she had to
cross the terminal, follow the arrows on the signs hung up
high. She had to walk and move up in the line till she reached
the check-in counter, hold out her ticket to the smiling hostess. She had to show her passport and her boarding pass to the
stern policeman sitting in the glass cage. And wait, wait for
him to leaf through the pages in the passport, verify its

authenticity, stare at her as if he were looking for another woman, another Mina Montério behind her weary traits. Attempt a smile and then, without trembling, put her carry-on baggage on the conveyor belt and watch it disappear for a second into the black X-ray box that detected arms of all sorts, but not fears, or ghosts either. She had to look like a normal person who knows where she is going, when in truth she felt as if she'd slipped out of the body that was straining toward the homeland with every fiber.

"It's okay!" she kept telling herself in order to exorcise the fear of Guadeloupe that came and went like a bad smell, passed in and out of her heart as painfully as a rusty needle, thudded and throbbed in her head like a three-worded song.

Return to Guadeloupe after twenty-one years in France. What insanity! She had a fit of dizziness. Looked for a free bench in the departure lounge. Creole words were flying, whirling around on all sides, filling the air with forgotten smells. People laughed among themselves. Several times, she thought she heard her name, recognized certain faces. Felt as if they were all making fun of her, knew before she did, that her trip home was pure madness. Boisterous encounters here, calls or whispers there, hugs galore. And she, backed into her corner, shying away from the crowd, was like one of those old rootless negresses, with outlandish clothes and too much make-up, that have lived over forty years in the metropolis and are going back to their native island to bury their poor mama or to retire back in the homeland, in their country, in the house they built with the money they saved day after day, penny after penny in France. No, Mina couldn't really recall what spurred her to take this trip. She felt as though she'd prepared for it too hurriedly. Confused and half-finished thoughts were crowding through her mind when the voice of a hostess was already informing the passengers to proceed with boarding. I should have waited a little longer, she thought to herself. Maybe it would be better if I didn't go on this trip. But

I've got plenty of presents. A porcelain dinner set, an embroidered tablecloth, made in China, three nightgowns, two flowered dresses, a handbag to give to Suzon. Maybe it isn't too late . . . An Adidas tracksuit for Tibert. Maybe I could sell my ticket to someone, make a reservation for another date . . . On the telephone Tibert said he'd taken up sports again and announced the good news at the same time: Suzon was still alive, she was waiting for her—Mina Montério—didn't hold it against her for keeping quiet for these last twenty-one years.

I'm not afraid anymore! Everything is fine!

She heard snatches of sentences bereft of all meaning, disparate words. Crazed images besieged her, then collided and exploded inside her head in a thousand vivid colors. People are happy to be going home, she repeated to herself to put her mind at rest. I'm happy too. I'm happy too. I'm happy . . .

I'm not afraid anymore! Everything is fine!

She opened Victor's letter that she'd found in the mailbox that very morning. A sort of poem . . .

Mina,
Two flights
Two friends
Two different ends . . .
The same sky going past
We're off at last
Toward that waiting nation
To find our salvation
Thursday we will meet
As was decreed
As we agreed

I'm not afraid anymore
Far from the rumor
I'll wait for you Thursday
Far from the fray
In front of town hall
By the fountain
I'll be wearing a red hat
It's as simple as that
We're off at last
Victor

She rose to her feet. Walked toward the passenger bridge as if in a dream. Went into the airplane. Seat number 75. Buckled her seat belt and closed her eyes when the plane lifted off the ground.

I'm not afraid anymore! Everything is fine!

Victor's letter was pulsing in her mind to the tune of a rap song by some mongrel group from Secteur ä, a harsh mixture that came tumbling in waves out of open windows in summer, rumbling through the project apartments, rage bouncing around in the stairwells, burden of hate and resentment borne along by enormous boom boxes on the shoulders of spiteful, hateful kids from the high-rises, faces as hard as those of the dockers from the port in Basse-Terre. Lysia's daughters sometimes danced to those ruthless tunes and voices, after their English lessons, under Ashwina's steely gaze . . . "Nothing ever remains empty for long . . . It's like silence . . . People can't refrain from filling the silence . . . So they talk, play music, sing, and shout . . . All of that just to feel alive . . ." Were all of these people filling up the silence, fearing death and pretending to be happy? Mina wondered, pausing here and there to dwell on the exuberant faces of the passengers crowded into the Boeing.

169

I'm not afraid anymore! Everything is fine, everything is as fine as can be.

Yet there are days when death seems desirable and sweeter than life.

When the first islands appeared in the window of the plane, Mina was seized with nausea and, in spite of herself, began to pray that the plane would fall into the ocean. The person next to her, a child who had slept through the whole flight, suddenly couldn't sit still. He wiggled in his seat, craned his neck, fidgeted impatiently and, from time to time, cast a delighted look at Mina as if he wanted to find the same ecstasy in her eyes.

As soon as the doors opened, the damp, stifling heat rushed into the plane. Mina kept her wool jacket on all the same and paced slowly along with the docile herd of passengers.

Everything is fine! I'm not afraid anymore!

Tibert was there as promised. Threw himself at her. Took her in his arms and hugged her before she even had time to get a good look at him. Carried her suitcase to his pick-up, hopping around in front of her, so fresh and lighthearted while Mina was sweating from every pore in her body, wondering out loud if it was really her, Mina Montério, who'd come back to Guadeloupe, this grief-stricken land.

They drove for an hour. Tibert asked very few questions. He had a cheerful expression on his face, the carefree look of happy people. I'm happy. I'm happy too, Mina repeated to herself. They talked a little about winter in France, about the snow and the cold, in a silence punctuated with insignificant comments. Then abruptly, without anyone asking him to, Tibert began to paint the portrait of Guadeloupe in the '90s, as if to warn his cousin that the country had changed quite a bit since she'd left, as if to erase the previous image from her mind. Mentalities have evolved, he assured her, pointing out—as material proof of the evolution of mentalities—the villas under construction perched on the hilltops here and there as well as the new road over which shiny cars whizzed. He paused a moment, his left arm resting nonchalantly on the door, his right hand on the wheel, wagging his head to the cooing and bleating of a love-zouk playing on the radio. On either side, cane fields to contemplate.

Immutable fields of cane swayed by the immutable trade winds. Cane fields that greeted Mina in their own particular way. There, now I am going into the countryside, she thought as the car cut through the fields. I'm going deep into it, penetrating it just like men's penises in my belly. Everything is fine, I'm not afraid anymore! I've come back to my homeland . . . I'm going back to Piment.

They arrived at nightfall. Cousin Tibert parked in front of Suzon's cabin, set the suitcase down on the veranda, waited for the old woman to open the door and without further ado, slipped off into the dark town. Mina and Suzon fell into each other's arms. After many hugs and the customary effusions, they remained silent for a moment, facing one another, fearing the words that were to come. Then, slowly, despite the stench hovering in the room, Mina began to feel more comfortable, asked forgiveness for her long silence and said thank you for the welcome. She started to talk, ask harmless questions, enquire after the health of her hostess . . .

Suzon seemed reticent to engage in the improvised duo. Disconcerted from the beginning by the tone of the conversation, tripping over words that arose gravely and rang false, she started in on the litany of her solitude. Little by little, she finally managed to bring her voice into tune with Mina's clear timbre. And that is how, for nearly three hours, with dry throats and damp eyes, they told each other—both lying— about the twenty-one-year separation. But when the subject exhausted itself of its own accord, one word spurred another, and together they plunged into times past, those of people who were no more, of a long-gone Piment...

And as the past came rushing back, Mina watched the parlor take on the aspect of a sinister theater prop, as if disguised by some diabolical decorator. Hanging on the walls, old faces, nostalgic and yellowed in their gilt frames, were now grimacing. The dull mirrors, covered with stains, reflected somber and deformed faces. The worm-eaten boards, chipped graying paint, seemed to be holding back a scream. The curtains, thick with dust, told strange tales to the century-old, rickety, broken-legged furniture with unhinged doors. Dark, pestilential abode that suddenly inspired fear rather than confidence. As for old Suzon, she was the spitting image of a witch taken from a horror tale, a horrible shrew straight from some monstrous fable using her studied smiles to conceal her intention to devour Mina who suddenly stood up to shake herself, get out from under the spell.

The old woman proposed a revolting dinner: marinated *balarou*-pipefish and eggplant that was more burned than it was fried.

"The fault of my poor eyes!" she apologized.

"Now don't you worry about that!" said Mina as she set the table.

"*An pa ka manjé qwan zafè lé swa!* You go ahead and eat while you can!" sighed Suzon.

Mina thanked her, trying to drive away the dark images that were besieging her.

"You're so kind."

"I had no right to refuse you. You know I think of you as my daughter," answered the old woman, tightly gripping the three crosses hanging at her neck in her claw-like fingers.

A little later, with the spirit of self-sacrifice that grips the emigrant visiting her native land, Mina threw on the floor an ancient mattress that had witnessed last confessions and smelled

172

of stale urine, even after being covered with the sheet that Mignard offered her. *That's the way it is here, I'd forgotten. That's how I used to sleep up there in the cabin on Morne Calvaire too. We didn't have a private bedroom or a bed of our own. I'm back in Piment and that's all that counts . . .*

One, two, three.
  One, two, three.
  Go on! Keep going, Rosalia!
  One, two, three. You can do it.

She fell asleep with those words, her stomach heavy with the fried food that takes so long to digest. And for the first time, but only in dream, Rosalia began to count the boats on the sea. They were lying on the floor of the veranda, up there on the hill, just like in the old days, before the fire . . . Rosalia's face wasn't burned and she was wearing a little red gingham dress. Mina was clapping at the numbers that were forming naturally on her sister's lips.

  One, two, three, four, five . . .

The two little girls squealed joyfully and sang out the miracle of numbers.

  Six, seven, eight . . .

Suddenly, still reciting the numbers, Rosalia asked for her paintbrushes.

  Nine, ten, eleven . . .

Mina thought she wanted to paint the boats on the sea. But her sister, who had never painted a single face while she was alive, began a sort of portrait. Two eyes, a nose, a mouth. Every time she dipped her paintbrush in the pot of water, she looked at Mina, seemed to be waiting for her to recognize the face she'd begun.

  Twelve, thirteen, fourteen . . .

A sweet dream in which Mina was smiling blissfully. The blue sky was scattered with fluffy white clouds. And Rosalia was applying her colors.

Then, everything changed.

Fifteen, sixteen, seventeen, eighteen . . .

The red paint turned to blood. And Suzon's face, dripping with that blood loomed out of the painting. Her twisted mouth screamed in echo: "Eighteen! Eighteen! Eighteen!" Rosalia started to howl and suddenly turned back into a poor retarded child, crazed whirligig escaped from the burned cabin.

Mina awoke with a start, breathing hard, cold sweat on her temples. In the next room, Suzon Mignard was breathing noisily, whistling and belching with the regularity of a metronome. The flame of a candle trembled on her night table. Disturbing play of light that brought a terrifying ballet of shadows to life around the old woman.

XX

Tuesday December 21, 1999

Mina spent the morning cleaning the cabin. She sorted through the tattered and dirty laundry that Suzon kept under her bed. Emptied the bureau, the wardrobe, the closets. Hummed to herself as she washed dishes and clothes. Threw out five boxes of antediluvian newspapers. Shooed off a black rat and five gray mice. Squashed four centipedes and sixty cockroaches. She swept, dusted, scoured . . . And each of her gestures said thank you to her poor friend, expressed her joy at being back in Piment.

The old shrew never left her rocker. She anxiously observed Mina's every move. She scolded, "Leave that be! You didn't come here to work . . . I don't like people putting my mess in order. I'll never find anything now if you straighten things up the way you see fit. You forgetting I lost my eyesight. Go out for a walk! Go to the beach! Make the best of your visit! Don't hang around the cabin like this!"

Yet she ended up falling silent, defeated by Mina's good humor and enthusiasm. It was plain to see, even if you were blind, the girl suspected nothing about Suzon's past deeds. After all, the only things Suzon had to hide were under a floorboard in the bedroom where Mina couldn't get her paws on them. So, the old woman rocked peacefully, sunk in the torpor of her memories. While Mina polished the furniture and scrubbed the sheets in the dirt-black water, Suzon went back twenty years. She saw the sad little orphan asleep in her bed, the sole survivor of the war she was waging in those days against Melchior and her bad luck.

The book of her life opened to page September 12, 1978.
    The day of Rosalia's funeral.
    The grave faces.
    "We are all brothers", the priest said.
    The walk back from the cemetery.
    Long steps. Eyes downcast.
    And suddenly fear in Mina's eyes.
    "There's a fire in the cabin! There's a fire, friend Suzon! I see Rosalia! There's a fire! I don't want to die with Rose!"

Then night came.
    The night of September 12, 1978.

The doctor gave Mina a shot of sedative. There's nothing else we can do, he whispered, only wait. Suzon promised to sit by the child as she slept, just like a mother. In those days her eyes were still good. She hadn't seen Rosalia herself, but she could have sworn to God that Mina was telling the truth. Accustomed to having close connections with parallel worlds, Mignard could believe, without too much effort, in that type of manifestation. She therefore sprinkled water blessed by the priest of Piment around the cabin, lit candles, burned incense. Heart gone sour, head seething with ugly thoughts, she sat at the child's bedside and opened the Holy Bible to a page of Psalms. Mina slept, knocked out by the mixture of drugs they had administered her.

Observing the peaceful face of Melchior's daughter, her chest rising and falling with even breathing, Suzon felt more insulted than ever, resentment filled her heart. Her life was a huge waste. For more than forty years she had cherished and waited for a man. He had robbed her of her virginity under a blooming mango tree, kept her hanging on the line with stupid hopes before irrevocably repudiating her, nine days after the death of that bitch, Médée. With hard words, words that were offensive to her mother, crude words, tempered in absolute sin and the sordid story of their own parents, he finally consented to explain why their marriage was impossible. He severed the ties binding their destinies that she had sealed three hundred thousand times. He asked her to forget his seed, his promises of travels to the metropolis, and her pipedreams of love, as if forgetting the sweet fruits of Paradise were as simple as that.

Just when she was thinking about her last expedition to Morne Calvaire, about her past suffering, the taste of blood came to her lips, the eighteen little black babies—announced long ago in her youthful dreams—began hammering and clamoring in her entrails. Seized with labor pains, Suzon suddenly let go of the three crosses she so loved to fondle. She put her hands on the folds of her belly that was swelling as fast as one of those modern-day tires advertised by Trident.

She saw them pushing their way out, one after the other, one after the other.

Eighteen from between her legs.

Nine girls and nine boys.

Uncontrollable, they screamed for milk and demanded justice. Not one of them had been given a ticket for life. It was all the fault of vice, of the Demon . . . Not a single one! And Mina was still alive . . .

Suzon no longer knew whether she was awake or if she was giving birth in a nightmare. Between two fainting spells and three labor pains, her eyes fell upon Mina: the girl's soft flesh, her little sapodilla neck, her mouth working interior words and her nose where the breath was passing. She was greatly tempted to be rid of the race of Montérios . . . Be rid of them once and for all . . . but the risk she ran was even greater. What would people think if Mina was found dead at Mignard's house? They'd tie loose ends together in no time. The story would come around full circle pronto. So Suzon resisted the temptation and dozed off for a few moments reflecting bitterly on missed opportunities.

That night she awoke a hundred times. In a trance. Her hands gripping weapons, tools of revenge, that each of the babies handed her. Sometimes she was clutching a pillow or a cushion, then found herself ready to cudgel with a mallet, hammer, iron, rock, stick, kettle, bottle, or cutlass. Other times she was armed with a wire, a rope, a spike-heeled shoe, a knife, a phial of disfiguring liquid, a poison powder, a jar of hot peppers, a giant centipede . . . Eighteen instruments of death.

She could have murdered Mina a hundred times for the love of her cherubs. But a hundred times, her hands—driven by her sons' and daughters' hatred—were thrown off by a supernatural heat rising from the innocent child like an indomitable shield.

In exchange for large sums, Suzon had always left the dirty work to others. She had never killed anyone or drowned anyone with her own hands, which in fact were only practiced at applying sorcerers' evil oils and poison essences. She did nothing but delegate. Professionals took care of the tracking down, striking dead, alienating, bumping-off for her. Her own hands remained clean, more often than not joined in prayer.

"She was prowling around here not long ago . . . Last month . . . She came back shortly before you did . . . You remember that I told you never to set foot in the country again . . . She came back."

"Who?" asked Mina.

In one morning she'd succeeded in making the cabin look respectable again, it was now redolent with Cresyl disinfectant and La Croix bleach. Mina was kneading dough for dumplings, glancing from time to time back over at Suzon, pensive and silent in her rocker. She had done her best, the glasses were glittering in the buffet, the sheets and towels were drying on the line outside, the furniture had been thoroughly dusted. She still hadn't taken a walk through Piment, but she felt prepared to face the streets and raise her eyes to Morne Calvaire. Her heart was light and she was humming a little tune when Suzon started to talk as if she were continuing a monologue out loud that she'd started under her breath. The red beans were cooked to bursting and the salt had soaked out of the pigtails.

"Who? Rose! Rose, of course . . ." Suzon blurted out in a husky voice. "I prefer to break the news to you before you learn about it from other mouths. Make sure you don't go listening to folks, y'hear?"

"Rose!" Mina repeated.

"Yeh, Rose! Almost all Piment saw her. With her burned nightgown, her red eyes, her flames and the whole works . . . She went rambling about here and there. Some hunters even tracked her through the woods. She went and stood around by the church, in front of the school! Everywhere! She was everywhere! I heard she's now living up there on Morne Calvaire . . ."

"Rose is here in Piment!" Mina had to find a seat.

"Don't get worked up now," Suzon grumbled. "She didn't do no harm . . . All she did was appear."

Mina wasn't troubled, but relieved. She listened distractedly to Suzon's advice while her heart and mind were whispering that it was all part of the scheme, that Rose's return to Piment had been orchestrated in very high places, up where man's intelligence is but a small ripple in the vast sea of sagacity.

"She appeared, yes . . ."

"She appeared!" repeated Mina whose voice was trembling with joy that the blind woman mistook for dread.

178

Heart as cold as stone, Suzon rejoiced inwardly.

"Yeh, yeh, that's right, she appeared!" Suzon drove the words home. "I didn't see her myself, as you might imagine, because of my eyes that hardly see nothing anymore, even in the middle of the day. People claimed," she said, thumping on her chest, "that she didn't have a single wrinkle. We all grown older, right? It's God's way. My youth is long gone . . . But Rose, why she's remained a young girl, the same as the day of the fire . . ."

Suzon fell silent, then abruptly changed subjects. Her voice grew gentler, "*Fout manjé-aw ka santi bon*! What's on the stove, it smells good! I'm so happy you here with me. If you was going to stay, I'd ask to live fifty more years, even in the darkness I've fallen into . . . Give me your word you ain't going looking for Rose up on the hill! You come to enjoy the sun and the sea, right? Have fun! There are *chanté-Nwel* carol parties everywhere! They back in style nowadays. Give me your word you won't go poking around in the wood that burned twenty-one years ago and you won't get lost in your dead father's banana grove! Swear it on my three crosses . . ."

The town of Piment—miserable hovels, hideous shops, narrow sinuous streets—lay between the sea and the green hills scattered with banana groves. It had remained almost exactly the same as Mina remembered it, just slightly more dilapidated and shrunken with, in places, the bright glare of a modern building, like a new patch on a coat that had been mended ten times over.

Mina had walked all the way around it in barely an hour. The paintings in the church were fading between graffiti and local separatist slogans. The factory, abandoned now for over forty years, had lost even more of its sheet metal. Immense billboards had sprouted up on every corner between the cabins, touting tomorrows of indispensable cell phones, cars to drive away now and pay for at Easter, televisions for one hundred and ninety-nine francs a month, micro-wave ovens, computers to be had at bargain rates before 2000 . . . Imperturbable, the faded red, white, and blue flag floated from the balcony of the town hall. The gates to the primary school had also withstood the test of time. But the Palace had had no choice but to close down after a false ceiling, eaten away by termites, had collapsed on the audience right in the middle of a karate film in the late '80s. The posters of the last showing had survived the years, the cyclones, the rains. Like old worn skins, they flaked away in scales and shreds, creating a new tortured picture of faded colors covered with hardened lumpy crusts. For a minute, Mina tried to find a trace of the films Médée had loved, picking away at the old paper. She quickly gave up. People were watching her and she had the impression they recognized her, were saying to themselves, "Look, Melchior's daughter is back! You think she might be crazy too?"

Then all of a sudden, Rue Mortenol, filled with a forgotten smell that threw her back twenty-one years in time. The smell of warm bread, cooked in the wood-burning oven of the Dotémar Bakery. It smelled just as good as it used to. More eloquent than all the stones, planks, or sheet metal she had rediscovered, the smell of warm bread was paying honor to her return to Piment, welcoming her back home.

No, nothing had changed. It was still the same scenery, just a little older, a little more patched up. Just had different actors walking through it. She passed some young boys on scooters, the spitting image of kids in the project, Nike tennis shoes, same wasted looks on their faces. As she was strolling along with her nose in the air, a car almost ran her down. Many cars were driving up and down the narrow streets. It was incredible, there were traffic jams in Piment. The sidewalks were crawling with people. Unknown faces that reminded her of others. Here and there, small itinerant vendors hawking fresh local juices, chicken, cod, liver, or hot spicy mackerel sandwiches. Women proposed kibis or coconut patties they pulled out of large wicker baskets. Posted behind a folding table, a disheveled Rasta was selling trinkets—kauri necklaces, braided leather bracelets, prophet rings with lion's heads—and posters bearing the effigy of Bob Marley or Hailé Sélassié, colorful pants in African prints, red-green-yellow knit caps . . .

The doors of Habib's sewing shop—the one that furnished Médée's zippers, thread, and lace in the old days—now opened onto a gaudy fast food restaurant where patrons consumed, with genuine American avidity, Coca-Cola and hamburgers with oriental sauce.

A self-service now replaced old man Torman's hardware store. But there were still untouched vestals of bygone days: women selling snowballs, roasted pistachios and cassava on the sidewalk in front of the tax bureau and the post office. Nostalgic scene from a defunct Guadeloupe. Mina stopped in front of a *bâta*-Indian negress who was selling manioc flour and cassava cakes with coconut. After a bit of conversation, she learned that the young woman, Louise, was the granddaughter of Mam Simonne, who used to be called Momonne. "Yes, Mam Momonne is still making the flour and the cassavas . . ."

In 1975, after the death of their parents, Mina and Rosalia had eaten a lot of manioc flour and cakes made by Louise's grandmother. Every Friday night the two sisters went down Morne Calvaire around six o'clock, took the Cambrefort road and went to stand in line in front of the drying tray in Fond Tany. At the time, Momonne spent the whole night making cassava cakes in order to go and sell them on Saturday morning in the Saint-Antoine marketplace in Pointe-à-Pitre. The black people in Piment fought over the cassava cakes that Mommonne rationed out stingily because she said she preferred to save the best ones for the city folks with fine white teeth who knew how to appreciate and pay a fair price for her fine white cakes. Momonne didn't touch the money. She kept her hands clean for the flour. Her daughter Bertha managed the till and every Friday, in keeping with tradition, there were sharp arguments as people waited in line. It was first come, first served . . . Momonne didn't raise an eyebrow, didn't hear a thing. She was completely absorbed in her art, like a painter with his canvas. A large jute apron girdling her middle, she stood alone in front of the heat from the oven, endlessly turning her cakes the whole night through, brow and underarms streaming sweat, a vacant look in her eye. She loved to sing. Her voice, even and poised, rose over the curses and imprecations of the ordinary folk haggling over a couple of cassava cakes, three cups of flour, and a half pint of *grabiot*.

Venus, you my friend who's so sincere
By my bed you sit so near
Is it tonight he will appear
To give me life and love so dear?

Momonne, who feigned not to see anyone, broke off her song when the two orphans arrived. You would have thought she had eyes in the back of her head, just as Mina and Rosalia stepped up to Bertha, she called out, "How many for you, sweet girls?"

"Two!" answered Mina.

"One, two, three!" Rosalia tripped on.

"Then let's make it four!" decided Momonne. *"Dé ba zot chak!* Two for each of you!"

"Dé ba zot chak!" repeated Rose looking astounded. *"Dé ba zot chak!"*

When Mina pulled the ten-franc bill out of her pocket, Momonne glared at her as if she were offended. *"Ou savé bien an pé pa pran lajan-aw! Kan-mèm! Kan mèm! Rantré kaz a zot! E pa lésé diab-la pwan zot an chimen!* You know very well we can't take your money! After all! After all! Go on back home and don't let the devil catch you on the way!"

Accompanied by Momonne's languorous refrain, Mina and Rosalia cut through the envious crowd with their treasure, coveted by all, wrapped in gray paper. They broke the first cassava cake in two and ate it on their way, praying that the spirits and the demons in the neighborhood weren't too ravenous, would wait until they reached home to invest the roads and inhabit the trees. The second cassava cake, dipped in milk, made up their breakfast the next day. They resisted as long as possible before tackling the last two, already stiffening a little, but they always succumbed during the afternoon, as soon as hunger started croaking in their bellies.

"You got to go see her!" ordered Louise, running the hand that served the cassava cakes through her wavy hair, inherited from her black and Indian ancestors. "She hardly goes out no more. I'll tell her you came by. She'll be pleased."

Mina promised, then walked away very quickly. Suddenly overwhelmed with a yearning to go see the old people from her childhood, to sit down on a bit of bench next to them on the veranda. A yearning to sit and sip on the fruit punch that they would inevitably offer her. A yearning to listen to them bandying the Creole accent around in their mouths. Soak in it. A yearning to feel truly at home in Piment once again . . .

So, instead of walking over to the beach, Mina turned left into Rue Shœlcher, the street that led to Eleanor Rutice's white house. Her first grade school teacher, the first person who had made an impression on her.

The schoolmistress had taught her how to read and write. She'd also attempted to teach Rose the rudiments of literacy. One Saturday, streaming with sweat and breathing harder than an old cow, she had appeared atop Morne Calvaire. Her mission: to persuade Melchior that Rosalia should have access to reading and writing. He laughed in her face.

"With all due respect, Mamzell Rutice, if I understand you properly, you want to teach this big dummy? Ha! Ha! Ha!"

The sun made her squint, but Eleanor Rutice remained there straight as a board, standing her ground on those tree-trunk legs of hers, convinced that everyone had a right to schooling and that she had a moral duty to dispense it.

"Rosalia will be able to do it . . . You have to try before giving up, Mister Montério."

Melchior tightened his belt a notch, patted his green snake-skin wallet, planted his cutlass straight up between his boots and doubled over, splitting his sides with laughter.

"No offense, but you must have time to waste, Mamzell Rutice . . ."

"Don't laugh, Mister Montério. She's your daughter after all. Your own flesh and blood. It's not Rosalia's fault that she isn't normal . . . You should be happy I've taken an interest in her future. You really should have been the one to have thought . . ."

Just then, the laughter in Melchior's throat stopped abruptly. He interrupted the schoolteacher with an irreverent gesture that looked as if he were threatening to slap her and pinch her nipple at the same time. Three stern lines crossed his forehead. He cast a dark look at Médée who had stopped short, both hands closed over the broom handle. At her feet, Rosalia sorted through the dust, putting the roaches, beetles, and red spiders to one side. She heard her name, knew they were talking about her, but never lifted her head.

"My daughter! That poor depraved girl . . . My word, if I'm not mistaken—I don't have you're fancy education—you're lecturing me, Melchior Montério!"

"I didn't . . ." began the schoolteacher.

Melchior thumped his chest. "You come climbing up here on my territory! I believe I right to say I'm still the proprietor of this land. And without even making an appointment! You come putting me on trial . . . What you know about life, Mamzell Rutice? What in God's name is in your mind? It's a waste of my time listening to your little song—la di da, la di da—like a child, and I old enough to be your father! You'd best be off now, Mamzell Rutice . . . I don't want to treat you no disrespect . . . But I already feeling an itch in my throat."

Rosalia briskly ripped the feelers off a roach.

184

Being the obliging kind, Mamzell swallowed her tears and her good intentions. She wiped her forehead, smoothed her skirt over her round bottom and smiled apologetically to the assistance—Médée, Mina, and Rosalia. When she bid them goodbye, all that remained of the roach was a powder between Rose's fingers.

Was Miss Rutice still alive? If so, she would be almost sixty . . .

The façade of her concrete house was now painted pink. On the balcony off the first floor, huge panties were drying on a line strung over a tight row of potted succulent plants. The door that opened onto the veranda was half-open.

Mina stayed at the teacher's house for two hours. Eleanor's voice was still clear and steady, she hadn't forgotten a thing about the years she devoted to educating the people of Piment. She remembered Rose perfectly well . . .

"I can still see her in front of the school . . . Poor girl . . . It broke my heart . . . I could have done something for her . . . You remember, I tried . . ."

"It didn't interest her, Miss Rutice . . ."

"It didn't interest your father!" protested the ex-school-teacher, stamping her foot—something she used to do when faced with a difficult pupil. "God have pity on her soul," she went on. "I've often thought of your sister . . . In my prayers, I've always mentioned her to the Lord . . . And have they told you she came back to Piment?"

"Yes, I know . . ."

"When I learned of it, I started dreaming about her. You won't believe it, she came into my class, sat down and asked me to teach her how to read and write. It disturbed me to have those strange dreams. Everyone said she was wandering around the town and in the countryside. I never saw her my-self . . . You know, I don't usually give much credit to what's said in Piment. I know these people too well: they'll quickly make a mountain out of a molehill around here! But people

185

who don't usually repeat pointless stories assured me they'd seen her. You remember Mrs. Dauchamp, the postmistress and Mr. Jetty too, who works at the registry office—his son is now a doctor in Bordeaux . . . Well they saw her! So I told myself that I hadn't been mistaken back then. That child could have had elementary schooling. She was asking for it in my dreams, you should have seen her! Straight as a board in her chair, holding her pencil in her right hand. Should have seen her copying her letters! And counting, I swear! She was really applying herself, believe me . . . who told you she'd come back?"

"Suzon, I'm staying with her."

Miss Rutice frowned. After a moment's silence, she ended up offering something to drink and then suddenly turned her attention to France, talked of her last trip over to the metropolis, recited the names of a few departments and jokingly, like back in school, asked Mina if she remembered the prefectures.

Tomorrow I'll go to the beach, Mina promised herself as she left her former teacher. It's too late now. I have to see Silène before going back to Suzon's, Silène Couba . . .

Night was already spreading its dark cloak over Piment.

Silène Couba's cabin was identical to Suzon's. Same state of blatant disrepair, same solitude, same poverty. On either side the older buildings had given way to two new five-story structures. Two concrete sentinels that preserved it from ultimate collapse and fended off cyclones. In one glance you could see the sheet metal was hanging on by a single nail, the boards were rotten to the core. However, contrary to Suzon's cabin, this one was filled with voices and the cries of children cavorting from one room to the next. A reggae concert spitting out of a radio set the tempo for the questions on a TV quiz show.

Mina walked along the unlit gallery and announced herself by calling to Silène. The voices immediately fell silent, the shouts stopped short. After a moment—time enough for a

question thrown out to the rap chorus that fell into a trance—
a teenager with a rasta hairdo reached his face through an
open window.

"*Ki moun ki la?* Who's out there?" he asked.

"Mina! Mina Montério. I've come to say hello to Silène. I'm
on vacation and . . ."

"Wait a minute, all right? I'll tell her."

His head disappeared immediately, as if yanked in by an invisible hand.

There was some whispering, a rush of commotion, broken
dishes. After an interminable wait, a woman, barefoot and
pregnant under her Mickey Mouse T-shirt, swung the door
open wide. A baseball cap worn sideways sat roosting on her
neat braids and bony childish face.

"*Man Lèlène ka vini . . . Ou pé antré . . .* Mam Silène will be
right here . . . You can come in . . ."

The living room, with its bawling television niched in a cup-
board like a venerated Virgin in its chapel, seemed to be on the
eve of house moving. A rustic style sofa with chipped varnish
on the arms sagged under a mountain of ironing. Scattered
about the floor were mucky, abandoned tennis shoes and
moribund tongs of different sizes. A baby with a pacifier stuck
in its mouth slept on a yellow foam mattress thrown down at
the foot of an old console table. On the table an incalculable
number of plastic cups and aluminum tins formed a circle
around an empty bottle of Coca-Cola and a pizza box bleed-
ing thick tomato sauce.

Mina felt as if she'd walked into an arena. An army of eyes
were trained on her. Isa, Silène's daughter, lived at her mother's
with her seven children ranging in age between twenty-five and
twelve. She was herself already a grandmother, twice over. Her
eldest daughter, Doriane was expecting her third child. Isa was
fifty-one years old, Olga's age . . .

Those two had once been friends, before Olga went away to
Point-à-Pitre to go to secretary school. Isa still had the slightly

slanted eyes of her youth that—back in the '60s—had earned her the nickname "China" that she used to love to hear on men's lips. Elected Miss Piment in 1967, she was considered to be, without the shadow of a doubt, the prettiest girl in Guadeloupe. Having reached the height of her fame, depositary of many high hopes, she orchestrated her own downfall by first getting hooked on and then into trouble with a policeman she met one night at the fair in Petit-Canal where she'd gone to dance and lose her soul, hiking up her pastel flowered dress to the diabolical rhythms of the musicians of "Typical"—poor China . . .

The year of the fire, Isa was thirty, already three children from different fathers underfoot and two bitter lines like those of her mother, at each corner of her mouth. Her breasts had collapsed. Her bulging belly that she still showed boldly— dress with open panels—was marked with ugly stretch marks. People spoke of her with contempt, swore that China—Miss Piment of 1967!—truly was the daughter of Silène, The Crab, who had never had any other descendants because she'd performed seventy-five abortions in the lean-to of her courtyard, right in the middle of town, only a few feet from the church, Lord . . .

Back in the days when she thought of herself as Marilyn Monroe, Médée had been a close acquaintance of Silène's. She felt tied to the woman, seeing as how the upstanding folks of Piment refused to acknowledge her existence in any way. No one would ever have dared to say anything against Médée in front of Silène. At the time, Isa was her mother's pride and joy, Silène promised her a brilliant career as a lawyer or a doctor. Then at the age when the first blood runs, Isa turned her back on school. As if a crosswind had suddenly caused her to deviate from her predestined course. She suddenly began to pay much closer attention to her long legs that flatterers said had been modeled by God's hands. To her slanted eyes, inherited from the fortunate intermixing of populations. To her white teeth, pearls of the Orient. To her titties, firm and erect as two lead goblets. To her slim waist.

The books she had so cherished ended their reign in the chicken house. For a long time, rats and mice lived it up, feasting on the glossy paper and French words, the tales of Tom Thumb, Little Red Riding Hood, and Cinderella.

Silène, preceded by heavy clouds of eau de Cologne, made her royal entrance.

"Mina! It really is you! I only know one . . . Médée's Mina! Ah, sweetie! It's been such a long time . . . Come here honey, let me take you in my arms . . ."

Silène opened her arms and closed them over Mina whom she held close to her in a prolonged hug.

"How many, many years you been gone?"

"Twenty-one . . ."

"Twenty-one years," said Silène in astonishment. "I can't believe it. No, you ain't changed. You got any children?"

"No, no children."

"That's good," declared Silène flopping herself down into the only rocker in the living room. "I only had one, and look where it got me," she sighed and glanced remorsefully at Isa, her eyes sweeping over her daughter's offspring. "I was ahead of my day. Can you imagine if I'd had two? Thank you, Lord! Isa don't want to understand that but—you agree with me Mina!—farrowing every year like a mama pig just ain't done no more. Wiggling your bottom in bed is fine fun! But then what . . . But then what . . ."

She crossed herself, shaking her head. Her eyes began rolling pathetically in her head, her chin jerking at all of Isa's children—each in turn—who seemed destined to reproduce infinitely.

Silène Couba, The Crab of the past had not grown old in the way one might have expected. Repented from her wayward youth and her reputation as an abortionist, she was the incarnation of wisdom and serenity befitting her age. The furrows on her face had almost disappeared, as if she'd willed all of her rancor to Isa, who seemed even more wilted, more embittered than she.

Of course they spoke of Piment in the old days, its great legendary figures: Melchior, Médée, Rose . . . Indispensable preliminary passageway, a means of setting the scene in its historical context in order to reach out to one another, recognize one another after those twenty-one years. And, since memories always bring back still other, older recollections—ones that have been deeply buried, lost in the cortege of laughter, tears, and sighs—they lost track of time. When Mina looked at her watch, it was ten o'clock. Doriane had already put her children to bed. The TV continued to soliloquize and address the emptiness. Isa, who hadn't been invited to the reunion, was out on the gallery taking the cool night air.

"It's late, I have to get back . . ."

"Watch out for Mignard," advised Silène, abandoning the rocker. "You know I never liked her . . . When Rose came back to Piment, I even thought it was to make Suzon pay her debt. What jealousy did to your family is a true a tragedy, ain't that right? I swear . . . if I didn't have so many people at home, you could stay here . . . But you see! Isa learned too late that she'd had too many children. Some people just don't know when to stop . . . And Doriane is already on her third . . . You weren't so foolish . . ."

"I'm no better than your . . ." Mina began.

"Hush," Silène cut in. "Isa don't need no one to defend her." She lowered her voice.

"We can't talk now, but come back and see me in the daytime, when they won't be under our feet . . . I got more to tell you about Médée and Melchior . . . and Suzon . . . And promise you'll be careful, all right? Don't let her do you no harm."

XXI

Mina kept her ears open all night long, listening to the sound of the other woman breathing. Struggling to stay awake. She was haunted by strange thoughts mingled with dream-visions of Rose's paintings, Miss Rutice's pointed silences, and Silène

Couba's repeated warnings. She tried to fight them off, calling upon the aid of reason, but dark recollections drifted slowly back up into the light of her memory. Suzon's face growing gradually more distorted as the past emerged from the shadows. At first haltingly, stumbling, stammering, stagnating, then in furious waves, rushing to fill up Mina's head. And as fear and doubt gained ground, the cabin, plunged in darkness, seemed to be panting, suffocating, heaving, gasping.

When the sheet metal roof began to weep and the beams to creak, Mina thought she would die of fright. In Suzon's room, the flame of a votive candle began to flicker. That is when, in the play of shadows, the creatures appeared.

Médée, her mother, covered with blood.

Melchior, stricken by lightning.

Rose, surrounded with flames.

Marie-Perle, drowned and bedraggled.

All of them drug up from the earth's entrails. In tatters. Worms coming out of their eyes. Their mouths, filled with rocks, begging for justice and truth.

With a tight knot in her throat, controlling her movements so as not to frighten the shadows, Mina slowly pulled the sheet up over her head. But the creatures came forward, made a circle around her. At times they grew long and stretched up to the roof beams of the cabin, at times they enveloped her before crumpling to the floor, other times they disappeared, were whisked away, dissipated.

At three o'clock in the morning, Mina tried to overcome her fear. She sat up. Got to her feet. Tiptoed over to Suzon's room. The floorboards creaked several times under her steps. Bound to one another with the same fear, the creatures shrank quickly back to a corner of the parlor.

On her bed, Mignard lay drowsing, her clouded eyes open in the half-dark. Her left hand clutching the three crosses at her neck looked like an old lion's paw. Mina stood leaning over the evil woman for a long time, petrified, staring at her face.

Her brow bore the deep lines of past torments. The breath coming from her sunken mouth smelled of the slaughter-house and made the flame of the candle dance on the night table. Twenty-one years ago, Mina had been in that very room. In that very bed. Smelling that same fetid breath.

They had come back from the cemetery.

They had left Rosalia back there.

Under the shovelfuls of earth.

In the coffin that men — in a hurry to finish the job — had hammered noisily shut.

On the way back, Suzon had held her up like a mother.

And then Mina saw the flames.

Coming from inside Suzon's cabin.

High flames.

The house was on fire.

She screamed

But no one saw them.

No one.

So Suzon had the doctor called.

"Hey so and so, Melchior's child has lost her mind!"

And then the doctor's long needle was stuck into her buttocks. Her left buttocks.

Almost immediately, she began seeing double, sinking away.

Head and ears full of cotton.

Arms and legs numb.

And then sleep. She tried to keep her eyes open, to see how she was going to die, burn up like Rosalia. But the doctor stepped through the flames.

He left.

"Take good care of her, Suzon."

And Suzon had answered:

"Pa okipé-w dokté! Konsidéré sé fi an-mwen ki-la . . . Don't you worry about that doctor. That girl is like my own daugh-ter."

Suzon was sitting next to the bed. She glared at Mina as if

she were going to strangle her, chop her to bits, suffocate her. She repeated several times *"Pa okipé-w dokté! Pa okipé-w dokté!* Don't worry doctor!" Sounding more menacing each time. And there were curses mingled in with her muffled threats.

Mina was fourteen years old. She opened her eyes several times as she sank into oblivion. Suzon's words barely made their way into her mind before being engulfed in the rising darkness. The woman seemed to be conversing with invisibles.

"Don't go tempting me, my sweet things! My hands are clean. Don't make me do it, my little angels . . . Yes he used me . . ."

Suzon grabbed a cushion. Faded blue satin.

"Sweet as honey, my virgin *coucoune* . . . Yes he did, he thrust his rod in and got his thrills from my body. He said, 'You my wife, Suzon. My wife for life.' . . ."

Suzon was brandishing a cutlass.

"Yes you right, my loves . . . There we were the two of us, stuck fast together. The mango tree was in bloom. Yes, he promised he'd never set eyes on another woman. Said he wasn't no ladies man. Said there would be only me, his Suzon. Told me we would take a fine trip to the Metropolis . . ."

Suzon was shaking a jar of hot peppers threateningly.

"You absolutely right, sweethearts. He swore before God. Yes, my little ones, yes, I know . . . You thirsty for my milk. You hungering after justice."

Suzon was holding a huge mallet with both hands.

"I waited, like some poor dog, at his door. I counted the years. And the marriages. And the children, stupid fool. I kept my coucoune dry for him. I didn't spill none of the honey he was so fond of. I never let anyone but him know my honey . . ."

Twenty-one years later, Mina was in a sweat. Seventy-two-year-old Suzon belched. In the next room the shadows started whimpering.

Twenty-one years later, standing next to the old sorceress,

Mina clearly remembered the pillow pressed firmly against her face. The smell of old satin. And then Rosalia had thrown out her flames. A blast of heat engulfed Suzon. Burned her neck and fingers. She let out a hoarse cry. The shutter was flung open. Suzon's hands ripped apart. The cushion flew out into the street.

All night long Rosalia and her flames had stood guard over Mina, staving off Suzon's homicidal attempts. Cushion, cutlass, clothes iron, rope, hammer, rock, bottle, stick, centipede . . . The flames blazed furiously each time, burning Suzon's hands, neck, eyes a little more. In the morning she finally realized the child was protected.

Mina went back to her bed in the middle of the night. She felt like fleeing her old stepmother. Going back to France the next day. But the shadows made a circle around her, hand in hand. Their eyes said in the same breath, "Now you know . . . Now you know . . ."

XXII

"If you're alone, Victor, we'll find some friends for you," whispered the girl who had welcomed him and shown him to his room. "The hotel's real friendly, you'll see tomorrow!"

She had eyes like a curious rat.

"Are you more the beach boy or the hiker type? You'll need to sign up for activities and excursions too, I'm counting on you . . . And in the evening there's a karaoke. Are you a singer? The clients just love it. Oh! I forgot the most important thing, my name is Channel. If you need anything, any little thing, just ask for Channel. In the mornings, I'm in the fitness classes, relaxation, stretching, anti-stress . . . People really need it. Running around Paris all year long. It does wonders . . . I'm counting on you Victor, okay?"

Dazed from the eight-hour flight, washed out from three anxiety attacks (the first at takeoff, another at thirty thousand feet in the middle of an air pocket, and the last upon landing) that he'd survived thanks to a good dose of tranquilizers, Victor gave her a haggard look, wondering confusedly why the girl was counting on him so much. He, who'd come from no place in particular, and hardly knew where he was going.

"You're tired, that's understandable. The trip, jet lag, the heat, the local transportation . . . After a good night's sleep, you'll be in great shape. I'm counting on you, right? Room 108. How lucky you are! You're almost right on the beach . . . By the way, it's all right with you if we call each other by our first names, isn't it? It's so much more friendly on vacation, it helps break the ice faster . . ."

In a gesture she'd repeated a hundred times over, she drew aside the curtain to point out the sea just a few feet away. Her biceps are incredibly developed, Victor remarked.

"Be careful to lock up after yourself. Thieves are no rarity around here. They hold up the clients. We have guards, but you can never be too cautious. Use the safe . . ."

At those words, she switched on the button to the air conditioner briskly, tightened her pareo around her slim waist, looking like a black belt judoka standing on her tatami, and wished him a good night's sleep and a fine vacation. Then, with a Queen of the Bodybuilders smile, her sunburned face broke into a thousand tiny wrinkles.

It took him some time to get to sleep. Because of the noise the sea was making. Because of a couple of bloodthirsty mosquitoes—tropical nightmare promising fever, shivers and slow death. Because of the purring of the air conditioner that he had switched off and on several times. Because of Bénédicte's voice shouting in his head, "That a boy Victor. You've taken the first step. You're in Guadeloupe. You're going to get rid of your ghosts. All you got to do now is follow my instructions . . ." He slept a little even so, in fits and starts.

Tuesday 21. He got up before dawn. Went and stood at the window and watched the day break from the bay window with

195

hooded eyes. The sea was so close. In the event of a sudden tidal wave, no time to flee, he thought. In the distance, islands in animal shapes, rounded backs under the cloud-filled sky. A slight, fleeting sensation of anxiety shot through his chest. Weren't those islands really monsters? You never know what might happen in foreign lands, he thought ruefully, dragging himself to the sparkling white bathroom.

He rummaged through his cosmetic bag, swallowed some tranquilizers and other anti-depressants. He hadn't wanted to admit it to himself in Paris, but his initial euphoria was wearing thinner each day. His familiar antagonistic anxieties were charging back in full force. What became of my lofty hopes of finding a cure? Victor wondered, as he observed his reflection critically in the mirror, stomach held in, chest stuck out. Still, he'd gotten on that plane to Guadeloupe. Why? He wasn't really sure anymore. Maybe in remembrance of his time passed in Esquirol, of his meeting with Bénédicte, of the times when they shared the same bench and cigarette on the hospital grounds. He had really believed that three ghosts were walking behind him, just as Bénédicte claimed, wide-eyed. Three ghosts that were responsible for his illness. Was it enough to take this trip to Guadeloupe to be free of them? All of that seemed so far away now, so crazy. "You'll have to learn to live with your illness, Mr. Clément," his psychiatrist had told him. "You'll have to get used to the idea . . . And you must never go off your treatment! Think of yourself as being afflicted with a chronic illness . . ." If Channel but knew, if old age but could . . .

He put on a pair of shorts that made him look like the average tourist on vacation, a T-shirt and some plastic beach slippers, locked the door to his room thinking of rude intruders, and made his way to the vast patio with exotic décor that he'd already seen in the travel agent's brochure in Paris. He wandered around a while before finding an empty table by the pool, hidden in a jumble of plants that reminded him of the Mundo Night. The clients were all white, more or less well-tanned. Many sported bright red, ragged, and shredding backs. The men's legs were covered with hair. Smooth and golden, those of the women. There were whole tables full of them, veterans of various clubs and tourist circuits, they laughed loudly. Sparkling white false teeth. Lips painted blood red. Bracelets jangling at their wrists.

He felt very white amongst the whites, next to the blacks who were serving coffee, pushing a rake on the lawn, watering the plants, cleaning the pool. Before I take a present to Bénédicte's niece, I need to get a little tanned, he decided as he finished up his breakfast. Looking sullen and detached, he made his way over to the beach, contemplated the sea once again. In the distance, an ocean liner slipped along the line of the horizon. Small sailboats danced through the waves. Closer to shore, people swam and jumped around in the water. It was already very hot. Five thousand miles and his old depression was still with him, thriving like a tropical plant instead of drying up in the sun.

Everything around him seemed to be organized in a way that he couldn't grasp, that excluded him. No one is waiting for me here, he said in walking toward the sea with halting steps. No one feels like coming near me. He let the little waves come up and lap at his feet. Everyone has a role. And I stick out in the scene. People selling trinkets, souvenirs, and bathing suits. Cold drink vendors. Copper-colored jogger with slick, oiled pectorals crisscrossing the beach like a robot. Woman with round breasts lying languidly in the sun. Father building castles. Retired couple under straw hats. Eager lover. Nubile girls. Ageing Adonises and playboys.

A ball hit him right in the head just when he spotted an unoccupied straw umbrella a little off to one side from the others. It was as if he'd received the order to leave. He went immediately back to his room. Spent his first day between the bed and the rotin armchair placed on the narrow veranda that opened onto the beach, telling himself that he was still suffering from jetlag and travel weariness, that he'd feel better the next day.

At six o'clock the sun set abruptly. On the abandoned beach, the coconut trees began to look threatening. Victor thought he saw the shadow of a thief behind a hedge of hibiscus. He went quickly back into the room. Heart racing, he waited a little while standing guard at the bay window, imagining all sorts of catastrophic scenarios: being kidnapped and held for ransom by a fringe group of Guadeloupe separatists, a time-bomb hidden under his veranda, a heart attack, an earthquake, a plane crashing on his room, an attack of malaria . . .

After two–three minutes that seemed to him like hours, he heard people laughing. German tourists back from their excursion coming into the hotel to pilfer some food. His heart gradually regained its normal rhythm. Victor finally calmed down when a wild zouk tune filled his room. He would have liked to write a book about the story of his life. Someone had suggested it once. It was — people said — a form of therapy. He promised himself to start on it soon, maybe upon his return to Paris, and congratulated himself about having made the decision. Contemplating his reflection in the bathroom mirror, he found he looked a little less pitiful. He took a Stilnox and got into bed, stomach empty, heart uncertain. Outside at the karaoke, the vacationers all chimed in to sing the chorus of a Stone and Charden song about dairy cows and Normandy.

XXIII

Wednesday December 22, 1999

Mina got up as if everything were normal. She rolled up her mattress, folded her sheets and went to the kitchen to make coffee. Up since the peep of dawn, her Bible opened on her knees, the old woman sat praying in her rocker. Mina had to pretend to be the joyous, grateful Mina of yesterday. As if night had brought her nothing but sleep and sweet dreams.

198

"This afternoon I'm going to the funeral of a girl I went to school with long ago, Mina. Maybe you recall her, Mamzell Eloïse Borges. She knew your poor papa well . . ."

"What did you say her name was, friend?"

"Borges! Eloïse Borges! Her nephew coming to pick me up at three o'clock. There's room in the car for you . . . You . . ."

"Oh! I don't think I want to go to the funeral . . ."

"She knew your father! Even if you don't remember her, you should accompany her to the cemetery!"

"Next time, friend. Next time, I promise."

"What next time? I not talking about going to a dance . . ."

Suzon fidgeted a bit in her rocker.

"I have things to . . ."

"What things?" exclaimed Suzon, in a worried voice.

"People to . . ."

"I hope you ain't got no idea to go sit by those old gossip boxes in Piment! Why don't you go to the seashore?"

"That's precisely where I'm going this afternoon."

"Good. That's fine. I highly prefer that."

"What would you like to eat for lunch, friend?"

"Fish!" hissed the old woman.

Mina washed the bowls that had been left in the sink. The radio began to emit a vapid love zouk. She took up the refrain while Suzon's blind eyes dug between her shoulder blades.

Across the street from town hall, the market place was still the same as she remembered it. The same vendors sitting behind the same rotten wood stalls, offering the same fruits and vegetables arranged in pyramids. True, the women had grown older, thicker, or had shriveled. But they seemed fixed there for eternity. They remained both masters and slaves of this marketplace to which they returned every day of their lives, come wind or come rain, after cyclones and funerals, in the middle of the dry season or Carnival. They watched time passing, people passing, automobiles, marriages, and funeral processions, watched torments passing. They were all there, in their

199

same places . . . Gloria Destanges who sold Médée's yams, purslane, and spinach. The Indian woman Didi Ramoussamy, spice queen, who ground her own colombo curry. Théodora, who had the best avocados in Piment when the season was right. Bérénice, the hot-blooded chabine who called her customers Honey but hated to haggle over prices. Yvelle Compère, Marie-Camille, Féfé Radonis, Sylvaine Trouchamp, Bébé Cador, Mercuria Totémis, Pépette César, wife of a fisherman and inevitably a fishmonger.

Mina would have liked to introduce herself to each of the women, talk about Médée, but she didn't have much time. She went and stood in front of Pépette César who recognized her immediately.

"Is that really you, Médée's little *ti moun* child? Mina!"

"Yes, I'm on vacation. How are you, Mam Pépette?"

"My health is fragile. What about you? *Ou savé sè a w viré?* You know your sister came back?"

"Yes, I know. Suzon told me. I'm staying at her place . . ."

"Huh!!!!"

Pépette frowned, shook her head and picked up her cutlass.

"How much you want? A kilo? Two?"

"One kilo will do."

"You shouldn't be in that creature's house," groaned Pépette slicing the fish as if she were chopping up heathens.

"I know," whispered Mina.

"I'm adding a slice for your sister, you never know . . . And take care of yourself, hear?"

Other women had recognized her and were calling out, "Honey! Come buy from me! Sweetheart! Come see Sylvaine! Médée's Mina! Why you running off?"

Mina left the marketplace as fast as she could and went down Rue Hortense, pursued by the cries of the vendors in the market.

When she came up in front of Silène Couba's cabin, she was drenched in sweat and her legs felt wobbly. Even though she hadn't made an appointment, Silène seemed to be waiting for her.

"I can't stay long," Mina began. "I told Suzon I was only going to the market. She doesn't want me to talk with folks."

"That's no surprise," grumbled Silène. "She scared . . ."

"What did you want to tell me?"

"You got to hear the story of your parents. I learned it straight from your father's lips."

Silène signed herself, smoothed her hair down with both hands, as if she were putting her thoughts in order.

"I don't know where to start . . ."

"Start from the beginning," Mina suggested in Lysia's firm tone of voice.

"It goes back a long way, a very long way . . . Even before your father was born. I won't finish by nightfall . . ."

"Hurry up Silène!"

"It ain't easy child! Got to give time some time. I not even sure I should be telling you these things . . ."

Silène closed her eyes. Then opened them suddenly. Her gaze fixed on a vase sitting on a shelf, she remained silent for a long time. Sinking back into the past. Gathering together the images and the characters in her story.

"I having trouble finding the words. They running away from my tongue, Mina."

"Try again."

"I not sure now if I got the right to dig up all that . . ."

"Do it for me, Silène. Do it for Médée and Rosalia."

"Yes, you right . . . The evil ones must pay. Suzon must go to hell."

The old Crab swallowed a gulp of ice water and started talking.

"You know the story of your great-grandmother Séléna. Your ancestor who bought a homeland for her goats. I don't need to tell you about that, do I? She had a son, you know, Gabriel who married Nana Salibur, a girl from Grands-Fonds.

201

They had three boys: first Melchior, and then Ferdy, and Grégoire. You know all that, right? After ten years of marriage, Nana went back to live in Grands-Fonds with the two younger children. Melchior chose to live in Piment with his father Gabriel. I went to school with Melchior. We were the same age. Just like Suzon was. Those two fell in love as early as first grade, you can take my word for that. They were as interdependent as finger and thumb. I saw them petting on the playground. They couldn't stop their hands. There was a force drawing them to one another. They didn't hide it. Your father told everyone he was going to marry his Suzon and that he'd take her to France. It was just kid talk. The teachers laughed about it. We, the other kids, teased them. In those days, my heart beat a little faster for Melchior, but he only had eyes for his queen. Suzon's mama whipped her for that. She didn't want to have nothing to do with that nigger from the hills. Anyway, Suzon became a woman. One night, she went to bed a child and the next morning she woke up in a woman's body. Titties as big as two pumpkins! A large bottom split into two round apples! Eyes and mouth tempting enough to damn a saint! Melchior thought he'd sprouted wings. He'd inherited the most beautiful girl in Piment. So he fawned over her all day long . . . Suzon this, Suzon that . . . Sweetheart . . . Honeypie . . . When she gave him her flower, standing up at the foot of the mango tree, it seemed only natural. And then . . ."

"And then . . .," Mina murmured.

"And then . . . It was all over with! Adieu Suzon! Adieu, eternal love and life in France!!! Door shut, mouths closed . . ."

Silène took a swallow of water.

"And then, that was all. And that was when the misfortunes began. Your father turned his back on her, all of a sudden. He took back his fine promises and went off to find that Marie-Perle from Anse-Bertrand who gave him Olga while Suzon went crazy with her mama. Misfortunes and maledictions . . . The first time he was widowed, Suzon came to offer him her life and her body. But he didn't even look at her. You know she almost joined the Carmelite sisters? Broken heart. Now we getting to Médée, your poor mama. Poor woman, she didn't know what she was getting into . . . Suzon sure didn't spare nothing. People saw her faithfully visiting some fifty *gadèzafès* . . . Only two–three folk in Piment know that her only purpose in life was to destroy Melchior, his wives and their descendents. But who would stick their neck out? Who would hold up their hand at the courthouse and say, 'I was sitting in Serpicon or Botinious's waiting room and I saw Miss Mignard come out the consulting room?' Who would dare accuse that Suzon Mignard, who's constantly in the confessional box?"

"Why wasn't it possible?" asked Mina.

"Why! Why! There ain't no reason, except jealousy, spite, cowardice . . . You been in France too long, you can't understand . . ."

"Keep talking, Mam Silène . . ."

"Suzon wasn't no friend of mine . . . Yet one day I ran into your papa coming out of town. You was already born. That was in the early seventies. With his cutlass on his shoulder, he was walking along the road like a weary old soul, worn out from life, a resentful man that had just missed his destiny. I couldn't refrain, I asked him. Why you leave Suzon Mignard like that? Why you didn't want to marry her? Why you putting her through this pain? Did she deserve this punishment, Melchior? He glared at me like I was blind and crazy. 'You got no right to judge me, Crab!' he said. 'I an innocent victim. Go hunt down evil in a body from another time. I just a lamb and demons are devouring my flesh.' He raised his eyes to heaven. Swiped at the guinea grass with his cutlass. Wiped a tear from his face and said the words I'm going to repeat to you exactly, 'I never stopped loving Suzon Mignard and I still love her more than my life . . .'"

"That's what he said to you?" exclaimed Mina, who suddenly saw her father sitting on the steps of the veranda, waiting for Delos, Suzon's brother, and—or so everyone thought—a letter from Olga.

"I didn't know what to say to him," continued Silène. "I just stood there all stupid in front of him as he looked up at the sky and then down at the mud stuck to his boots. Then he took his green snakeskin wallet out his back pocket. You remember the wallet he always carried, Mina . . . Well you know what he told me? That it was his only protection, that the day that wallet would be completely worn out, he would be struck down by lightning. I didn't believe him. I didn't believe none of his stories . . . I thought he was like all the other men I'd run across: lying, cowardly, stupid . . . He hadn't told me the real reasons. Suzon had swallowed his fine tale hook line and sinker. She'd wasted her life for that scoundrel who didn't know nothing about love. I turned my back on him, but he grabbed my arm, 'I going to tell you a secret, Crab. I ain't forcing you to believe me. You see, when Rose was born, the cord was wound around her body. Some children is born with the cord around their neck. But this was spectacular . . . Her whole body! She was blue and the cord was green. Green and hard. Hard and longer than you can imagine. A snake that got into Médée's belly to snuff Rose out, squeeze her limbs, strangle her, keep her blood from flowing and her mind from forming. You should have seen it, Crab! When dame Sophie started unwinding that snake, cutting it up into pieces with a small razor blade as she went along, she glanced at me sideways just like she were looking at the very Devil's son. She didn't say nothing, but a shudder ran down my back, Crab. Médée was bellowing like a cow having its throat cut. And I couldn't see the end of the snake, I swear. There were marks on the child's face and body like those made by a whip. After three hours of cutting away, Sophie held out a piece of the snake to me. 'You got to make something out of it that you'll use every day. Something you must never lose or lend. Bury the rest of the cord under a young traveler's tree that you'll go fetch in the forest and plant in front of the door. This child won't live long, it's best I tell you that now . . . But if you bury the cord at the foot of the traveler's tree, she'll grow wings for the day she wants to fly away. Don't get attached to her, Melchior . . .'"

Silène let her voice rest a moment.

"And then what?"

"Then I went on my way. I didn't want to hear no more. All that waste, all that unhappiness made me sick . . ."

"All those deaths," Mina added.

"Marie-Perle, Médée and her stillborn children, Melchior and Rosalia . . . So many pointless deaths . . . And why?" exclaimed Silène, who suddenly seemed short of breath, as if she'd awoken from a long nightmare. "Why? Why? You got to ask some questions over Nana Salibur's way, Mina. She's still alive. She knows more than I do. If she's still sound of mind, she'll tell you what happened between her and your grandfather Gabriel. She'll tell you why she went back to Grands-Fonds . . ."

"Nana Salibur, my grandmother . . . In Grands-Fonds . . ."

"He who seeks shall find, Mina. Time is nothing. The past is at the tips of your fingers. The living will guide you and the dead will escort you along the path to truth. After Rose, you've come back to Piment too and it sure ain't to go and sleep on the beach or drown in the ocean."

Mina looked at her watch.

"All right, I have to go, Suzon will be wondering where I am."

"Let her stew for a while. I got one last thing to tell you. About Médée. She's a woman I respected. She wanted your papa to be happy, but she could do nothing against the forces of evil. She paid for it with her life. I'm happy I talked with you, Mina. I feel relieved of a great weight. Seek and ye shall find! Now off with you! You are protected. If you've lived till now, it's so you can learn the truth," concluded Silène as solemnly as a venerable prophetess.

205

Suzon was fidgeting impatiently in her rocker. She got up several times to go out on the veranda. She called out to the passing shadows asking if they saw Mina coming, yes Melchior's Mina, sister to Rose who had created havoc in Piment the month before, the Mina who used to live up on Morne Calvaire . . .

"What you been up to?" she roared. "Where you been all this time? Just what you come back here for, eh? What you doing in my house if you . . . ?"

"I had to wait for the vendors. I was at the marketplace, friend. Don't be angry. Everything's all right, friend. Everything's all right . . . I'll go scale the fish and start the court-bouillon."

Suzon settled herself in the rocker, watching Mina walk away. Her wilted fingers trembled between the pages of her Bible as she tried to feel out the girl's mood and motivations from the sounds coming from the kitchen. Nothing to be alarmed about.

Relieved, she asked Mina to put the radio on the table so she could listen to the obituary notices, listen once again to the names of Eloïse Borges' parents, friends and allies.

At three o'clock sharp, the nephew of the deceased, a black man of fifty, came to Suzon's door. The jealous old woman had put on a purple satin and lace dress that stank of naphthalene. Her immense black hat was lumpy in several places and moth-eaten on the ribbon and the edges. Her patent leather pumps that dated back at least forty years were the work of a shoemaker from Piment whom Mina had forgotten. Her hose were covered with dust. She hadn't washed.

Suzon locked the door to the cabin and turned to face Mina. For an instant they stood motionless on the veranda, thrown back twenty-one years in time. Fixed in the same place; the same stance. Both of them realized in that instant, that they had everything to fear from the days to come. They gauged each other, estimating one another's strength. Suzon seemed to hesitate between going and staying. She tapped the three crosses at her neck with her fingertips. The cloud over her eyes turned green.

As soon as the car had gone, Mina went around to the back of the cabin and sat on the trunk of the avocado tree that a cyclone had flung to the ground in the '80s. She needed to wait a little, be cautious.

"Time is nothing," Silène had told her.

Heart racing, she nudged the door to the kitchen open with her foot at ten past three.

When it was closed up, despite the thorough cleaning she'd given it, Suzon's cabin stank even worse. Encrusted stench of old piss, vile prayers, ancient dust, demoniacal perfumes, diabolic incense, putrid thoughts . . .

First of all search the Hag's room. Empty the dresser drawers. Pull up the mattress and sink your fingers into its filthy forty-year old innards. She knew every move she would make, she had gone over them so many times in her mind. She had to act quickly, not dissipate her efforts, not panic, not tremble. Listen to her instinct, follow her intuition, trust in luck. And convince herself that she was going to find something . . . He who seeks shall find, Silène Couba had said to her.

He who seeks shall find!

He who seeks shall find!

He who seeks shall find!

XXIV

When he awoke, Victor was hungry. His night had been restless, filled with confusing dreams. He was around three or four years old, was holding a candle in his hand and watching his parents lying side by side on a bed that was floating above a cloud. Emilie and Edmond were wearing their Sunday clothes. Edmond was dead. His face was blue. His black lace-up shoes were shiny. Emilie was crying, crying, crying . . . And she kept saying, "O Dear God, I don't want to go on living! Take me along with my poor love! I want to die too."

That morning on the patio, the clients already seated around their tables seemed less unreal than the day before. Channel gave him a distant little wave. Victor responded with a friendly nod of the head, filled his tray at the buffet and walked to his table. He'd already swallowed a cup of coffee, two tranquilizers, his favorite antidepressant, and eaten three hard-boiled eggs when one of the waitresses came to ask him his room number.

"Number 108."

She was already walking away. He called her back. "Miss! Please could you tell me how to get to Goyave?"

"Well, you'll need to take the bus, Sir."

"Is there a bus station near here?"

"A station! There's no station, there's no bus here in town . . . You stand on the side of the road . . . When you see a bus coming, you wave it down and it will stop . . ."

"I could stand in front of the hotel. The bus will stop for me?"

"In front of the hotel or further down the road, whatever you like!"

"Oh good! And what time does the bus come by?"

"There's no fixed time. You just have to wait. When you see it coming, you raise your arm and it will stop."

"It will stop just for me, no matter where?"

"Yes, it will stop for you and you climb on board."

The woman seemed irritated. But Victor went on, "And do you have any idea how long I might have to wait?"

"Ah, my good man! I'm not in the transportation line!"

"Yes, but . . . If I might ask you one last question . . . And what happens then?"

"What happens then?"

"Yes, when I climb on board the bus?"

"Oh! Well, you simply tell him where you want him to let you off in Goyave. Do you have the address?"

Victor started rifling around in his wallet.

"I just arrived yesterday. This is the first time I've been in Guadeloupe. I have a package to give to a young . . ."

"They'll give you directions, Sir!" she cut in with a weary look on her face. "Get on the bus and ask the driver! It's as simple as that. You won't get lost around here."

At those words she made an about face.

She has every right to not smile, thought Victor, watching her walk away in her madras uniform that she evidently wore begrudgingly.

As he passed the sentry box at the entrance to the hotel, Victor felt as if he were leaving a fenced compound and entering the real world. He rejoiced. Once again believing he would soon be cured. Once again being absolutely convinced that three ghosts were walking in his steps and that their days were numbered ... Here I am in Guadeloupe at last, Bénédicte! The spell can be broken, at last. I'm going to make it, he kept thinking, as if he were trying to convince himself. And with a blissful smile lighting his face, he marched swiftly along, surprised to find himself in a state of such exuberance that—he was certain of it now—would bear him toward a bright future and painless tomorrows.

"Why you laughing like that, man?" asked the man who was walking toward him.

"Huh?" said Victor, startled.

The man before him, a tall black Rasta with the face of a strict judge, grabbed his arm.

"You laughing at me, man?"

"Not at all," protested Victor. "I didn't even see you."

"Ha! That's just what I thought."

He shook Victor, whipped him with his Rasta locks like the tentacles of an octopus and bit his lips before spitting out more accusations that seemed to multiply in his head as quickly as sewer rats in Paris.

"So you don't see me, eh? I not visible, eh man? I a man all the same ... Yet you saying I ain't one ... Look! I got two arms and two legs ... You already dead! You a white ghost! Hoo! Hoo!"

209

His breath smelled like a dead cat.

Across the street, two men were watching the scene, looking amused. Victor shuddered.

"I the invisible man, eh, man?"

"No, no! I can see you. Let go of me!"

"How much you got in your wallet, man? You came to get some kicks in the West Indies eh? Beaches and coconut trees! You came to buy some women, eh? Negresses and chabines . . . How much you willing to pay so I don't knock your head in?"

He tightened his grip a little and his dirty fingernails dug into Victor's flesh. The whites of his eyes were greenish and bloodshot.

"I'm not a tourist. I didn't come for that, believe me. I have no intention of indulging in sexual tourism . . ."

"Lay off the song and dance," Mister Jungle cut in.

"I'm sick you know . . . I came for a cure . . ."

"I don't give a shit!" snapped Jungle. "I want the bread . . . Gimme your bread . . ."

"I swear . . ."

The Rasta's jaw clenched tighter.

"The bread! You hear me?"

"I don't have much on me," said Victor.

A lump of anxiety was stuck in his throat.

"What's not much? You come to this country empty-handed . . . Come on! Bring out the money and let's get it over with . . ."

"Wait, let me look . . ."

A sly smile spread over the black man's lips.

"Come on! Cough up the bread! And we'll forget the whole thing. They call me Mister Jungle. Welcome to Guadeloupe, man."

Victor eased away. Pretended to be opening his backpack, looking for his billfold. And then, in a surge of bravery, he took off in a beeline, pursued by Mister Jungle's curses and the cheers of the onlookers, who had suddenly turned into his fervent supporters. Jungle vomited a few platefuls of insults on them and waved his arms like a Don Quixote from the tropics. He stood there for a moment rooted to the sidewalk, dazed, vacillating, before going on his way, hunger gnawing at his stomach and his brain eaten away by the daily crack.

Panting like an ox that's been grazing all day in a field of ganja, Victor came bursting into a small grocery and odds and ends store where three dull-eyed men sat in a dark corner, swigging down glasses of rum. Old ads and political posters papered the walls. A chandelier draped with spider webs sat on a rickety shelf. Empty boxes were piled on one of the tables in the bar and a three-legged chair with a broken cane seat was pushed under it. Above a door hung a crucifix with a palm branch stuck in it. The storekeeper, Gracieuse Palmort, was filling plastic bottles with kerosene.

"Good morning!" exclaimed Victor.

The woman didn't bother to answer and remained focused on her task.

"Excuse me, please. Do you serve lemonade?"

Gracieuse growled.

"Excuse me, ma'am, excuse me . . ."

"I heard you, no need to shout! Ain't no rush after all!" interrupted the woman with a sigh.

"Have a drink while you waiting. Can't be in no hurry around here. Cool it! You not in Paris!" shot one of the men from a corner of the bar.

"*I tro bonè ba sé mesyé!* It's too early for that gentleman to be coming to a bar!" his companion responded, pulling on the visor of his baseball cap. "*Ou ka di Blan pa ka bwè? Sé nèg ki invanté ronm!* Who says white folk don't drink? Black man invented rum." exclaimed Julien.

"Hey! Drink some rum! Pay for a drop! Raymond says that white folk don't drink this early . . ."

Old lady Gracieuse still had around ten bottles to fill. Victor could have left, just asked for directions in passing. He knew perfectly well that Guadeloupe was not all fun and games. Somewhat exhilarated from his victory in the confrontation with Mister Jungle, he suddenly felt like celebrating his arrival in the country, mingling with people. He didn't want to pass up an opportunity to drink with the locals.

He pulled up a chair defiantly. With knowing smiles, the three men opened up the circle, scooting their stools back in short thrusts. Victor sat down amongst them. With a glance, Edmond ordered Old Lady Palmort to make sure they had everything they needed. She immediately abandoned her bottle-filling activities and came back with a dented, chipped tray upon which danced a bottle of Trois-Rivières rum, a clean glass, and a pitcher of ice-water.

The men served themselves each in turn, copiously. Victor imitated them, lifting his elbow gingerly to show he was truly one of them: a man amongst men. A real man that could toss off a half glass of 110 proof rum in one gulp. He imitated them to melt the hard lump that was stuck in his throat, forgetting his promise of abstinence and, even more importantly, the fact that he swallowed a heavy dose of medicines every day.

"This the finest!" Raymond, the black with the baseball cap, promised him.

"Ain't no respect for tourists in this country!" railed Julien, glaring at Gracieuse.

"Tourists is king everywhere in the world. But here in Guadeloupe, this damn country full of Creole dogs, got no consideration."

"What your name?" asked Edmond.

"Victor . . . And you, Sir?"

"Victor, don't call me sir. We don't know that fancy French talk here. My name is Edmond."

"You on vacation here, Victor? At the hotel!"

"Yes, at the Tropicana Beach . . ."

"How many days you been here?"

"I arrived yesterday . . ."

"Ho! You don't want to go to the hotel!" advised Raymond.

He shook his head in disapproval.

"You won't see Guadeloupe if you stay at the hotel. Whites with Whites. You need to stay with a real family!"

"No! You sure don't want to go to no hotel!" Julien agreed, pouring down his rum in one clean swig. A gesture each of his drinking partners imitated one after the other.

"Why shouldn't I go to the hotel?" asked Victor in a worried tone as he savored his rum taking small sips, thinking that it certainly wasn't pure chance that he was sitting there drinking with Edmond. A sign . . .

"Drink it all in one gulp, Victor! Bottoms up!" urged Raymond fiddling with his cap.

Victor obeyed.

"My sister takes in vacationers, Victor. I can take you to her place if you like. Let's have a couple of drinks and then we'll go over there. You can have a tour of the place, right? The tour is free. Then you pick up your things at the hotel. And everything will be fine."

"You don't want to stay at the hotel!" repeated Julien.

"How much you pay a day, Victor?" asked Raymond.

He smiled amenably. He was missing at least three front teeth.

The rum slowly made its way through Victor's body. His thoughts were still straight, but he felt touched by the divine warmth that enters the blessed, traversed by extraordinary waves of energy, overwhelmed by a great wheel of joy, plunged into a bath of tropical flowers with heady fragrances.

"Somewhere around four hundred and fifty francs, I think."

"*Mesyé! Mesyé! Mesyé! A pa ti volè*! Man oh man! You being robbed!"

"A day?"

"Yes, that's about right, a day," stammered Victor.

"Four hundred and fifty francs? Four hundred and fifty francs! They robbing you Victor. You know how much she asking, my sister? And! And she'll feed you . . . Feed you local food! Fresh goat in curried colombo sauce! Fresh sea bream in court

213

bouillon! Fresh breakfast, lunch, and dinner! You know how much she asking?

"You don't want to stay at the hotel!" added Julien for emphasis.

"You know how much she asking, Victor?"

"No, I don't know. How much does she ask?" said Victor.

A fire had just started at the back of his neck. Antidepressants, tranquilizers, and rum.

"Get this, Victor! She asking two hundred and fifty francs. She has eight bungalows. Full all year round. The tourists pass her address around. If they wasn't satisfied, they wouldn't come back, right? They wouldn't go giving her address to their friends, right? The walls of the living room are covered with post cards from France. And! And! And even from Switzerland, Belgium, and Canada . . ."

"Two hundred and fifty francs! Room and board . . . When people leave they in tears, ain't that so, Julien?"

"That's right. The people is in tears . . ."

"But she might not have any room left," said Victor hazily.

"There's always a bungalow for a friend, Victor. My sister been working in tourism for ten years, fifteen years, what I'm saying? Sixteen years . . . She knows how to welcome folks. Don't worry about that! We'll get you a bungalow. You'll be happy as a lark in a park, Mark! And! And! And I didn't tell you the best part! You got the beach a hundred meters away . . . You decide, Victor . . . You the king . . ."

Raymond grasped the bottle. The three served themselves and pushed the rum toward Victor. His ears were red. Tiny bloodred threads were spreading through the whites of his eyes. A fire was roaring in his brain. He grabbed the bottle by the neck, welcomed himself to Guadeloupe again and poured out a healthy drink.

"Just two–three more drinks," Julien suggested. "Then we'll go over to Raymond's sister's house. You want to see the place, don't you?"

"It's up to Edmond to decide," answered Victor.

His tongue felt heavy, but he remained alert, trying harder than ever to watch for the signs of his destiny.

"Why it up to Edmond to decide? You a man ain't you?"

"My papa's name was Edmond," confided Victor.

"Ah! If your papa was named Edmond, then I don't hold it against you, Victor. That's respect for you . . . Gimme five, Victor! You a good guy, you are! No getting around it, you a good guy . . . and that's a rare thing with white folk . . ."

Three hours later they were still there, stuck in the bar, unable to abandon the rum and break the bond of friendship. They'd made the world over three times and rewrote History. In the end, each in turn had attempted to relate his tormented life in minute detail.

"Now we got to go to Georgette's," Raymond decided reluctantly, giving one last glance at the bottle to make sure there wasn't a dribble left for communion.

Edmond shook Victor who more or less succeeded in getting to his feet.

"The spell on me will soon be broken!" he declared to the company at large.

Then under the stunned gaze of Gracieuse, who was dusting off her counter, he put his arms around Edmond, called him papa, and burst into tears.

"Victor, you got to pay!" Julien whispered after a moment of respectful silence.

"In my bag. The black billfold," sniffled Victor between two sobs.

"Don't cry, son! You going to rest up at Georgette's."

"I have to go to Goyave. I promised Bénédicte. I have a date with Mina on Thursday. What day is it?"

"You'll go tomorrow. You in Guadeloupe here. We in no hurry."

"The spell on me will soon be broken," repeated Victor.

"I going to be the Pope soon!" scoffed Julien.

XXV

When Mina found the hammer and the small crowbar hidden under a handkerchief in the drawer of Suzon's night table, she knew immediately she had almost found what she was looking for.

She grabbed the tools. Swung around. Glanced about looking for a chest to wrench open or pick the lock to. If I had something to hide, she thought . . . Then she put herself in Suzon's place. Tore herself out of it immediately, terror-stricken and clawed by the sordid creatures she had awakened. Horrified, covered with thick spider webs, it seemed as if, in a quarter of a second, she had roamed three centuries through a labyrinth of caves. Had passed a thousand phantoms. Sloshed through rank waters in which swollen corpses floated that rats and monstrous fish were vying over. Mind racked with vociferations, weeping, gasping, she was on the verge of giving up. When a floorboard creaked underfoot. Like a painful cry . . . She squatted and felt with her fingertips first, the board that started moaning like a woman in labor.

"Do you have something to tell me?" Mina managed. "Are you the one who keeps Suzon's secrets? That's it, isn't it?"

Three fat rusty nails lifted their bent heads. Mina pried them up. Pulled on the board that came easily out, lifting at the same time, the two boards next to it. A wooden chest, made to fit the exact dimensions of the hole, was hidden there.

The chest contained two Princess shoeboxes, one tied up with twine, the second wound with a raw silk ribbon.

In the first box, lying in tight rows, were eighteen little black dolls. Nine of them were wrapped in blue cloth and placed on the left. Arranged on the right side, the other half were clothed in pink. A piece of cardboard separated them. At their feet, in a piece of tissue paper, were folded—very carefully—small pieces of clothing of every color, and shoes of all kinds.

The second box held Mignard's archives.

Fifty years of suffering. Fifty years of waiting.

Mortal prayers. Love letters. Proverbs, sayings.

Poems in verse and in prose. Psalms revised and corrected. Endless Jeremiads.

And . . .

A manual of black and white magic. Incantations. Supplications. Maledictions.

Strands of hair. Nail clippings.

And more . . .

Torn out of magazines, catalogs, newspapers, advice to mothers, the photo of a young bride (long wedding dress and trail 548 Francs), articles from *France Antilles.* "Death in the Curve."

And still more . . .

Couplets shamelessly satyric. Verse blatantly diabolic. Recipes vile and satanic. Phials filled with arsenic. Powdered gold, downright malefic. Bouquets of flowers wilted, sick.

Horror, nausea, and then, quickly, a feeling of pity seeing the meager relics of the love that had poisoned Suzon Mignard's life. Love denied, scorned, aborted eighteen times over. Passion that was both fierce and naïve at the same time. Madness . . .

Stunned, Mina set aside her fear, felt her anger—the resentment and the desire for vengeance that for an instant had consumed her heart—melt away. What use was it? It was all finished and done now. Adding more hate to so much hate wouldn't bring back the dead, she told herself. So she sat down on the bare floor and began gently caressing the eighteen dolls—nine girls and nine boys—as she contemplated her life in France, the parade of men she had met to fill up the emptiness, the ghosts she had cherished to overcome her unhappiness. Hadn't Suzon done the same? "We always find something to put into our body or our heart," Ashawina had said to her. "All of that just to feel alive . . ."

When Suzon came back from Eloïse Borges's funeral, her room was turned upside down and the two Princess shoeboxes were on her bed. Mina, who seemed astonishingly calm, was rocking in the old rocking chair that had known fifty years of criminal ruminations and murderous prayers.

"Forgive me, I regret everything," Mignard began in a sniveling voice. "Forgive me poor girl. I didn't want all this devastation. But there was a force here," she said pointing to her solar plexus, "way down deep in my soul that commanded my acts . . . And my steps always led me to the *gadèzafè* . . . Those beasts promised I would marry your papa . . . I believed them every time, every time . . . 'It's only a matter of a week, they won't suffer,' that's what they said. I believed them every time. Every time, Melchior drove another spike into my heart when he went in front of the Mayor with a new woman on his arm . . . Forgive me dear . . . I swear I tried prayers, but Evil in sheep's clothing always came forward before Our Lord did. 'This time is the right time, Suzon! This time, he'll be all yours, for the rest of your lives, till the end of time . . .' And I, stupid blame fool, thanked them in advance and sold my soul at a discount, in bits and pieces, like beef from a maroon butcher's stall. I swear I didn't want the death of your family . . . Alas, it come simpering up to me making like it would be deliverance . . . I didn't see the pain coming, Mina . . . Only my dreams coming true and the promises your father made me under a flowering mango tree . . . When love gets you in its grips—but you heard all that before, ain't you? You can't imagine a woman's body robbed of love, Mina . . . It's not something you can easily explain with ordinary words. It's worse than a sickness that eats out your brain and the inside of your bones and feeds on the blood lost each month for nothing, just to use up sanitary napkins. The blood let for nothing, like that of the lamb for the humans on this earth. For nothing . . . The blood I watched running down between my thighs, for nothing. Running out along with my dreams . . . And my belly that I carried around like an empty ship's hold. And my two titties where no milk never flowed, Mina. My woman's body that I lived with and that was good for nothing. And the shame, Mina. The shame of not bearing children, of walking over God's earth under the gaze of women who were glorying in their reign. And the time that was passing. So quickly, Mina. No matter how much I hoped and prayed to God every day . . . But the Good Lord couldn't care less. Nothing in the cards for me. Nothing but drying out and spider webs.

"Jealousy, that is all I was able to give birth to. It wormed its way into my body in place of the beloved babies I seen a hundred thousand times in my dreams. When the blood stopped running, I drank bitter decoctions to make it come back. Alas, I finally realized that the time for childbearing was behind me, like all the alluring charms of my youth.

"Could you have waited fifty years for a man who had sworn his loyalty to you? You don't know what loyalty is, do you? Would you have accepted to see him living happily in a fine family, without a worry, or a pain? Would you have been able to endure the looks, the silences, the muffled words under the laughter of the mother hens in Piment?

"He promised me. And then, mystery . . . He turned away from me as if he was seeing the Great Beelzebub come down to earth in his black cape . . .

"After your mama's death, I went to offer myself to Melchior. The last time . . . I asked him why he didn't want me . . . He declared he couldn't say anything, that's just the way it was. It was the fault of those who came before. That was all. But I could see in his eyes he was lying. He knew . . . I begged him, 'For pity's sake, Melchior! For pity's sake! I got to know why I been jinxed like this . . . You'd even take pity on a dog . . .' I took a knife from my pocket and stuck the point to my heart. 'Melchior, you got to talk now if you don't want to see me die right here today!' He tightened his belt one notch. He was always doing that . . . And he started talking, but he would have done best to keep quiet, believe me. I can't repeat his words to you. I hope that horrid story dies with me. It's not worth it. I'm willing to go before the judge. Rot in jail, Mina. Burn in hell . . .

Today I an old woman. I took justice into my own hands. I not proud of it. I know that too many innocent people paid for the guilty ones. I asking for your forgiveness. An honest request that comes straight from my heart. I asking for your forgiveness even though this small pardon can't help me bring back the dead. I know your words won't erase the evil I done or absolve me. Believe me, I have my conscience to torment me. But I swear to you, Mina, the forgiveness I asking for is all I got left—that, my silence, and a bitter taste in my mouth—the bile that Satan left on my tongue so that I will remember even after death my evil thoughts and my cruel acts. I know the Devil's din is waiting for me down below . . .

"Now that I'm blind, I can finally see clear. I tell myself that I used my life—the only one I had—to work Evil, instead of trying to get over this overwhelming grief and devote myself to Good, which is so precious in this world. I could have thrown out this pile of trash before you, before Rose came back. I knew you wasn't coming back just for the sun and sea. I was even expecting you earlier, believe it or not . . . After the fire, Lautréamont promised me twenty years of malediction for you and Olga. You let one whole year go by, Mina . . .

"I waiting for your judgment without trembling. It's the sentence of my Father watching me from heaven that I fearing most. You can beat me or kill me Mina. You got the right! You got every right now that you know . . . And maybe you won't believe this, but even so I got to admit that I'm relieved that you know what I been through . . . I not being pretentious, but it makes me glad, deep in my heart, to think that someone on this earth can tell my story.

"I put your name on my testament, girl. I leaving you my old cabin to replace the one on the hill that went up in smoke. You can do what you want with it . . . Tear it down, if you want, as soon as they've thrown my body in the grave . . . Burn the boards so my passage on this earth will be forgotten . . . You can live the rest of your life in Piment . . . And I not asking for your thanks. You know I got no descendents . . .

"Here, look! I taking off my three crosses . . . You see, I not protected now. The man who sold them to me died long ago. I could never make up my mind to take them off. I remember, he told me, 'The wooden cross is to give you roots on the earth, black woman. The gold cross with the living Christ in solid silver, is for riches and eternal life. The cross made of twigs bound together with a red ribbon, is love, it's Melchior and Suzon . . .'"

Putting her words to action, Mignard tried to unfasten the leather thongs that were tangled and almost glued together with grime, hair, sweat, and ages and ages of diabolical prayers.

"Your papa died along with my last hopes, Mina. Still, I always believed that these three crosses had true power, see how silly we can be, eh? Here, look! I taking them off . . ."

"Do you want me to help you, Suzon?" asked Mina suddenly, looking as if she'd awoken from a long sleep.

"Use the knife in the right-hand drawer . . ."

"Don't you have any scissors?"

"No, need a knife for this job. A nice sharp knife. That's what you need . . ."

"I might hurt you . . ."

"You'll do what you have to do, Mina. Take the knife with the black handle. Over there in the drawer of the buffet, on the right-hand side."

"You wanted to kill me a long time ago, the night the doctor gave me a shot . . ."

"Yes," admitted Mignard. "To finally rid myself of you Montérios. My little ones were calling for justice."

"Why didn't you do it?" asked Mina as she opened the drawer.

"You know why, Rosalia was there, burning high as a bonfire in the cabin."

"But you didn't try anything against Olga . . ."

"Why do you think her belly could never hold on to a single

221

child? You must have wondered ... Sometimes death is sweeter than life, you know that, right? Some went too quickly, without suffering, ain't that so? Not even time to understand that the dance was over. Not even time to see themselves dying ... And meanwhile I lived on, endured ... I wasn't allowed to have children, so deep in my heart, I needed the consolation of knowing that another woman was suffering the same fate ..."

"And Douglas?" murmured Mina, suddenly wondering whether her passion for Olga's husband could be explained by a recipe cooked up in some witch's den.

"Douglas too," sighed Suzon, "and the other men you went running after. Not out of love, but just so your flesh could touch their flesh, ain't that right? If that ain't a dog's life! I wanted you to be deprived of love, never find it. I asked for you to be smitten with twenty years of malediction ... Twenty years ..." And, in saying that, a slight smile lifted the corners of her mouth.

"And Rosalia?" Mina continued.

"Oh! Her! She was a tough one. She shouldn't ever been born ... But she held on for you as long as she could. To protect you ... That was her mission on this earth ..."

Mina opened the drawer, picked up the knife with the black handle.

"You'll keep a steady hand, won't you?" Suzon asked worriedly.

"Yes, don't worry, you won't feel anything."

Suzon closed her eyes.

"Wait! First I got to tell you that my mama wasn't a mean woman, you know. If folks tell you bad things about her, don't you believe them, hear? She never did no one no harm. She walked a straight line in life ... I want to go join her now," whined the old woman in a childish voice. "She left me alone so long ago ... She went too quickly, like your own mama, eh Mina? You know I think of her every day ..."

"You ready, Suzon?!" Spat Mina through clenched jaws.

"Ready."

"Throw down the crosses!" said Mina as soon as she had cut the thongs. "Burn the boxes and the old dolls!"

"No! Not my children, no . . ."

"Burn them or I'll do it myself."

"I'd rather die," groaned Suzon. "It's all I got left of your papa . . . Our poor babies . . . My orphans . . ."

They remained facing each other for an instant, frozen. The knife between the two of them. Quite a risible weapon to slice into the flesh of time, kill the past, cut out the pain.

Tibert pulled them from their mute confrontation.

Three knocks, like at the theater, just at the moment of reckoning.

Three knocks at the door that brought them suddenly back to the miserable present.

Tibert had been in the neighborhood, was just dropping by for a visit.

After allowing herself to be kissed, Mignard went to her room grumbling. Mina invited her cousin to sit down in the parlor but—as a precautionary and preventive measure—kept her eyes fixed on the old woman. Squatting in front of her bed, rocking back and forth, Suzon mumbled, hummed, reread the papers in the Princess shoebox, dressed and undressed the dolls, sniffed at the phials, fondled her titties and pinched their wilted nipples.

Tibert was talking, talking . . . A stream of words from which, every so often, one would stand out more sharply than the others, heavily accented, a double *r*, a lisped *s* . . . Mina truly began listening to what he was saying when he started talking about his father and his grandmother Nana.

Tibert and Mina being first cousins, they had been kept at a respectful distance during their youth. One might have thought that their two fathers, Melchior and Ferdy—though the same woman had carried them in her belly and they were blood brothers in the state registers—had turned their back on all their kin. With the years, the ties between them had grown slack, and then were cut—out of sight, out of mind—due to a sticky, unspeakable secret. While Melchior was alive, he never spoke of his mama Nana, who had gone back to Grands-Fonds, where her family came from. Nor did he ever mention his brothers in Grande-Terre, or at least very infrequently. A few uncomfortable words for people to gossip about. First names torn from his lips. Illusive shadows pulled out of a repudiated, banished past.

"Oh Mina! You just have to come and give our grandmother a kiss . . . You have to come before it's too late. She's been waiting for you for so long. She surely has things to tell you . . . If you like, we'll make a date and I'll take you over . . ."

"She won't say nothing!" screamed Suzon from her room. "Stop telling stories, Mister grave-robber! Let the past rest in peace! What give you the right to come plotting under my roof? In any case, Nana won't say nothing! Nothing at all! No point in going out and asking her questions . . . Don't listen to him, Mina! Old Nana ain't let out a peep all this time, she's not going to start talking the day before she dies . . . My mama preferred losing her speech so she could keep the truth from falling into Piment's gossip mill. Don't go, Mina! Don't listen to him! Tell him to get out of our house! Oh! Don't go see Nana! She got nothing to tell you, I swear. Nothing, no secrets to reveal . . . No, no, no . . ."

With a sheet over her head, Suzon had got to her feet and started whimpering like a little girl awakened by the Devil in the blackest of midnight bacchanalias.

"Are you sure you still want to stay here?" whispered Tibert, who didn't in the least enjoy finding himself in this kind of predicament.

"I'm not afraid of her. I'd very much like to go to Grands-Fonds tomorrow."

Tibert stared at his cousin in admiration. She wasn't trembling. Her voice was firm. Her dry eyes reflected a steady, unshakeable soul. He had already promised to take his sweetheart, Cindy, to Pointe-à-Pitre the next day, but she'd understand that this was a critical situation and the stakes were high. Suddenly he was convinced that Nana would open up to Mina. And he, Tibert, didn't want to miss this episode of the family epic, this reunion between the last Montérios.

"Tomorrow, Thursday, at what time, Mina?"

"Three o'clock."

"Go for three o'clock . . . We'll be in Grands-Fonds around four."

"Perfect."

They both seemed relieved. They felt as if they were reaching the end of a long road strewn with doubts and disasters. They were still walking blindly through the cursed past, groping, clinging to intangible things, trusting in chance. However, they sensed they were nearing their goal, and that words that had once been so jealously guarded were now simply waiting to be harvested.

It was already six o'clock in the evening. On the veranda, Tibert hugged his cousin, telling himself that there were good aspects to living in France, regardless of what people from here said. Twenty-one years earlier, he'd never have thought that the little orphan he put on a one-way plane would have made this upright woman.

"I'm proud of you," he murmured.

"See you tomorrow, Tibert, see you tomorrow . . ."

XXVI

Victor awoke around six o'clock in the evening, just at the time when in Piment, on the other side of the island, Mignard was getting back under her sheets. His head was like a blast oven and his body was numb. In a moment of panic, he thought he'd been thrown back a few months earlier, and was on his hospital bed in Esquirol.

There were people on the other side of the wall. They were laughing and talking in a language he didn't know, but that he'd already heard somewhere . . . I'm in hell. Good God, I'm dead. I didn't get to see the year 2000 . . . I promised I wouldn't drink. I went drinking with some men. I didn't have time to get the spell broken . . . "I believe in God!" he screamed. If he's around here, he thought to himself again, the Devil will send me back from where I came. No, I'm in a nightmare, I'm dead. My God, please let me not be dead!

"Get a hold of yourself, Victor. Collect your thoughts!" whispered a voice from beyond the rum.

"Is anybody out there? Answer me! Is anybody out there?"

His saliva was sour-tasting. Alcohol fumes came wafting from his mouth. I got drunk at the Mundo Night . . . No! Now I remember. I'm in Guadeloupe. I listened to some men telling me their life-story. Three black men . . . We finished off a bottle of rum. We talked about women, Georgette, Marie-Denise, Sophie . . . Now I remember, I remember little snatches . . .

"Hey, Victor!"

Head craning through the half-open door, toothless smile, Raymond looked the epitome of the Devil's jail keeper.

"Georgette made you *on di té*."

"Where am I? I can't move . . ."

"What you mean you can't move? You came in here on your own two feet, an upright man! Try and sit up! It's because you ain't used to drinking rum from here. It was your rum christening . . ."

"Where am I?" repeated Victor, trying to sit up.

"Why you at Georgette's, in your bungalow. We been waiting for you outside on the veranda. Georgette made some *dombré*-dumplings and *ouassou*-crayfish in your honor, Victor. I told you she knew how to make folks feel welcome.

"My things at the hotel . . . My backpack . . . The presents for Bénédicte's niece . . . And I have to see Mina . . ."

"*Pa okpè-w! Tout ti zafè-aw ké fet . . .*"

"What?"

"We taken care of everything. We called Claude. He's Georgette's nephew. He got a car. He'll take you to the hotel in

226

a little while. You can get your suitcase and then head for Goyave. It won't take long, just go make the delivery and come back. *Sa ké fet*! It'll all get done!" concluded Raymond, who evidently was unable to stick to the French language.

"Help me get up," begged Victor. "I need to take a shower. Now I remember. Yeah, the Rasta, the woman with her bottles of kerosene, Georgette's bungalows . . ."

"You remember my name?"

"Yeah, Raymond. And the others: Edmond, like my father, and . . . Julien, that's it."

"The tea get you cleared you up, you'll see."

Georgette had a generous smile. Part male and part female. As a child she must have looked a lot like her brother Raymond. But the paths of their lives had traced wrinkles of joy on Georgette's face, whereas bitter folds had been dug into her brother's. Georgette's thick hands told of a life of labor. A life of striving toward one single dream: building Georgette's Club. She had worked 25 years in a hotel on the Caribbean coast before buying a large plot of land—for peanuts, as she pointed out.

"Back then nothing want to grow here. Land was poor, cracked and dry in all seasons. People made fun of me: 'You'll never get nothing out of it!' they said. 'You can't raise goats or plant breadfruit trees . . .' I laid the cinderblocks for the house in 1979. The first bungalow was built in 1986. Now there are eight! And I ain't finished . . . Next year there'll be a pool. Three girls work with me. It's a family atmosphere around here. And I rent out cars too. I don't charge high fees and I earn an honest living. And there are flowers, and plants and trees everywhere . . ."

She lent Victor one of her dead husband's shirts. Forced him to drink three tall glasses of local tea, recommended for problems related to indigestion and alcoholic ingestion.

"There's nothing you can't ask me for, Victor. If you want to eat lobster, you'll have it. If you want to go out fishing, I'll

227

introduce you to my cousin who's a fisherman. If you want to sleep, it's your prerogative . . . If you're lost, just ask for Georgette's Club, everyone knows where it is . . . If something is bothering you, come and see me any time. Here we take better care of you than at your own mama's."

No sooner said than done. Victor went back to the hotel to pick up his bags with Edmond, Raymond, Julien, and Claude, Georgette's nephew. He paid his bill under Channel's icy stare and protected by his four bodyguards, who got an eyeful of the women clientele while making loud comments in Creole.

Victor got into Claude's car and put the package intended for Francine Tudor between his feet. He felt strangely calm, his mind blank and appeased, light-hearted, trusting, and already in a hurry to rejoin his friends who promised to wait for him at Georgette's, while sipping on the Devil's concoction as Julien put it.

The brand-new BMW with direct fuel injection started up with a roar.

"Just a few minutes by car and we'll be there!" assured Claude who was taking the curves on the left, driving with his headlights on, passing without putting on his turn signal, and carrying on a conversation by himself, not keeping his eyes on the road.

Victor wasn't afraid. His ideas were slowly beginning to fall into place. Before, he never would have gotten into a stranger's car so quickly. He would have been wary. Would have asked questions, laid traps, done some crosschecking, maneuvering between logic and reason. Emilie had warned him. "Beware of strangers. Kindness is always suspicious, Victor. People never act out of sheer benevolence or generosity of spirit. They scheme. They harbor evil intentions and pursue . . ."

Claude's life unfurled in less than thirty minutes, the time it took to get to Goyave. Women, gambling, politics. The words rocked Victor gently as he watched tiny yellow lights piercing the darkness, shadows stretching out here and there. It was the first time he'd been immersed in the Creole night. Mina had mentioned it when she told him of the cabin burning down on Morne Calvaire. For Victor, each lamp was the promise of a fire, the desire for a fire. He saw himself rewriting history, the knight in shining armor suddenly appearing from the future to turn back the tide of time and save Rose.

"You said there was a fountain out front? Here we are!"

After having knocked at several doors and having asked six different people for Francine Tudor, Bénédicte's niece, they came up in front of a small cabin, quite far from the fountain. Stacked up on the veranda were about ten bags of cement under an oilcloth that must have once served to cover a table. An armchair—Emmanuel style—upon which no one seemed to sit anymore, but which no one could make up their mind to throw away, presided over a table guarded by two old benches with gnawed down legs. Fragmented light shone through a curtain of half-broken seashells that, in a highly symbolic fashion, barred the entrance to the main room.

They found Francine sitting in front of the TV host Julien Lepers and the lucky contestant of the day.

"I was expecting you earlier! Come in!" She shouted by way of a welcome. "Aunt Béné told me you were coming. You're the white man, a friend of hers."

She wiped her mouth and hands with a rag, but remained sitting, eyes glued to the television, deaf to the meowing of a little cat begging for the fish bones in the plate sitting on her knees.

"We had a hard time finding the place . . ." Claude began.

"Wait a minute! I want to see if he's coming back tomorrow," cut in Francine, motioning him to keep quiet.

Claude settled himself in a rocker looking totally absorbed. Mouth hanging half-open, thighs closed tight, he suddenly seemed gripped by the program. That must be the way he looks when the races are coming in, imagined Victor, who had

229

not been asked to sit down. He therefore remained standing, arms dangling at his sides, planted between the seashell curtain and a mahogany cozy-corner decorated with several spotless white doilies. Sitting on a shelf, a bouquet of red roses contemplated itself in a mirror supported by two angels with gilt wings. Victor took a step forward and his face appeared amongst the angels and the flowers. The image delighted him. He started to play with it, trying to catch himself off-guard. He turned his eyes away for a minute. Then with a flutter of his lashes, looked back at the mirror. He was surprised every time. Sometimes he looked like a dumbfounded tourist, a wayward, traveling, amateur sociologist, sometimes like a hunted animal or a dead person freshly arrived in Paradise.

"Stay Honey!" whispered Francine to the winning contestant who was weighing the pros and cons.

Suspense, polite smiles, muffled laughter.

On a buffet, a collection of photos showed Francine at all ages in her life. She was smiling in all of the pictures. Chaperone to a boy squinting against the sun who was stuffed into a blue suit and tie, she held him around the neck. A black and white shot, undoubtedly in the company of her parents, thought Victor. As a child in the arms of her Aunt Bénédicte one day at the beach. Greasy mouthed, eating a drumstick. In France, standing before the Eiffel Tower next to a young, starry-eyed couple in her Sunday best . . .

At forty, Francine was still a handsome woman. But she had sworn off using her charms. That was obvious by the way she had welcomed them. She couldn't have cared less that two men came upon her in the brightly-lit solitude of a good–humored Julien Lepers show. In the old days, she must have sat in the Emmanuelle armchair and pushed her suitors away with the back of her hand, the tip of her toes. Today, she had nothing left to give.

"How much is the jackpot?" asked Claude who was unable keep quiet for long and was forcing himself to show an interest in the quiz show.

Francine knit her brow; the champion of the day was just going to make his decision. Climax: "I'll stay!" he boomed. "He's staying!" confirmed Julien.

"He's staying!" Francine repeated in utter delight.

She was bobbing up and down, hitting herself on the forehead, knocking loose the huge blue hair-rollers—like Beaubourg pipes—that covered her head. The theme music began. Handshakes, close-up of Julien smiling, applause, credits, the end.

"Sit down!" Claude suggested, spreading his legs and throwing them out in front of himself.

One might have thought he was Dame Francine's long-awaited guest and was ready to spend a good while at her place, swallow a couple of drinks while he was at it.

"We're not far from Piment?" asked Victor.

"Five miles, no more. Don't worry, I'm taking you tomorrow. I'm your guide, Victor. I want you to have good memories of Guadeloupe. Too many people come here and then criticize the country afterward . . . This way, when I come to Paris, you'll be my guide in turn."

Flashes of anxiety.

The kid in the blue suit is him, at eleven, posing next to his mother the day of his solemn communion.

Anxiety mounting.

The scissors hanging over the door are the same ones that Emilie stuck into the blue materials that she brought back from Fine Fabrics . . . One day when he was reluctant to practice the piano, she threatened him with them. That night he had dreamt she stabbed him in the skull with them to turn him into a prodigy. "You're going to learn to read your notes! You have to recognize them, Victor. Go on! Play your father's piece! He's watching and listening to you, Victor! Play, Victor, More! More!" And each time she screamed "More", she jabbed him again with the scissors. When he awoke, he ran his hand through his hair and looked for traces of blood on the pillow.

Torrents of anxiety. Dizziness, cold sweat.

231

The Eiffel tower, in front of which Francine was posing, reminded him of one summer afternoon when he was out on a walk with Emilie —he must have been seven years old —, Victor had felt his first dizzy symptoms.

Relentless ...

Francine's Beaubourg-curlers ... He was twenty-one when the desire to do away with himself grabbed him by the scruff of the neck in the covered marketplace in Paris. Die to find deliverance. The feeling of imminent death ... Die to escape suffering.

Pitiless ...

He had had visions of his face framed by angels and flowers several times while in the hospital, at Esquirol. He saw himself dead, like his father. When he told Bénédicte about his nights of insomnia, the woman sighed and looked over his shoulder as if she could see the three ghosts. They're not really attached yet Victor. If you go to Guadeloupe, they'll go back to their shadow-world before you can turn around. All you have to do is turn them over to a good old *gadèzafè*-sorcerer who knows the remedies.

Flashes of anxiety.

"Don't worry," Claude repeated. "I'm entirely at your service. I'm your guide ... I won't leave your side ..."

"No," said Victor, wiping his forehead. "Tomorrow I have to be alone. I promised. Take me to Piment if you like. I'm going to spend the afternoon there. I'll come back in the evening ..." He almost added, "I already have a guide."

Claude squinted his eyes and put on a knowing look. "Woman!" he ventured.

"It's not what you think, I ..."

Francine was already coming back with a tray of drinks.

"Gentlemen, serve yourselves!" she ordered.

They stayed another fifteen minutes with their hostess, who wasn't a great conversationalist. She reluctantly thanked Victor for having come out, set the package he had brought her on a chair, and offered him lunch one of these days. But faced with her obvious lack of enthusiasm, Victor refused the invitation.

"I have an address for you," she suggested to Victor during a moment of silence, and her eyes plunged into his like daggers. Since his attack, Victor had been doing his best to compose himself. "Aunt Béné sent it. She said you should not leave Guadeloupe without going there. It's for your well-being, to help solve your problem . . . Don't wait too long . . ."

She searched in one of her pockets and extended a piece of paper folded in four.

"Well then, we'll be going now," Claude said.

On the way back, the two men exchanged very few words. Victor unfolded and refolded the piece of paper several times, read and reread the name and the address written on it. Claude was burning with curiosity to know what was on his friend's mind, but didn't dare ask him.

They arrived at Georgette's around nine o'clock in the evening.

"What you come looking for in Guadeloupe?" Julien asked immediately, without taking the slightest oratorical precautions. "Tell us!"

"I made a promise. And . . . and I also came to cure myself," he confided.

"To cure yourself of what?"

"A hereditary illness . . . A family illness . . ." a shudder ran through the audience.

"What you talking about?" asked Julien, visibly moved. "You been with us since this morning. You drank with us. You ate with us. You left the hotel to come to Georgette's bungalow . . . You don't seem so bad off . . ."

"Let him speak!" grumbled Edmond.

"Wait, let's have a drink first. Serve yourself, Victor." Julien was the kind who firmly believed in the tongue-loosening virtues of rum.

Victor wanted to remain sober.

233

"I mustn't drink anymore, Julien ... I made a promise ... My father Edmond died," he went on. "I don't think my mother ever got over it. She laid down next to him on the bed. Next to him, a dead man. She spent half of her life in that bed, smoking and wasting away, talking about him, her lost love. And I was there listening to her. My father was a pianist. He hung himself. She never told me why ... She called me Bunny ..."

As he was talking, Victor laughed at himself and was shaken with sobs twice. He portrayed himself first as predator, then as victim. He saw shreds of his father's sheet music coming from Julien's eyes. He thought he heard Emilie's voice, "Please Edmond! It's Victor's party! You should play something for Bunny!" He hugged Raymond's arm and his voice broke up when he spoke of his first anxiety attacks, his dizzy spells, and his multiple attempts at putting an end to it all ... The relaxation sessions, talk groups, psychiatrists, Bénédicte and the three demons ... He played his last card, his joker.

"I came to have the spell broken," he repeated as a conclusion. "To heal this wound once and for all."

And he fell silent, like one closes a door on the indecency of a body accidentally caught naked.

The three companions had no idea that white folk in France endured such calamities, were equally pursued by demons. They had allowed him to speak without interrupting him even once. Between themselves, they were in the habit of commenting every point, in order to bring words to the storyteller's mouth. They opened a parenthesis on their own lives. Traded hard-luck stories. Cursed. Raged. And the rum always punctuated the darkest hours, broke the silence, absolved them, consoled them, comforted them. Not one of them reached out for the bottle while Victor was telling his story. When he finished, they remained frozen by the truth of those words come straight from the heart, dazzled by the tears wept, the strange laughter that had sprung up like flowers on arid memories. Torn between sadness and compassion, their backs bent under the weight of emotions they had never felt, they were grateful to Victor, the France-White, for having abandoned himself so, for having found them worthy of hearing the story brought back from childhood, for not having held back his tears.

"A man who cries in front of a woman is good-for-nothing!" declared Raymond.

"Yeh, but a man who cries in front of men, is a hell of a male!" added Edmond, who, more than ever, had adopted Victor as his son.

"Now we'll drink!" Julien decided.

Long pinkish strands suddenly stood out in the black sky that was slowly turning blue. The first rooster crowed. Then the sun tore itself from the sea like a golden nugget and rose, rose, in the tow of the white birds tracing arabesques in the sky. In the distance, coupled with the horizon, an ocean liner set in dazzling light moved slowly along. A sailboat landed on the Saintes. It was four o'clock in the morning.

XXVII

Thursday December 23, 1999

The dreams we remember come in the early morning hours. That's something one should know. Creatures seem more alive than the living, their words go straight to the heart, their smell lingers.

It was four o'clock in the morning when Suzon Mignard was visited by her mother, Lucinda, who had been wandering in the kingdom of the dead for some forty years. Twenty-five years looking for the door to Paradise, ten years praying in Purgatory, et cetera years deferring her entrance into hell. The poor woman was wearing the dress she was buried in. Suzon jumped out of her bed. She landed at age twenty-five. A firm body, strong bones, and all of her teeth. Barely surprised, she cupped her young-lass breasts, smoothed her hand over the flat of her stomach, and felt her rounded buttocks. I'm going to start all over again, she thought, sincerely believing she'd been given another chance. This time, I won't fall in love with Melchior. This time, I'll find the kind of man I deserve, one that can make a mother out of me ... eighteen little black babies that I'll ask him to plant in my belly ... And she was ready to go off into that fine life and swore she would to her mama, poor gaunt woman come up from the shadows. Suzon already imagined herself on the arm of a young man that all the women in Piment would envy her for.

As she was talking to herself, buzzing like a mosquito, time started going by on her body. Each second counted for a year and she quickly found herself back in her wilted years, with her flaccid skin, seventy-two-year-old titties, flat buttocks and dead eyes. That was the moment her mother chose to hold out her hand to Suzon. An invitation to finish with this world. Mignard threw everything into reverse gear, as if she still had some dirty business to take care of. Was her time up?

"No! Lord, no!" she cried just like a condemned man on the scaffold. A deep feeling of injustice pierced her breast.

"No, I don't want to drink of that cup!"

But Lucinda hadn't taken that long trip to come back empty-handed. She'd come to get her Suzon.

"No! I ain't ready yet! I got to go before the priest! You got to leave me time to confess! I got to ..."

She was sweating, gasping worse than an old donkey at high noon halfway up a steep hill.

"I got to get married ..."

She dove under the bed sheet, covered her head with it. Bride's veil ... She waited ... Cruel minutes. Both of her hands over her mouth to hold back the screams that were filling her throat. Why hang around? Mass had already been said. After all, the time had been well-chosen, Suzon could have taken the opportunity to disappear with dignity, die a gentle death. Who

236

would have mourned her? Neither you nor I. She could have gone away holding her mama's hand, abandon herself to that serene ending.

Even though she'd been called three times—the voices came from the floorboards—Lucinda held out hope, pitiful scarecrow standing very straight in the morning twilight. Alas, Suzon was the stubborn type, cracked in the head, lacerated from the inside, entrails whirlwinded. She wanted to live and live some more despite all the words she'd spoken that very afternoon. She wanted to breathe in Piment's poison air. She still wanted a husband . . .

"A husband, dear Lord! Just once in my life . . ."

A husband! And, repeating that word to herself: "Husband! Husband! Husband!" She began to laugh at herself, laughing up her sleeve and into her sheets. If the vision of the huge pyre that was being prepared for her under the earth had been less terrifying, she would have let her laughter reach Mina's ears, who was sleeping with one eye open in the next room. She would have grabbed Lucinda by the collar and danced a frolicking farandole with her. Bawl out, at the top of her lungs, the lament of manless women.

~

After his three companions had left, Victor stretched out on his bed. He slept two hours, but he felt refreshed, all excited with the prospect of seeing Mina that Thursday. Sitting on the veranda of his pink and blue bungalow, dubbed Butterfly, sipping a strong cup of coffee, he let his gaze wander and lifted his eyes to the sky every now and again, trying to catch a glimpse of beyond the clouds like Bénédicte had mentioned.

Suddenly Claude appeared.

"It's old reliable me! A promise is a promise! See, I as good as my word, Victor. So when you get back home to Paris, you can say people from Guadeloupe is responsible, and not jokers, right?"

"Yes, that's what I'll say," said Victor.

"So you happy to be at Aunt Georgette's? You sleep well? Where I taking you today?" asked Claude.

Victor handed him the address that Francine had given him.

"It looks to be between Goyave and Piment. It's on our way. How you feel about it? You sure you want to see this Mister Verity? You don't know him? You know why you going there?"

"No, I don't really know . . ."

"You don't know!" exclaimed Claude. "You the easy going sort, you are . . . And if they sending you to your death, Victor?"

"It has something to do with breaking the spell . . ."

"That Francine woman didn't seem all that nice . . ."

"Stop it! It was her Aunt Bénédicte that helped me when I was in the hospital. I trust her."

"You the judge . . . Don't let people manipulate you! You a free man, Victor!"

"I know . . . But I have to see this man, Claude . . ."

"You have to, or you want to?" insisted Claude, as if he wished to instill the poison of doubt in Victor's mind."

"I . . . WANT TO. I want to! I want to!"

"OK! OK! OK! What time you want to leave?"

"But don't you have any obligations, a job?" asked Victor worriedly. "I can take a bus . . ."

"Don't worry. I on vacation. I your guide . . . Every once in a while, you pay for gas, a *dankit*-cake and the booze . . . We always find a way of working things out around here."

Mister Verity lived at Trois-Sources.

The hamlet called Trois-Sources was not marked on any map. And the people they asked for directions from here and there couldn't tell them exactly where it was.

"Go right after the first mango tree, follow the road down, you come to a crossroads, keep going and you'll see a big hog plum tree, go left there, you pass one-two-three-four-five cabins and a one-story white cement house, with a green

238

wrought-iron gate, keep going slow, slow so you won't miss the turn, you can't miss it, afterward there's a trace, that's where Verity built his house, at the end of the dirt trace . . ." explained an honest, good-natured man who was busily tying up his ox.

Someone else told them to take a road that was a dead end.

One woman stood with her nose in the air for a good five minutes before declaring that she couldn't help them.

An old, one-eyed, limping woman told them to go to the devil and his three hundred acolytes and then signed herself four times over. That vision in the rear view mirror made Victor's blood run cold.

"Verity! Verityyyy! Ve-ri-ty!" spat one man between two shots of rum, scratching himself, cra-cra-cra, chanting Verity's name the whole while.

Then, miraculously, they ran into a young mulatress who reconciled them with the whole of the human race.

"You're not far. I'm going there too. I can show you the way, if you like."

It was a three-story house. A red truck, a blue Mercedes and a white pick-up were parked under an immense concrete slab held up by narrow pylons. Old Verity's living quarters and consulting room were on the second floor. A balcony laden with potted plants wrapped all the way around the house.

"Come on up!" shouted a faceless voice.

They climbed the steps on the exterior.

I'm not afraid.

Everything is fine.

Everything is as fine as can be.

Two women were waiting for them at the top of the stairs.

I'm not afraid.

Everything is fine.

Everything is as fine as can be.

One of them, a dark woman, was emaciated. Skin stretched over a bony face. Neck twice as long as usual. She was wearing

239

a drab yellowish-brown alb belted with a cord from which dangled a large wooden cross. Her hair looked like an old, used broom head.

"Master Verity will be seeing you," she announced.

Victor gulped painfully. Claude gave him a jab in the ribs with his elbow.

"Come along!" the other woman said.

She, an Indian, had a fixed gaze. Around her ankles she wore bracelets of dried leaves that wrapped up her calf. Her black dress fell to her knees. Thousands of black hairs covered her legs. She asked them to sit down in a sort of waiting room and disappeared.

The room was dark and — they soon realized — guarded by a caged monkey that screeched and knocked its head against the bars of the cage whenever he felt a move was suspicious, a word pronounced too loudly. The two men remained quiet for a moment. But Claude couldn't keep himself from throwing his legs out in front of himself, or suddenly bringing them back under his chair, or else looking at his watch with an irritating tic. The monkey went wild. Victor was sitting up stiff, straight, a brave sailor weathering the storm. Only his head moved, slowly, to keep from frightening the monkey. And his eyes rolled from left to right.

Victor wasn't even wondering why he was there anymore. He was letting himself be swept along in the tide of events. More fatalistic than an old black man living the last fifteen minutes of his life, he was no longer surprised, was prepared to see anything, hear anything, accept anything. More and more relaxed, thanks to the Tranxene he'd swallowed earlier in preparation for this scene, he was simply observing without judging anything, not letting any anxious, metaphysical, or poetic thoughts assail him. Counting the slats of the venetian blinds at the windows, the mildew stains on the ceiling. Contemplating his toes in his sandals. Staring at a ray of sunshine that lit the coffee table in front of him. Waiting for what life had in store for him. Waiting for his turn like at the doctor's office, hands folded quietly in his lap.

"Please follow me," said the vestal in black.

Claude and Victor stood up together, which set the monkey off.

"One at a time, please!"

"He can't go in there alone," protested Claude, who took his role very seriously.

"That's the rule. The master does not give group consultations."

With her lips curled into a disdainful sneer, the girl leaned against the doorframe and waited for them to decide. It was either take it or leave it. There was no bargaining with Mister Verity. She had centuries of patience before her . . .

At Mister Verity's first glance, Victor suddenly forgot he was a former inmate at Esquirol, a chronic depressive, working temporary jobs, a red-blooded Parisian . . . As soon as the door closed behind him, he sunk into a dark hole.

Do not laugh, ladies and gentlemen!

Do not jeer!

Certain lucky people run smack into that exceptional moment when time wavers and vacillates. Everything becomes meaningful and appears in its original nudity. Childhood fears become clear. The key to dreams and mysteries is put in their hands.

Do not laugh!

Do not jeer!

Mister Verity did not say a word. He wore a gray suit and a blue lavaliere over a white shirt. He had a bald little bird's head, a piercing look, and—the only indication of his belonging to the brotherhood of *gadèzafè*—sorcerer's claws. Aside from that detail, he looked exactly like a civil servant at his desk, upon which were stacked, not pending files, but prayer books, images of the Virgin, and bundles of tapers.

Do not laugh!

Do not jeer, ladies and gentlemen!

Mister Verity was an affable and benevolent man. His silence went back to his childhood. Already, when in his mother's womb, he stamped his foot to warn of a danger, give directions, or denounce an innocent-looking enemy. At three years of age—when he still hadn't started talking, and people thought he was worthless in this world—Mister Verity, whose name was Michel, was found in deep conversation with someone only he could see.

Do not laugh!

Do not jeer!

Mister Verity set himself up in business at twenty-two years of age, which is quite rare in the profession. Ordinarily, *gadèzafès* open shop around thirty or forty.

"Bénédicte sent me," stammered Victor who was slowly coming back to his senses.

"I know," Verity answered.

"I'm not sure what I'm doing here," Victor continued.

"I know what you're doing here."

The man must have been over eighty years old, but his voice was firm and its tone self-assured.

"Could you explain a little what it's all about . . .?"

"What did you see when you walked in here?" asked Verity.

Victor scratched the side of his head.

"I saw you and your desk . . ."

"No! What did you see in your head? Did an image pop into your head?"

"Yes . . ."

His father hanging at the end of a rope tied to the fixture in the living room.

Three men in black taking him down.

"Get the kid out of here!" they said.

Emilie crying.

"Get the kid out of here while we take his father down."

"You will find peace of mind, I'm sure of it . . . And you will be cured . . . Sister Clara will tell you how much you owe."

"What time is your appointment in Piment? We won't have time to go back to Georgette's to eat."

Victor had just been relieved of nine hundred francs, but it wasn't too high a price to pay for a memory that had been sealed in forgotten time for nearly forty years. When he was leaving Verity's place, he felt at first as if he were a bronze tyrant whose bolts had been loosened by the masses. Then he felt like a treasure-hunter, a prospector who'd discovered a river of gold. Now, with the rap music spitting out of the car radio and penetrating his body in warm gentle waves, he was floating like an astronaut in the immensity of space, his senses heightened, feeling light, so very light.

Did Mister Verity really have the gift of seeing what ordinary people could not?

Wasn't his plunge into the past due to the barrage of emotions he'd been through since he'd arrived in Guadeloupe?

His run-in with Mister Jungle.

His visit to dame Francine's place.

His confession the day before.

Abusing rum.

Antidepressants.

The heat.

Tranquilizers.

The sun.

Hadn't the accumulation of signs . . . the photos at Francine's, meeting old Edmond, the scissors stabbing into his head . . . created an opening on to that scene from his childhood?

"Here we are! We're in Piment!" said Claude loudly. "There are some good restaurants here."

Victor raised his eyes immediately toward the sky, the clouds, the hills.

"Have you ever heard of Morne Calvaire?"

"You some strange tourist!" the other responded wrinkling his nose. "I ain't never seen a vacationer like you."

Victor started laughing.

"We make a good team, don't we?" suggested Claude.

"I almost missed all of this . . . Thank you. Thank you for helping me . . ."

"It ain't nothing, Victor . . ." Claude said biting his lip.

He would have liked to utter more brotherly words, show Victor his affection with a gesture, a friendly word, but being too reserved, he was unable to do so. To break the tide of emotions, he started singing.

They chose a restaurant on the beach. A jetty of coconut and palm trees, the straw hut didn't look like much, but Claude guaranteed that the owner could grill fish better than anyone. The chairs were the white plastic type you see everywhere since they started catching on in Guadeloupe. Shaded with Coca-Cola parasols, the tables were covered with gaudy-colored oilcloths.

"That's it right in front of you, Morne Calvaire!" snapped Claude when they had taken their places at a table. "At the end of the road is the town of Piment. It's real close . . . You got time to take a dip before eating if you want. I going to order some punch . . ."

Morne Calvaire stood out like a little round nose in the hills above Piment. Other hills of similar size, planted with banana groves or colonized with houses, stood around it.

"I'll go to my appointment on foot. I'll see you back at Georgette's tonight. I'll take a bus back."

"Be careful! There's no transportation after seven o'clock . . ."

"I'll make out," assured Victor.

"Don't hitchhike, all right? You might end up in a cane field cut up in little pieces . . . I'll come pick you up, if you want. Call Georgette's and I'll nip right over . . ."

Victor took his first dip between the rum and the fish dinner. He swam for almost a half hour without taking his eyes off of Morne Calvaire, feeling no anxiety or dizziness. At times, he thought he caught a glimpse of the ruins of the burned-down

244

cabin and a white shape coming and going busily. At times a cloud detached itself from the others and came down so low that it was harpooned on the branches of one of the trees guarding the hill. You could see the old path to the stations of the cross perfectly. It seemed to move in the sunlight like a long black snake between the clumps of yellowed grass, the jagged rocks and the bushes from where white birds flew.

Most of the stores didn't open till three. Victor had some time to kill. Haphazardly, in search of a postcard, he went down a few narrow streets lined with desolate cabins and came out at the marketplace. There, the last vendors were packing up their vegetables, they didn't even try calling to the tall white man, who was whistling through his teeth and looking lost.

There was a post-colonial, deserted, neglected kind of sadness about the town of Piment, a heart that had never been loved, a soulless ghost town. It was Christmas time, so there were Christmas trees and artificial snow in the shop windows, strings of colored lights and gold and red balls. But the streets were rutted, the sidewalks unpaved, and the old cabins seemed rejected by the very earth they stood upon, like teeth that betray, come loose over the years and end up deforming a smile. The newer buildings clashed with the general décor.

The primary school.

Victor couldn't help but stop there, lay his fingers on the bars of the tall iron gate. Imagining Rose, he remained like that for long minutes, under the gaze of old Clarissa who, on the other side of the street, was keeping an eye on him, nodding her head in her rocker. Not a breath of wind in the leaves of the almond trees planted in the middle of the courtyard. Not a child to be seen. But scores of pigeons. The shuttered doors to the classes were closed. On the surrounding wall, a fresco in primitive style spun out colorful flowers and animals.

Victor closed his eyes, the cries of children immediately filled his head. He saw Mina in her apron of orange material.

He heard poems, grammar rules, and multiplication tables being recited. And then, he felt someone prying his fingers one after the other off the bars of the gate. One after the other.

When he opened his eyes, a few feathers still fluttered in the courtyard. The pigeons had disappeared. Victor looked for them in the sky, on the roof of the school, and in the deserted street.

At one minute to three, he was in the main square, fearing already that Mina had forgotten their appointment. His shirt was drenched with sweat. I'm a sorry sight, he thought. He sat down on the stone bench, facing Piment's war memorial.

When the church bell struck three, he suddenly realized he'd forgotten his red ball cap and was panic-stricken.

XXVIII

The morning of that same Thursday, Suzon woke up in sheets soaked with piss. Even more foul-smelling than usual. She was alive and to really make sure, she pinched the fat on her arm. Winced with pain. She immediately regretted not having had the courage to give in to her mother's request, to the temptation of death . . . Yes, she'd survived, steeping in her sour solution. Who would have believed it? Then she was struck with a profound feeling of injustice. No, she wasn't dead. Very early, she had heard Mina moving and walking around in the cabin. The girl had even called her from a distance to make sure she was alive. Steeping in her juice of piss and sweat mixed together, Suzon had mumbled some words with no backwards or forwards and then she'd purred. And Mina had gone out, may it do her a world of good. The day of reckoning had come. She was sure Nana Salibur would spit out the whole story. Truth always comes out in it's own time. And the hour has struck, moaned Suzon on her pissy pallet.

Why delay it? The wheel of fortune had already been turned.

But you know, when the Devil takes possession of one of the Good Lord's creatures, he uses it to the very end. Believe it or

246

not—infidels that you are—Suzon left her bed of filthy humors. The bell tower in town struck noon. Out of precaution, even though she knew Mina had gone out, she called to her, sniffed into the dimness, opened her ears to the noises in the cabin. No one . . . So she got up, gathered her eighteen dolls and found the strength to place them one at a time, one after the other, on the shelves in the living room, on the sofa, the buffet, the chairs and the table. And then, as if everything were perfectly normal, she went back to bed, leaving trails of nauseating piss on the floor.

At a quarter to three, cousin Tibert parked his pick-up on Suzon's street and gave a quick honk of the horn. After the scene of the day-before-yesterday, he no longer dared venture into the old woman's den. He opened his *France-Antilles* and looked for the obituary page. Too bad, Suzon's name wasn't mentioned. In the sports column, he forced himself to read a chauvinistic article about the game pitting Morne-à-l'Eau against Capesterre-Belle-Eau. Zero to zero. Oh! On page four, they announced the opening of a new clothing store in Point-à-Pitre. He promised himself to take Cindy. He leafed through the paper glancing up at his rear-view mirror from time to time, foot ready to jam down the clutch if some Rasta danger appeared on the horizon. That very morning he'd gone to prepare Grand-Mother Salibur for her granddaughter Mina's visit, and he was inwardly delighted at how he had handled the whole matter.

Nana was now eighty-nine years old. She had been living with her son Ferdy—Tibert's father—ever since one morning in 1987 when she'd been hit on the head by a cacao pod—which had made her completely *ababa* for a time. In the space of one day she could attain the heights of ecstatic euphoria, or fall into the pink depths of childhood, black holes of amnesia, gray pits of melancholy. Sometimes, rubbing the bump that the pod had incurred, she relived the birth of her three children. At certain times, her hands were oddly agitated, her fingers kneading the invisible. People thought she believed she was shelling peas, fingering her rosary, squashing ants, or scaling fish.

The old woman recovered some of her faculties. She wasn't able to live alone, but she still pursued her sewing activities at the Municipal Office for Youth and Culture and continued to pray with her Christian women-friends. Sometimes she still said things that were devoid of all reason but that Ferdy and his family ended up growing accustomed to, thanking God for having granted them a grandma who wasn't too terribly disabled.

In the evening, after his work at the butcher shop, Ferdy sat down next to her on the veranda. They had a nice talk just like two old bodies sharing the same yesteryear. As long as they spoke of life in general and nostalgic faraway times, Nana was never at a loss for words. But as soon as Ferdy started down the paths of the family history in Piment, Nana lost the thread of her words. Like Ancestor Selena, her eyes became veiled. She began to stammer. Then fell silent, squaring herself in her rocker as if to better perceive the rumors of the past that still lived within her. She remained a few instants in that position, sitting helplessly, hands knotted in her lap.

For thirteen long years Ferdy had tried in vain to find out the truth about the Montérios, bring an end to the old secrets that had been rotting the family tree from its roots to its crown.

Without laughing or crying, feigning innocence, Nana kept him in ignorance. At eighty-nine, she was still alert; Doctor Finger predicted that she still had a good deal of time and fine days ahead of her. Words of a false prophet that Ferdy didn't give much credit to. What did it mean when he said she had a good deal of time ahead of her? Ferdy had seen old folks disappear from Guadeloupe in a thousand different ways. Some were snuffed out quicker than a cheap candle. Others looked wonderful up until the very last breath, even though they were totally moth-eaten on the inside. There were those who picked the day they would die themselves, refusing to tell anyone about it, and sneaked off in secret with the pension that thirty-five mouths depended on for survival. Many left in their sleep, slipping quietly away, taking along with them the country's memory, the folktales from back in slave days that no one had taken the trouble to write down, *neg mawon* songs lost to future generations, recipes inherited from the Caribbean world, dreams of jars full of gold, of . . . So you'll understand that Ferdy was wary of death coming up unexpectedly. And simply the thought of having to close Nana's coffin one day without having learned the notorious secret was downright unbearable. Opportunity makes the thief. When Tibert told his father that Melchior's Mina had written him to announce her forthcoming visit, Ferdy was eager to see her come face to face with Nana finally. He pestered Tibert.

"Good Lord! What day you going to bring her? You talk to her about it yet? She going to leave without having come to visit us and it will be your fault! You got to think of the family, understand? You in love lately . . . Lord, your Cindy not going to fly away! *Koké byen bon mé sé pa tou sa* . . . Having a poke is fine, but that's not all there is to life . . ."

"She coming tomorrow, Thursday! I going to pick her up in Piment! We'll be here around four o'clock . . ."

Ferdy was in the butcher shop cutting up a piece of meat with a cutlass. Fifine was counting the money in the cash register. The man jumped, but continued slicing the side of meat.

"You sure, eh? You really sure, Tibert? Hmph!"

"Well that's what I said . . . Mina needs to know the whole story too . . . You should just see her . . .

"Mam Nana has been driving me crazy about that . . . Hmph!"

"Twenty years in France really changes people."

"Don't go filling Mam Nana's head with stories . . ." growled Ferdy, talking more to himself than to his son. "What time you say you'd get here? Hmph!" The slabs of beef quivered on the butcher board. Blood spurted everywhere.

"Four o'clock! I'll come by tomorrow morning to fill Mam Nana in . . ."

"Four o'clock sharp, then! We be waiting for you . . . Hmph!"

"You think she's really going to tell Mina the truth?"

"I got no idea for God's sake! You sure, then? You said four o'clock . . ."

"Yes! Four o'clock . . . And Cindy sends her regards . . ."

"Right, say hello to her too. And don't forget! Four o'clock tomorrow . . ."

During the discussion, Ferdy had continued to cut up the meat and his excitement and apprehension so impaired the mechanical gestures he'd been repeating since he was seventeen years old, Tibert thought his father would end up leaving one of his fingers or half his hand on the chopping block.

At the second honk of the horn, Mina glanced at her watch. Three o'clock. What day? Thursday! Good Lord! Victor . . . She'd forgotten about him. Had been thinking only of her appointment with Tibert. She'd had lunch with Miss Rutice. The old schoolteacher had brought out her crystal, porcelain, and silver for the occasion. They spoke of Rose again, the old schooldays, the benefits of a good education . . . Lunch had lasted longer than anticipated. After the old rum—aged twenty-five years—which Miss Rutice served her without asking, Mina had run, head heavy and stomach laden with too much grub. She felt a little drunk and had just gotten back to Suzon's to change her dress, freshen up a bit, powder her nose. She recognized Tibert's pick-up at the street corner. He hadn't seen her.

Victor, she thought in the dim light of the living room as she took off her dress with perspiration stains under the arms. Would he be there? They had agreed upon three o'clock . . . What had he been doing since his arrival? She pictured him, suntanned body, stretched out on the beach like a piece of dead wood polished by the waves. She tried to revive the feeling inside, down in her abdomen, at the tips of her breasts. Yes, she felt something . . .

Victor, how could she have forgotten him? And what would she do with him if he was really at the meeting place? No, he couldn't come on the trip. This was a very special day. The true story of the Montério family was going to come out in broad daylight.

Victor . . . Suddenly she heard Mignard groaning. Mina finished slipping on her dress and spun around, imprisoned in an invisible web. Overhead, the sheet metal roof seemed to be inching downward. The cabin was closing in around her like a vice. The furniture in the room was jerking around in the half-light. Shivering in spite of the humid heat, Mina suddenly found herself staring one of the dolls straight in the eyes. Then a second one. They were everywhere. On the sofa, stuffed tightly between the faded pink cushions. On the shelves, the buffet. They all had their arms stretched out, menacing, staring at her. Eighteen dolls. Nine girls in worn lace dresses and nine boys in threadbare pants. An evil legion prepared to rise up and avenge their mama who had to keep them closed up in the Princess shoebox for such a long time . . .

Mina was seized with dizziness and nausea. For a moment, eyes closed, she held herself up on the table. Her legs wobbling and her heart racing. She tried to get out of the cabin, but staggered, like a drunken woman. When she cracked open her eyes, sweat dampening her temples, she thought she saw the dolls getting to their feet, one after the other. They were all standing on their little brown plastic legs that were so shiny you might have thought Suzon greased them with thick carapate oil. Sinister, bitter dolls, as wrinkled as old people. Sunken cheeks of the last days of life, dry, cracked skin, runny eyes, flabby mouths, sparse, unkempt hair. Old bodies suddenly animated with a last burst of energy, baring their teeth — black stumps — ready to bite and rip apart. The sad debris of flesh and blood that had had its share of hard knocks and that now was rising up against life, God's injustice, and the promises that a hundred and some demons had made to their Mama Suzon. At the ends of their gnarled fingers, thick black

251

nails had grown. They clawed. Penetrated Mina's flesh.

She closed her eyes and called out, pleaded.

Rose!

Come save me my little Rose!

Don't abandon me.

Dear God! Rose! Save me!

I'm not afraid. My eyes are deceiving me, she kept telling herself. Nothing I'm seeing is real . . . I don't feel their hands on me.

Words she strung out and recited to boost her courage, help her grab her purse, walk out of the cabin. I'm not afraid, my eyes are deceiving me, nothing I'm seeing is real . . .

Words chanted despite her shortness of breath, her dry mouth. I'm not afraid. My eyes are deceiving me. Nothing is real . . . Nothing I'm seeing is real. I don't feel their hands on me.

She suddenly found herself flung onto the veranda. Safe, purse under her arm. Dumbfounded at having been able to escape this last nightmare.

Outside, the street was still and white, petrified. Not a hint of wind. The sun burned high in the sky.

Tibert was getting ready to honk one last time when Mina finally appeared in his rearview mirror. He closed his newspaper thinking to himself she wouldn't refuse an invitation to dinner at his place after the visit with Mam Nana.

"I didn't want to go in," he said apologetically.

"That's all right, I understand . . ."

Mina put on her sunglasses and climbed into the truck.

"We're going to Mam Nana's house. After that, I'm inviting you over to my new place. Cindy's doing the cooking and . . ."

"I'm not sure I can stay. We have to go past the town hall. I have an appointment with a French guy and . . ."

"No problem, there'll be enough food for everyone . . ."

At seventeen minutes past three Mina spied Victor sitting on the edge of the fountain that dominated the square in front of Piment's city hall. A bright red Victor, hair stuck to his head, arms and legs exposed, covered with long, light brown hair. Mina's heart started beating harder. Her eyes got bleary. A shudder ran through her.

"That the white man over there?" asked Tibert.

"He's waiting for me," answered Mina. "He's waiting for me," she repeated to herself, surprised to find him there, as they had agreed upon.

~   .

Nana Salibur had asked Ferdy a hundred times what the name of the person coming to visit that afternoon was.

"Who? Mina? What Mina?"

"Mina, my niece, Melchior's daughter who went to France after the cabin burned down."

"Mina, you say. Mi-Na . . ."

If Ferdy had just been your usual ill-mannered old nigger, he would have cursed his mama. He would have given her two–three smacks up the side the head, just to clear up her memories. He would have shaken her like a prune tree in order to bring down the truth. But he held his tongue and his hands. Judging from her sly looks, he could tell that Nana was playing with his nerves, was taking him for a first-class idiot.

"She's coming at four o'clock with Tibert. You do what you like. I'm washing my hands of this whole business," he sighed looking at his watch.

He sat down beside her with a frown. He slipped into an unbearable sort of silence, but the kind that, in his opinion, would inspire regrets and the confession he'd been waiting for since that cursed day in 1937 when he left Piment.

XXIX

"So this is the big day!" Victor exclaimed, getting into the pickup truck. "Today's the day we're going up on the hill? I'm so glad to see you again . . ."

"What hill?" Mina interrupted abruptly.

"The place where your house was . . . The one that burned down . . ."

"It's called a *morne*. Morne Calvaire. And we didn't have a house, but a cabin."

"We're going to Grandmother Nana's place," said Tibert.

"Ah! Grandmother Nana . . . You didn't mention her, Mina . . ."

"She wants to see me. She has some things to tell me about my family. You don't have to come. We can leave you in town, if you like . . . If I'd known how to get a hold of you, I would have cancelled our appointment . . ."

"No, it's fine. I'd like to meet your grandmother Nana."

Mina couldn't keep from smiling. That was good old Victor for you. She relaxed a little and let the bumps in the road jostle her up against his body.

"After we see Mam Nana, we're going to my house. My wife Cindy is making us a fine dinner," said Tibert proudly.

"Maybe Victor has other plans," objected Mina.

"No, no, thank you very much for the invitation, Tibert. I'd be delighted to meet your wife."

"Relax, we can be less formal with each other. You're Mina's friend, aren't you?"

"Yes, of course, I'd love to, thank you thank you very much . . ."

"Have you had any colombo curry since you got here, Victor?" asked Tibert.

"No, not yet."

"And what have you seen? Castle Point, Saint-François, le Gosier . . ."

"Stop it Tibert, he's not a tourist."

Jammed in between the two men, Mina was having gloomy thoughts, suddenly feeling trapped at the idea of visiting her grandmother Nana. She had only run into her at the family funerals. A woman she had never seen smile, hiding an old wound. She wondered what could be the connection between Suzon and Mam Nana. What could have triggered that avalanche of hate in Suzon's heart. And then there was this man, this cumbersome stranger. Victor! What was he doing in the middle of this mess?

"We're not far now," exclaimed Tibert, just to loosen up the atmosphere in the vehicle.

The tone of voice had been gay, but the two passengers were little inclined to conversation. Tibert turned up the sound on the radio.

Victor had so much to tell Mina about. He wanted to talk to her about the incredible things that had happened to him since he arrived. But they had to be alone. He sensed she was disgruntled.

As soon as they'd left Pointe-à-Pitre and the Gosier beltway, a more rugged landscape opened out before them. Arid hills over which ruled ancient mango trees, reedy coconut trees with their palms in the wind, and immense red and yellow flamboyant trees. Cattle in savannas ruminating old hardships. Goats, goats, goats . . . Wooden cabins that had resisted cyclones and seemed to be counting their remaining days. Creole cabins held over from another era; cabins that, elsewhere, people had eradicated from the landscape with a quick swipe of a bulldozer and new concrete villas. Mina wasn't familiar with this side of the island, this wing of the butterfly on which her mother Médée had been born and where the largest colony of Indians in Guadeloupe lives.

"Here we are in Grands-Fonds!" blurted Tibert. At those words he gripped the steering wheel more firmly.

"We're in Grands-Fonds," repeated Victor who seemed delighted to be part of the expedition.

"Yes, we're in Grands-Fonds," murmured Mina answering the male chorus.

"Just three more kilometers and we're there. What time is it?" asked Tibert looking at his watch. "Ten minutes to four; we're on time."

"Victor, it might be best if you left us after the greetings.

Mam Nana wants to talk with me. She won't say anything in front of a stranger . . ."

"And we been waiting for so long now," Tibert added. "You understand . . ."

Victor nodded with a grave expression on his face. Since he'd been in Guadeloupe he'd just been following the tide of events and letting himself be guided by the signs. It had brought him luck. He was still alive. He had succeeded in surmounting some old fears. He had faced ghosts. He had made friends, was beginning to feel as though the spell had been somewhat broken. His anxiety had not really disappeared. He still needed tranquilizers . . . But he was now sure that Mister Verity had unlocked a door — as one of his psychiatrists put it — that opened onto the road to healing.

"I have to buy a post card," he said. "A card for Bénédicte," he repeated to himself.

"You'll find a shop not far away."

"And a stamp too . . ."

"Just say hello to Mam Nana and then go take a stroll over to the Post Office. We won't be long . . ."

When Ferdy heard Tibert's pick-up, he was seized with a terrible stomachache.

"If he didn't bring her back with him, he might as well not come in!" he grumbled to his companion.

Fifine sighed. Since morning the whole house had been in an uproar. Everything had to be ready at four o'clock for the arrival of Mina, brother Melchior's daughter. Ferdy had been bawling people out constantly, coming and going as he inspected every nook and cranny in the house, griping, and flattering his mother who was sitting on a bench on the veranda, telling her over and over again that Mina would be there at four o'clock sharp. When the old woman had had enough, she'd closed herself up in her room from where, listening closely, they could hear her singing psalms in Latin for over two hours now.

"Look! Look and see if she's here!" Ferdy ordered Fifine.

Dragging her feet, the woman went to stand guard at a window with venetian blinds.

"I see a white man in shorts."

"What!"

"A white man talking hard with Tibert."

"She's not here!" raved Ferdy. "She's not here!"

"Look yourself!" whimpered Fifine.

"I'll disinherit him! He'll get nothing! I'll give everything to the church!"

"Wait a minute, there's someone else with them. Yeh, a woman. She getting out of the truck . . . Yeh, it looks like her all right . . ."

"Let me see!"

Ferdy posted himself behind another window, trembling from head to foot, both hands holding up his stomach.

"She not very tall," observed Fifine.

"He made it. Thank the Lord! The spitting image of her grandmother. I going out to greet them. You go tell Mam Nana they here."

Fifine pushed open the door to the room and found Nana kneeling at the foot of her bed, mumbling one last prayer to order the words that would come from her mouth. She was asking God to tame the hatred that had filled her heart ever since that day in 1937 when she had unmasked her husband Gabriel, father of her children, a scoundrel . . . After having made the sign of the cross, she unstiffened, stood up, repeating to herself that the time had come for her to leave this world. Fifine took her arm.

Nana had powdered her face and put on a heavy, white, immaculate dress that she had made herself and never worn. Her hair was braided and held up with tortoise shell combs. She came before them, serene and straight, lips pursed. First she kissed her son Ferdy, as if she hadn't seen him in a decade. Then she turned toward Tibert and held his hands in hers for a long time. Standing in front of Victor, she gave him her cheek. When it was Mina's turn, she looked her up and down, finally opened her mouth and in a high-pitched voice exclaimed, "Yes, it's you! It's really you, Melchior's Mina!"

Ferdy's dream come true: the family circle around a little formica table spread with a table mat upon which a bouquet of red roses was embroidered. Each of them silent, imbued with the gravity of the occasion. And the words ready to spill from Nana's lips.

The only sour note, Victor, the outsider, grinning widely.

"You had some things to buy," Mina reminded him, glaring at Victor.

Cousin Tibert nudged him with his elbow.

"Yeh!"

"Stamps, post cards . . ."

Victor stood up looking haggard, eyes blank. Three generations of Montérios watched him cross the room, stiff-necked, arms dangling, like a zombie. But when everyone thought he was already outside, he swung around and since he had some time to kill, asked if anyone knew anything about a certain poet that had written *Beyond the Clouds*.

Tibert jumped, but remained silent. Each thing in its own time. They were assembled to listen to what Mam Nana had to reveal. Ferdy contemplated his son. Ah! He had always said that Cindy Farétina could only bring trouble. Mina and Nana were looking each other straight in the eye.

"Let him stay!" Nana declared. "Today is the day for revealing secrets. Is he your husband, Mina?"

"No, not at all," she said. "We met by accident and he wanted to . . ."

"Come sit down, son!" interrupted Nana. "One person less, one person more . . ."

Victor sat back down in his place thanking Nana with a nod of the head. The others looked at him in disgust.

"I can serve some drinks, punch, or some papaya juice," offered Fifine.

258

"Afterwards!" grumbled Ferdy. "Afterwards!"

Nana cleared her throat and without any frills or beating around the bush, she plunged into the past.

"I was born in 1911. Right here in Grands-Fonds. In 1927, I followed Gabriel across Rivière Salée because a woman who is married in the church of our Lord and in the town hall has a right to do so. My parents wept sorely, but what else could I do?"

With words that had been trapped in the net of her soul for et cetera years, Nana opened her heart at last. Ferdy couldn't believe his ears. He was writhing and wriggling in his chair.

"I didn't know nothing about Gabriel and even less about his mama Séléna, the land of the goats, and her dealings with the priest in Piment who hoped to set up a calvary in Guadeloupe on a desolate hill.

"I entered the land of demons like an innocent lamb. And you got no idea how they tore me apart . . .

"Mam Séléna was already deep into her mental illness. She only had ten years left to live. Ten years to tell over and over again, the story of her goats and the battle she waged for her land. Ten years of watching people on pilgrimages climbing the flanks of the hill and kneeling at the foot of each cross.

"And my youth that was wilting away in that cabin. I was married in January 1927 and in December I gave birth to Melchior, my first son. You came in '29, Ferdy. Gregoire in '32.

"I swear I tried to get used to the way of life the folks from Piment led. But they didn't want nothing to do with me. I could tell by their looks, the words that went between them when they watched me walk by on Gabriel's arm. Of course they would have preferred he marry a girl from Piment, a woman from Basse-Terre. There wasn't nothing about me to their liking. They even said I didn't speak their Creole.

"I stuck it out until Séléna's death in 1937. God have pity on her soul. The day after her death, Gaby pulled up all the crosses on Morne Calvaire and he made a big pyre. It's no lie, the smoke was black. It rose high into the sky and hovered over the town for three full days. Black folk signed themselves when they crossed our path. It made Gabriel laugh. After that, he put up the "private property" sign at the beginning of the dirt path that the pilgrims used. Well, you know, people didn't hesitate to say that I had been behind his acts, that it was heresy, even blasphemy to have dared to break Séléna's vow.

"Everywhere people spoke of the curse on the Montério family. In every rum bar, in every corner store. The Montério name was ripped apart in the marketplace and in the town square, during mass, and at vespers.

"That period of disgrace and downfall lasted the year long. Finally, one morning, I found a note slipped under the door. A letter with shaky words written on it that said Gabriel had a daughter, a girl named Suzon, who was supposedly born the same year as Melchior, in 1927. The name of the woman was also given. Lucinda Mignard. And the two children never left each others' side and were beginning to play games they weren't yet ripe for. And I had best leave with my children before Lucifer's fork ran us through. That was the words that were written. I had best leave with my children before Lucifer's fork ran me through.

"Believe me, it was some shock. I stuffed the letter into my blouse and went down to town in a flash. I didn't say nothing to Gabriel. I still thought it was all a bunch of lies, the work of jealous folk. I couldn't believe it, by that time I had been living as best I could in Piment for ten years—that's how old my Melchior was. I wasn't going to let no one run me around. Oh, I said to myself, I'm going to teach these folks who I am!

"I could situate her perfectly, that Lucinda Mignard. Cross-eyed. I hadn't run into her often, but I sensed she was a bad sort.

"When I burst into her courtyard, I called out to let her know I was there. I heard the blinds rattle but no one came out. I called her name several times . . . Lucinda Mignard!

Lucinda Mignard! Lucinda Mignard! And she ended up coming out, that bitch of a ..."

At that point in the story, Nana's voice cracked.

"Water! Bring Mam Nana some water, Fifine!" cried Ferdy, who was afraid he would never hear the end of the story.

"She motioned me to stop yelling her name and come sit with her under the breadfruit tree in her courtyard. She looked like a woman pursued by the satans," Nana continued.

"'Why you coming now? All that was in the past. It was finished long ago. My poor husband is sick. He can't hear this.' She flung herself to her knees and hugged my legs. Suddenly my head went blank, *flap!*

"'So it's true what they writing in the letter ...'

"'What letter? Good God, Lord! What letter?'

"I threw it in her face. 'Oh! I don't know how to read. Forgive me, forgive me, forgive me ...' I felt her tears running down my legs.

"'You tell your Suzon not to come round my Melchior no more! You tell your husband what you did with ...'

"'Oh forgive me. A thousand pardons ... —I don't need your forgiveness—we were young. Gabriel had been drinking. We danced all night long. Neither of us was married yet. He was going to get you up at your place two days later. We only did it once. Just one time, I swear ... When he came back to Piment, we didn't try to see each other again. And then I missed my blood. And I started living with Région who'd been hanging around and asking after me for a while. He doesn't know that Suzon is someone else's ... After that I had my son Délos and ...'

"'I don't believe you ... How come people know about it if you only did it one time? Maybe Délos is Gabriel's child too... And why they dragging up this story after ten years, eh? Whose hand wrote the letter?'

"'You don't know the folks in Piment ... Nothing can ever

261

remain a secret for long here. You think you alone, but the earth, the water and the wind have eyes and ears. They hear and see everything. One day or another what you done blows up right in your face. The seeds you buried grow stems and branches and even fruit. The wind blows the seeds to the right and left. The river overflows and washes down a stream of bitter words. Only Fire can . . .'

"'Enough of your parables! Melchior never said nothing to me about your Suzon.'

"'Melchior and Suzon are brother and sister, that's as far as it goes. That's as far as it goes, I swear by the cross.'

"'Blasphemy!'

"'Suzon knows the secret,' that's what that liar said.

"'Are you really sure?'

"'Yes I swear to it. She knows he her brother. She knows, I can swear to that by the cross. She known since they been in first grade . . .'

"'And Gabriel? Did Gabriel tell Melchior the secret?'

"'I not the one sleeping with Gabriel. I can't guarantee nothing. In any case he knows Suzon is his daughter . . . His one and only daughter . . .'

"When I went back up to the top of the hill," Nana went on, wiping her forehead with a white handkerchief, "I felt betrayed in every cranny of my body. Ten years that I'd left my Grands-Fonds to set my life down far from my people. And what was I harvesting? Cheating and the contempt of that Lucinda who bragged about having given Gabriel a daughter. What was keeping me up on that hill? Nothing at all . . . Nothing at all . . . And what was I being promised? Lucifer's fork . . .

"'I going back home,' I said to Gabriel. 'I taking my children. And you'll never see us again.' I was trembling all over.

"He looked at me like I was sick in the head. 'My word, you had too much sun on your noggin.'

"'Remember what you did with Lucinda Mignard two days before our marriage,' I said to him.

"He played the innocent. 'What did I do, God damn it to hell!'

"'You lost your memory, Gabriel Montério! Well I going to tell you some hot news, you got a daughter that's ten who's called Suzon. So, your memory coming back?' Suddenly he started screaming like a man possessed.

"Ferdy, you were eight and your brother Gregory was barely six.

"'You can get the hell out,' he said. 'I keeping my boys!'

"'You'll regret it, Gabriel Montério, you'll regret it . . .'

"'Get the hell out of my house.'

"'I won't leave without my kids. I won't abandon them . . .'

"'Get out! Go back to Grands-Fonds! You been hanging around here too long already . . .'

"Ferdy and Grégoire heard us shouting but they was too young to understand. Only Melchior broke in on our argument. 'I staying with my father,' he said. 'I don't want to leave Piment.' Just then, Gabriel started laughing and he ordered me to leave immediately with my two younger children. He said it was an even split. He wouldn't change his mind.

"After that, I didn't get many chances to see my son Melchior. I know all about the torments he endured because of Lucinda Mignard and her daughter that he was madly in love with. When Gabriel told him, it was already too late. Melchior didn't sin again with his sister. But the evil had been consummated and the fruit has been poisoned. She's dead today, that bitch Lucinda . . . Died with her lies. She hadn't talked to her daughter, that's the truth of the matter. She waited for the two of them to mingle their bodies. That's what made her lose her speech and her mind as well . . . She always did enjoy the company of sorcerers, but her illegitimate daughter had even closer ties with them. Just look at what happened to poor Melchior . . ."

Ferdy couldn't believe his ears. A whole life of imagining a thousand hypothetical tragedies for only this . . . This measly story . . . A seventy-three-year-old half-sister . . . And he examined Mina furtively, as if she'd stolen half of his life.

As for Tibert, he felt relieved. He had accomplished his mission on earth and had the feeling he owed nothing more to anyone. What is done is well done, he said to himself. It was just a little unpleasant to think that Suzon Mignard was his aunt and to remember he'd wished she were dead only that afternoon. But all's well that ends well.

"Let's have a drink to bolster our spirits!" he exclaimed.

His voice was immediately covered by that of his father.

"Why you make us wait all this time, mama? Why you have to see Mina? I your son too . . ."

"She knows why. You were spared. Her father, my son, my sweet Melchior, suffered and paid for Gabriel. He paid a hundred, two hundred times over . . . Everyone he loved died because of a woman who thought he'd abandoned her. Nothing on earth is worse than that. You never wondered why Melchior was surrounded by so much disaster?"

"I chalked it all up to fate," sighed Ferdy.

"When did he find out about Suzon?" asked Mina with a tight throat.

"Too late," moaned Nana.

"Why didn't you tell him?"

"I thought Gabriel had already told him. Don't forget, I was in Grands-Fonds. It was his duty as a father to inform his son. He was the sinner . . ."

"You could have stopped Suzon's hand . . .," began Mina.

"Stop what?" thundered Mam Nana. "She didn't strike with a saber, you know! She had allies in the shadows. She prayed to the forces of Evil. Can you stop spirits? Can you call the police on demons that leave no traces?"

"And Rosalia? You know about Rosalia . . ."

"I don't want to hear no more about it all . . . It's finished, I won't say another word. I didn't bring on the disasters . . . I didn't call up the demons . . ."

264

At those last words, Mam Nana closed her eyes and crossed her hands on her stomach.

"Let's have a drink," repeated Tibert.

His father stared at him in profound disgust, wondering how he, Ferdy Montério, could have engendered such scum. And what, Ferdy suddenly wondered, was that white man doing amongst them? He glanced at Victor, who had felt anxiety flashes whenever anyone mentioned demons, but who then sank back into his own thoughts. Everyone had forgotten about him while Nana was telling her story. And now he was like a stain in the middle of a white tablecloth. Why in the devil had Nana allowed him to stay?

"We'll be going soon," Tibert went on. "Cindy's waiting for us at the house."

"I fixed some papaya juice, you can't just leave like that," exclaimed Fifine half-heartedly. Crazy about soap-operas that she watched every day on television, Fifine hadn't found Nana's story all that fascinating or the characters very interesting either. The intrigues and endless new developments in *Love, Fame & Fortune* were something else altogether...

"I already knew that Suzon was passionately in love with my father, but I never would have imagined she was my aunt..."

"Half-aunt," rectified Tibert. "Only a half-aunt..."

"Shut up, Tibert!" grumbled Ferdy. "You don't understand anything."

"I would have imagined anything but that. What a waste, after all. So much pain..." said Mina.

"Get a hold of yourself, girl. You can't change the past," whispered Fifine handing her a glass of papaya juice.

XXX

Tibert lived in an apartment in a new part of town. He parked at the foot of the five-story building and pointed out a balcony on the third floor.

"Above all, don't say anything to Cindy about our family problems! She's young, I don't want to worry her with all that. Also, she's expecting my child . . . I'm starting a new life with her. You understand . . . Witchcraft, jealousy, and curses, aren't the nicest things to discuss in front of a pregnant woman . . . Victor, you're one of our generation, you've got thick-skin. It doesn't faze you, but my Cindy doesn't know anything about all that . . . Take it easy with her, understand?"

Mina and Victor nodded in silence.

"We'll take a little walk and we'll be right there," said Mina. "Five minutes. We've got some things to talk over."

"I'll be waiting for you, eh? No tricks! Third floor on the left. My name's on the door. I'll make some punch . . . And I've got a surprise for you, Victor . . ."

At last alone, Mina and Victor sat down on a bench. The sounds of a *chanté-Nwèl* Christmas carol party arose nearby. It was already late.

"I dragged you into one very strange story," Mina began.

"We promised to help each other."

"I haven't helped you much up to now."

"There are signs. So many strange things have happened to me since I got here. You have no idea. If I told you . . ."

"Oh nothing can surprise me now!"

"The tourists that travel up and down the roads of Guadeloupe don't realize what's going on in the country," Victor went on. "They're hypnotized by the sun, the white sand, and the blue sea. They wonder at the abundant and luxuriant vegetation. They're in Paradise and don't seem to believe that people really live in this décor . . ."

"Yes, I know, Victor."

"I met people. They talked to me."

"I believe you. You see, you didn't need a guide."

The voices of the Christmas carolers grew stronger, ringing out ever more fervently toward the heavens.

"I think the spell has been broken a little," declared Victor after taking a big sigh. "I know who the three demons walking behind me are. Bénédicte was right. I saw them again. My father hung himself from the light fixture in the living room. I was four years old. I had forgotten them. There were three of them, dressed in black. They unstrung him in front of me . . ."

"You haven't sent the post card yet?"

"Tomorrow morning, maybe. I haven't seen beyond the clouds, but it doesn't matter . . . And your sister Rosalia, you haven't seen her again?"

"Not yet, no . . . I don't think I will see her again . . ."

"And when are we going up on the morne, Mina? The morne of your childhood . . .

As soon as he saw Cindy, Tibert asked her to add a place at the table for Mina's friend, Victor . . . Victor Clément, a white man who's kind of strange and who was asking about Grandfather Farétina. Why? It was a mystery! Cindy picked up the phone immediately and called her grandfather who was deaf in one ear. He made her repeat the name five times and ended up saying he didn't know any white men by that name—as a matter of fact, he hadn't spoken to a single white man since the last World War. Those he had known were either dead or had gone crazy. Cindy pleaded so much that he finally accepted to meet the man. A *chanté-Nwèl* carol party was being given at his place that evening and he wouldn't have much time to devote to him. Though he was seventy-five years old, Grandfather Farétina—known as Dodo—enjoyed life and hadn't given up music. He still played the trumpet in the municipal band and paraded through the streets of Mordeuil every July 14 before going to kneel at the tomb of the Unknown Soldier who had given his life for France, along with the mayor, his cronies and the town's three surviving veterans from the last World War.

The prospect of having dinner at Tibert's was beginning to feel like a bit of a chore to Mina. Her cousin didn't seem affected by what had been said that afternoon. He had barely been fazed by Mam Nana's revelations, as if the family story no longer concerned him. The reasons that drove their grandmother to leave Piment didn't carry the same weight in their minds. Even though they now had the same blood aunt. Suzon . . . Suzon who could have also been spared if the truth had come out earlier. Tibert hadn't understood any of it. He had no idea of the extent of the disaster.

The family being torn apart
Incest
Suzon driven mad with love
Sorcerers
Evil
Death
Its recurrence
Death
Its relentlessness
Death
Marie-Perle
Drowned in the Goyave River
Médée
Run down by the Titan truck
Melchior
Struck by lightning
And the spirits that lingered on this earth
Suzon's eighteen little black babies
Olga's sterile womb
And Rosalia
Rosalia's lunacy
Rosalia, the protectress
Despite the fire that struck
Despite crossing the seas
Love lying dead in Mina's heart

At the beginning of the dinner—a delicious colombo curry—Tibert and Cindy were like perfect caricatures of starstruck lovers. Mina found them despicable. Their hands were end-lessly intertwining and there was an unbearable gleam in their eyes. Is that what love was? She wondered.

Cindy, thanks to Tibert's shenanigans, was extremely preg-nant and wore a dress that showed off her large titties and her calabash belly. At twenty years of age, one might have thought she was barely sixteen, with her smooth face, her cornrow braids, and her childish laughter. She was joyful, luminous. At first Mina tried to maintain a certain distance from the young woman, thinking she had nothing to share with that child. No dead, or phantoms either. No pain, or lovers either. No tor-ments, or revelations either. But for lack of an adversary, she finally let down her guard. She began to relax in the middle of the meal. And in spite of everything, found herself laughing with Cindy, relating bits of her life in France to Tibert, and even singing. From time to time, she cast a worried glance at Victor, as if at a judge who would condemn her laughter. But he was in heaven. He was talking, smiling, and chiming in with the chorus to the Creole Christmas songs without under-standing them. The rum and the wine had reddened his cheeks.

"We'll carry on at Mordeuil," Tibert, already well-soused, exclaimed after the desert.

"There's a *chanté-Nwèl* carol party at my grandfather's place," explained Cindy.

"You're going to be mindblown, Victor. I swear you're really going to be stunned . . . You ain't here by accident, believe me, brother. Some things are bigger than we are, that's the honest truth. And you couldn't have come to a better place . . ."

Tibert had gotten up from the table. He was having trouble staying on his feet. Mina glanced at him gloomily. He's had too much to drink, she thought. Everyone knows that rum and wine don't mix.

"You need to get some sleep, Tibert. It's already late and Vic-tor has to . . . It's only the twenty-third. We'll come back to-morrow for the real Christmas celebration."

"No, you'll see, Mina . . . There are some strange coincidences in life," interrupted Cindy.

"We have a surprise for you! A big, big, big surprise," whispered Tibert, sounding like a conspirator sitting on a branch that is about to break.

Victor turned toward Mina as if the decision was in her hands. But his eyes said the contrary. He was following the course of events.

The old man barely lived seven miles from them. But the road was so deeply rutted, Tibert so terribly drunk, and the night so densely dark, that it took them a good hour to get to the hamlet called Mordeuil where the chanté-Nwèl awaited them.

There were at least a hundred people, young and old, at Dominique Farétina's place. Some were eating, others singing at the top of their lungs, noses buried in songbooks. They were all drinking, or had had more to drink than was reasonable, or were going to drink more until they'd even forgotten their names. It was Christmas! A time for feasting and thanking the Good Lord because he had sent his only son to earth to save men of good will, sinners of all kinds, and the blacks in Guadeloupe. It was Christmas! Christmas the likes of which Victor had never seen. With no stockings, or Santa Clause. No snow, or toys, or Christmas trees . . . Christmas in Creole sauce. And Victor felt he was bursting with painful joy. He felt like throwing his arms around someone, kissing people, getting drunk, to forget . . . The old fears he couldn't shake, the dizzy spells that came over him without warning, the frozen desert of his despair, sweet desirable death, probably never being able to see beyond the clouds.

Forget
The Bunny he had been
Edmond's black piano
His sheet music
The light fixture in the living room
Emilie's large, cold bed . . .

270

"Victor! Wake up! You're asleep! I'm going to introduce you to Cindy's grandfather!" shouted Tibert, shoving a glass of rum into his hand. "Drink, brother! Drink! You're going to be mindblown! Follow me!"

They made their way through a clamorous crowd and found the man in the kitchen in the process of tasting the sauce in an enormous stewpot of browned pork-meat. Dominique Farétina was wearing a pink Dacron shirt and spotless white twill pants. A belt styled out of imitation crocodile skin was around his waist. His black patent leather shoes were impeccable. He had the body of country black men that have slaved forty years in the cane fields. You never would have thought he'd traveled in his youth. He never talked about his war days.

"Hey! Grandfather Dodo! Good evening!"

"Good evening . . ." answered Farétina without even lifting his head.

"Come closer, Victor! I want to introduce you . . . Grandfather Dodo, this gentleman is from France. He's my cousin Mina's friend. Come closer, Victor! No one's going to eat you! That's no white man grandfather's browning in his stewpot!"

Tibert, in top form, was exulting while Faréntina remained stone faced, concentrating on his sauce.

"Don't insist, Tibert," whispered Victor. "You can see he's busy . . ."

"Be quiet!" Motioned Tibert. "I tell you it's a surprise."

"All right, you can take in the meat and start serving," said Dodo to two young boys wearing Reebok and Nike T-shirts.

Finally, he turned toward Victor looking at him sharply.

"Where do you know me from?"

Tibert was doubled over laughing. A lump formed in Victor's throat.

"I don't know you."

"You don't know me, and just why were you asking about me?"

Tibert was grimacing with delight and slapping himself on the thighs. He was playing up the suspense. Dodo ran one hand through his gray hair and looked at Tibert—the good-for-nothing that Cindy had fallen for—sadly.

"*On pas las joué kon sa! On gwan mal-chyen kon-w . . .* You ain't tired of playing like that! A big male dog like you!"

Tibert straightened up immediately. Every joke had a beginning and an end. He couldn't afford to lose too much of grandfather's esteem.

He cleared his throat, forced himself to put on a straight face and said to Victor, "What'd you say to me this afternoon? Who were you looking for? Didn't you ask after a poet who wrote *Beyond the Clouds*?"

"Yes that's true," admitted Victor, thinking this just wasn't possible.

Chance could not have brought him face to face with this poet. It was too much . . . He was being taken in. Bénédicte, Mr. Verity, Tibert, and Cindy . . . They were all in on it.

"Well, that's him! Right there in front of you . . . Dominique Farétina, Cindy's grandfather. See what a small world this is . . ."

At those words, Tibert fell silent, enjoying his victory.

"Where do you know me from?" asked Dodo once again.

Victor's throat was tightening around his heart like a vice, but this was no time for procrastinating. He had reached the end of the road.

"It's Bénédicte," he began. "She's the one who told me about you. I have to see beyond the clouds and I'll be healed."

Grandfather Dodo's eyes widened and he hurriedly looked around for a place to sit down.

"Mina has got to hear this, Tibert. Quick, go get her!" whispered Cindy.

Dominique Farétina remembered his war days in France perfectly well. Winter time. Forced marches through the snow-covered fields. The trumpet he carried with him everywhere and that cried out in the night to comfort his companions in misery. He had made friends and exchanged addresses with American soldiers, and with them he had relearned his mother's language. She was from the English island of Dominica, which is where he got his name. After the war, he promised himself to move to New York and become as famous as Duke Ellington, Sidney Bechet, Louis Armstrong, Earl Bines, or Jelly Roll Morton . . . As soon as he was on leave, Dodo created melodies, wrote songs. One evening they occupied an abandoned farm. Dodo went out into the field alone. The earth still carried the marks of old furrows. Stumbling at each step, he nevertheless kept walking and began to play, with his trumpet pointing toward the dark sky. And suddenly, something incredible happened. He saw beyond the clouds. That is when the poem, *Beyond the Clouds*, sprung from his lips.

In the courtyard people were singing loudly. Laughter and the clinking of glasses rang out. But in the kitchen, right before the eyes of Mina, Victor, Cindy, Tibert, and a few others, Dominique Farétina had traveled back fifty years, to his youth in the French countryside.

"At the end of the war, I was demobilized and I came back to Guadeloupe without further ado. I never went back to France. However, I never could forget what the sky had shown me that night. I started reciting my poem in the *léwose*-gatherings. It made people cry. One day a schoolteacher was there. She listened to *Beyond the Clouds*. She came to see me at the end of the evening and asked for permission to copy down the verses. The next day, she taught it to her class. That's how I became famous and all the children in Guadeloupe know my poem. That's how I became a poet . . ."

Farétina's tale had completely sobered Tibert up, and he wanted the old man to play his trumpet to top off the evening, in a manner of speaking. But it was five o'clock in the morning on December 24.

"Some other time," Cindy whispered to him.

The first crowing roosters were already rivaling with the survivors of the *chanté-Nwèl* who continued to bawl out their songs beside others who'd fallen asleep, exhausted, on benches and old lawn chairs. The floor of tamped earth was littered with plastic plates and cups, empty bottles of rum, Pshcitt, or Coke.

Victor received a hug from Farétina, who couldn't get over the fact that a Frenchman from France had heard of his fame. And Victor decided it wasn't the right time to ask him to give a precise description of beyond the clouds. Can you ask a poet to supply technical explanations for his inspiration? Everything had been said. The nature of beyond the clouds would undoubtedly remain an unfathomable mystery. He walked out of the cabin, a bit disoriented, escorted by Mina, Tibert, and Cindy, waving goodbye to the remaining singers, who seemed to be hungering and thirsting after God more than ever.

"That ain't the end of it," said Tibert as he climbed into his pick-up. "What's on the program for today? Piment! Morne Calvaire! And tonight we're invited to another chanté-Nwèl . . ."

"First we're going to get some sleep. We'll see about the rest later," said Mina.

"I have to buy my post card. For Bénédicte. I have to send it today."

"It won't get to France before you do. It's the holiday season, Victor. The mail is running slow," Tibert declared.

"It's always running slow. Holidays or not," groaned Cindy letting out a yawn.

"It doesn't matter, I'll mail it today anyway. I'm cured now. It's almost certain . . . I didn't feel anxious once tonight . . ."

"Cured of what?" asked Cindy.

"It's too complicated to explain. We need to sleep now," sighed Mina.

And she lay her head on Victor's shoulder.

The road opened out before them, friendly and serene, like the dawning day. The sky was growing light. Very pale pink and blue clouds streaked with orange reflections seemed to spring into being at the horizon. Here and there the first rays of sun shot over the humpbacked hills. Sandwiched between Cindy's huge belly and Mina's breasts, Victor smiled at the landscape. Inspected the clouds.

XXXI

January 1, 2000

He woke up at noon.

A voice in his ear.

A familiar voice that wasn't a dream.

A continuous murmur.

"Let's go. Let's go. Let's go . . ."

She was leaning over him with her cross slowly dangling before him, her black skin with golden sparkles.

"Let's go. Let's go. Let's go . . ."

She had arranged everything. They would go alone. Had to go alone. By bus. Leave the bungalow in Georgette's Club where they'd been staying for a week.

They reached the foot of Morne Calvaire around three o'clock. They had to make a stopover at Suzon's and tell her that the truth was no longer a secret. Tell her that she was forgiven, old Aunt Suzon.

Victor took her arm. As promised, as planned. And they climbed the hill together, like two pilgrims, back in the days of Ancestor Séléna and her beloved priest. Like two convalescents.

They stopped at the stations. Seven stations. Mina didn't say

275

much, just that she didn't recall Morne Calvaire being that steep. So many treacherous little stones underfoot.

Short of breath, they stopped at the foot of the traveler's tree that opened out its immense fan of leaves.

There was not a trace of the old cabin. Not even a charred plank on which to sit. Not even an old square-cut stone with the mark of Melchior's cutlass. Not even broken bits of the jar Médée dipped the water from. But gradually, the view from the top of the hill was revealed. Her father's banana grove. The river at the foot of the morne. All of Piment. The infinite sea. The islands in the distance.

One, two, three.
Rosalia's boats.
One, two, three.
The birds in the sky.
One, two, three.
Beyond the clouds

In the EUROPEAN WOMEN WRITERS series

The Human Family
By Lou Andreas-Salomé
Translated and with an introduction by Raleigh Whitinger

Artemisia
By Anna Banti
Translated by Shirley D'Ardia Caracciolo

Bitter Healing
German Women Writers, 1700–1830
An Anthology
Edited by Jeannine Blackwell and Susanne Zantop

The Edge of Europe
By Angela Bianchini
Translated by Angela M. Jeannet and David Castronuovo

The Maravillas District
By Rosa Chacel
Translated by d. a. démers

Memoirs of Leticia Valle
By Rosa Chacel
Translated by Carol Maier

There Are No Letters Like Yours: The Correspondence of Isabelle
de Charrière and Constant d'Hermenches
By Isabelle de Charrière
Translated and with an introduction and annotations by Janet
Whatley and Malcolm Whatley

The Book of Promethea
By Hélène Cixous
Translated by Betsy Wing

The Terrible but Unfinished Story of Norodom Sihanouk, King
of Cambodia
By Hélène Cixous
Translated by Juliet Flower MacCannell, Judith Pike, and Lollie
Groth

The Governor's Daughter
By Paule Constant
Translated by Betsy Wing

Hôtel Splendid
By Marie Redonnet
Translated by Jordan Stump

Nevermore
By Marie Redonnet
Translated by Jordan Stump

Rose Mellie Rose
By Marie Redonnet
Translated by Jordan Stump

The Man in the Pulpit
Questions for a Father
By Ruth Rehmann
Translated by Christoph Lohmann and Pamela Lohmann

Abelard's Love
By Luise Rinser
Translated by Jean M. Snook

A Broken Mirror
By Mercè Rodoreda
Translated and with an introduction by Josep Miquel Sobrer

Why Is There Salt in the Sea?
By Brigitte Schwaiger
Translated by Sieglinde Lug

The Same Sea As Every Summer
By Esther Tusquets
Translated and with an afterword by Margaret E. W. Jones

Never to Return
By Esther Tusquets
Translated and with an afterword by Barbara F. Ichiishi

The Life of High Countess Gritta von Ratsinourhouse
By Bettine von Arnim and Gisela von Arnim Grimm
Translated and with an introduction by Lisa Ohm